AZURA GHOST

Book Two of The Graven

ESSA HANSEN

orbit

orbitbooks.net

ORBIT

First published in Great Britain in 2022 by Orbit

1 3 5 7 9 10 8 6 4 2

A CIP catalogue record for this book
is available from the British Library.

ISBN 978-0-356-51559-5

Typeset in Garamond by M Rules
Printed and bound in Great Britain by Clays Ltd, Elcograf, S.p.A.

Papers used by Orbit are from well-managed forests
and other responsible sources.

MIX
Paper from
responsible sources
FSC® C104740

Orbit
An imprint of
Little, Brown Book Group
Carmelite House
50 Victoria Embankment
London EC4Y 0DZ

An Hachette UK Company
www.hachette.co.uk

www.orbitbooks.net

To hidden unities and overdue reunions.
To all the luminiferous echoes interacting with us,
whether we recognize them or not.

CHAPTER 1

REUNION

No weapons, no masks—those were the rules of seedy places like this. Caiden tilted his hooded face down as he leaned his elbows on the bar. He scratched impatiently at his morphcoat sleeve, watching the material transform from thermal fur to leather and back again.

His bounty was plastered in every venue across the multiverse except here in Unity, the central universe. That was a trap—and so far, no more creative than the traps he'd evaded before.

The crowded bar was not a room but an open platform with seats, surrounded by darkness. Creeper boughs laced overhead through trellises, cascading lambent lichen and fungus, bright as lanterns. Up past them, on the trunk of one of the forest's massive trees—kilometers tall and so dense they created constant night below—there bobbed the rare, absurdly expensive flowers he'd traveled all this risky way for.

Not traveled. Driven. Caiden grimaced and sipped the purple fire of his drink. It tasted like fuel and anxiety, stinging across his tongue, vapor heavy in the lungs.

Across a series of ambushes, Casthen hunters had been targeting the chemical packs on C's collar, spilling enough to deplete Caiden's supply of the rare elements that kept the nophek alive. The sayro flower Caiden needed in order to synthesize more life-sustaining chems grew nowhere but this planet, only during the glessing season, when leaves filled the canopy and blotted light below so bizarre things could grow. The plant's short shelf life excluded it from distribution. So—Caiden was driven into the trap of Unity.

At least the lack of walls here would make it easier to flee. Darkness meant easier to hide. He gazed unfocused into his glass, peripheral vision broadening, brain parsing species-specific body vocabulary. Arguments and gossip fizzed. In ten years on the run, he hadn't once stayed in a populated venue for this long.

It took, on average, twelve arcminutes before someone recognized him.

He'd already wasted three.

If the scholar isn't here to translate in five…

Caiden side-eyed the security clustered on another platform past a bridge. They stood so dense together he couldn't see the sacred sayro keeper—"merchant" for the right price—behind them. Not the first disreputable purchase he'd made alone. Unarmed. Languageless.

Four arcminutes.

Ephemeris time weighed heavier with meaning in Unity. The multiverse's time measurements, as he understood them, were based off arc degrees correlated with atomic frequencies, using the frame of reference of the center of the whole multiverse, which was Unity's central planet Solthar. An antiquated, sentimental Dynast system. A way to remember that the multiverse, pre-cataclysm, used to be just one world, one Unity of consistent physics.

Scents of ozone, mushroom, and resin permeated the air. Water drops pattered and far-off boughs moaned. Roosting birds crooned atop percussion insects, music enough for the Andalvian who danced hypnotically onstage. Beautiful chromatophoric patterns flowed across their skin. As Caiden had hoped, the patrons were engrossed, and even the bounty hunters lurking in the mix seemed distracted. Just two to worry about: the tall saisn, his eyes shut, tuned in to broad sensory landscapes. And a hunter in a split surcoat in Dynast colors. Her eyes glinted amber under the glow.

Caiden tucked a snarl of ashy hair behind his ear. Ten years had distanced him from the bounty photo: he wasn't that crisp, twenty-year-old thing. A bit of scruff on his cheeks and jaw helped hide his freckles. Bruises, scrapes, cuts—all over—scars. A lot.

No more associating with fellow passagers in sparkling white Cartographer settings. He was endlessly on the run from Threi Cetre, the Casthen Prime, who was imprisoned in a universe with an impassable rind. Caiden had stranded him in there by using the universe generated by his starship, the *Azura*, as a bridge inside. That miraculous technology remained the only key to get the man out.

Caiden ran with the key. He skimmed seamy systems and dark markets, evading notice and procuring what he needed to keep the ship and himself moving. Befriending no one, revisiting nowhere twice. He hadn't seen his family in ten years, not since he'd been ambushed on the planet that was supposed to have been his haven for a while. He couldn't risk them being made targets too.

If they still watched him from afar, they'd know the truth behind rumor and moniker.

The glass Graven star.

The Ghost of *Azura*.

The Butcher of Prixia.

I can't run forever.

The lonely thought rattled in a well-worn groove.

The Casthen had made a hollow in Caiden, and the years since had carved it deeper. Monstrous things burrowed inside. Violence. Deceit.

Five arcminutes—enough. Nerves danced under Caiden's skin. He would do this the harder way, then run again. He took a final drag of liquor, tucked his head down, and swiveled from his seat.

A woman stood in his way. "Can I 'ave yer drink, if you're leavin'?"

She fit the scholar archive photo. Human, twice his age. Her smile tried to pull up the wrinkles of a well-carved scowl. Her thick hair was as white as the lichen and lit into a halo that contrasted with her cool-toned black skin.

"Scholar Faramei?" Caiden asked.

She tried to squint her large eyes at him, but it didn't quite work with the delicate tech impeding on the sockets. White eyelashes quivered instead. "You're Anixellan, then. Obviously, if ya have to ask who I am. All these slods know me."

Anixellan, worldwender. The moniker he'd provided her. Was a name still considered fake if someone gave it to you once? They called him worldwender on the outer fringes of the multiverse, as far from here as you could get.

Caiden fidgeted at the attention. Most eyes still fixated on the dancer, but it was halfway to twelve arcminutes now. "You've already been paid, but you can have my drink too. Afterward. One sayro."

"Patience'd be good for ya, young thing."

He snorted a laugh. If ten years wasn't patient, maybe he misunderstood the word.

The laugh withered.

It wasn't patience if you weren't waiting for anything. He was just a man on the run.

The scholar rolled her eyes, but Caiden wasn't sure if it was reaction or activation: light swelled into her dilated pupils and shimmered over a morphing corneal membrane.

She snatched his drink and chugged the remainder, then strode through the bar, across a bridge, to the platform of market stalls.

Caiden followed only to the bridge, pretending to observe the forest while he sensed the rhythm of the air, the shape of the dark. His body tingled with anxious instinct, never relaxed long enough to enjoy the scenery of his travels.

This planet's soil was completely transparent. Vast root networks knotted below. Underground river systems roared, bright with schools of fish. Overhead, swarms of lightflies and bioluminescent rays cruised the dark.

Faramei made it through the security phalanx to a counter with the gelese merchant, a photosensitive species native to the planet. They had ropy bodies with long limbs, their dark skin clustered with candescent pink blisters that matched their huge glowing eyes. Faramei's tech let her perceive their language and replicate the mechanics of it: an optical luminescence filtered by multi-membrane blink combinations, invisible to unaugmented human eyes like Caiden's. But clearly, the deal wasn't going well.

Sayro wasn't advertised for sale. To gelese who weren't shady merchants, it was sacred. This gelese seemed less shady than Caiden had been informed.

The crowd cheered as the Andalvian finished their dance. The spectators unknit, attention roving.

"Out of time," Caiden muttered. *Should have done this the usual way. Blood and fangs and speed.*

Faramei spread her arms to calm the bristling security, but more than one fidgeted their hands around hidden glaves.

The darkness pitched inward to this one point in time. Caiden strode for the merchant just as the ten security officers folded in. Their paralytic glaves rose to the scholar's throat. Caiden yanked her back while still striding forward, taking her place in the ring of weapons. Fingers half-squeezed triggers. Glave muzzles shoveled into Caiden's neck.

"Leave, Faramei," he said. "You were never here."

He threw off his hood. Lifted his chin. Pinched his shoulders back and crammed a regal bearing into his frame. Soreness striped his muscles from other fights, his stitches and bandages twinged, and his bloodstream pulsed around the hollow in him.

And a burst of rancid shame, but there wasn't any choice. This was a last resort.

The security hesitated at the sight of his face.

Caiden gathered up and sharpened his Graven will, hot as a blade. Reality, soft as tallow. He cleared his mind of anything other than his desire and met each of their gazes, pouring his energy into their obedience, fostering whatever cursed resonance it was that bent their emotions, that ripened curiosity into awe and festered awe into love.

Caiden said gently, to the group, "No fighting, I'm here for the sayro, that's all. Just one. You can stand down for me."

Squared shoulders rounded. The glaves eased off his neck. Eyes stared, fawning.

The gelese's tight posture sagged and their pupils brightened, reverent.

Caiden swiped at the holosplay on the desk, inputting fund-transfer details while a sourness seeped across his tongue. He pointed up to where the sayro blossoms bobbed and held out his palm, hoping his Graven intention communicated something too.

The gelese scurried off their stool and climbed the trunk behind them. Their weedy fingers, tipped in bulbous pads and claws, easily scaled the bark.

One of the security cocked their head and glanced at the others, perplexed. A species less harmonized by Caiden's Graven hormones or bioresonance or whatever it was. Usually the most affected in a group influenced their peers while confusion filled the gaps.

Caiden swallowed the sour taste and stared into the guard's eyes. Years of evasion had forced him to learn that his Graven effect, paltry as it was, grew stronger with focus, like a muscle flexed. *Or a monster fed*.

He still wasn't sure *what* he was made of that constituted the Graven part of his space-garbage genetics, except that it felt foreign and wrong, infesting him with a power he didn't want but was too often forced to unleash. As if he'd struck a bargain with the Graven in him.

The truth about his hybrid genes lay kilometers deep in the Casthen Harvest and a classified organic matter or set of data called only "the Dominant." The project's scientists were dead and the subject itself lay locked behind impassable biosecurity.

The Harvest was the last place Caiden would ever go. Threi was imprisoned there, and the whole point of Caiden keeping on the move was to keep the *Azura* away. To hobble the Casthen's exploitation of the multiverse and limit the reach of a Graven man who innately wielded too much power.

The gelese plucked a sayro and whisked back down the tree.

The flower head was a ruffled cone with gossamer filaments weeping off. The chemical it had concentrated from the tree fungus gave it a cyan luminescence. Now plucked, the filaments began drying up from the bottom like fuses. Five arcminutes or so and it would be worthless.

The gelese sealed the sayro in a padded bag before lowering it into Caiden's hand.

"On with your business." Caiden forced the words.

The security bowed to him.

The acid in Caiden's stomach curdled into an ache. He pulled his hood up and strode back to the bridge. As proximity widened, the sight, sound, and scent of him gone, the Graven effect faded and the merchant's group began to mutter. Ahead, the bar crowd of several hundred buzzed with inebriated energy. The bounty hunters were lost in the mass.

Faramei had fled—good. He didn't need liabilities.

Caiden nestled the sayro in his coat, then looked up and halted. The amber-eyed hunter stood at the other end of the bridge.

She stared, unnaturally still. Uncertainty frowned over the bridge of her nose.

Caiden froze, too, puzzled by unrecognizable machine components and biology. She wasn't a xenid, but clearly only an approximation of humanoid. Heavily augmented? Lustrous metal, obsidian, ashen hair, patchwork face.

"*Butcher!*" screamed one of the gelese's security, pointing at Caiden.

The crowd swiveled, hushed. Insects hummed in the gap of sound. Amber Eyes took a step forward and the whole place erupted in action. The crowd became chaos. Bodies clotted the bar's fenced exits. Bewildered drunks brawled with anyone nearby, and drinks became weapons, flying across the space, liquor igniting.

"Crimes," Caiden swore as he darted into the fray.

A shadow poured after him—fast. Her forearm snapped around his neck from behind and his momentum yanked. He rammed an elbow into his attacker's belly with all the strength in his augmented left arm. Amber Eyes doubled over. He twirled her hold down to lock her arm in front of him, then snapped it at the elbow. The juicy *crack* suggested organic bone.

She didn't blink or make a sound as she grappled for a hold with her good hand. Zero pain recognition—a massive problem—plus her flat stare wasn't a Graven-loyal look.

He flipped his position and kicked her knee hard enough to break it.

A glass drink shattered against the side of Caiden's head. He swore and dodged the bodies flooding off the bar platform. His morphcoat puffed and hardened into armor.

Fully equipped security forces streamed in on illuminated walkways. The saisn hunter finally spotted Caiden, nicked a glave off the security, and fired first. A scarlet blast roared through the night. The darkness hissed in revolt. The energy bolt skimmed the edge of Caiden's hip as he rolled aside and floundered to his feet, biting back a cry. Heat keeled into a sudden chill.

Caiden smashed a quick-heal pack onto his hip and dodged behind a tree trunk. The fall had angered an old fractured rib.

The saisn hunter's aim targeted everyone's attention on Caiden. But chaos was familiar to him. All his tension snapped into action. Reflexes glittered with the deadly precision and speed that had built his reputation. He was the Ghost of *Azura*. Charging through the fray, he snapped limbs, cracked skulls, snatched drunks to shield himself from glave fire, pinched pressure points, made weapons of glass and stones, matched violence with bloodshed while an involuntary mirth bubbled up in his chest, forming a grin on his face—and the volume rose on that empty voice that said Caiden was *better* this way.

Uncompromised. Alone. Blood and violence and a hot blade through tallow.

He plowed through the confused riot and sprinted into the lightless forest. His hip burned with pain, ribs sparked.

Behind him, Amber Eyes tore out of the brawl, stopped hard, and leaned into the air, crookedly—tracking him? Her arm was fixed, somehow, the knee still bowed but bearing her weight.

Caiden weaved around massive tree trunks, dodging clouds of lightflies that might betray his position in the dark. He slowed to desperately fumble the sayro from his pocket. It was squished and the filaments three-quarters charred. He unbuckled a chemical canister of fluid off his belt, flicked the lid open, and shoved the sayro inside. The flower melted and a reaction fizzed up. Caiden snapped the lid closed as the liquid boiled bright. He sighed in relief: this part wasn't a waste, at least. He could make the medicaments he needed.

The *Azura* was docked on a landing platform a quarter kilometer away in a giant clearing. He aimed for the unnatural gridded plantings of fungus that illuminated a flight path into the canopy. Behind him echoed the rasping sound of Amber Eyes dragging her leg as she tried to follow him at speed.

But no one knew running like Caiden.

At fourteen years old, he'd run for his life. Then he ran from the memory of the slaughter. Ran from nightmares on repeat. Now he ran from Threi Cetre's bounty hunters, and there was nothing more to life than feet pounding, wings sailing, heart beating.

He leaped from root to root, avoiding the transparent soil because what was solid or gel or liquid all looked the same. Bioluminescent fish coursed deep below and hinted at the planet's freshwater veins. It meant absolute drowning if he lost his step.

The sounds of fight and pursuit faded off into a mush of echoes.

The ship dock was a series of platforms. Caiden stumbled with relief when he spotted the *Azura*'s disguised backside among the vessels. Paces from his ship, the neural connection congealed. Serenity glowed into his mind, wrapping his muscles around the vanes and thrusters of the *Azura*, sparking his mirror neurons with the components of her engine.

Bay doors—all it took was the thought command. The alterskin disguising the ship tore and flickered as the back iris folded open. Caiden dashed inside. He was greeted by monstrous darkness. A huge body rushed at him, maw gaping, paws slamming the ship as lethal muscle rippled.

"Stay!" Caiden yelled at C.

The nophek whined. Rough skin roared across metal as he whipped his tail back and forth in frantic greeting.

Caiden barreled for the storage wall, yanked a drawer out, and dumped the contents of his chemical canister into a waiting tub of culture. The sayro light purled through inky tissue inside. Caiden gushed another sigh of relief and refocused, popping the engines online with a mental command. Then the bay door—

C roared, earsplitting. Caiden swiveled around to see him leap at Amber Eyes as she dashed inside. The ship shook when he landed, and Caiden pitched to the floor. The nophek took up a sixth of the whole ship's bay, and he bore that weight on the bounty hunter to pin her down. Her hands flew up, stopping his sharp-toothed mouth inches from her windpipe. This time, she screamed.

Caiden scrambled upright, swearing. Out the back of the bay, between the trees, small security vessels jetted toward the dock like a school of fish, glinting as they veered in the dark.

He signaled the iris door shut and limped to the cockpit, shouting, "C! Keep!"

The nophek's giant paw pinned the hunter's chest to the floor. He snarled in her face, and she winced and twitched more than she'd done when Caiden broke her limbs.

He plunged one hand into the cockpit's misty glow. Particulate light gathered up into bright nerves, threading his fingers and forearm, whispering under his skin. Thrusters fired and the *Azura* detangled from the berthing. The other half of Caiden's control was mental, the ship linked to him as if he were armored in it, its muscles cladding his, engine thrumming with his pulse. He had little attention to spare for the ruckus in the bay.

The ship's alterskin disengaged—no point in it now. The *Azura*'s liquid-glass shell showed some of the forest surrounding them, distorted past the transparent contours of the Glasliq material. The security ships spiraled in their wake.

Amber Eyes twisted to elbow C's nose and wriggle free. She launched at Caiden, and he could only catch her in his augmented left arm. His machine muscles plumped and the shock system wheezed as he crushed her in a one-armed choke hold. "C!"

The nophek whimpered, sliding to one side as the ship veered. Light-studded tree trunks slithered past. Caiden clawed his right hand in the drive guides. The ship crashed upward like a water drop through a lattice. Its glass wings splashed into liquid around three-meter-thick tree limbs, re-forming on the other side, speed dropping. Flocks of luminous creatures swerved from their path.

The nophek fought for purchase to get near. Amber Eyes struggled. Small muscle groups dissolved, joints dislocated, and she melted out of Caiden's hold. He flipped her to the floor while his other arm was still raised and shaking, orchestrating the *Azura*'s flight out of the forest.

"Brace, C!"

He tipped the *Azura* vertical and kicked the bounty hunter toward the nophek, who crushed her under a paw. C's other limbs braced, claws crunching into gaps in the wall plating as the ship yawed sideways.

Caiden vaulted into the pilot seat and pulled both arms through the light guides, heaving the ship around tangled boughs and slapping leaves. The *Azura*'s Glasliq wings splashed. Her inner scaffold skeleton tightened, ribs folding together to forge a sleek glass blade cutting the forest open.

Blips in the cockpit holosplays marked the security flock, which scattered and were quickly lost in the canopy.

The hunter was jellying again, joints rotating, more flexible than any augmentation Caiden knew. She broke half her body to squirm free from C's claws. The nophek snarled and bit her ankle, but the slim running blade of her foot hissed through his teeth. She kicked off C's skull to propel herself at Caiden again.

The whole ship jarred as she crashed into his side. Resonance armor screeched and dragged bumps across Caiden's skin as the neural link mirrored the *Azura*'s impacts against the canopy. He clawed his hands into fists to power upward.

Rain clouds, sunlight, water drops. The ship jetted through lightning and out of the atmosphere, streaking into empty space.

Unity's rind filled the cockpit view. A glossy, vaporous membrane, the vast surface formed the border between Unity and smaller outer bubble universes with micro-differences of physics.

Velocity peeled the hunter off his side. She clung to the seat and wrapped him in a choke hold much more effective than his had been: whatever she was didn't feel pain, could go without breathing, and regenerated rapidly.

Five seconds before he lost consciousness.

"Listen," the hunter said through gritted teeth.

Choking, Caiden corkscrewed his fingers in the guides, boosting the *Azura*'s speed.

Unity's rind bowled over the ship's nose, an iridescent storm licking the windows, colors birthing and dying through the pane, suffusing the cockpit. The bounty hunter seized up and emitted a hacking sound. Her arm slackened. Caiden turned to see her eyeballs glazing turquoise like oxidized copper.

As the *Azura* cruised out the other side of the rind, the hunter crumpled to the floor. Swirled patterns started splitting open in her skin, bleeding fluids as inner tendons melted. Strips of her skin foamed and sloughed off.

Unexpected.

The *Azura* sailed on smoothly while Caiden looked over the hunter's twitching biomechanical body.

Tightness whittled his voice to a whisper: "Too close of a call this time."

Multiple factions chased him now, a new type of hunter, a trap he couldn't avoid. His previous wounds were barely healed before each next encounter.

He couldn't keep this up. It was changing him. Turning him toward a fondness for brutality and a reliance on his Graven will.

Caiden crept close to kick the bounty hunter in her hip. No response.

C stalked over and sniffed her disheveled white hair as the ends crisped black. More than half her parts didn't seem built to exist in the physics outside of Unity.

"Watch her, in case she's still alive." Adrenaline fizzled into clammy pains. Massaging his throat, Caiden turned back to the cockpit. Then froze, cursing, "*Nine crimes.*"

Just across the rind, a Casthen armada of hundreds waited for him, netted out across space.

CHAPTER 2

THE PROXY OF HER

The Casthen ships scattered across space in a pattern Caiden recognized: a trick they'd tried in a fringe universe. Star-bright encrustations on their bellies built up a knockout wave that would disable even the *Azura*'s special systems.

Measurements chirped red in the cockpit holosplays. Arcseconds ticked. Heat prickled up Caiden's ribs as he stared at the Casthen net. He had installed weapons and could bash the ships into one another, but he'd done that in the fringes and they'd be wise to it now.

He'd never outrun them.

But he could hide.

"C! Come!" he shouted. The nophek bounded over, filling up the left side of the cockpit. Caiden yanked a pen syringe off a slot in C's collar and plunged it into the nophek's shoulder. "Sorry, just for a bit. Baby dose."

The nophek pinned back his ears, shook his head, and slumped to the floor as the injection changed his blood chemistry. It was the only way he'd be safe to cross over the *Azura*'s rind, incompatible with his rare species.

With the pup safe, Caiden smacked his hand on the florescer above his head. The smooth crystal peak fit his palm, bulging from a larger liquid-crystalline and lightseep obsidian spine that stretched inside the length of the vessel's ceiling and glowed through the Glasliq layers. Its impossible quantum technology activated at his touch: a new universe blossomed, expanding to encapsulate the *Azura*.

The fiery rind washed through and past Caiden. Golds and blues murmured in the expanding energy membrane. When it pushed through the ship walls, new substances plumped into the carapace of the hull, loose components cinched and hollows filled. The engine's song merged into happy tones, and Caiden smiled. His breath tasted sweeter, tension massaged, biology simply *better* here.

Moments until the knockout blast—Caiden raked his hands through the light guides and spun the ship, thrusting back inside Unity's rind but not all the way through the other side. This rind was wider than the breadth of the *Azura*, so Caiden turned to fly sideways. The ship's own universe clashed with Unity's in a roil of hues, energy blistering all around. Any other vessel would have been dismantled by the consistent flux of flying inside a rind, but the *Azura* remained cozy in her own world, a tiny bubble inside the membrane of an even vaster spherical world.

Caiden exhaled and dropped his fingers from the guides, which dissolved back into luminous fog. The ship would be undetectable until the Casthen managed to track disruption patterns on the rind surface and find some way to blast him out of it.

He set auto-course and a timer for a few hundred arcminutes, well within the fuel he had to keep the rind active. He peeled his mind from the controls. Adrenaline twinkled away, leaving him lightheaded and trembling, muscles heavy and energized at the same time. New and old pains twinged.

"We can't run forever." Caiden rolled out of the seat and placed his palm on the *Azura*'s console. Buzzes coiled beneath his fingertips. He smiled and trailed his hand along the wall as he turned to the ship's bay. The buzzes followed like a little swarm.

At a distance, he inspected the wrecked bounty hunter. Whatever her biomechanical body was, she wasn't designed for a crossover between universes.

She appeared dead. If true, that was the rind's fault.

C roused as the injection of protective drugs wore off. The crossover through the *Azura*'s specific rind would destroy nophek physiology, though C was fine once *inside* the universe itself. Caiden's heart had nearly exploded the first time he had to test the safety meds on the pup.

C raised his big boxy head and purred deep in his throat until he noticed the hunter. Purr turned to growl. He pinned her under a paw as broad as her chest, with sharp nails as long as a human finger.

"Good boy." Caiden petted C's short, cropped-looking ears, receiving a head-butt and a rumble of purrs. He scritched the thick muscle ridges running up C's forehead. Felid and canid traits combined with monster, and the nophek's powerful body tapered from hulking shoulders to a slimmer backside and long, thick tail with fins. Dark-skinned muscle rippled under fine black fur and scaly patches. His eyes were vicious round moons of reflective shine. A sweetheart nightmare.

"We don't have much time, so let's gather clues before chucking her out the back." Caiden hugged C's big head. A glass chicory flower jingled on his collar. "Sorry this hunter isn't one you can eat."

To this day, Caiden's every dream was filled with teeth and tearing, with the razor stench of nophek blood and roars blurred with the shrieks of his slaughtered people. The memory stimulus and recording—or "memory jog"—he'd undergone as a child left him with the side effect of a memory loop, his brain repeating the events of the horror every time he slept.

"All right, release."

C lifted his paw. The nophek had been a fast learner since he was a small pup, and as the gloss in his brain matured, he was growing more intelligent and grasped meaning behind Caiden's languages.

Caiden crouched to examine the hunter. "Hybrid organic-inorganic. Viral bioassembly? Not an augmented human...but completely machine beings don't have consciousness or operate with bioresonance like she did. So?" He pressed a palm on her sternum. Alloy materials pinged deep in her torso. The twitches of a dead animal?

Her clothing was Dynast shades of black and blue, even the copper of her eyes was a Dynast color. More perplexing, part of her construction looked to be lightseep obsidian, that rare, incongruent, phase-pliable material left scattered around the multiverse from the Graven civilization. Many lightseep structures had been recolonized for other purposes, and the technology within hoarded by the Dynast for their Graven research. But lightseep famously could not be tooled or broken—how could it get inside a mobile body?

The nophek huffed into Caiden's hair.

"All damned, three of the most powerful factions in the multiverse are after us now, C."

Threi had sent the Casthen chasing Caiden for ten years across the multiverse. The Cartographers' passagers gunned for the bounty Threi had placed on him.

Threi's sister was Abriss Cetre, the Dynast's Prime. Her unique astrologian expertise allowed her to divine information based on the alignment of stars, as well as the location and birth pattern of individuals, groups, and events. Within Unity, where Threi had driven Caiden, she could have tracked him down precisely. Despite Threi's murderous relationship with his sister, it made sense they would work together, because there was nothing the Dynast, obsessed with Graven relics and knowledge, would want more than the *Azura*: phenomenally unique, with modern components patched around ancient bones, origin unknown, and a universe-generating mass like nothing Caiden had seen in all the multiverse.

He straightened to his feet. Ache called up in his sinew and bones. C's nose whistled with worry as he leaned into Caiden's thigh. "You and I might have to take on all the worlds, little boy. You doing all right?"

The nophek yowled and licked Caiden's face with a serrated tongue, mashing his hair with meat-sweet saliva. Caiden wrestled C's head and scratched through his dense mane. He swept the fur aside to check the chemical levels in C's intravenous collar. Most universes were inhospitable to nophek, but ingenuity and care kept C alive.

The beast stank of brine and sea-stuff from the last planet they'd been on, and his belly was still full of fish. The top height of his shoulders reached Caiden's chest, and he was over twice as long from nose to tail tip—much too large to fit in the scour and wash the stink off.

"Watch her while I clean up."

C stretched his full length, then plopped down on the bay floor. He crossed his paws and licked them while his moon eyes fixated on the hunter.

Caiden jogged down the ramp in the middle of the bay to the lower level. A short hallway housed the cylindrical scour chamber. He peeled off his clothes and chucked them in, then ran the scour while he probed his wounds.

His body was a patchwork of injuries, and his augmented arm needed tuning. He signaled the pigment from flesh-colored to transparent, exposing crystal and sapphire pins, porous bone bundled in plump blue muscle and lustrous white tendons. It stretched from the cervical vertebrae, over his shoulder, and down to his fingertips, the actuators feeling clunky lately and the variable hyperdiamond stiff.

Caiden squeezed his eyes shut. He missed En. And Panca—she would have recalibrated it in moments. Ksiñe would scowl at Caiden's dropped weight. Laythan would secretly be impressed by all the scars. And Taitn would just be happy to have him back.

Caiden rushed into the scour. Radiance blazed. Heat flushed then chilled. Waves of dense air rolled down his body. He stepped out cleaned, insides emptied, bruises gone, skin newborn soft and stripped of a dark tan. Freckles dotted his skin beneath.

He surveyed himself with distaste, remembering why he scoured so infrequently. The dirt, wounds, and tinier scars returned him to a normal creature. Wear and tear clothed him in some of the humanity he'd lost while embroiled with the Casthen. The evidence of time was erased by the scour, and he found it unsettling to be reverted to a former state, as if to underline how pointless the intervening moments had been.

He yanked clothes on, grabbed a toolkit, and marched back up to the bay to squat by the bounty hunter again. He would harvest lucrative components, then chuck the rest outside.

The hunter's features were feminine but with mixed aesthetics—brutish and soft, warrior and spy. She had strong brows and a small nose, deep eyes streaked with dark pigment. Scars scratched her up all over, healed in with an artificial white tissue. Her skin was patchworked with black materials and textured plate armor. Her lower jaw and her neck were fitted with a skeletal copy, sharp teeth cutting into plush lips.

How many more strange fighters did the Dynast possess?

Caiden dismantled the mangled construct, setting aside the most valuable parts to sell. By the time he was done, she no longer looked humanoid: necklace bones, peeled organs, and plucked tendon.

"Time to be quick." He treaded to the cockpit and reached a hand in the light guides to swerve the *Azura* out of the rind and back into Unity. One arcminute was long enough to dispose of the hunter, burying her in the vacuum of her own universe. He could do that much for her. Then he'd be a ghost again, well before the Casthen located him.

At a mental signal, a violet atmoseal membrane spread across the bay's back, and the glass door iris pleated open. Beyond the atmoseal's luminous particles lay empty space. Distant stars pinned back the void.

For safety against the vacuum, he pulled on a cloudsuit harness and activated it: a skintight membrane grew across him. Its material puffed out so much it became a transparent gaseous field. Caiden gathered up the Dynast hunter's remains. The cloud surrounded them both, faintly sparkling.

He stepped through the atmoseal, then past the ship's scalar gravity field. Pressure patterns shed off him, body lightweight. His boots magnetized to the floor while the body he held floated up. Hair and nerves ribboned out. Caiden let go, and the corpse lifted toward nothingness.

It drifted there in the dark, lit by the *Azura*'s idle lights.

Guilt curled through him but another universe's physics had done this to her, and she'd been gunning for him, inviting trouble. *Listen*, she'd said . . .

He reached out to prod the thing away. It'd be obliterated when he fired up the jets.

Listen.

A susurration . . .

There could be no sound in the void. But a chill stitched down Caiden's spine.

Something grazed him like a noise.

"Cloudsuit glitches." He reached to the suit-controller pad, then froze, staring ahead.

Petal layers hummed inside the organic machine's mangled throat. Spongy tissue sloughed off its frame. The void squeezed glittering marrow from porous rods of the clavicle, droplets levitating away. Crushed down inside, her vocal folds quivered.

Leave it, she's dead.

Random dead animal twitches, electric impulses lagging through broken matter.

Caiden's cloudsuit field fizzed to cool his body heating. *Get out of Unity.*

But he couldn't look away from the syntactic rhythm of that void-eaten voice: *Hmmm. Mm. Thmmm.*

He widened the cloudsuit oxygen field. Packs on his shoulder blades wheezed gases, bubbling out the atmosphere cloud to encompass the mangled corpse. As air slicked back over the hunter's frame, marrow crusted, tissues stopped liquefying, and those thrumming vocal folds emitted sudden sound.

Words half-born. Whistle braided around her murmur, and he thought he heard the word "wind." Her intact rib cage splintered under the strain of forcing air out.

"Where sssss." Gill-like vocal folds went slack into whisper.

Caiden flinched backward, which slipped the atmosphere field off the body, robbing sound waves of medium. Silence engulfed him, except his heartbeat thudding.

She couldn't possibly have anything to say that would be worth hearing. Every moment's delay was a moment longer for the Dynast to track him down. Every star that glittered in the expanse was a data point for the Dynast Prime to extrapolate into Caiden's location using her astrological insight.

He tugged the body back into the oxygen field and gripped either side of the mangled torso. His fingers bolstered ribs around lungs. A sigh wheezed, and words, "Wwwwhere's thhhe wind..."

Caiden went rigid. Sharp memories bristled, stabbing the rest of the phrase into his brain: *Where's the wind come from?*

He no longer remembered what Leta's voice sounded like, but his mind had kept her words.

Scents and sensation kicked up. Lying beneath the oak tree, cold grass under his back. Sweet, sunbaked alfalfa flooded his nose. There had always been a breeze on their childhood planet.

He blinked back to the present, the void. The cloudsuit whined warnings. Tanks low.

Trembling, he answered the phrase, the same words from when they were children: "It just makes a big circuit."

Tension deflated in the rib cage between his palms.

This is absurd. This thing has no way to hear me.

Atop the torso, the rent skull plates resembled a limp flower. Lightseep glinted in the brain case, fracturing starlight as the body swayed in space. Bits of auditory system remained.

Caiden's heartbeat counted loud, waiting for a response.

Tiny spasms formed whimpers. A tight, hoarse hum, "So it's...the ssssame—"

—wind every time?

Memories lashed up again.

"Where did you hear this?"

A trick. Threi had tried to use empty promises before to lure Caiden into traps. Fragments of Caiden's childhood memories lay buried in the data of his memory jog: easy for Threi to dig into now that his Casthen were allied with the Cartographers who owned that footage.

Cinched sounds emitted from the hunter. Gills fluttered, too weak to hold a shape.

Caiden tried inverting Leta's words. "I can't fix everything," he said— she had said to him, accusing him, *You can't fix everything, Caiden.*

The hum of the hunter's flowery throat replied, "You can...try."

Anger stamped up his spine, making his fingers fidget. Another test: "This is just the way..."

"...it's always...been," she replied correctly.

"Tricks," he snarled. *These* memories were still recent enough to have been part of his memory jog. His enemies had bent incomplete phrases into the shape of hooks. It wouldn't snare him. "You aren't her, and your lies aren't welcome here."

For ten years, Caiden had watched ten-year-old Leta die a thousand times in his dreams: trampled, chewed, crushed, eaten whole. It had taken the entire length of her life again for him to let her go.

This wasn't his Leta. His fingers squeezed the filigree frame of the hunter's torso so hard it snapped. He shoved the whole mess into the void.

Debris glittered off into space. Tiny machine functions died, and soft materials shed away as the body glided beyond the cloudsuit border.

Two final words quivered into the air between her and him.

"Break...stuff..."

Cold sheeted through Caiden.

That memory hadn't been recorded.

Leta had been eight.

It was raining. She'd been left to handle an impossible task alone, and finally gave up in tears. Afterward, Caiden told her, *Whenever you're running into trouble, break the machinery. I'm closest to this sector and always get sent out for the small fixes, I'll come help you. And sometimes smashing feels good, you know.*

Leta had smiled shyly and picked more flowers.

I'll come help you.

Before inertia took the hunter's body out of reach, Caiden lunged to the end of the ramp and snatched her wrist. Scraps and fluids scattered as he yanked the rest of her back into his arms.

Whatever consciousness had been animating the body was gone now. No more twitches.

Confused tears sparkled off his cheeks. His breathlessness hazed white, loud in his ears.

Ten years ago, Threi had dangled the first bait, saying he'd salvaged more than nophek from RM28, the desert where Caiden's people were sent to slaughter. In Emporia, Caiden had seen Threi handing off a child-sized body to the Dynast Prime in exchange for information.

Caiden's nightmares had conjured every possible way Leta could have died on RM28, but he hadn't really seen it. His final memory was her huddled in the corner of the dark transport box: a tear slithering down her bruised cheek as she closed her eyes and managed a brave smile. His promise to come back for her blazed a lifeline between them.

He swallowed, something coiling in his throat. He did not *want* it to be possible.

"Nine crimes," he swore, "what are you?"

He gathered as much of her materials as he could and stepped backward through the atmoseal. Scalar gravity patterns snared them both and pulled parts to the floor. Liquid splashed, heaviness filled Caiden's arms, and he folded to his knees with her across his lap.

Whenever you're running into trouble, he'd said to Leta. *I'll come help you.*

This wasn't his childhood friend, but either she had access to parts of his mind he'd buried leagues deep, or she knew a truth he didn't.

CHAPTER 3

THE ECHO OF HIM

After the devastation of her Proxy body, Leta's consciousness was ejected, her spirit unraveled from its anchor. She entered the luminiferity, a nonphysical dimension brimming with energy and information, where a conscious spirit could travel independent of space and time. Or hurtle, in Leta's case.

Untethered, her spirit blasted like a lightning bolt back to her real flesh-and-blood body in the Dynast's palace on the planet Solthar, the center of Unity. Leta crossed the immensity of galaxies and the laborious curve of time between her Proxy and her real body, the two vessels she could inhabit—though only one at a time.

She slammed back with a force. Eyes flying open, Leta shrieked and jerked backward hard enough to slip from the scalar gravity levitating her body over her Away station. She hit the floor with a *crack*, skull bouncing, dizzy in a burst.

The pain signals that her machine Proxy had stifled came roaring into her far more fragile human cells. Injuries mapped into her, convinced her body that ribs had snapped, vertebrae cracked, skin melted.

Leta clenched her teeth and tried to slow her breaths. She peered, dazed, over the room and the ten bright quartz plates of the Away stations. A couple of the other Graves' real bodies levitated comfortably, as if asleep, while their consciousnesses were off in their own Proxies on missions or local tasks. The Graves had a single Proxy each, crafted by Abriss using sacred geometries and bioresonance so that, like rods built to call down one specific bolt of lightning, they drew in a Grave's consciousness from the luminiferity.

If that Proxy wasn't wrecked, as Leta's was now.

Dejin Eight's real body wasn't there levitating, and he rarely strayed far—

"Dej?" Leta called, voice breaking.

She rolled on her side and yelped at the pain.

That brought him. "Saa ol bri!" Eight boomed, lumbering in through the archway of a connected alcove. The ursgen had a sinewy face, jaw wider than a human's, nose broader, eyes small and glittering. Skin almost black. His hairless head was thick with patterned muscle, and his long, wide ears twitched with worry. His longer tail skated anxiously across the floor.

"Leta Nine!" rang Dynast Prime Abriss Cetre's beautiful voice as she swept past Eight from behind him, swift with alarm.

Leta's whole body tingled like a sleeping limb awoken. Her mind, expanded while within the luminiferity, tried to fit itself back into her limited physical brain. Human gray matter felt jagged and cramped compared to the airiness of nonphysical being, where all things were interconnected. Eternity in every second, and every second stretched to eternity. Accessing the luminiferity cost one's individuality—and sanity—if they weren't trained to endure it. A consciousness could expand so much it would dissolve into the plenum forever.

The Graves *were* trained, but Leta hissed swears in her head and wondered when training would ever feel like enough.

Dejin Eight hesitated to touch her, asking, "Consent?"

The Prime knelt and cradled Leta's head off the floor. "She's hurting, Eight, you don't need to ask consent to help now. Lift her, please."

Dejin scooped his long, rangy arm under her. With spread fingers, his hand was big enough to engulf her whole head. "Saa ai, you are safe, mae li sistra." The ursgen words fit his throat better, like pebbles tumbling across his tongue.

Abriss said to Leta, "Take your time to come back wholly." She pushed short waves of Leta's hair away as she probed skull and neck. "We're holding space for you."

In the woman's Graven proximity, with the spell of voice and touch,

Leta's convulsions stilled and temperature equalized. Abriss's gravitas swaddled Leta in harmony, and the world could end, for all she cared, as long as it ended like this.

Abriss Cetre was elegant and sharp with energy, with confident intelligence and boundless empathy. A pale copper cloak she wore over her blue-and-black flight suit draped down her back and pooled around them both like molten metal. It caught the light to cast watery ripples across the walls and fire her brown eyes into amber. It sparkled on the legions of freckles on her tawny skin. She was wreathed in fragrances of sage, earth, and rain, as if she spent more time outdoors than in labs and libraries. Leta adored her.

Behind Abriss, the main entrance door opened and another form strolled in, picking up speed toward Leta's side. They peered down, backlit by the ceiling's glow. Sisorro Seven, in-Proxy.

Seven's real body hovered above their Away station farther in the room. The prinna looked nothing like their humanoid Proxy, which had perfectly sculpted, crystalline skin over the organics within. Textiles draped them, all brilliant colors and fractal patterns.

Including Leta, there were only seven Graves left. Their genetic reconditioning utilized Abriss's Dynast strain of genetics, which was forging them into creatures approximating what the Graven had been. Intensive training on top of that made them capable of navigating the luminiferity to harvest the knowledge accumulated by that ancient civilization. Ultimately, they meant to access the spirits of the Graven beings themselves, which Abriss believed could re-cohere in the luminiferity, where nothing was dead, only diffused.

Pale shoulder-length curls brush-stroked the air as Sisorro Seven tilted their head side to side. "You look ghastly, Nine."

"Ol!" Dejin chastised, ears pinning back.

"I've felt better," Leta murmured.

The Prime said softly, "No damage, but lie still."

Seven asked, "You got the ship?"

"He didn't believe me," Leta whispered.

Caiden, her childhood hero. Alive and real.

Winn—that name she knew by his reputation, the name Threi had passed along.

Her memories of him had only recently returned. She knew a life with the Dynast, raised under Abriss's care for the past ten years. The Graves' conditioning had erased everything prior, yet mere days ago she'd recognized Caiden from footage presented during the Prime's remote comm meeting with Threi Cetre. The recognition had opened a pathway in Leta's mind. Recollection of a former life trickled in: the place she'd once thought of as home with pastures as vast as a sea. The spicy fragrance of oaks. Ripples of grass. Wildflowers. Wind.

She remembered the mechanic boy's laugh, his bright smile, his scent of metal and grease. The man who'd shoved her Proxy into the void was wounded and violent, and Leta didn't know him at all. He'd smelled of blood and fire and starship fuel, as if all the extra years between them had poured that fuel on his temper, charring a pit of violence.

Leta squeezed her eyes shut and groaned. "He is so much stronger than we expected. I couldn't steal the *Azura* alone, and my Proxy... stars forfend, he shattered it and tossed it into space. I failed us and won't get another chance."

The Prime frowned. "Unity should not have let you fail."

Sisorro's syrupy voice drawled, "Should have let me go too. I wanted to go. Prime, we should all have gone. *He is stronger.* Sounds fun."

Everything was fun to Sisorro Seven. Leta hadn't minded the challenge of chasing and fighting Caiden but... everything after went wrong.

"Sending you all would have made us fail for sure." Abriss pulled out a small device that opened above her palm. The tech jetted sharp rays and rainbow waves that arranged into a sphere mapping all of Unity: a tiny orrery. "I did not send you after the *Azura* to fail, Nine. Winn has slippery astrology, which is why Threi's failed to catch him all these years. But you, meeting him in-Proxy at that exact place and time, should have all but guaranteed our success."

The alignment of large-scale energetic structures, affecting all the unified fabric of space, was a language that gave Abriss information on people and events. It illustrated the future and showed her the bones of the past.

Eyes soft, Abriss delved through the celestial figures. "Tell me exactly what happened, when you're ready."

With Dejin's help, Leta straightened to her feet. Waves of pain crashed on shores in her body. Sawtooth shapes blared in her skull, where a squishy sensation pulsed between her ears. Part of it was her Proxy sensations mapping onto her, but part of it was just . . . her.

Out of Proxy, the Graves had a day or two to live. Her body and spirit separated slowly, oil and water. She and the others were still imperfect: whenever Leta's detached spirit returned to her body, she brought back a channel of energy that she was incapable of wielding as the real Graven had. It overfilled her body instead, corroding her nervous system.

The Proxies were a temporary shelter, giving their real bodies time to heal back up while "empty." But the longer the Graves spent in-Proxy, the more disorienting and destructive it was to return. So they lived in a delicate balance: their spirits didn't mesh with their biological bodies anymore, they couldn't live in Proxies forever, and they couldn't survive bodiless in the luminiferity for long.

The Graves' evolution had hit a biological impasse that only the *Azura* could fix. Abriss promised it was the key. And this was Leta's chance to give back something to the effort to save them, to lift one burden off Abriss's shoulders and not just bide time until healed.

Leta took a deep breath, ready to explain just how badly she'd failed.

"Wait!" Sisorro chimed, and whisked to another room, light on their feet in a flurry of colors. They dashed back and whooshed a weighted thermal cloak around Leta's shoulders. Soothing heat poured into her. Sisorro draped their arms over Leta from behind, curls tickling her cheek as they flopped their chin on her shoulder. "All right, tell us."

Leta sighed out her held breath and leaned her head against Seven's.

The plan had seemed simple. Talk to Caiden. Convince him of who she was so he'd feel safe. Steal the *Azura*.

She hadn't even managed the talking part.

"Someone recognized him and a riot broke out. I knew if I let him go, he would never be forced back into Unity again. I slipped onto his ship, but the crossover through the rind . . ."

The Proxies weren't designed to leave Unity. Passing through in-Proxy had severed her mind's connection with her Proxy body and thrown her back to her real one. Besides that, the rinds themselves may as well have been borders for consciousness. The energy membranes described and projected Unity's contents, a density of information that Leta struggled to sense past—not that there had ever been a need to seek outside of Unity.

Leta skipped the gruesome details. "He flew back into Unity, where I could reconnect, barely a few words…but I failed to convince him I was the real Leta."

His voice hurt and afire: *You aren't her.*

Given how different her Proxy looked compared to her real body, she didn't blame his skepticism. The real her would have been better bait, but she was hardly in any shape to fly away with a starship, much less fight him or a nophek if it came to that.

She shoved thoughts of the nophek away.

Still frowning, Abriss said, "You did everything you were meant to. I can't see yet why the rest didn't unfold as anticipated, but events are still in motion." She flicked a little planet in the projection, its arc twisting through a peppery dust field.

An idea occurred to Leta. "Dian Six can see whether my Proxy is lost."

The Graves had different strengths and weaknesses when it came to using the luminiferity. Sisorro Seven could watch dreams, Aohm One could fan through time and glimpse memories, and Dian Six could view a subject in remote locations. Leta excelled at gathering ideas and individual consciousnesses from the luminiferity, defining separate units out of that vast blur of interpenetrating reality. She'd saved some of the other Graves that way when their minds started to diffuse. Not that such a skill would have helped her confront Caiden.

Abriss cocked her head, a brown braid sliding off her shoulder. "Worth an attempt, yes. Wake Six gently."

Eight and Seven made way for Leta as she walked to the line of Away stations. The luminous crystalline plates emitted hums that braided through space, knotting gravity up around the Graves' sleeping forms. Dejin Eight's big silver-armored Proxy—humanoid like Sisorro's—knelt inactive in front of his plate. So did Aohm One's even more massive Proxy, Tayen Five's beetle-black shell, and Isme Two's, veiled in waterfalls of silky hair. Their real bodies were elsewhere in the Dynast Hold.

Leta stopped in front of Dian Six. The long, kinked waves of his onyx hair froze upward in the scalar field. His muscular torso was bare, the garments tugged loose by gravity nodes as he tossed and turned while away, ever restless.

The Graven treatments had affected the seven of them differently by species: Dian was a variety of human, his dark skin mottled with scars where the radiation split him, burn heals sketched his ribs, and bumpy venous patterns striped his face. His flesh was built of layers of transformed cells in freckling, both darkened and lightened in swaths. Leta's skin didn't have the swaths but was similarly freckled in every shade, following the swirling patterns of energy currents. She thought it looked better on Dian.

Leta grazed the back of his hand. A real body touched would bring the Grave's consciousness back. Six was in-Proxy with the Dynast military on a distant planet handling an unseasonable hatching of dangerous creatures. He had joked that he could use the stretch.

Dian's eyes snapped open. The levitation patterns unknit, lowering him. Even his hard-lined features softened when he glimpsed the Prime. Then he riveted on Leta and read her face. She was never sure that her face was emoting correctly, but fear must've shown through because Dian flipped to protectiveness in an instant. A snarl wrinkled his brow and he crouched to grab Leta's hand.

"Ah ri! Consent!" Dejin boomed from behind.

Dian glared and only squeezed Leta's fingers harder. She found the contact grounding. "What happened?"

She knew to be blunt. Impatience and scattered thoughts were already infesting him, making his hand quake. "I need you to try to locate my Proxy, from the luminiferity."

His sharp gaze inferred meaning in an instant. He leaped backward so the scalar gravity caught him again, twisting up his clothing and hair. He shut his eyes and the roughness of his expression mellowed out as his consciousness sought away.

Please find it. The swiftness of his help warmed her. She imagined his awareness flying across dimensions, shifting and discarding details of place as he tried to home in on her Proxy specifically in space and time.

"Eight and Seven," Abriss said, "join the others to eat, please."

An unnecessary *please*, set like a jewel. Every being would do as she requested, but gratitude and invitations still adorned her speech—it was part of what Leta loved about her. Abriss's Graven coercion always laced Leta so gently, she couldn't separate genuine affection from that which might have been genetically imposed.

Sisorro Seven pouted, exaggerating their Proxy's human face. "I would like to hear what Six finds."

"You will hear it later."

Seven dragged a quartz-skinned hand through their curls as they whisked over to their Away station. They plopped down on folded knees and flared their draped garments out. The dramatics did always cheer Leta up.

With Seven's real body only a meter behind them, the transfer of consciousness was instantaneous. Sisorro's Proxy slumped and their real body stirred. They were a prinna temporid xenid: their inner body spindly and featherlight while the rest of them spread in gauzy tissues that refracted light. Their sleek, birdlike face always looked smiling yet was unreadable like a faded painting, temporally vibrating too fast to make out.

"Dian is about to wake," they reported. Temporids had special relationships to time. Seven oscillated between multiple windows of it—lagging in the past and slipping to the future—and their voice simultaneously chorused, "Chilly in here," among less coherent futures that trilled, "See you there. Famished."

Their gauzy body caught up to their future echoes as they swished out the doorway. Imprints of their shape trailed in space behind them, gradually fading.

Dejin Eight straightened, long ears upright. The ursgen loomed a meter taller than Leta on lanky animal legs, a tower of worry in the dark.

Go, Leta mouthed. She nodded outside.

Ursgen culture was built on a language of touch and synced heartbeats, and Leta enjoyed pressure, so the two of them had bonded quickly. But he was too clingy sometimes. "Consent" requests helped him curb his instincts.

Dejin folded his body and tail up to fit out the doorway as he left.

Dian Six opened his eyes and lowered. Leta's pulse rate sped. Variations of his potential words crowded up in her head, all saying her Proxy was floating in space at the edge of the universe, completely destroyed.

"I could not find it," he said. "Nine's Proxy is outside of Unity."

Leta's fears dropped to her stomach. "Winn tossed me into space the other direction. This means he retrieved my Proxy and flew through the rind again. Second thoughts?"

As long as her Proxy was outside of Unity, her consciousness couldn't inhabit it. It was dead material and no use for getting through to him.

"I traced its last location," Dian offered. "The Casthen could start there and track Winn outside of Unity, drive him back to this side."

The Prime had a removed look on her face as she calculated. "No... but if he's kept the Proxy with him, there is hope. Second thoughts, as Nine said. A second chance."

Abriss smiled, half-forced, perhaps only for the effect it wrought: Leta and Dian both thawed, anxieties easing, responding to the harmonious gravitas Abriss impressed.

She said, "I'll examine the situation in the large orrery. You two join the others. Nine—you especially need care and family now."

Family. Abriss spoke the word as if trying it out. It was a rather new idea to Leta too. In the original group of twenty-nine Graves, she'd been scared to make friends who were likely to die, before the remaining ten had received numbers. Abriss had also forced herself to disconnect, as one might with a litter of sickly kits, preparing for the ones that might not make it despite effort and love. But the fewer Graves who remained, the more hope and attachment she seemed to pour into each of them. Seven left...

When Leta and Caiden were children, they'd had no real concept of family, just their respective parental units who were assigned to train them. Besides the animals, Caiden was the only thing in that world worth keeping—she had admired him and relied on his kindness—but she and Caiden weren't connected by blood. He'd been a fancy Casthen hybrid living there by mistake, and Leta was a far-from-fancy hybrid orphaned from a random world or grown in a labor lab—she didn't really know.

She thought of him again, but the spark didn't catch. Caiden was a speck in the immensity of her purpose. She couldn't allow the suddenness of him to strike her off course.

Leta and Dian followed the Prime out to the hallway. Coppery light from Abriss's cloak moved with her, peeling away from the darkness. When she parted from them, her Graven serenity ebbed away with the distance.

Dian Six swept along the hallway arcade in the opposite direction. Always impatient, as if his activity in-Proxy piled up in his body and he was desperate to expel it every time he returned. "We will not let you die."

"I've heard that before and said it myself." Leta followed him and smiled, knowing he meant well but was unequipped to *say* it well.

If her Proxy never returned to Unity, if the stars said definitively that she had failed their one chance... her spirit would corrode her own body within a day or two, and Caiden would fly off with the *Azura*, and the other Graves would suffer her same fate eventually.

"Did you defeat all the hatchlings on Falthent yet?" she asked, to dodge down-spiraling thoughts.

"I'm no good at stories."

"That's all right. I like the gory bits too. You're good at those."

CHAPTER 4

ENGRAVED

Caiden shifted his cramped legs in the nest he'd made of tools, machine parts, and chemical kits. Some bits hovered in scalar gravity nets as he worked on the wreckage of the hunter's body. He needed to repair only the brain and voice box enough for her to speak.

A bright holosplay showed neuromorphic circuit function and coupled energetic networks. It—she—was a complex adaptive system, a monster of quantum computing.

He'd arranged the mangled parts into what resembled a person again: a muscular human his height, with a broad build and feminine face. Her torso resembled a smashed bouquet of lilies wrapped in chipped black knives armoring transparent lightseep bones. Hair-thin wires threaded the mess. Some of the humanoid design had been improved by running blades, balance tensors of an exotic material, and xenid organs.

She was a very fancy hook with very irritating bait.

Leta.

If it was a trick, it was a dirty one, and he needed to know who was responsible. This area of his past was off-limits.

Caiden tossed an awl into the levitation field and plucked out a welding stick. To keep himself awake and to put C to sleep, he sang. He didn't have a great singing voice or know wholesome songs, but it worked: he'd been up past exhaustion for hours, and the nophek sprawled across half of the *Azura's* bay.

He got the hunter's windpipe padded with foam spray and her aural sensors active. Some parts of her construct had been *grown* and couldn't simply be reattached. Caiden was a mechanic, not a gardener.

He rubbed at a headache deep behind his eyes and admitted, "This is the best I can do."

The nophek huffed and got up, his footfalls jittering the machine bits on the floor. He nuzzled his head under Caiden's arm while his pupils dilated. The glass chicory flower jingled on his collar: a memento meant to remind Caiden of the person he'd been in Leta's eyes. A hero and protector, someone who stepped in when it was needed, who didn't keep walking when they saw injustice. He'd been trying, as an adult, to keep hold of that even as he let her go.

"If this doesn't work, I'm getting some damn sleep."

Caiden slid into the pilot's seat and raised his hands. The light guides congealed to twine around his fingers and the *Azura* stirred, thrusters waking.

He had evaded the Casthen armada by cruising farther through Unity's rind, then jumping to another side of Unity completely through a stellar egress, a portal between locations. He'd stayed outside of the universal bounds of Unity, but the hunter's materials were designed *specifically* for Unity's physics. The cerebral function she needed in order to talk depended on him putting himself at risk for a moment.

Caiden turned the *Azura* through the rind. Brilliant hues crashed over the translucent Glasliq shell. Fractal clouds split, chewed each other up, then whorled into darkness before the ship pierced through the other side in Unity. Caiden fixed a course parallel to the rind for a fast bail.

He stared ahead, listening behind him to her body's crackling diamond and fizzy chems as Unity's physics altered her materials for better or worse, a foul music of mechanical parts.

Caiden waited for a voice, watching the stars instead of looking back at her, as if observation would break some quantum alignment and determine that he'd failed.

Bumps prickled down his arms. His morphcoat grew tighter and heavier to soothe.

C growled.

"I'm not nervous!" Caiden shoved up from the seat. "Fine. Just get ready to bite her."

He swiveled around. Some parts of the hunter had healed, others crumbled. Pearlescent fluid leaked from somewhere.

Caiden knelt by the torso. C sniffed the skull, rustling sticky white hair. The holosplay schematics hovering over her showed life functions. Her lungs fluttered and changed color as air cycled. Her machine heart pumped. Energy levels stabilized. Rhythms good.

No cognition.

The nophek yawned, then bumped Caiden's shoulder. Caiden pushed him away. "I know I need sleep. But this—It has to work. The signal flow..."

Looked perfect. All systems linked, the holosplay reported.

The body didn't stir.

Caiden groaned and pored through different analysis modes, but none of the outlandish technology the Dynast had devised made sense, and he had neither skill nor parts to do better. Caiden hurled his tool, which the gravity field caught, denying him the satisfaction of striking a wall.

If he had to toss her out to space again, he would forever be haunted by *why* Leta's consciousness or memories were supposedly inside a weapon like this.

The nophek nestled his big forehead against Caiden's back.

"It didn't work."

C purred. Even the *Azura*'s hums changed tune, thick and comforting in Caiden's neural link.

"It's a trap anyway. Whether they've bottled up a ghost in order to bait me, or really have Leta—" That shut him up. He hadn't spoken her name in...how many years?

Caiden lifted his arm, and C wriggled his head under it. He cuddled into the nophek's mane.

A wretched temptation burgeoned in Caiden's mind as it often did when he felt desperate and alone: family.

Caiden stroked the velvety fur behind C's ear as sweet memories floated up to entice him: all the ways his family crew had guided and restored him, holding his hands as he accelerated age from fourteen to twenty in a flash and raced after childish notions of justice.

En might know how to externally stimulate the hunter's memory content. Panca would recognize the obscure machine parts. Ksifie could understand the biology. Taitn's partner was a Cartographer, and Laythan had Dynast contacts. But Caiden had lost count of all the dangers nipping at his heels. The last thing he wanted was to put loved ones in that line of fire.

Leta was a loved one too.

"Abandon the possibility of Leta forever..." Her name hurt to say, like the sound of it brought something of her alive just so he would have to bury it again. "Or put my friends at risk to help me reach the truth. If you and I were our younger selves, C, we would have rushed into this trap alone by now."

C whined and snuggled his head against Caiden's stomach.

Caiden remembered walking down the row of all the tiny nophek pups' cages stacked to head height, ready to transport to a safe planet after he'd nicked them all from the Casthen. Their eyes were closed, little faces less fearsome with Ksifie's special sedatives. But one still growled cutely at Caiden as he passed by. Caiden had laughed and peered in. The groggy nophek tried its best to be vicious.

"Nothing can keep you down, huh?" Caiden stuck his finger in the cage, and sure enough, tiny C bit him, weak jaw but razor-sharp teeth. Caiden didn't flinch—he'd been bitten by adult nophek teeth countless times.

He opened the cage door. The pup cowered but snarled. Caiden had been the same, when younger, before he understood that anger and violence really stemmed from fears.

The nophek lunged mightily and bit onto Caiden's shoulder. He caught the beast with both arms. This baby's bite was so much smaller than that of adults who had chomped the same place.

"It's tough fighting alone against something bigger than you. I would know."

The little nophek started shaking, its adrenaline battling the sedatives. Caiden wrapped his arms around the animal and squeezed, firm but gentle. Calming pressure was something Leta had taught him.

Caiden was jabbed out of reminiscence by the thought of her.

C yowled halfheartedly then sprawled. His claws scraped the floor as his forelimbs flattened, and Caiden chuckled. "Ten years and you're still a baby. The crew would be surprised how big you've gotten."

Crimes, I miss them.

Laythan's crew hadn't stayed together. Caiden had been their temporary glue, as children often were. Or it had been his Graven effect, which seemed to bind people to him.

Any one of them would rush to his side the moment he reached out for help. The problem would be getting them to leave afterward. He would have to kick hard, and it would injure his heart as much as theirs to part ways again. Yet it would hurt less than living with this mystery of Leta twisted into his mind for the rest of his life. She might be alive and in need, had cried for help only for him to maim and abandon her for good.

"Just one," he murmured aloud. C sleepily twitched an ear. "I won't call everyone. Just En's help for a matter of hours will be safe enough."

En had augmentation knowledge, could obtain the parts needed, and understood stealth and cunning. But En flitted around the multiverse almost as much as Caiden. A message, even in the proper channels, might take too long to reach them.

Caiden was holding his breath. He released it in a rush and scrubbed his fingers through his hair, then grabbed fistfuls until it stung. Seeing family meant wading into the shame of his avoidance and risking whether the gentle parts of him were dead for good, whether they would recognize the man he'd become, whether his Gravenness was so strong now it transformed their care into—

"Enough. Leta's memory matters."

Caiden dropped his hands, and while the pain ebbed in his brain he encoded a message using his neural link. Brief, only the basics of what he needed. He sent it, then doubled over C's back, cuddling his forehead into fur and letting the *Azura*'s idle tones blanket him.

Almost immediately, a sparkle cast through the neural link and the cockpit chirped with a response. Caiden startled upright, pulse hammering.

He peered over the words sketched in light across the holosplay and sensed, in En's charming phrasing, a hundred written then deleted words, an anxiousness over what tiny misstep might change Caiden's mind and send him running like a skittish animal. The message ended with rendezvous coordinates, and Caiden almost laughed at En's cleverness: Melynhon, a planet bifurcated by Unity's rind, half inside it and half in another universe.

"Perfect. Why didn't I think of that? I'm not Endirion Day, that's why."

His eyes misted. He hurried to the cockpit and flight maps.

This was happening too fast, yet many years delayed. He could be quick. Safe. Get the hunter to explain, or rip the answer from her brain, then he'd be back on the run before his heart had time to crave more of family.

———

The Graves' Away Room was halfway up the Dynast Hold's towering levels, and the long walkway outside had an open wall overlooking the palace and the planet—Solthar—Leta's home.

Tree trunks reached to this level, with lacy canopies and bulbous rain-catcher flowers that dribbled streams of water to gardens below. Forty meters away was another wing of the Dynast Hold shooting upward, many stories high. Tiny vines grew across the translucent lightseep obsidian, which fractured their reflections into different time periods, from bursting blooms to withered dry.

A distant evening sun-shower rained droplets lighter than air, snared in kilometer-wide beams of light. Dusty galactic structures peppered the sky.

As Leta strode beside Dian Six toward the meal, she couldn't help glum thoughts intruding. She imagined her Proxy—her other half, artificial though it was—far past those stars, beyond the border of her world.

Abriss is reading these stars. Soon she'll tell me how much I've ruined things.

"Leta?" called Isme Two from a terrace where the Graves had gathered. He curled around his knees on the bench, self-conscious of his state. His human body had been diaphonized by the Graven treatments: translucent flesh and glassy gold organs, silken white muscle, sparkling nerves, sinew like veins of gemstone. Rosy sparks danced under his skin: the freckling hadn't ever cooled in him, and it swirled painfully when he moved.

Sitting very still, he cradled a chalice of broth between crystalline hands. Buoyant waves of short hair obscured his face, forming a veil with the steam.

Of the seven of them, he looked most like what Leta pictured in her mind when she imagined the ancient Graven species, beautiful and full of light. The Prime had never confirmed they would end up *looking* like the Graven had, only that they would gain the same abilities.

Isme cleared his throat.

"Yes." Leta flushed, stopped staring, and sat between him and Dejin. She squeezed one of her hands, watching the deep layers of speckling shift. To become Graven seemed to mean gradually peeling away from herself, a tempest of sparks clothed in a skin that was all oscillating string, twisted too tight and out of tune.

The seven of them were freshly out of Proxy, meaning the disintegration of their nervous systems was in the early stages, bearable and easy to mask. The ambiance was almost lively, even. The crowd of bodies on the small terrace was a comfort. Leta felt at home and not so *other*. They'd all been through the same fires, into chaotic luminiferity and back again countless times. They'd suffered twenty-two losses together.

Dian Six sat next to Tayen Five and piled up a plate with food from the surrounding spread.

Tayen was a human variant, with a round face and butch features, cropped ears, close-shaved hair, cliff-face cheekbones, and a natural frown like Leta's—although honestly more of a scowl.

Aohm One was yraga, a muscular, flowery xenid: all white, silver-freckled skin with scarlet cilia frilled up inside bony and liliaceous folds. They had a head but not quite a face, no limbs as such, no voice except a presence in the mind. Their speech-thoughts were like a forest in fast motion, syntax budding and decomposing, many parts working to form a whole, of which Leta captured a gist: *Take time, little one. You are lost but there is hope.*

Isme Two said more plainly, "Something went wrong on-mission. Do you need to talk?"

Leta shook her head and tucked loose waves of hair behind her ears. "Better already."

What was there to say?

His empathy warmed her all the same.

Dejin rearranged his huge height and long limbs, spiraling his smooth tail around his waist and down one bent leg. He assembled Leta's plate with delicate foam, stringy herbs, hard yolks, and disks of pink fruit. Many flowers. A cautious diet designed to not upset them with how quickly their physiologies were changing.

"Are you sure, Treasure?" Isme asked.

Leta chewed on a bitter flower and leaned sideways to bump her shoulder into his. "Yeah."

Dian shoveled food into his mouth in a mix, done with the taste of it in one go. "Why this fuss. I still say we could live in Proxies all the time, never come back."

Leta shrugged. Six liked to believe that simple solutions never had repercussions.

Tayen smacked Dian's arm. "Insensitivvvvvvv"—the sound dribbled between her teeth until she blinked and finished—"to say when hers is wrecked wrek re eh." Tayen Five's parasite tripped her up and colonized her words with silence.

She was from a border planet where strange beings sometimes wended through Unity's rind. Her culture had revered this alerid-type parasite as a deity and selected Tayen as a host. She almost died from it before the Dynast rescued her. With Graven treatments she became stable, then symbiotic, and now there was no distinction between Tayen and the alerid. The most harm it did was rewire her speech and wriggle her memories into a different order, whether she was in-Proxy or not. Of all the Graves, she had to be the most thankful for how the treatments had transformed her, though she'd denied it when Leta asked. Not the softie, Tay.

"Eat. Eat," said Sisorro Seven, vibrating across time: arms spread invitingly to the feast moments before, and them already gorging. "Eat," they said, chorusing atop the words "delicious" and "skinny Nine."

Leta wrinkled her nose at them. "Who is skinny, bird arms?"

Sisorro fluttered happily, gauzy body curdling as they settled in place. Echoes of them still stood while some were already pouring her a drink of her favorite creamy beverage.

Leta reclined, calmed by the familiar background of Tayen and Dian arguing. Now and then they shut up at the same time as Aohm said something in their minds.

She sipped her drink and ate more, worries dissolving until her gaze found her plate and one of the flowers. It was the purplish-blue color of chicory.

Caiden. Winn.

"Leta," Isme prodded gently. His glazed, translucent features were hard to make out, but Leta imagined a youthful face as sweet as his manner. She'd forgotten his age, except that it might've been close to hers, disguised by unusual maturity. Leta hardly recalled Isme's prior self or deadname. She adored his white lashes and sun-bright irises, perfect zippering teeth, and messy, honey-colored curls. In the center of his skull, the crystalline pineal gland blazed like a third eye through his forehead. "Just tell us."

Stars forfend, he's keen.

Dejin Eight puffed up, his beady eyes widening and ears flicking. "Let her relax! Ahh bri."

"It's all right." Leta picked blue petals off the stem as she shared, "Even if my Proxy's safe, even if I get a chance to talk to Winn again, maybe the man is so different from the boy, no number of memories could make him care again."

Isme Two inhaled the vapor of his drink. It filled his diaphanous throat like pink fire and ruffled when he spoke. "Well...Whatever happens, if you return to your Proxy and are still compromised, come back safe. Abandon him and the ship. The Prime will find another way to heal us."

Leta didn't say it, but if the *Azura* would save the others' lives, it was worth hers. She was just one of seven, after all. She smiled, but Isme's sideways look said he knew the thoughts she hid.

Dian said, "If your Proxy reenters Unity and you make contact again, lie. Lie through your teeth. Lie like our lives depend on it, Nine. Do better."

Tayen Five smacked him again. "She is doing her besttttttt—"

Abriss's voice from behind them rang out, "She has." The Prime looked breathless but her eyes sparkled. "You didn't fail, Nine. You simply are not done yet."

"Prime?"

"My stars tell me you'll get the chance to talk to him soon, Proxy or not. Your weapon will be words."

Or not? Another chance to fail spectacularly. "Words. I've never been great with those."

"No," Abriss said in a soft chuckle, "but you're good at feeling. And you have memories to weaponize against him, make him feel safe enough to trust you. *I* trust you. We will have another chance to snatch the *Azura*."

CHAPTER 5

HEARTSWITCH

Melynhon was as close as Unity came to having a battleground. Unity's expanding rind was engulfing the planet with aching slowness, now about half and half. The portion *outside* of Unity was within a large universe that blistered off Unity's side and had a hospitable yet interesting variation in physics.

The Dynast Prime had immigrated half of Melynhon into Unity's philosophy of living. This made the planet both a trial ground for integration and a front of anti-Unity sentiment. Weaved into the cracks of this was commerce: traders in Unity and passagers from the multiverse capitalized on the physics transformations between sides to turn cheap commodities expensive.

Caiden flew the *Azura* along the non-Unity side down the fashionable "conversion belt" of Melynhon: buildings, courts, and plateaus clustered alongside the rind like one narrow city stretched out to the horizon. A few port hubs with vertical saisn architecture maximized rind exposure. Structures bored underground and towered up through the atmosphere to provide docking for ships in orbit.

The rest of the architecture was grown from a coral-looking mineral. Long tubes, tanks, and channels fit in seamlessly to accommodate xenids needing alternate environments. Fiery-colored plants and trees grew messily all around the Unity side, while green vines tangled the other. A dilapidated trail of structures crumbled back into the earth in Unity, the city tapering to dust in the wake of the conversion belt expanding to keep up with the rind pushing outward ever so slowly.

Nervousness blitzed Caiden as he approached the coordinates. He memorized topography and cataloged risks. There were Casthen vessels around, mostly big ones unloading large cargo. Some areas had drone patrol of civilians. The *Azura*'s alterskin was functioning fine.

He reminded himself that En had carefully picked the rendezvous point as well as who knew they were there and why—a delicate orchestration of nonchalance, trickery, and blending in. Caiden would be fast and alert, backup plans at the ready.

The *Azura*'s atmospherics cooled in response to his anxious heat. Even his morphcoat grew plush to counteract his stiffness. C ambled over, ears wiggling, and curled around the pilot's seat, walling Caiden in muscle and purrs. This tiny world knew him well.

"I know. I'm getting ahead of myself. As always, be ready to bite."

The weather changed as the *Azura* jetted onward. A bank of storm clouds dumped rain in Unity while the droplets transformed through the rind, becoming long ribbons of reddish vapor.

The coordinates were at a seamier part of the belt, not bustling but not so abandoned that ship traffic would look out of place. The crumbling architecture was filled in with other cultures' styles in a patchwork for many kilometers. Suggestive signage and strange code and small pockets of vibrant activity all looked fun and dangerous in equal measure. The sort of district En knew how to navigate best.

Caiden's pulse ratcheted up as the rendezvous point drew closer in the cockpit's map overlay. Veils of rain-vapor shed through the rind, obscuring his view. Proximity numbers dropped to zero.

"That—" Caiden stalled the *Azura* in a hover, gaping.

There at the meeting point, parked expertly in a canyon of cramped buildings, was a small, sleek, exceedingly handsome warship. Maltaean design, the color of blued steel, with faint hexagonal shielding scales. It was designed for all types of flight, aquatic included. In hidden visual spectra, a name sketched across one of the vessel's seams: the *Wintra*.

"Wow."

En wasn't a pilot. When had they bought such a fancy ship? A friend or partner must have picked them up for a ride.

With proximity, the security key he'd received opened a comm link.

Caiden took a deep breath of silence.

Through the aural devices: "Hi, hero." En's voice, crisp and feminine. The sound of it sledgehammered cracks in Caiden's resolve. *Crimes, what will I say? A decade delayed.*

En said, "Get down here."

There was a spot beside the unusual warship with just enough room between buildings for the *Azura* to fit. Caiden's hands shook in the light guides as he dropped his palms to descend.

A cluster of figures stood beside the *Wintra*. En was unmistakably the animated one on the winning side of a game of tiles spread out atop crates. Looking beautiful and deadly and entirely in her element, En laughed sweetly as her losing opponent fumed.

Several other xenids grouped around, and their faces swiveled to the *Azura*. En waved merrily at Caiden, then turned back to send her playmates away. Even the loser looked reluctant to go.

Landing gear unfolded from the *Azura*'s belly. The ship touched down, engine noise fading to a sigh, and a gentle sensation lapped through Caiden's neural link, fluffing around his jabbing thoughts and that violent hollow in him that was too deep to fill up or pave over and he hadn't ever needed to before and what if En saw it when she looked at him?

Caiden exhaled forcibly, then levered to his feet. He gestured to C. "Sit."

The nophek had to bow his head to clear the ceiling when he sat on his haunches.

"Just in case you forgot your manners," Caiden said, fitting an invisible leash bracelet on his own wrist. "You were small enough to carry, last time the crew saw you."

Goodbyes on a black-sand beach. *No gallivanting until we get back*, En had said. And Taitn, *See you later, brother.*

Caiden opened the bay-door iris. The muted rainstorm rumbled beyond Unity's rind eighty meters away. Red vapor trails on this side sizzled as they dissolved and gave off a peppery scent. Storm clouds hung puffier here and made everything dim. The physics allowed for Andalvian lighting: lazy brushstrokes of luminous jelly-stuff that levitated, lighter than air.

Caiden straightened his morphcoat, strode for the ramp, and nearly tripped, heart already tumbling. He caught himself and slowed. Exhaled. Beside him C groaned in annoyance and snapped his teeth once.

"Right. No cowardice now." He exited the *Azura*.

The *Wintra*'s side hatch opened. A figure walked out, and Caiden's jaw dropped once again.

Taitn Maray Artensi froze as he spotted Caiden in turn.

The *Wintra* was his—of course. One of the best pilots in the multiverse would have a vessel better than military spec. Caiden ached at the sight of both: emblems of so much that had happened in the intervening time that he was unaware of. He had *chosen* not to share his family's lives in order to protect them. That had always seemed the better choice... when he didn't have to see what he was missing.

And now the stakes of this rendezvous for "help" expanded, messier than Caiden wanted even though his heart soared at the sight of a brother. *Two to risk, but another getaway pilot isn't a bad thing. En wouldn't have added extra risk without care.*

Neither he nor Taitn moved until Endirion Day strolled to Taitn's side and clapped the man on the back, teetering him forward to walk with her.

En whistled as she neared. "Pup's not so young anymore. The nophek's grown too."

C lunged with a snarl. Caiden swore and caught C's momentum on the invisible leash, his bicep bulging as the nophek yanked, hackles up. "*Pace*," Caiden commanded, and the pup huffed, stepping behind Caiden's hip.

Caiden looked up and dithered in place. *What do I say?*

Taitn looked older. Smile lines framed his deep-blue eyes. That was a good sign, wasn't it? His dark hair and beard were neatly trimmed short. He had a filled-out look, healthier than Caiden recalled.

En hadn't aged at all—being completely augmented, she could look like whatever she pleased—but that put her around the same age as Taitn now, in the whereabouts of forty to fifty human years. Piles of loosely tied black hair sprang over her shoulder, ruffled by flexfield armor that thickened the air. Her dark-bronze skin glistened, and transparent strips revealed machine parts within. Streaks of smoky color around En's eyes made her disappointed gray gaze all the sharper.

Caiden reminded himself to breathe. "I..."

En took three big strides and smashed him in a hug. Her augmented strength crackled his vertebrae and pinched a fractured rib. The pain was worth it.

Caiden hugged her back hard. "En."

"Missed ya, kid."

He would always be a kid to them. Even now at thirty, he was the boy the crew had found at fourteen.

En pulled away, patted him on the shoulder, then shoved him into Taitn's embrace. Caiden inhaled nostalgic scents of starship fuel and alcohol, and leaned into the cold, textured leather of Taitn's pilot's jacket, green as a blackbird's wing.

Taitn pushed Caiden away to see. "Haven't been kind to yourself, huh? You look..." He hesitated before settling on, "Intimidating."

Caiden backed away and sank a hand into C's soft mane. "That's useful in some places."

En scowled, looking Caiden over from head to toe and back again. He was underfed for his thick build. His clothing hid most of the scars, bruises, and bandages. His hair was too short for a tie and too long to keep out of his face except with the clips that now sat askew.

"No reason to look presentable," he said, "with no one to see."

En snorted. "No one to look presentable for, and you couldn't scour once for us."

Caiden winced. "I did scour." Before hours of sweat and grease and no sleep.

"You look fine." Taitn smiled. "Worse for wear, but better than the rumors."

"Ah." En gave an elegant mock bow. "We're in the presence of the famous—"

"*Infamous*," Taitn said.

"Infamous! Legendary. Enigma. The man the entire multiverse is looking for, bounty higher than a heap o' gloss."

Heat flushed Caiden's cheeks. "Stop."

En laughed. "There are those embarrassed blue eyes I've missed. We've known you're safe—I've been tracking you when I can. But it's something else to see up close that you're still you."

Am I? Caiden forgot who he'd been, sometimes. He scritched under C's collar, the glass chicory flower jingling there. "I didn't want to draw you all into this."

"All?" En crossed her muscular arms. "Could've brought just me along. I love the sort of heroics you've been up to. Isn't that why you chose me to finally call? I'm flattered, by the way."

Taitn added, "We would've fought with you," which chipped another shard off Caiden's heart. "You can have a life, Winn. Pan made designs to outfit a new ship around the *Azura*'s spine and the Glasliq material. The alterskins you've been using to hide are unreliable."

Winn. Caiden hadn't heard his passager name in a long time. He twisted to peer up at the *Azura*. He didn't need a life—she was it. The alterskin disguised her as a beat-up security cruiser, but Caiden's mind's eye always saw the real thing: the Glasliq blazing, light fractured through it, her body perched like a sharp glass bird with too many wings folded up.

Taitn extended a hand for C to sniff, and continued, "Ksiñe's been working on ways to use nareid research to perceptually mask faces. Together we can make it easier for you to hide, rather than run."

The nophek gave Taitn's fist an approving nose bump.

Caiden smiled, tired. "The *Azura*'s more important. I can't stop running. The Casthen will dig me up if I hide. I came here for your help this once, please."

En threw her arms up. "How c—"

Taitn elbowed En away. "Don't scare him off again. And crimes, Winn, just spend some time with us before you run again, keep it as simple as that for now. We—" He swallowed, throat bobbing. "We missed you. I have a present for you from Ksiñe while En's doing repairs. I think it'll change your mind about coming home."

The Azura *is home.* Caiden returned a tight smile. "Fine. Sorry."

"That's our boy!" En wrapped an arm around him, ignoring C's growl.

"If Laythan was here, he'd smack you—rightly so—but he's not, so let's get on with the repairs you need. Show me this Dynast construct allegedly housing the consciousness of your dead little sister."

They headed for the *Azura*. Caiden's whole body hummed, his instincts trying to tear his attention away to every alley shadow and ricocheted sound. *En's wrong. I'm not the old me.*

He strode into the *Azura's* bay and gestured at the hunter.

"Nine crimes," En swore, "you did make a mess of it."

"Can you fix what I couldn't?"

"Just need her listening and talking, eh?"

"Please. Keep the rest of her broken so she can't attack."

Some of the flowery skull plates were still open in the back and down the neck. The hunter's nerves flickered with faulty impulse. Some skin still striped her face, including most of her pink upper lip and half of the lower, which was held in place by metal armor carved into the fangs of a lower jaw.

En tenderly stroked a lock of the hunter's white hair over her ear, then tilted the skull gingerly to see the back.

Caiden hadn't been that kind. He'd treated the enemy so much less like she was valuable. So unlike it could've been Leta in there.

"Pretty." En brushed debris from the white eyelashes. Oxidized eyes glinted unconscious behind. "Pretty features and gorgeous design. You're right about this being a Dynast construction, but that doesn't mean it's not still a Casthen trap. I poked through the Dynast's communication records: no envoy between the two since you went on the run. No unusual positioning of Dynast military. Nothing unusual at all, in fact. The Dynast Prime runs a tight operation. The Casthen Prime runs a chaotic one, but it lets him hide more."

Caiden added that to the puzzle. "She was followed up by a Casthen net. And Threi is the only person who knew Leta was part of my past."

Even imprisoned, Threi Cetre was still able to command his people, oversee research, and build up power while he festered in his isolated universe. Trying to catch Caiden and the *Azura* was a challenge that helped stave off boredom—or so the little personal notes Threi left for Caiden every year or so suggested. But the Threi that Caiden knew had been obsessed with murdering Abriss, and there was no way that obsession hadn't festered too.

"Something doesn't line up," Caiden said. "Or lines up *too much*. For years Threi's been poking around RM28, the planet where Leta and I had been sent to slaughter, where I thought she'd died, where I found the *Azura*. Me and her and the ship…I don't know."

"You're tired," En said, raising her voice as she made a racket rifling through his tools.

"I think he's been hoping to find more tech like the *Azura* there so he can bridge out of his universe on his own. I still worry it's only a matter of time before he finds a way out."

Taitn fixed Caiden with a dark gaze. "If he does, then you're free to give up running. Is that so horrible to think of?"

"This isn't about me. You didn't see what Threi is capable of."

"If you've been keeping tabs on him, you can admit he's changed. The Casthen's new deeds have benefited the multiver—"

"He'll snatch the *Azura* right away, you know that."

Taitn fell silent.

Caiden regretted his bark, but it was the truth. "I have edges again, sorry."

When no one took up the silence he'd made, he said, "Çydanza, remember? Threi's scheme to depose her and do good by it was concealing his true desire to kill Abriss. Threi will take the *Azura* no matter how he gets released, and we don't know what he'll do with it. All these 'new deeds' of his may be him biding his time."

"All right." Taitn raised his hands in surrender. "You know him."

En hummed. "Let's focus on what's in front of us. This body's got the weirdest synthetic brain I've ever seen, but if I can't get her talking, I can mine some information from it."

Caiden exhaled. *I have help now.*

Help was dangerous. He might crave more.

"Be quick, En."

She rolled her eyes. "Don't rush art, kid."

Taitn had unpocketed a handful of salty protein bombs and sidled over to offer them to C. Instant friends, the two of them. He raked his fingers up and down the nophek's bristly, ridged back, and laid his other hand on the *Azura*'s glassy wall while gazing across her ceiling. The broad crystalline spine running the length glowed a soft blue from organic processes within.

"Sorry," Caiden said. "You missed the ship too."

"Yeah." The pilot's slight smile reached his eyes. "You can stop apologizing. We know you've been hurting. Come on, I've been ordered to feed you."

Taitn strode out and C—who knew the word "feed"—yanked Caiden along by the invisible leash.

Caiden marveled at the *Wintra* up close as he followed Taitn inside to a floor table with a food case atop it. He sat on a gel cushion and tried to ignore the strangeness of being civil, of not looking over his shoulder.

Taitn flipped the lid on the case, and the fragrance of Ksiñe's cooking struck Caiden immediately. Warm spices and tangy supplements, a floral note and edgy citrus. His mouth watered and tears brimmed in his eyes. "Smells like family."

He should have known that En would reach out to everyone else, even as Caiden tried to minimize contact.

Taitn passed over three ramia: cylindrical wraps with twenty tight layers of meats, grains, sauces, shredded plant, and fried flakes. "Ksiñe said you were a creature of habit and he could guess your exact malnutrition."

Caiden couldn't respond between mouthfuls. The ramia was a perfect blend of textures with each hot bite, the flavors balanced impeccably in a journey from sour-sweet to creamy, salty spice.

Taitn added, "Ksiñe told me you'd been in touch once, just before you took off to the fringes. Once more than with the rest of us, anyway." A hint of hurt in that.

Caiden closed his eyes and started into the second ramia. His gut was cramping, confused by a meal as good as this. "I gave him the Casthen's data on my genetics, hoping he'd unravel what the Graven part is. That's all I needed."

Taitn unwrapped his own ramia but ate much slower, staring at the colorful layers. "You're still worried about that?"

"Something feels wrong, foreign, the more time passes. Like I'm a genetic cocktail poorly mixed and it's starting to separate."

"And finding out what the source is will help how?"

"Threi said he had a secret the Dynast must never know about, and the Dynast are obsessed with Graven things. My origin has to be that same thing, and I'm leery of what Threi means to do with a secret of that caliber."

C scooted closer. His nostrils flared pink, and his pupils were wide, bright circles. Caiden teased out a strip of meat from the ramia and tossed it to the monster. C swallowed it whole and licked his teeth.

Low, Taitn said, "You're still taking responsibility for these big factions. You don't need to forgive the Casthen for what they put you through—that's unforgivable. But you do need to *release* yourself from it. Why can't you let yourself live?"

"First I need to ensure there keeps being a safe multiverse to live *in*."

"Why does it have to be you?"

In the beat of stillness that followed, Caiden grew aware of his body and the shape of its Graven energy fitting him poorly, layering up in the wrong places and leaching out in others. Distantly he answered, "Why *not* me?"

C noticed the invisible shift whenever Caiden flexed that Gravenness. He grumbled deep in his chest and pressed his big head against Caiden's ribs.

Caiden cleared this throat. "Tell me about you. Is..."

Crimes, I even let my curiosity die all these years. Couldn't check on their lives, couldn't smile for them without hurting too much.

Taitn chuckled and a blush crept above his beard. Shyness didn't fit how brutish his features looked. "Lyli's still with the Cartographers. We're still partnered and have a...have one daughter. She—"

Caiden dropped his food and slapped his hands on the table. "A *daughter*?"

Taitn laughed, and his gaze fell to the table. "She's about four now."

"Four." Caiden's mood plummeted and he whispered, "You shouldn't be here. This is why I didn't want to drag you into this. You have another family."

"That doesn't invalidate you. Besides, Lyli has everything handled while

I'm gone." Taitn drew a familiar lacquered flask from his jacket and pushed it Caiden's way.

Caiden traced a finger over the flask's blue flowers and the cracks En had put there long ago. Caiden had watched and thought that cracks once made couldn't be mended.

"What's your daughter's name?"

Taitn leaned back with a happy, far-off look on his face. "Aredis. Ari, for short. The bedtime tales she asks for every time are about you, the Ghost of *Azura*."

Caiden grinned until he thought about what those tales might contain. Bloodshed. Evasion. Lies. Heroics too... Salvation, revolution, economic resuscitation, but often those results weren't bought in pretty ways.

He took a deep drag from the flask, let the fire tear down his throat, let the ugly side of him swallow this attachment cropping up. He wanted to know everything about Taitn's life, and En's, but that would pull them closer and right into risk. New lives like Ari's were on the line, and Caiden would keep happily paying the costs of securing her future.

Before he'd formed a response, En yelled from *Azura*'s back opening, "Ready to test!" She emerged with the hunter draped in her arms.

"Fast." Caiden got up and met her halfway, between the two vessels.

"Helps when you have superb skill. And rare parts." En winked and dumped the body into Caiden's arms. "You do the honors. I'll stay back with the ships and keep tabs on the area while you walk her into Unity to check cognition. If that fails, bring her back and I'll crack her brain open."

Caiden shifted the hunter against him, struggling with the limp assembly of her limbs. Her throat and chest had been neatly repaired with new materials. C huffed and shoved his muzzle through the hunter's hair, sniffing the nape of her neck.

"I'll give her two hundred arcminutes."

Quietly, Taitn said, "Then you run."

"And then I run."

Caiden marched off toward Unity's thick rind past a couple warehouses. It rose out of sight like a massive wall splitting the storm clouds. Taitn and C followed, stopping in front of it beside him. The physics shift was visible in the street stretching across: its smooth mineral crumbled to sand, then a fluffy substance, then more and more green mosaic tile on the other side.

"Ready for a trap." The rind's feathery flux edge waved over Caiden, tickling his morphcoat's leather into tiny spikes. Rain poured through the rind and turned to hot wisps across his skin.

"A trap. She's not a bomb, right?" Taitn unholstered a small glave anyway. "And no transmitter."

"I just have a bad feeling." Caiden strode through.

Unity's fluctuations whisked through his organs and bloodstream. It didn't change much of his biology—that he could tell—but the body in his arms shifted. Musculature tightened, wrinkled skin smoothed, and her lightseep obsidian bones made a pinging sound like cracking ice.

She belonged here. Unity's creature.

C followed in—Unity was safe for him—and growled low while pinning back his ears. Something had changed in the hunter's body that only the nophek could perceive.

Caiden hurried out of the rind. Rain fell in fat droplets on Unity's side, plastering his hair down and slithering through his morphcoat's weave before it could transform to waterproof feathers.

Taitn pulled out a device that spread a field of agitation overhead and funneled rain to the sides. Caiden knelt beneath and set the hunter's body down, soaked by puddles as he propped her head against his knee.

All of En's fine repairs still looked good. The materials held up perfectly. She could speak. Her brain was intact.

A chill quested into him, and his morphcoat bristled a wool layer in response. He couldn't stop his hands trembling. Couldn't tell if the quivers he felt were in his palm or her shoulders he held.

No, she's alive… Small processes whirred inside the torso. Bloodstream coursed. Nanopiezo bits harvested energy, and the organic skin coverings started to warm under his touch.

Caiden braced himself. "Tell me who you are."

CHAPTER 6

CURVED TRUTHS

The hunter's snowy eyelashes shivered, the pupils behind them adjusted, coppery rings dilating.

Caiden tensed, which made C's hackles raise, his monstrous bulk towering void-black in the dim weather. The hunter's eyes flew open at the sight and she choked on a startled noise. Her limbs' nerve lines were cut, but the flight impulse jerked her torso. Caiden, surprised, grasped her so she wouldn't slide off his propped knee, but two slim ribs snapped at the force.

He swore. "C! Step back."

If this *was* Leta's consciousness, then nophek meant trauma. Caiden had overcome his own, but Leta would not have.

If she was faking, it was a convincing detail.

C shuffled backward with an annoyed huff, ridged back bristling.

The hunter's gaze was pinned on the nophek, repaired lungs flushing between hues as she panted. Caiden adjusted his grip to her shoulders, which pulled her focus to him.

"*Caiden...*" It wasn't Leta's voice, or even a very human-sounding voice—more saisn, airy—but for all the hours Caiden had toiled trying to fix her, he'd fueled the fantasy of Leta having lived after all. Now his heart lurched at the possibility. "You're real." Her words came out with a croak as the voice box adjusted to its repairs. The filigree crackled and fast-grown tissues sounded sore. "Caiden, the sweet boy with...an awful temper, who liked to fight and called it 'protecting.' Haven't changed much?" A smile quivered through her cheeks.

Caiden struggled to fit this voice and face to the girl she was intending to be. He scrutinized for signs that she was reading a script or somehow digging through his mind.

Taitn asked, "*Caiden?*"

"My name from before. But Threi knows it, and anyone could guess my temperament." He cleared Leta from his mind. This was a Dynast construct, and he had the advantage now. To her he asked, "What did we find, the day we went beyond the pasture blocks?"

She laughed brokenly. "When you stole the duster? I'm happy to see... you got to be a pilot after all."

"What did we find?"

"The ocean."

He'd helped her climb to the top of the duster vehicle. Once she saw the view, she promptly lost her fear of heights. The sea wind tasted heavy. Water stretched to a horizon where it met the gray of their planet's vapor-filled atmosphere. That gray had sheltered them from knowledge of other worlds.

Memories webbed around him, making his voice quaver, "What did you say?"

The hunter's gaze hadn't unlocked from his. The real Leta wouldn't have made this eye contact, but she replied correctly, if hesitant, "I said... I said I would have built floats, like ships wide and flat, and put pastures on those. All that water was a waste of space."

Caiden looked up desperately at Taitn. "The memories are real. The question is—"

"How she came to possess them." Taitn frowned and lowered his glave.

C curled farther under the rain shelter. The hunter flinched hard again and shut her eyes. No longer the fierce bounty hunter that had chased him single-mindedly before.

Caiden asked, "How do you know my sister's past, and why did you pursue me?"

"Sister..." Her forehead frowned at the same time her lips smiled. "I looked up to you. When I heard about you recently... when I remembered you again..." There was a short in her voice, the glitch of a forced lie. "Cai. I remembered your promise to come back for me."

"I—" He worked a dry mouth, but his retort stuck there.

"I'm Leta," she said. "This body is a Proxy that my consciousness inhabits remotely. I'm really your Leta, a Dynast captive, my real body imprisoned on their homeworld Solthar here in Unity."

Questions crowded his mind. There was barely space for the idea of her survival after years living with the reality of her death. And in all Caiden's travels, he'd never heard of such an absurd thing as a Proxy. Parasitism and forms of remote viewing, yes, but not a consciousness inhabiting a different body remotely.

His grip slackened and his knee drooped. The Proxy slid to the ground with a *crack*. Her throat's filigree frame snapped, slicing into her cry. Caiden swore and gathered her back up, clamping a palm around her neck to support her voice box enough to keep speaking.

She gasped and blinked up at him.

Taitn asked first, "How's remote consciousness possible? You exist in two places at once?"

"Not at once," she answered, the sound buzzy. "I have two bodies, but I can only inhabit one at a time. I project my consciousness through the luminiferity."

Luminiferity. The luminiferous dimension was a plenum outside of linear spacetime, a wellspring from which the content of reality folded and unfolded. So the Dynast *had* been studying how to access the accumulated knowledge there.

Ten years ago, Caiden had devoted himself to consuming everything he could find on the Dynast's beliefs, in order to decide whether to release Threi Cetre from imprisonment. The man had lent him a book—*Graven Intention of Prima Luminiferia*—which outlined the Dynast's true aims to restore a Graven world. Caiden grasped the science of the luminiferity, but the text veered into flowery prose, romantic epithets, and spiritual obfuscation.

Threi rejected the Dynast's aim and believed the Dynast Prime to be a terror of unfathomable ability. Caiden didn't see any inherent wrongness in wanting to understand what the Graven were or intended. He'd chosen to believe Abriss could be kindhearted. The world she'd created showed it clearly.

Just because you can't see treachery, Threi had said, *doesn't mean it's not there. And who better to hide it than the woman every being is genetically programmed to adore and never question?*

"A captive of the Dynast," Caiden repeated her claim, "your real body imprisoned. Why do you have *this* body?"

"There were twenty-nine of us, at the start, various xenids. We're the Prime's Graven experiments. Now able to operate remotely in-Proxy, we carry out missions for her within Unity."

"Graven experiments?"

"It's...why I forgot about you. They used liquid gloss to infuse us with biophotonic fields. It imprinted the Dynast type of Graven strain on our own genes, derived from the Prime's. Our biology changed. I...I grew up among horrors. Bones splintered through flesh, skin desiccated, comatose brains, insanity, suicide. We all lived in dread of what would happen to us and when."

Her voice chafed down to a whisper as she forced the words. Caiden, with one hand holding her neck together and the other supporting her snapped ribs, felt both the heartfelt push and the vibration of her syllables. Her emotions didn't feel fake.

"It scoured our memories. I didn't know there was more to me until I saw you and some of those memories returned. Caiden...There's seven of us left. I don't know how long...how long I'll last." Her eyelashes fluttered as her stare dulled. "I'm so sorry I forgot about you."

Caiden bent under the heft of her words and closed his eyes to remove the wrong vision of her—that mature, inhuman face, the structure of it all wrong. The vishkant he'd encountered before had shown him exactly what a twenty-year-old Leta would have looked like. That imagery filled his mind instead, and he couldn't help superimposing the suffering she'd described. His fault.

Taitn's warm palm landed on Caiden's shoulder. "Even if it's true that a consciousness can drive this thing remotely, how could your girl have lived?"

"Threi—" Caiden and the Proxy answered at almost the same time. The name hummed against Caiden's fingers as he held her disjointed throat together.

The timeline… Chills skated across his skin. "Threi took you from the slaughter on the nophek planet. He sold you to Abriss. That *was* you, that day."

Caiden had seen Threi trade a child's body to Abriss in Emporia. It had been packed on the Dynast flagship in a pod among so many others. More than that, the Casthen's gloss operation that spawned Caiden and Leta's world had been secretly funded by the Dynast because at that time, Abriss Cetre was desperate for gloss: she'd started a special Graven project that required phenomenal energy.

This batch of twenty-nine that the Proxy described.

Caiden couldn't hear any more. He lifted his hand from her neck, which loosened the parts enough to clip off her verbal capacity.

Threi saved her. Threi *did.*

All the dusty, long-ago fantasies Caiden had secreted away about him saving Leta from the slaughter… his mind now rewrote them with Threi the hero. Striding in toward that little girl in the corner of a lightless, reeking transport box and carrying her out to the light. Threi getting to say the words, *I'm here. You're safe.*

"He sold her. From one enslavement to the next." Caiden's vision watered as he peered up at Taitn. "Because I—"

He couldn't say it aloud, refused to give it form.

Taitn offered a sympathetic and calculating look, brows drawn tight. "The memories and the timeline work, but…" His expression changed to a rare fierceness that fit his naturally brutish features. He asked the Proxy, "What do you want with Winn—with Caiden?"

Caiden curled his palm back around the stressed materials of her larynx so she could answer.

"Cai…" Emotion shivered against Caiden's fingers. "You promised you'd come back. Come save the real me from Solthar. If you'll fix my Proxy more, we can save me together."

Ache swelled in Caiden's jaw. If she was real, the splintered promise lodged in his heart could be pried out. "Leta—"

Taitn, in one smooth move, ducked to pull the two of them apart and pinned the Proxy to the ground while holding her neck. The air-shelter device faded, and Caiden was thrust aside, battered by rainfall.

Taitn's deep, soft voice took on a strange calm that Caiden hadn't heard before but befitted the former military pilot's title, *Commander*. "If you have a flesh-and-blood body in the Dynast Hold, then the Prime controls you, even now."

She tried to smile, upper lip twitching. "Our Proxies are immune to her gravitas—that is what we call the Graven effect."

"But your *real* body cannot be immune," Caiden said, sobered by the icy rain. He'd seen Leta bent to others' influence and caught in patterns of abuse before. Even her parental unit had convinced her she was broken. Was this any different? The Dynast had swept her up—with Graven influence, no less—and reshaped the vulnerable parts of her. "What are the Proxies, then? Dolls?"

Her smile died. "When my consciousness inhabits my Proxy instead of my real body, I think for myself."

Tone still that of a strategist, Taitn said, "Gravitas-immune Proxy body. Vulnerable real body. If you're suffering so much, why don't you save yourself? Pick up your own body and carry it away?"

"You understand the Prime's astrological precognizance. We Graves are precious to her, invested with all the Dynast's time and resources. Innumerable gloss, each worth a world. She's watching us too closely and would notice if we meant to defect. But she *won't* be looking for a thief from the outside." The Proxy tilted her head to look at Caiden with fresh energy. "This is a rare chance to strike so fast the Dynast Prime doesn't see it coming. I can be in-Proxy, where I'm meant to, and no one will suspect my real body's being spirited away."

Caiden probed her plan for holes. He wanted to deny his secret delusion that the multiverse really did draw individuals together, link them in a way that space and time and even death couldn't sever.

Her voice was fading to airiness as materials wore out. "I remember you like there's no time between us. I care about you, just as then."

Caiden tilted his head back to let the rainfall smack his face. It drove the sting of tears out of his cheeks. He'd given up on Leta being alive, and she'd suffered for a *decade* because he hadn't been strong enough to carry hope with him.

Taitn moved away from the Proxy, letting her larynx seize up and cut off any more she might speak. He turned to Caiden. "Do you trust her?"

"I have to," Caiden blurted, and the immediacy surprised even him. "You're all telling me I run too much—well, now I might try to follow something that feels real. She's not the girl I knew, she's been influenced and reshaped...but there's a lifeline between us that I thought her death had severed..." He sighed and concluded, "If it's really her and I do nothing, I'll never forgive myself."

"All right, brother." Taitn offered Caiden a hand up. "Good enough for now."

CHAPTER 7

VOWS MADE

Leta opened her eyes underwater, her awareness slowly glowing back through her real brain.

Rather than in levitation, this time she'd left her body in a radiation bath in the Away Room while she'd been adrift in the luminiferity, her spirit wandering like a streak of lightning never finding ground. Finally Caiden had brought her Proxy through to Unity so she could sense it and reconnect.

While her spirit was away, her unconscious body had a long time to heal up. A lattice of vibrations carried through the casket liquid and suffused the meat of her, whispering to her cells to differentiate, to become more Graven like Abriss was. None of the treatments had ever given them gravitas, but Leta didn't want it anyway. The Dynast Prime seemed abysmally unhappy knowing that she could never trust affection to be real.

Leta sat up, groggy. The crystalline water rolled off in rainbow drops, leaving her freckled skin quite dry and hair too frizzy. She raked her fingers through the waves and winced at a dull ache, a thread-thin migraine, and tendons that felt too tight for her bones. Despite her body's recovery, a slow disintegration began anew with her spirit back inside, undoing everything her time away had healed.

Perfect Graven bodies were indestructible, timeless, omniscient, and had creative control of reality. Sometimes, in the luminiferity, Leta could taste what this would be like. Most of the time, she felt very far from that ideal: half-constructed, lopsided, leaking. The *Azura* was the complementary

Graven strain that the Dynast Graves needed to reverse their disintegration. Now Leta had brought them one step closer.

"I did it," she said.

"Leta!" called the ashy voice of Isme Two, muffled by his Proxy's faceless mask. He strode over to the bathing alcove from the line of Away stations. "You reconnected?"

Leta beamed at him. "I did. Stars forfend, I even convinced Winn to trust me."

This time, once he'd caught on to the belief that it might really be her, she *had* seen the sweet boy in the grown man. Her memory matched the sight, and she had hope.

Two offered his hand down to help her stand. "Yet you're not pleased?"

He was the most empathically keen of the Graves. It annoyed Five and Six, but Leta appreciated how it shortcut their conversations, how he could read her emotions even when they didn't show on her face—which was most of the time.

Leta said, "I've never lied so much in my life."

"Doesn't it matter less to lie to a stranger?" Isme Two chuckled, a fleece-soft sound that shook his torso and fluttered butterflies and spiders webbed up in the art painted across his shoulders. "I watch you mask your real feelings all the time to anyone who's not us."

Leta curved her feelings around that thought. "He's not a stranger. He called me 'sister,' though I never imagined him as a sibling, to be honest. He was my only friend, in that awful place."

"Protector?"

"Comforter. He often arrived too late."

She rose from the casket. Her nervous system unlinked from invisible harmonic patterns, tickling all over. Half the freckles in her flesh sparkled white from the radiation. She tapped the metal collar around her neck to signal a sheath of morphfabric spreading down her naked body to her ankles. The compression of it made all the tingles in her muscles take flight. Out of Proxy, she felt like a raw creature bereft of shell. Or something with the skin peeled off, nerves bare.

"I hate lying," Leta grumbled. She was *too* blunt and honest, some told her.

Lying to Caiden to get him to trust her put a strange type of sick in her belly. The memories they shared had been true, but her account of her life with the Dynast was all false. Yes, Threi had sold her to the Dynast at ten years old, and yes, the treatments had been painful at first, and twenty-two had died, some in awful ways, but they'd consented to their life here and were taken care of. Abriss's gravitas *did* harmonize them to her will, but her will was always gentle and to the betterment of Unity and—"Isme," Leta said, cutting off that line of thought. "Can we get some air?"

They weren't lies she had told Caiden. They were bent truths.

"You're shivering, Treasure." Two fetched her a floor-length coat and whirled it around her shoulders as they walked out. Layers of thermal veil and knitted spider silk sorted out as she moved, bunching or billowing to fashion her a comfy dress of sorts.

"I need to report to the Prime." Leta wanted to sprint all three corridors and six rooms away to Abriss's soothing presence. To be shown she'd been dishonest for good reason. "I fabricated a new plan on the spot while convincing Winn but I...I think it'll work."

Two said, "Quick and smart, you."

"Only smart. My Proxy gives me processing time to be quick."

"Your mind is always quick even if your words aren't."

Isme's Proxy was, in Leta's opinion, the most stunning of the seven. He was the last Abriss had crafted, and perhaps had all her skill in him. A solid mask contoured like a skull with the holes filled in. Delicate veins melted on. Hair, gossamer flame down to the floor. He wore a draped shirt of see-through spider-silk weave and a stiff pleated skirt with armor encircling his hips, an antiquated Dynast style. His synthetic skin was inked with a labyrinth of insects and webs. He was gorgeous like a—

Caiden's phrase intruded in her mind: *What are the Proxies, then? Dolls?*

She drove that thought out fast. *We're Abriss's family, not toys. She needs us because she can't do this all alone.*

The Prime dedicated herself to the Graves so fervently because she'd lost so many of them already. Every success was a step toward a future where every person belonged—including her.

The day outside was soft: a mostly eclipsed sun dimmed the light, and no field training meant less noise, less motion. Leta's Graven body's disintegration caused her sensory systems to work overtime to process more input, including information from unperceived dimensions. But beyond that, she'd always been a highly sensitive person, her experiences so lush and detailed she was easily overwhelmed, sometimes to the point she simply shut down.

Now her proprioception unraveled. Sounds in her environment called her to inhabit them across kilometers, as if each molecule could be a Proxy body. She was snared by the roar of distant hot springs waterfalls, the patter of rain-laden gardens, and the passing wingbeat of morning birds.

Isme kept up with her quickening pace. Shortly they reached the Prime's private workroom, where Aohm One's Proxy towered at the entrance on guard. Osseous armor encrusted their muscular body, which seemed human to a human eye but was really all the wrong proportions. Scarlet tissues beneath showed at the seams. A cloak of disguising matter draped off them in sticky plumes of smoke.

"The Prime is expecting you," One said, their voice as rough as a thunder-crack. The faceless skull resonated their voice. "Her astrology described your good news." They made a sort of bow as they stepped aside.

Leta bowed back before entering. The Prime's workroom floor was a milky, ancient wood—one piece from some gigantic tree—with spiral grain mottled by the passing of feet. Three walls heaved with relic books, printed with inks on papers. They filled the room with a musty vanilla scent she'd encountered nowhere else.

The sides of the workroom held instruments of Graven research, the Prime's efforts having redoubled since Threi explained the *Azura*'s existence. Dust motes lazed in the air. A waterfall curtain glittered soundlessly out the south windows. The northern view showed rolling hills and rivers and stars in full daylight. Close by, a gigantic, winged phantasm flew as slow as a whale, its body making the air sing.

Sleepless Abriss sprawled on the floor as if wilted by fatigue. Ideas cocooned her: stacks of books, golden holosplays, and the faint tracings of a reference orrery in the air. Tools hovered in small scalar gravity webs.

She plucked an orb of translucent gloss out of a basket brimming with them and fed it into the crucible of a machine nearby. She retrieved a fresh vial of melted glossalith liquid, then with a stylus in her nicked, callused fingers, she hooked up fresh strands of gloss from the chalice, hardening them like spun sugar.

Leta was happy to watch, silent and unnoticed. She relished any moment when the Prime was acting natural, even if still driven and burdened by responsibility, by past and future but never the present. Leta found Abriss's obsessive focus easy to relate to.

Sunshine turned the woman's brown eyes amber, her tawny skin bronze, and motes of light caught in her braid. Her movements were elegant and energized. She was treating Aohm One's real body, which levitated at the back of the room, unconscious while they guarded the door in-Proxy. Their xenid body faced away, all curled up like a flower at night. Abriss relaced the nerve-bright glossalith threads down their complicated spine while Leta imagined a spider weaving a web to catch energy. Her own stitchings had fused to her body weeks ago, not needing replacement yet.

A featherlight Graven magnetism entwined Leta's body in this proximity to Abriss. Reality fell into alignment. Tension unlaced around her middle and a sunny feeling spread. The disintegrative sensations ebbed away, harmonized—or at least overridden by nicer things. This was Leta's comfort place: with Abriss, the heart of Unity, on Solthar, the Dynast homeworld, in the very center of the known multiverse. There were no lies here.

Some of Leta's fondness was Graven-induced, as Caiden had accused, but if that was supposed to feel different from affinity of other kinds, Leta couldn't tell. She had grown up feeling included, not compelled.

Abriss had incredible and involuntary power over those around her, but she was always soft with it, always deliberate, respectful, patient. Everyone adored Abriss Cetre of the Seventh Primal Etheric Line of the Dynast Lineage. And she was alone in a crowd. Leta noticed how Abriss died a little inside each time someone melted into obeisance in her presence—she didn't *want* to rob others of their original feelings.

"Nine!" Abriss noticed finally once she turned around. "You're awake."

The *relief* in those words soared through Leta.

"And *you*," sweet Isme accused, "should sleep sometime, Prime. In your bedroom perhaps. Try it once? You'll never rest with work nearby."

"Bed?" Abriss always fell asleep in a book, or engrossed in her work, or her orrery, or at the council-room desk. Her expression shuttered for a moment, then she replied, "I cannot think of a lonelier place. Now, Nine— my stars told me you reached your Proxy?"

"I also convinced Winn that I'm really the Leta he knew."

Abriss smiled and smoothed her braid over one shoulder. "But there is a problem?"

"He'll repair my Proxy. But he has an ally and a noph—" *Forfend, I wasn't ready for a nophek. Those memories can stay erased!* "A nophek pet. Maybe a chance will arise to catch them all by surprise and steal the *Azura*, but I bet he doesn't part from it often."

Isme reclined on a long seat nearby. "He's spent more than ten years with that ship, yes? With a neural link that steel-strong and sensitive, he'd be alerted the moment you lay a finger on the controls."

Leta nodded. "I think I managed to persuade Winn to bring the ship *here*. I'm bait, aren't I? So I've baited him to Solthar to rescue me."

The Prime's face lit up and it was all the gratitude Leta needed. "You wonderful girl, well done. I know this hasn't been an easy task."

Leta flushed and folded her hands in her lap. Eyes down, she pinched her freckled skin. Her flesh had a shadow in it, as if remembering darker pigment, and it tingled, the harmonies in her loosened like an ill-fitting corset. Her spirit vibrated subtly past the boundaries of her body.

This is some of the torture I told Caiden I was enduring. Crooked truths.

"Ensure he brings the *Azura*. While the Graven hybridization of his own genetics interests me—a Casthen abomination though he is—the ship contains the missing strain of energy we need."

Isme leaned forward, long hair refracting sunlight. "Forgive me, Prime, I understand the ship's technology is important, but what can it do that is worth ignobility? Deceit and theft? The Dynast may claim it rightly owns all Graven technology, but you've never before taken actions even remotely close to *theft*."

"For the glorious thing that lies within that ship, even I will sully myself with low means. If my brother's data is correct, the *Azura* is a complementary type of Graven to the Dynast type—which is myself, Threi, and you Graves—the enharmonic strain to our harmonic, creating a perfect balance together. It's what you've been lacking all along, and it is what I've been searching for my whole life." Abriss stood, cringing as several joints crackled. How long had she been at work? "Let me show you. I haven't explained before because...I didn't want to raise your hopes."

She gestured to bring up a holosplay that superimposed around Aohm One's body, displaying the yraga's biological rhythms and etheric composition, their nervous system coupled to higher octaves. Three different energy strains were distinguished by color. Aohm's system was almost entirely the Dynast type, conditioned into all the Graves from Abriss's genetics.

"The Dynast bioresonance, a force of attraction and affinity. *Unity*, right?" Abriss's eyes crinkled in a smile. She gestured to filter out that strain in the diagrams, leaving the other two—the *Azura* and a third strain— mere trickles among the rich data of Aohm One's being. "The *Azura's* Graven force is the opposite: expansive and dispersive. With it, I can balance your nervous systems and solve the disintegration issue. Spirit no longer separating from body."

"What's the third?" Leta ventured. *Dear stars, are we only one-third complete? After twenty-two losses? Seven chances left to get it right.*

"I believe it will emerge from the synergy of the two complementary strains once we combine the *Azura's* energy into your Dynast bodies. This will make you complete Graven beings, unaging, impervious to harm. They lived in co-creative balance with the manifest universe, such that what seemed like miracles were the natural order of things, the way things are supposed to be. My Graves, you would not just survive, you would *thrive*."

Abriss's eyes softened, and though she spoke often in monotone, without charisma, her syllables twirled Leta up in a buoyant certainty. Impossibilities felt real.

Gravitas netted around Leta as Abriss approached. Fragrances of fresh rain and sage filled Leta's head, and the woman's touch, picking up her hands, was like sunbeams but all layered up to the density of flesh, warm and radiating power.

"I promise the *Azura* will heal you. I will work tirelessly to make it so. And I wish it hadn't taken so many losses to get this far, but if I can make the seven of you perfectly Graven, I will have a means of gifting that same perfection to all of Unity. To eliminate borders and restore the Graven world: one predictable universe, mapped by science, ruled by co-creation and shared consciousness, eliminating disease and war forever."

"So they can be your equal," Leta said reflexively. Despite being the political center of a universe, Abriss was achingly lonely. Leta couldn't help but see the woman's intense focus as a race toward a future with Graven peers where her gravitas was nullified, where she could share genuine feelings. She would be free.

"So *all* of us can be equal," Abriss corrected. "I haven't been enhancing my own Gravenness, after all. I don't want power. I wish to give it to others."

Us. There was something incredibly sad whenever Abriss said "us" or "we."

Leta had told Caiden, *I remember you like there's no time between us.*

"Stealing and lying..." she began, combing through the recent encounter to isolate what still felt wrong, beyond the fact that she'd never had to steal or lie on previous missions. She pulled away from Abriss and sat on the long, cushioned seat beside Isme. "I don't want to be the one who captures or betrays him once he's here. I don't want to hurt him that much. He doesn't deserve it."

"He does not," Abriss agreed. "The others can handle him, and I promise he'll be released forthwith. All he'll lose is his starship."

And me. The idea of me.

"Thank you, Prime."

"Don't think of it as harming him. Sometimes a thing needs to break in order to grow. Winn is chasing the past, and I can see in his stars that's exactly what is keeping him from having a *future.* To keep my brother imprisoned, Winn has been stuck keeping everything in his life the same. Who has ever lived or evolved, doing that? These events may break Winn into the future he's meant for."

That resolved Leta's last hesitation. Isme Two added, "This is all temporary, Treasure. You'll be able to forget him again soon."

"I'm still worried he'll change his mind," Leta confessed. "I should cement this whole plan soon, back in-Proxy."

"Here then." Two snatched a pillow and laid it on his lap. "I'll watch over you, if you consent."

Leta settled on her back, head on the pillow. Two's hands wrapped her skull and forehead through waves of her hair. His fingers felt electric.

"Thank you, Nine," Abriss said.

Leta glanced over shyly. She'd never been such a focus of the Prime's attention, picked out of the group. The original twenty-nine had been a crowd she could hide in.

She straightened her head and left the slight smile on her lips for Isme, then closed her eyes to focus.

Each of the Graves had a different method for unlinking from their body and entering the luminiferity. Leta sensed in such detail, she could easily lose her awareness in one sensation—it wasn't much of a leap to unravel the rest of the way from there. She closed her eyes and focused on the texture of Isme Two's synthetic fingers. Slight chill, skin smooth as leaves, with dendritic patterns, gentle pressure.

Her consciousness detangled from humming flesh and snapping nerves. Her spirit unfurled from where it had scrunched in the smallness of her body. Her mind stretched wings, catching the air of the luminiferity, and soared.

She entered the true nature of the world: a monster of boundless energy, infinite magnitude of force, constantly conserved and transforming.

Isme Two once said the luminiferity felt like a sea of dead spirit, a collective field of dissimulated consciousness into which individuals dispersed upon death, to one day condense into singular points of awareness, reborn. A cradle of being, brimming with potential.

Tayen Five complained that it was a whole lot of chatter.

Aohm One claimed it was simply a multidimensional holographic field.

Leta thought it was peaceful, most of the time. She sensed participation, oneness, as if here she could never be alone. This was the world the Graven had harnessed, the world that Abriss Cetre meant to comprehend and control once more.

Leta focused on her Proxy and traveled, expanding her consciousness carefully. Too much and she would dissolve, spread too thin, never gather herself back. She was everywhere and nothing and no one, but she could hear the voices of the future and the presence of the past crowding close as time unwove into strings.

She didn't sense her Proxy. Outside of Unity again? Or the repairs went wrong?

Everyone was counting on her. Even if her Proxy was destroyed, Leta would carve a path to Caiden somehow. She gripped memories like reins and bent truths into barbed lies. She imagined Caiden with everything she knew. Blood and fire. Hard eyes, soft heart.

She concentrated on the far past to utilize memories of Caiden as a boy. Their last contact, young hands shaking, swamped in a terror that was too big for them.

There.

His presence pierced her awareness, far-off, then she sensed her Proxy and instantly it pulled her in, calling down the expanse of her into a body. Her spirit bundled up and she crashed into the machine's mess of lightning circuits and gardens of code.

Leta opened her Proxy's eyes. The lenses adjusted, crushing rainbows into shapes and answering light with shadow. The world started to materialize as she blinked, and she already felt easier than she had in her real body. Sounds slipped past her skin instead of digging under it. Light sat correctly on surfaces. Colors took on a limited range of hues.

Someone bent over her seated body.

Caiden. Damage signals still blipped all over, but she sighed and relaxed in her secure Proxy shell. The light bloom cleared—

It wasn't Caiden's silhouette crouched over her.

CHAPTER 8

BARBED LIES

Leta didn't speak or react. The stranger hadn't noticed her awareness return, or was ignoring it, while they micro-welded new bands to the frame of her ribs. Most likely this was either one of Caiden's allies or someone he'd sold her Proxy to.

About 40 percent of her damage was repaired—enough to fight. Statistics flooded her mind from joints, fibers, and nerve lines, ready for her examination if she wished.

Toolkits and parts heaped all around. She was propped against the interior hull of a parked vessel. The person pulled away to fetch muscle swaths from a bin of liquid. Their silhouette suggested a human with a feminine shape and elegant build. Leta's vision shuffled through electromagnetic ranges that revealed an almost completely biomechanical construction. Not a Proxy, but similar. Leta shuddered, which clacked a few of her own loose metallic parts.

The augmented person turned around and paused. "There you are."

Flexfield armor striped their body around vitals. Stealthy glaves and blades hugged their figure all over, outlined cold in Leta's thermal vision. She recognized a few rare organically modeled weapons—an interest of hers—which spiked the person's threat level substantially.

Who are you was too obvious a question, so Leta shuffled five inches to the right to peer through an open side hatch. Outside was a clearing in a copse of spindly trees. Vast layered platforms overhead cast deep shade. They were part of an abandoned-looking city structure all around, and through the gaps, the distinct colors of Unity's rind shifted. Since Leta was conscious, they were on Unity's side now, yet a foul feeling slithered through her at the sight of that border.

Sunbeams speared the gloom and illuminated a starship in the clearing. Leta's unique Proxy senses let her recognize the *Azura* straightaway despite its alterskin. Caiden leaned against the ship next to another figure. His short hair was braided against his scalp now, and he was relaxed, brushing the fur of the monster sprawled over his legs.

"When you didn't wake again, he thought I'd broken you." The augmented person crouched by Leta's legs to apply a new soleus muscle. "I thought about it." They snared Leta's eye contact while a lovely smile spread across their face. "I may still be thinking about it."

Leta recognized the look behind those gray eyes: it was the sort of look Tayen Five had when she was considering a bad deed for a good purpose, when she was fighting the parasite in her brain telling her there was a simple action that would solve a whole lot of complication.

Leta's mind was quick—now her Proxy's function kept up. "What would *he* think of that, and what are you to him?"

They straightened and raked their long black hair into a magnetic tie. "If you were familiar with the wider multiverse, you'd likely know a scoundrel like me by name. I'll indulge you the secret. Endirion Day, at your service—for now."

"Your pronouns, Endirion?"

"I like the Andalvian handling of pronouns," Endirion said, "but in Shihl you can use she or whichever you want. I'll let you know if I prefer something."

Leta switched languages and murmured, "I can speak Andalvian."

Flis Ten had taught her, before dying. Right after the Graves had been numbered and Leta imagined it was safe to make friends.

Endirion curled over to meld Leta's new muscles into place. Though her Proxy inhibited the sensations of the repair, the proximity and intimacy of Endirion's work was...unnerving. Proxy repairs and tuning were usually performed *without* Leta's consciousness inside.

This means I survive long enough to bring the Azura *home.*

With Andalvian nuance, Leta asked, "And what are you to him?" She hated asking questions twice.

"Isn't that a fun mystery?" Endirion strung Leta's tendons on, fast but shoddy, the same sort of post-fight repairs her own augmented body showed. "Am I his progenitor, his sibling, his lover, his friend, his bodyguard, his hired help?"

Leta couldn't tell, but it was clear she would have to pass this judge before she'd get a chance to talk to Caiden. And Endirion wouldn't be swayed by emotions or memories.

Out in the clearing, Caiden's softer side showed through as he conversed with his friend and scratched the nophek's ears.

This was the time for a quip to Endirion's dagger words, but Leta wasn't great at them. And she didn't know how much Caiden had told this person or even what Leta herself meant to him exactly. Instead of a quip, she breathed deeper, testing auxiliary lungs. New biometrics sparkled online. Endirion's mechanical craft was not as delicate as the Prime's, but it would do. Leta flexed both arms to help the muscle fabric gain tensile strength. Piezoelectric sensors sparkled all over.

"It's the lightseep in you, isn't it?" Endirion asked, her voice humming strangely into Leta's chest cavity where she bent.

"What is?"

"Lightseep absorbs and embodies consciousness, is my guess. No one in the multiverse has succeeded in creating completely biomechanical beings that can generate or contain consciousness. In my case, my brain and spinal cord are original. But you're something else, and lightseep—which you're full of—is supposed to be impossible to tool."

"Abriss."

Endirion stopped and cocked her head.

"Abriss crafted the Proxies herself."

"Multitalented and hands-on, huh? Frightening woman."

Frightening was not an adjective Leta would have ever used for the Dynast Prime. *Selfless and caring. She loves us Graves enough to save us.*

Welling with pride, Leta countered, "Abriss Cetre calculated the precise celestial transits in a point of space and time perfectly attuned to each

Grave's natal and engineered nature, so the very atoms of our Proxies and the sacred geometries of their constructs are predisposed to drawing in and containing our individual consciousnesses."

"Is that so?" Endirion stared into Leta's eyes, and Leta matched without blinks. In her real body, this eye contact would've been overwhelming—she'd sense Endirion's thought processes and feel layers of emotion.

More proud words lined up for her tongue, but her mission wasn't to convince anyone to empathize with the Dynast. It was to draw Caiden and the *Azura* to Solthar.

Leta shifted her gaze over Endirion's shoulder. Caiden's friend said something that made him laugh so hard he doubled over the nophek's back in his lap. The sound and the warmth were palpable across the distance.

I'm not part of his world. But he wants me to be, doesn't he? Is he ready to risk everything for my lies? Perhaps her lies were doing good, as Abriss had said. This reunion with his friends looked healing and long overdue. After the Dynast captured the ship and threw him out of Unity, he would still have these friends of his. *Trust Unity to bring each person what they need.*

Endirion moved to block her view. She propped up one of Leta's legs and began to refit the diamond pins. Her posture and tension shifted, her hands firmer. Her augmented body transformed to a muscular male physique, bones making a slick sound as they changed. The baggy, cinched clothes he'd worn made sense as they filled out. His skin lightened to a rich tan, locks of hair shrank and slipped out of the tie. Leta grew starkly aware of their closeness, his breath hot on her raw nerves. How easily Endirion could snap her.

These repairs were being done as a courtesy to Caiden.

He would decide whether Caiden rushed to Leta's rescue or not, because no Proxy meant no plan.

"So," Endirion began, his voice deeper and rusty now, "Abriss and the Dynast raised you—your real, captive self—and you drive this Proxy to carry out Abriss's will?"

Leta blurted a defensive reply, "We carry out peace missions for the Outer Immigration Initiative as well as—" She cut off and winced as Endirion's scalpel jammed against a nerve bundle in her knee.

"And you just happened to see Winn at a backwater bar and suddenly needed to reconnect."

This, Leta had an answer for, and though it wasn't how she'd learned about Caiden, it wasn't a complete lie either. "My consciousness travels a medium between bodies: the luminiferity. It's a higher dimension of reality and I can harvest information from it. I learned of Winn through rumors and old imagery, and recognized him, then felt the moment he entered Unity."

Her luminiferous capabilities weren't yet good enough to gather *specific* information she wanted or to view locations remotely like Dian Six could. She hadn't sensed Caiden the moment he entered Unity. Her Proxy had already been in position to intercept him.

Endirion sprayed a coating up her leg, then moved to the other. "You didn't answer *why*."

Even in-Proxy, Leta struggled to interpret vocal tones, and Endirion's face gave nothing away. But the longer she paused, the harder his thumb dug into the nerves of her calf as he refit the pieces.

"When...when we were children, he saved me from abuse and was always a safe shelter when I needed it most." Not a lie. Leta gazed at the clearing where Caiden wore that crooked smile she remembered. He listened to his friend and picked burrs out of the nophek's massive paw. "I thought he might save me again."

"He told me about that," Endirion said. "Torture. Genetic conditioning. Memories scoured away. Convenient."

Leta had used ugly words for Caiden's benefit to describe the years. Some might see what the Graves had endured as torturous, but was it torture if Leta consented and the outcome benefited the universe as a whole?

Abriss's energized explanations of the Graven trinity swelled back to her mind, softening her face—not quite a smile, but Endirion noticed and narrowed his eyes.

Dear stars, he's sharp. Leta tried to salvage her reaction by saying, "I didn't mean to forget him. I thought he was dead. My heart let him go, that's all."

"And he worked very hard to let you go, too, to forgive himself for leaving you on that desert. He's seen you die countless times. Now that whole scab's off and he's hurting. So if you're lying..." Endirion rested his arm on his knee and twirled the tool in his hand. He watched Leta's face, his own pupils adjusting minutely. Was her face fixed enough to show microexpressions that might betray her?

Leta replied, "I've never been good at lying. On the contrary, I tend to overshare. You can ask him."

Endirion knelt at Leta's back and pressed her forward, popping open the armoring at her lower back. As he tinkered there, nothing had ever felt so dangerous as the subtle nerve twinges that carried through her lower body.

One slip and Endirion could "accidentally" sever something in her spine.

"Say it's true and our boy rescues you...then what? You travel along with him? Make a life somewhere else? And in none of these scenarios does the Dynast attempt to recover their stolen property?"

Leta hesitated. The plan ended before she was "rescued." The Dynast was her home, and she was family, not property. Besides, she didn't have a "then what"—without the *Azura* to balance their Dynast biology, she and the other Graves would keep dying off one by one.

It hadn't been a lie when she'd told Caiden she didn't know how long she'd last.

Her brain raced for a verbal answer that would palliate Caiden's protector. "I hadn't dared to dream much further because I didn't hope he would believe me. I know how different my Proxy appears. He doesn't see *me* when he looks at it."

Endirion snapped her spine plates closed harder than he needed to, then moved in front of her. "You've thought as far as your rescue, though?"

This answer was easy. "We Proxies possess the highest rank in the Dynast military." Endirion raised an eyebrow at that. "I'll proceed to a scheduled audience with the Prime, in-Proxy, so that I'm accounted for. The other Graves will be there in-Proxy, preoccupied, while Winn escapes with my real body. The Dynast ignores everything outside of Unity, so as long as my real body gets across the rind, no one will miss one Grave."

Lies.

"And just like that," Endirion drawled, "you would abandon your Proxy forever?"

The idea shot ice through Leta. "Yes," she replied, but her musculature tensed. Endirion's palm pressed in as if he could feel that lie wriggling.

Leta tried again, "I'll manage without, no matter how comforting I find it. My Proxy can't handle the crossover out of Unity anyway. As you know."

Endirion didn't relent. "If the real you is found missing, will the Dynast assume you've defected and your Proxy is a threat, or that you've been kidnapped and you might reconnect to your Proxy to explain?"

"Kidnapped. They would never think I'd defect."

"Because your real self, the one driving this Proxy, is a Graven-influenced adorant of Abriss Cetre."

Stars forfend! He'll pluck up every stitch of logic if I let this continue. Leta closed her eyes. It would look suspicious, but she just needed a moment to focus entirely on what she wanted: speaking to Caiden, the two of them linked up. She held that one idea tight, offering it up to the luminiferity so that reality might rearrange...

Endirion ran his fingers down a freshly strung tendon. "Not going to deny it, Proxy? If I were to—"

"Shit!" Caiden's shout rang out in the clearing. "Drone swarm!"

From inside the ship, Leta saw only the drones' fist-sized shadows flit through sunbeams. Sprays of gossamer threads trailed from each one to taste the topography of spaces, including the mass of the two ships, the body heat, the voices. They were only surveilling, and they carried on to disappear through narrow lanes between the city's platforms.

Caiden had jumped up in a perfect fighting stance, all energy and instinct. The nophek's snarl ended in a hiss as he curled protectively around Caiden. Leta shuddered at the sound.

The bearded man beside Caiden raised a placating hand. "We're doing nothing illegal. Trades happen all the time in tucked-away spots like this. They'll have registered *a ship*, not that it's the *Azura*."

"Sorry, Taitn, this means it's time to run. I've paid every single time I wasn't overcautious. C, load!" The nophek bounded inside the *Azura* while Caiden shouted, "En!"

Endirion growled in frustration as he stood and extended a hand to Leta. "Up."

She levered to her feet without assistance. Clunky legs. Muscles tight. But the new grips on her running blades were improved, her joints cleared of dross, actuators tuned, and all in all—better. She wriggled her uniform back on. The textiles tightened down, the surcoat draped, and she felt appropriate again. Abriss would fix her Proxy once she got home.

Caiden was arguing with his friend Taitn: "—be looking for exactly that, even in this spot. Don't forget how high the bounty is." He was already backing up toward the *Azura* when he turned to Leta. His gaze flicked across her and his mouth opened to say something but hung as she approached.

Leta's Proxy was the same height as him. Just as strong. Their past rammed an ill fit to the present. Their memories of each other begged to be lies.

"Those repairs will have to be enough," he said.

Leta rolled her shoulders, then cracked a little adjustment to the lower-jaw-shaped brace on her skull. The fanged teeth pressed into her lower lip. "Endirion does good work."

"Yeah, he does." Caiden nodded gratefully at Endirion while he clenched his left fist and the skin-colored pigmentation grew transparent up his forearm, revealing the augmented components inside: all black and blue and glassy, like his *Azura*.

Endirion grinned. "Compliments will get you everywhere, kids. But I can keep working on her while we go."

"No," Caiden said. "Thank Panca for the parts, will you? Taitn, tell Lyli that—"

"Hang on," Taitn interrupted, "you're not doing this alone."

"No, I'm doing it with her and C."

Endirion swept over and threw an arm around Caiden's shoulders, both startling him and stopping his backward retreat. "I can manage the infiltration with her as well as you could, then bring Leta to you. No one's ever stormed the Dynast-damned-Hold—I wouldn't mind having that story to tell."

Caiden countered, "I'm the only one who will recognize her."

Endirion snorted. "Does she have a brand like you did?"

"Those can be faked or removed."

Leta struggled to parse the body language and expressions of the three of them at once. Clearly Caiden didn't fully trust her yet if he thought she might be leading him to a fake. *What do I need to ensure happens? Only that the* Azura *becomes accessible on Solthar.*

Caiden pinched the bridge of his nose. "En... I won't risk you or Taitn."

"You don't get to make that call for us."

Caiden shook Endirion's arm off, backed up another step, and looked pleadingly between his two friends.

Taitn deployed a soft voice. "At least let us take you there. Leave the *Azura* somewhere safe and I'll fly you to Solthar on the *Wintra*."

"Nowhere in the multiverse is 'safe,' Taitn. The *Azura*'s only safe with me. This isn't negotiable."

Leta picked up all the minutiae of Caiden's separation anxiety. All but quivering, he peered where the drone swarm had headed, then at all the gaps in the city's layered structure where sky showed through and he might catch a glimpse of the enemy.

For ten years Caiden had shaped his life around keeping his *Azura* safe. That was the whole of Leta's time with the Dynast, and she wasn't about to leave them either.

Taitn whispered, "You don't trust us."

Snarl wrinkles curled across Endirion's nose. "He hasn't trusted us for years. The stray pup has his bite back."

Leta was caught in the middle. *What do I need?*

She assembled the pieces of the broader situation quickly, a feat she'd always been good at. The puzzle of it locked into a solution in a flash. With new confidence she spoke up: "The *Azura* will be safe enough on Solthar." All three pivoted to face her. "I've heard rumors about a starship able to fly straight through lightseep obsidian structures out in the multiverse. That's the *Azura*, isn't it?"

Caiden nodded, his brows furrowed. "Her universe changes the phase of lightseep."

"That is our way into the Dynast Hold without being seen. No need to fly through the orbital checkpoint, no need to park the ship far away while we walk in. The Hold is a gigantic lightseep structure that extends beneath the mantle, branching out and down to the planet's core. We can enter unseen, many kilometers from the Hold, and fly under Solthar's crust through the lightseep. Then exit it into one of the Hold's subterranean caverns used for storage and take a lift up from there."

It was a brilliant solution. She would've been proud of it if this rescue had been real.

Caiden blinked at her.

Endirion burst out a laugh. "Treat solid matter like a river? Not the strangest plan I've ever heard. Taitn flew the *Azura* into the core of an actual star, if you recall, Winn."

This might work. Leta locked stares with Caiden and could see his mind mulling over this strategy. *Agree, agree.*

A steady crackling sound itched Leta's aural sensors from the left. She turned her head several moments before the others did.

Miniature streams of thunder, four distinct ones weaving through the city. They were hard to place by the sound. Leta's vision adjusted for distance and through the trees: the vessels resembled long ax blades, their edges all glowing, pitted strips. *Casthen traders.*

Far overhead above the city plates, the belly of a much larger vessel cut off every shaft of sunlight in the clearing.

Caiden became a blur of action. He smashed Taitn in a hug with a hasty "Goodbye," and he whirled away but Taitn caught his morphcoat sleeve.

"Stop running," the man pleaded.

"No." Caiden's word had teeth. "I needed help desperately, that's all."

"And if you save Leta? Then what? Drag her with you as you bolt again? Dump her on us and flee on your own?"

Then what…

Caiden gently tugged his sleeve free, but his hands were fists. The smaller Casthen ships weaved in the distance, forming a perimeter around the clearing. "*This* is why I don't want any of you involved."

"It's our choice if—"

"*No,*" Caiden snarled again, this time with all of his being: a rich Graven word that resonated from his chest, spiced with gravitas. It shut Endirion and Taitn up hard. Leta wasn't affected by gravitas in-Proxy, but it startled her too.

Caiden's dose of Graven genetics—mosaic and experimental—was obvious from the freckles on his skin, but how was he *this* strong? None of the Graves had gravitas, and they were certainly more Graven than he. Leta recalled Abriss's diagram of the three flows and wondered what Caiden's makeup was.

The nophek roared from the ramp of the ship, piercing enough to make Caiden jump and realize what he'd just done. He covered his mouth with a hand, eyes teary as he saw how his Graven whip had struck his own friends.

Endirion recovered first, an injured cringe on his face. "So this is how you've been getting around. Remember what you were worried about, before you left us last time? You didn't want to turn into Threi, irreverent and reckless, muscling through life with Graven arrogance. Especially since your effect is subtler, you use it without thinking"—he dragged out his words, looping them like nooses—"and stop noticing your influence. Without us around to say anything, how would you know?"

"If it saves bloodshed, is that so bad?" Caiden took another step back.

How different this Graven creature was from the Prime. Abriss's Graven will was like soft veils of light she wafted around her. Caiden had brandished his will as if it cut him too, and he had to pour salt in the severed spaces. A haunted thing showed in his face, and his energy changed shape, as if his spirit were made of blades that now shifted edge-out.

Caiden inhaled, shuddering. "As much as I hate it, my Graven genetics are useful. An alternative to violence, getting me out of tight situations before anyone realizes I've been there. But right now that won't help, so we need to fly out of here. I'm sorry, En."

A sharp sound cracked overhead, then a wash of muddy tones cascaded into the city. Something started to fall and expand from the belly of the large ship overhead: a dark-red field of particles, spreading slowly and filling up the open spaces between buildings.

Caiden cursed. "I don't know what that is but go—now!"

Taitn darted for the *Wintra*. Caiden snatched Leta's wrist and hauled her through the open back of the *Azura*. He fired the engines through his neural link. Leta stumbled on her new legs, falling against one wall as she tore from Caiden's momentum. Endirion dashed inside the *Azura* beside her and hit the bay doors closed.

Caiden whirled. *"En!"*

"Stuck with me now, kid."

Caiden roared in frustration as he threw himself in the pilot seat and cast his hands into the air. Foggy light coalesced into guides instantly, the thrusters bellowed, and the ship lifted.

The nophek's claws screeched into the metal floor as it dug in for stability.

Leta clung to the wall opposite the beast, dizzied by memories of nophek pulling bodies out of the transport vessel while she huddled in the corner. The *sound* of them. The smell.

The *Azura* pitched up sharply, then sideways as Caiden evaded pursuit. Unity's rind's roiling hues filled the cockpit view, approaching fast.

Caiden spared a side-eye to Leta, then apologized, "Sorry," and sped straight through.

Leta's consciousness smacked the wall that was the rind, slathering her back into the luminiferity.

CHAPTER 9

SOLTHAR

Caiden's doubts persisted through the uneventful travel from Melynchon through Unity to the edge of the Dynast homeworld. Their safe journey seemed to confirm the Proxy's claims that the Dynast wasn't after Caiden, but he couldn't shake his caution. He decelerated to a stop, staring at the vista of Solthar, the planet not only at the center of Unity but at the heart of the wider multiverse. The outer universes had bubbled off from vast Unity long ago, and this spot was the nucleus of it all.

A field of lightseep obsidian shards surrounded the entire planet. He could barely see beyond its glittering as space itself fractured and refracted. Starlight reflections flamed across the planet's aura, the cadence of light melodic. Something changed in the *Azura* too: the flux of her universe rind hushed and tightened around the fuselage.

"Oh," En said behind him, "you've never been here before, have you?"

Caiden had little to say after the stunt En had pulled. C padded over, giving fluttering huffs that asked if Caiden was all right despite his mood. Caiden reached out of the pilot seat to wrap C's big head in one arm and press his face in soft fur. The nophek's purr filled his head.

The lightseep shard field was usually impassable for ships, with one narrow checkpoint gap that allowed traffic through. The *Azura* rested in orbit opposite that checkpoint. With her universe active, Caiden could fly through the lightseep wherever he wanted, as if it weren't solid matter. No other vessels were in sight. The Proxy's strategy had been a good one.

She lay unconscious near the cockpit. The *Azura*'s universe formed a bubble within Unity, a barrier between her consciousness and Proxy. Her own impossible lightseep bits caught Caiden's attention. The absurdity of her construction did nothing to help his lingering doubts. She looked more like a weapon than the kind girl Caiden remembered.

The Proxy's head rested in En's lap as he reapplied skin media to her face and fixed oxidization. She needed to look uninjured for long enough to be a distraction while Caiden whisked her real body away.

En cocked his head at Caiden, wearing a pensive look. His face now was clean-lined but rounded, eyes heavy-lidded and swiped with smoky pigment that made his gray irises brighter.

Caiden tried to regather the sweet moments: the ramia meal, Taitn's stories, En insisting on braiding Caiden's hair if he wouldn't cut it. Caiden ran his fingertips down the three tight weaves against his skull and remembered the Graven shout he'd brandished on his own family.

His Graven effect, he'd realized, was more of a bonding force than a purely attractive one like Threi's Dynast gravitas, but either way, he hated the ease of it. Hated how it felt autonomous and he needed to wrestle it back. Hated his lack of control. Hated how it stole others' consent.

"En," Caiden started. "It's not that I've been trying to keep you all out of danger. I think...I meant to keep you all from *me*."

"Sacrifice in and of itself doesn't count as 'good'—you learned this before. So can you prove you've prevented any wrong by running?"

"Back then it was almost glamorous, fighting head-on against a terror that was visible, rather than quietly suffering to keep contained a terror that no one sees." Caiden looked up at the *Azura*'s ceiling, her spine glistening sleepily through the Glasliq. "I've done good while on the run."

En smiled. "I gathered together the rumors. Anixellan, the Butcher of Prixia, the Ghost of *Azura*, the fellsweep—all accredited with liberations, daring rescues of the downtrodden, stopping the heartbeat of wars, transporting precious cargo through impossible routes. If anyone stitched gossip together, it would paint quite the hero."

"I'm trying, En."

It wasn't enough. Small acts of valiance could affect entire populations or planets, but given the scale of the multiverse, the rhythms of the Casthen, the immensity of Unity...that valiance was too little. He'd been a boy when he overthrew the Casthen from its core, but he'd had Threi's help. On his own he was no match for either Threi or Abriss.

En hummed and leaned against the wall. "It seems to me that Threi has won. He may be imprisoned, but he controls your life. You never broke away from that man after all the events in the Casthen Harvest."

"I saw the raw side of Threi Cetre, behind all his smiles. You really don't know him or what being Graven means."

Threi's words had carved on Caiden's walls: *Welcome to a life of lies, Winn.*

"This Graven part of me was weak and buried when I was a boy, but now...It's like it's growing up as I do, becoming stronger than the leashes I put on it."

C snorted and pulled away at the word "leash." Caiden waved him back over and murmured soothing things as he injected a higher dose of the solution that altered C's biology. Caiden would be deactivating and reactivating the *Azura*'s universe a few times for this whole plan.

The nophek shook, then settled down to sleep. Caiden rolled the empty vial in his palm, watching the Graven freckles in his skin distend behind the glass.

Tenderly, En said, "You're not a monster, Winn."

"Yet."

"You're allowed to live, like the rest of us."

What is living? He'd experienced impossible vistas, seen a plethora of species, fought vicious monsters, and wildcrafted delicacies. There was a lot to want to protect, out there. Was that all his life was, ensuring others could live well? "I've seen more of the multiverse than most have."

En shifted. "From a distance, briefly, before you whisk off into space again. That's not living—that's not even sightseeing."

Caiden became lost in thought, feeling even more like he was one layer removed from life. He wanted to blame his Gravenness, as if it were a magnetism turning him the wrong way against reality.

En hauled the Proxy to a sitting position, then walked behind Caiden's seat. "Speaking of sights...Wait until you see the actual planet."

Caiden crept the *Azura* through the thick veil of lightseep shards. The ship's reflection was fractured all around into strange new versions: a black void, a wisp of ghost, a swarm of sparks.

Once through the field completely, Caiden made a sound and gaped out the cockpit at Solthar. En sniggered at him.

Caiden said, "I'd read about this, but..."

The Dynast had repurposed the shards as satellites to bounce energies and create a prismatic, holographic world, hybrid of phantom and real. Solthar's atmosphere was luminous blue and aflame with incandescent pink curls. A partially eclipsed sun scythed the far side of the planet with brilliance but cast no shadow. Starburst-shaped cities constellated the surface between swaths of nature.

The lightseep projections blended biomes that shouldn't have mixed. Velvety forests covered the hills. Waterfalls curtained off their boughs. Rain fell from tiny stars not as drops but long silver threads, while windy curls of fog serpentined the plains. Translucent megafauna flew as slow as clouds.

Enemy territory, Caiden chastised himself. He was in a beautiful cage teeming with Dynast military, right next to the Prime and all her strange powers. The *Azura* had an alterskin applied, a false scan print, and concealed energy signatures, but risk was still risk.

He brushed his hand overhead, where the florescer plumed out from the crystalline spine in the ceiling. A mental command would have worked, but habit was in his body and he enjoyed the familiar warmth that rippled through his fingertips. The *Azura*'s universe contracted, dulcet tones grew rougher, and things loosened in the walls. Caiden began descent.

After a while the Proxy's connection was restored and she murmured, "Caiden."

An impulse kicked in him at the name. "Y-yes?"

She got her bearings, pushed back white waves of hair, and peered out the cockpit. Her smile bloomed instantly, fitting oddly against the armored jaw that rimmed her face.

Caiden tried to look past her features, imagining a grown version of Leta. What would it be like to have her back? The other children had teased him that he only wanted something to protect, treating her like an object, but they didn't try to know Leta enough to realize the reason Caiden stuck by her: her intellect, the way she engaged with the world in so much detail, the things she noticed that slipped past everyone else.

"Relieved?" En asked her, voice thick with suspicion.

The Proxy's smile caved. "Solthar is objectively beautiful."

"How much of the landscape we're seeing is real?" Caiden asked.

"All? It's part of your consciousness, so it's real."

That was the most Dynast answer he could imagine.

Her copper eyes glittered as she took in the sight. She'd lived here a decade. Captive or not, she'd made a life, and her years had been spent belonging.

Impossible ravines cracked into black caverns at impossible angles, and plants moved a hundred times the speed they should, and... Caiden admitted his elevated heart rate was real. Lightseep towers bladed up like jagged bones spearing the flesh of a broken creature. They ribbed thicker, gripping towering peaks and kilometer-high trees, until—crowning all Solthar—the Dynast Hold nestled in nature.

Caiden stalled the ship again.

The palace was a jewel chiseled from spacetime. The world refracted and bent on its lightseep planes. Mineral growth muscled the obsidian bones to make a more recognizable architecture, something that could be lived in.

"Is that where you are?" he asked.

"Yes."

He frowned, imagining Leta inside, trapped like a creature in amber.

Caiden had studied the extent of Abriss Cetre's influence, the countless planets loyal to her, and the history of the Dynast family, but *seeing* it was different entirely. The carved plateaus surrounding the Hold teemed with vessels. They were specks across the distance, but that only magnified the visual immensity of the forces she controlled.

If Abriss ever turned eye or ambition to the multiverse outside of Unity, she possessed unspeakable power to bring to bear against it.

"Given this sight," he said quietly, "Threi's obsession with murdering the Dynast Prime doesn't seem like such an overreaction."

"What?" A surprised scoff in the Proxy's voice.

Caiden studied her. "Threi has bent countless years toward it. Does Abriss not realize?"

She hesitated. "The Prime doesn't speak with her brother anymore."

"Not at all?"

En added, "I'm surprised she'd think so little of him, given that he's half immune to her and now commands equally vast forces."

One of Threi's first moves after imprisonment had been allying the Casthen to the Cartographers. He'd traded the Casthen's immense resources and multiversal reach to gain access to Cartographer databases.

The Proxy frowned, one finger picking nervously at a seam in her cheek. "Threi is galaxies away, locked in a universe to which only you have the key. Besides, Abriss's astrology would tell her if he was a threat."

Caiden shook his head. "She can be wrong, you know. She can read *Unity*, but Threi isn't in Unity, is he? Abriss knows nothing of Casthen stars."

"If she died," En thought aloud, "would the Dynast's power dissolve with her? She's their last Graven ruler, besides Threi."

"Threi would seize the reins and have the Dynast, Casthen, and Cartographers all wrapped around his fingers. That's exactly what I've been trying to stop."

"But did you ever ask what he would do after his obsession was over? With that much power...Maybe he would do good."

Caiden shot En a glare.

En raised his palms. "You can be sour, but I know you've been keeping an eye on him, looking to snip off corrupt operations before they get started. So you've seen how different he is from Çydanza, how much actual improvement he's made in the multiverse. The sort of improvement you're fighting for."

Caiden wrinkled his nose. "I know more than I want to about Threi. Any goodness he's shown the world is a cover to keep spreading his leverage farther." He side-eyed the Proxy. "What is Abriss like?"

"She's kept Unity stable and harmonious, and welcomes outside worlds. Dynast immigration policies are ones she'd implemented as a child. She's streamlined the peacekeeping factions of the Dynast military. She's relaxed the signal flow of command to strengthen the endarchy and reduce the influence of her gravitas on critical freethinking—that part is important to her."

"I didn't ask about her deeds. I asked for your opinion."

Abriss's *deeds* were magnanimous to a fault. Unity was the most peaceful and equitable universe of any Caiden had been in. But he knew absolutely nothing about Abriss's heart.

The Proxy answered softly, "She is selfless and kind."

Caiden swiveled to face her. "And your treatments? The pain? The dead? Is that her *kindness*?"

The Proxy flinched. "She's acting with a higher purpose. Besides...kind and cruel can go together. Remember my parental unit? No one knew about the abuse except you because they were kind on the outside."

Caiden slowed the *Azura* in the clouds. An armada took off from a city nearby, clotting the traffic flows that stalled to watch. Magnificent Dynast ships skewered the atmosphere. The air ripped into thunder and light.

"Where to?"

A holosplay map of Solthar ghosted across the cockpit.

The Proxy said, "Toward the sun. Those knobby peaks."

Caiden veered from populated areas and headed for the massif. The ship torched above a glossy salt flat, rippling the reflected clouds.

And if you save Leta? Taitn had asked. *Then what?*

Caiden, after ten years on the move trying to harness his own Graven nature before it turned him into a terror. Her, after ten years raised as an experiment by the Dynast, chiseled into a Graven creature.

We'd have to start over.

Mountains heaved up ahead to form canyons. Waterfalls spilled down either side, the amethyst water splitting to form the trunks of trees with vapor foliage. Roots seeped into the earth like branching rivers. Caiden disengaged the *Azura*'s alterskin so he could marvel at the sight blurred beyond the Glasliq material.

En drooped over the back of Caiden's seat. "This brings back memories, these Solthar trees."

"Sordid, violent, or romantic memories?"

"Romantic." En sighed.

The forest of amethyst liquid-trees was perforated by rays of light, which made Caiden guess it was projected reality. Except that the waterfall mist kissing the cockpit windows actually beaded up and rolled away. With all the strange things he'd seen out in the multiverse, he could believe this lightseep was so powerful it didn't make illusions but manifested impossible, reified things.

En added, "The violence came later."

Caiden snorted. He slowed the ship as a deck of perfectly smooth lightseep began to push out of the ground. "Is this the spot?" he asked the Proxy. He scrolled across a map of the area. One overlay showed the lightseep deck's subterraneous extension. Big channels of it *did* connect to the base of the Dynast Hold.

"May I?" She sidled over and commandeered the map to show him the route she had in mind and which underground parking cavern. The *Azura*'s universe would be active for the whole trip, cutting off Proxy connection.

Caiden asked, "Everyone in the Hold is human?"

She blinked. "There are...all variety of human raciation and hybridization here—the spectrum of sexes and gender, skin shades and texture, hair of all densities and length, every height and—oh. You mean nonhuman xenids, don't you? Few. The Graves, we're all xenids and hybrids."

"I mean that the Dynast family keeps closest the subjects they can easily control."

Graven influence was completely effective on human physiology. For many other species it was attenuated to varying degrees.

En patted Caiden's shoulder but looked sad. "That'll make it easier for you."

"Well," the Proxy said, pulling away, "if you're ready, I'm rather tired of getting kicked out of this body. Do you mind if I leave it *before* you initiate the universe and go? I'll be able to sense when it's available again and meet up with you."

"Back to your real body in the meantime?" En asked.

Caiden caught on. Every time she—Leta—returned to her real body was another chance for the lovely spider Abriss to come along and web her up again.

"No," the Proxy said, and smiled. "As long as you're fast, my spirit and consciousness can drift in the luminiferity, bodiless and unanchored, until I sense my Proxy again."

She sounded sincere.

Caiden still struggled to trust the incredible mechanics of what she claimed she could do—spirit independent of body. She walked back to one wall of the bay, where there were a few pillows, and settled there, copper eyes closed and milky hair pushed against the wall.

Despite doubts, closure felt near. The path through the lightseep was clear and rife with alternate escape routes. En and C could guard the *Azura*. He would teach En C's battle commands. Caiden was confident in his own abilities. And he was Graven, if all else failed.

I'm coming, Leta. Ten years late, but I promised.

CHAPTER 10

RESCUE

Leta and Caiden traveled up from the Hold's subterranean levels through a wide concourse sparsely traveled at this time of day. The onlookers bowed to her while Caiden received stares. He walked as if there were something nipping at his heels.

Leta had lent Caiden her Dynast surcoat to wear over his base layers, so he resembled an Arbiter. It looked dashing and dangerous on him if she were honest. Meanwhile she'd borrowed garments from him and Endirion to fill out her missing pieces. It was enough to convince the pair that she was committed to the plan. The lie.

The tempo of Solthar's reality soothed her. She was home, and the *Azura* was in position. Caiden was the biggest obstacle to capturing the ship, but she didn't need to draw him very far apart from it before he could be detained.

Catch and release, unharmed.

"Side archway," she said, steering him into a narrow passage.

"Proxy?"

She looked over. Caiden hadn't yet called her Leta. Maybe doubt was what nipped at his heels, and he was rushing toward the proof of her. What would he think if he saw her real body?

He asked, "Where do we split up?"

"Just beyond the atrium. I'll point you toward the Away Room, not far from there, while I head to the audience." Sweetening the ruse, she smiled and asked, "Have you really memorized the route back to the *Azura*?"

He nodded without returning the smile. The Dynast coat swished around his legs with his brisk pace. He carried a sharp, observant energy now, his fire-blue eyes bright.

Will I forget him again, afterward? Will the new Azura-*derived treatments gradually erase the memory of this?*

Leta let herself be charmed by his competence for this short moment, side by side. He had a smart head even though his foolish heart was too devoted to truth. Her childhood rescuer had grown up well. He would be all right, afterward.

They reached the atrium hall where soaring ceilings chiseled to a light-seep peak. The angles tessellated one another into a black-hole spire with a refracted star of light in the center. The obsidian walls were a hundred meters away, but appeared to extend galaxies beyond that, filled with ghostly inclusions of a mysterious vista.

She led Caiden on and veered for the training hall, jogging across a bridge between towers, over fathoms of plants. Shafts of light speared through the garden and cracked open time, showing the same plants blossoming or withered, dewy or snow-laden.

Leta swept into the huge hall, where she was buoyed by the sight of three Proxies standing in the center. Tayen Five, her Proxy oil-black and glistening, armored and faceless. Sisorro Seven, sculpted quartz dermis sheathing organics, body draped in colorful textiles. Dejin Eight stood two heads taller, muscular and clad in engraved armor, somewhat storybook, like the golden scrollwork on the spines in Abriss's library. A faceless woven mesh of silver helmeted his head, and a cowl over that. A white cloak covered his back with copper embroidery of beasts and stars.

All three were improved humanoid designs, but only Sisorro had requested a face—perhaps because they were a xenid with the least human features of the seven. They exaggerated their expressions, like this eager smile crimping their cheeks too wide.

Caiden eyed Leta. "Proxies like you? Will they stop us?"

He'd spoken soft enough for her ears only, but he didn't know Proxy hearing. Sisorro called over the distance, "Thought you could outrun stars? Fast rabbit."

Leta's lungs prickled as they flushed excess heat, her anxiety starting to leach past the suppressors. *They'll capture him so I don't have to. Abriss agreed. Goodbye, Caiden.*

He slipped into a fighting stance, summoning up that sharp energy that needed release. Now Leta wondered if it was actually a *Graven* energy. He glanced over and smiled... his first smile for her... and it was exactly as she remembered. The knife of guilt twisted.

"Strange to think of you... *fighting*," he whispered quieter. Finally he alluded to truly thinking of her as his childhood friend.

Leta couldn't help but smile back, then realized she would have to fight the other Graves, too, otherwise Caiden would realize her complicity when the Proxies apprehended him. *Stars forfend, what a mess. But he doesn't deserve his heart broken on top of this.*

The Prime had said, *Sometimes a thing needs to break in order to grow.*

She could keep the ruse up a little longer and simply pretend to fight back. Sparring. Like old times. Leta eased her running blades into a ready stance. Seven cocked their head at her, Five and Eight exchanged glances.

The Graves used to spar every day when their Proxies were new and needed tuning and tests, stretching out and breaking in. They hadn't known their own strength or lack of it, and the only safe training was with one another. There were as many laughs and smiles as there were cuts and bruises. Isme Two was the undisputed best fighter among them, in-Proxy, but Leta was near the top.

Clang. Clang. Tayen Five's sword beat the ground to the tempo of her impatience, blunt from days of the habit. The dents all over the training hall were ten years of Tayen. Leta found the sound soothing.

The three Proxies spread out while stalking forward. Leta drew her own weapon—an electric white ribbon, blade and whip—from its sheath along the length of her spine. She advanced on Sisorro Seven—arguably the most dangerous. They weren't just a brute, and of the three, they were the most likely to want to toy with Caiden first, against orders.

Seven laughed as if they knew her thinking. Their gaze saccaded across her, cataloging every weak joint and tender patch of nerve.

Leta danced in, flicking the energy lash around her body. It cracked the air with tiny pressure bursts. Sisorro's delicate-looking quartz skin was a deceit; it behaved more like morphable Glasliq, and the little snipes Leta landed glanced off. With each of Sisorro's agile dodges, they rapped a sharp knuckle on some sensitive or mal-repaired piece of Leta. The strikes barked at her nervous system, warning of imminent failures.

Seven's shoulder-length curls swished across their grin as they stopped suddenly. "This is delightful, but you always keep distance, Nine. Get right into it, like your boy there. He is doing a delightful job not being rabbit-caught."

She peered at Caiden. He'd chosen to fight hand-to-hand with only one augmented arm against fully augmented fighters, but he was blocking well against Tayen Five—who *was* the brute.

Tay's Proxy was an ooze of shadow at this speed. Space fluttered in the wake of her translucent sword. The blade wasn't truly lightseep, nor was the substance in the Proxies' bodies: Abriss had developed an imitation. Tayen's blade cleaved space itself. And when she slammed it against the real light-seep obsidian sections of the floor, they rippled into flickers of visions: a pit, a jungle, a mire, a cloudscape.

Caiden continued holding his own, and Leta realized where his confidence came from: the strange glave packs over his shoulder blades and hips were mini scalar gravity generators, patterning nodes in the air around him. Not strong enough to *hold* Tayen but enough to deflect and control her momentum. He angled precisely and tripped Tayen's legs as he ducked the sweep of her blade.

Dejin Eight stalked around the tangle of Caiden and Tayen, waiting for a chance to grab or strike.

Sisorro gave a fluttery chuckle. "Maybe we should switch. He looks like fun."

"Just catch him! No playing."

"Oh? Ah. Dian said you would be too protective. The rabbit does need to be caught, but the Prime did not say no playing. What are you doing now if not playing with his feelings?"

Leta flicked her lash out and snapped its barbed end on a quartz plate. Glitter exploded around Sisorro's chest as their skin fractured. They stumbled back in a flourish of fabrics and beamed at her. "Then you and I can play, and you will appear to be on his side still. That will be nice for your conscience."

Leta fixed her stance and shook the lash, its energy crackling. *Conscience...*

Sisorro Seven's eyes flicked to Caiden over her shoulder. "Well, well."

Leta glanced. Even Dejin paused to watch the smaller opponent take on a fury of oil-slick shadow.

Tayen Five still hadn't made contact with Caiden and was getting more furious by the moment. He was patient. Precise. Using the nodes to accelerate Tayen's own momentum and smash her fingers into the ground... repeatedly enough that tendons dangled.

Five swung and Caiden rolled aside to kick her wrist. The lightseep blade clattered from her broken-fingered grip: his plan all along. He snatched it and launched up as she curved over him with a fist. He impaled her chest with their combined momentums and carried both her and weapon to the ground. With the added discharge of his augmented arm's energy, he slammed Five on her back and drove the blade into a stony patch of floor, pinning her there.

Howling filled her skull behind her mask. Her snapped fingers flopped as she scrabbled for the sword hilt, not gaining enough purchase to pull it out.

Clever.

Sisorro Seven clapped their hands, grinning from ear to ear.

Leta gaped, caught between the alarm of seeing Tayen's Proxy impaled and the knowledge that she couldn't be killed in this body.

Caiden, panting, backed away from Five, glanced at Leta and Sisorro, then faced off Dejin Eight. Leta stalled while Seven's applause slapped her ears. She had fought Caiden on the sayro planet, knew his speed and shrewdness, but now the violence in him was loose, coiling him up, marching to a rhythm that maybe he couldn't stop.

Leta realized, inexplicably but deeply, that no net could catch Caiden. He was an arrow streaming toward a target that had been denied him for ten long years. If there was anything Unity rewarded, it was the energized combination of desire and idea. Focused strong enough, the two would bend reality to manifest that desire. Caiden was gaining control of events now.

Dejin grunted and engaged him. He wore elaborate gauntlets full of charged force. His body was heavy and he was wise to the momentum trick, holding his ground until he released one well-timed punch that threw Caiden several meters across the floor, screaming. Caiden's augmented arm popped with electricity.

Tayen Five was still pinned by her own blade, painlessly twisting her long, glossy body to try to wrench free from the floor.

Sisorro snatched Leta's arm and whirled her up against their side. Their curls tickled her cheek and their voice poured into her ear: "Are you going to watch him the whole time? Playing is no fun if you are not paying attention."

"You're supposed to be catch—"

Sisorro kicked her stumbling toward Dejin before she could finish. They sauntered over to Caiden, colors swaying around their body, fingers and knuckles curved into hooks.

"Nine." Dejin drew her attention as he towered between her and the fight. He reached to grab her, playing his role, but hesitated and whispered, "Consent?" as if this were any time to be courteous.

"Yes!" Leta snarled. He hauled her up by her arm like he'd caught her, halfheartedly. She said, "Can you stop Sis and just catch Winn? He's not supposed to be harmed."

Sisorro Seven was a flurry of colors. Caiden blocked with quick gravity patterns. He reversed the nodes with perfect timing to sling Seven's hands to the ground or forward off balance, or he caught them straight in the air inches from vital points. He shot glances back at Leta. Worried for her?

Dejin rumbled, "He was not supposed to be this strong."

"Then stop him before Sisorro gets hurt! Dej, *please*."

Dimpled air nodes clustered around Seven, turning their figure into a blot of round, distorted colors. *Crack!* The gravity inverted, space sundered, shattering every inch of Sisorro's quartz surface. Leta and Dejin both startled.

Sisorro's eyes widened. They fell to all fours, levered upright, then sat right back down, curled over laughing. Sparkling dust wheezed from the ruptured sculpture of them.

Caiden backed off, breathless. His hands were raised, ready for another flurry of attacks.

But Seven just giggled, managing to say, "Delightful! A prize, then: run, rabbit." They flapped their hands in a shooing gesture toward the hall exit.

Leta cursed. Sisorro had changed games. They wouldn't fight or capture.

Five ripped herself free from her sword, grunting an animal sound of frustration. She was fine—her organs not in human locations—but her left side glitched hard enough that she had to stay sitting.

Eight dropped Leta, flexed more charge into his gauntlets, and advanced on Caiden. His bulk was a bad match against Caiden's speed and determination and having *everything* to lose. Caiden sprang into a kick perfectly timed to slam Dej's charged uppercut right back into the Proxy's own face. The impact exploded off Dejin's helmet, staggering him back with more surprise than damage.

He's monstrous. Leta's brain, confused, buzzed with adrenaline while she also struggled to parse a foreign, luminiferous sensation that tried to convince her this was all meant to be. She wasn't supposed to get pulled into his unstoppable energy or feel so included in the depths of his need, but alarmingly, it didn't feel intuitively *wrong*.

Caiden ran past her with a desperate look. Leta dashed beside him, out the archway, while she struggled to sort her feelings. The past echoed into her, tilling up her old affinity for Caiden. Abriss had pointed out that he was chasing the past. It felt more like he brought the past with him.

"I understand you couldn't hurt them," he said, panting. "Family."

Leta's rhythm tripped up. She fell and skidded on the causeway's stone.

Caiden reached a hand down to her. "Do we still have a chance? Where do I find you?"

She stared at his palm: a choice.

He *smiled* again. "Which way do we go?"

Leta let him pull her up. "Here. Left. The room's close." The words floated from her lips, heard dizzily in her own ears. This wasn't how the mission was meant to proceed.

They turned a corner to a long walkway. Gardens sprawled below in multiple levels, with green bridges and catwalks and trees of every height.

Who am I? This me he's so desperate to save, a me that the years haven't corroded...

He could make it to the Away Room, at this rate. What would happen if they met for real? The past wanted to know.

Or she could grab him now, knock him out or bind him, and that betrayal would inhabit him forever. He would lose the *Azura* and his one chance to make amends for abandoning her before.

I don't want this choice. Unity—guide us, make it for me.

"The lift." Leta gestured and Caiden ran, stormed up in his own violent energy.

He bundled them both into the small lift platform, meant for one person. Leta leaned against the wall near his shoulder.

"Caiden. Why am I worth this to you?"

He looked over. There was that smile again. That crooked, wary thing. Just as she remembered. The world shifted and the past crashed over her with that smile.

"When you were dead in my mind, it meant you never had to suffer again." A lump hitched in his throat.

Ah. The fact that I'm alive erased that grim comfort.

She murmured, "I was never your responsibility to protect."

"I took it on myself."

"*Why?*"

"Selfishness," Caiden answered. "When your shivers stopped, when I could ease the pain, when I made you laugh, when you felt I was safe enough to come to when in need, I had a purpose. It was enough."

Wisps of memory reminded her she had survived because of him.

"We're close?" he asked while the lift sang.

"We're close." *Forfend, we are. Two corridors and four rooms away.*

He was rushing to meet the real her. She hadn't yet met the real him, either—the unfiltered, human frequencies, the scents and colors. Their proximity to each other now was the lie. The intentionally filtered design of her Proxy's sensory systems usually soothed her, but she had never been so aware of such a *lack* of experience. Until she could meet him, he was as unreal to her as the promise of her was to him, and this strange inkling pushing her onward whispered that something important would unlock at their meeting.

The lift stopped. Door opened.

They trundled out.

"Having fun?" Dian Six waited just outside. "You got quite far."

His ankle-length skirt panels rustled as he shifted to the balls of his feet. His bare-chested Proxy's "skin" was a vitrified, translucent ceramic painted to represent the sacred geometries that built his inner mechanics: a vast web of progressions and paths, a tree growing up him. Abriss had spent days with each of the Graves designing exactly the sort of meaning they wanted in their ideal bodies. Dian wanted power and complexity.

Caiden's scalar gravity field surged online as he lunged toward Six, but the Proxy twisted himself up, joints dislocating, and curved around while locking Caiden's arms behind him. "You really think we'll let you take her? My little sister?"

Caiden froze at that term.

Dian Six snapped a blow into Caiden's cheek. It staggered him into a wall, which jarred the side of his skull. He crumpled to the floor, woozily cradling his jaw. A dribble of blood leaked out of his lips.

Six hauled Leta out of earshot. "You lead him to the sword, but you don't want blood on your hands. Can't you tell you're injuring him the most by stringing him along?"

"I know." Whatever expression she was making caused Six to soften. "Something feels off, and I need to place it. A luminiferous will, a pressure to see this through. These memories feel like something buried that shouldn't have been unearthed."

Dian looked over her shoulder to Caiden, who was rising slowly. He yanked Leta close and scoffed, "Something *off*. Is this another brief obsession of yours? Or a childhood crush?"

Leta landed a rapid surprise knee in Six's smallest rib, smashing it against one of his hearts. He doubled against her, recovered fast, and sneered. "Is that a yes or no?"

"It's a no. Dian, he can't realize that I betrayed him."

"And that makes all this better?"

"It's not for my conscience. It's for him."

Caiden trudged toward them from the lift, full of fight. Leta needed to plunge toward a choice. She hooked Six's ankle and tripped him to the ground, locking his limbs tight with hers as he struggled. She looked up at Caiden and nodded a direction. "Two corridors and four rooms away. Black door."

He hesitated only a beat before sprinting to the Away Room.

Leta disconnected emotionally as she watched him run. Something had gone terribly wrong or right, but she had lost track of which.

Dian Six relaxed beneath her and whispered by her ear, "Aren't you going too? Slip away from your Proxy. I can tell…you want to be there when he finds you."

CHAPTER 11

ANSWER

The jet-black door dissolved open in front of Caiden. No locks. No guards.

His unadjusted eyes struggled as he stepped inside, darkness closing around. Sounds diffused, cocooning him in a soft thrumming that he couldn't place. Warm, unscented air. An innocuous space.

Caiden flexed his hands open and closed, prepared for attack. Tiny gravity wells spiraled against his palms.

"Leta?" he whispered.

His vision weaved something out of the dark: ten translucent, luminescent plates lay in a row on the floor. Hovering above them: seven bodies, unconscious.

Caiden's chest seized up as he crept down the row.

The first one was a xenid he didn't recognize: a curled-up garden of a body, lily-white flesh, frilly tendrils, red cilia blooming in folds of skin. Freckles spotted them all over in silver and crimson.

The second was a human male, diaphonized to the extreme. Translucent flesh, organs bright gold. His whole body was a tapestry of texture. Freckles throughout like fire sparks.

The third and fourth plates were empty. Leta's words itched up in his head: *Twenty-nine of us.* Twenty-two horrifically dead.

The fifth was a woman with ruddy, close-shorn hair and a hard face, mottled freckles burned white in her umber skin. Older, not Leta.

Sixth: a muscular man covered in burnlike scars, sable skin bleached in places by galaxies of compounded speckling. Long black hair levitated and obscured his face. The seventh Grave was a spindly xenid wreathed in gauzy tissues as if they were clothed in the gossamer skins of a hundred ghosts. Eighth: a huge, thickly built ursgen. His limbs were folded up, long tail coiled down one leg.

Nine. The last was his Leta.

He stared up at her, transformed and twenty but *it was really her.* Her soft face. Lips naturally frowning like she was always cross. Fawn waves of hair tangled upward in the gravity suspending her. She had freckles now, from the treatments. Sparks of bioradiance had burned layers and layers of spots into her flesh, light and dark both—a landscape of stars swirled across her.

As much as he'd wished for it, Caiden wasn't prepared for this truth. Not that she still existed and not the state of her transformation, which harkened back to all the childhood bruises she'd explained away. This was the same all over again.

"I'm here," he said in exhale. He wrapped his arms around her waist and pulled her out of the field. She sagged against him, and his knees gave out not from the slight weight of her but from the weight of *this.* The reality of holding her.

"I'm sorry. Crimes, Leta, I'm so sorry." He supported her limp neck in his hand, his fingers catching in her hair. The softness of it and the realness of her... Then he jolted as he felt, against his palm, the knotty impression of the Casthen slave brand on the nape of her neck. A swear sizzled between his teeth. "Leta. Leta, I need you to wake up and say it's all right."

She seemed delicate, all dead weight. Did her real body still work, or was she just a mind they kept captive to pilot Proxy weapons?

Leta's eyelashes quivered. She opened one eye and then the other, and though the color had paled, they were the honey gray-green he remembered.

"Cai," she whispered.

Fissures burst through his heart.

She gazed up at him, searching his face, while a slow gasp filled her lungs.

"Hi," Caiden quavered. "You're real."

Leta winced as she struggled to sit up, and Caiden's heart broke a little more. Her sides were so ribby. The effort made her quake. She grasped a handful of his sleeve as if she were slipping. *What did they do to you?* he wanted to ask, but that heavy question could wait until she was safe.

A shadow glided across them both, and Leta's gaze flicked over his shoulder. Like a switch, her expression changed. A flash of guilt, then her frown smoothed out and adoration filled her features.

"Hello, Winn of Casthen," said the Dynast Prime. Her voice flooded Caiden with cold dread, then an instant, searing bliss. Harmony wrapped around and relaxed his tense muscles, and the worried words that gummed up in his brain melted away.

Abriss Cetre stood in the doorway, flanked by six Proxies. The injured one leaned on another while the one who had been by the lift cradled Leta's limp Proxy body.

"No." Caiden whimpered and tore his focus back down to the girl in his arms. "Leta?"

She wouldn't meet his gaze. The frown crept back into her face.

Before Abriss's Graven proximity could snare Leta completely, he grasped her shoulders and squared her to face him, summoned up every sickening shred of his own gravitas, and poured it into her, voice cracking as he asked, he *ordered*, "Do you really want to escape?"

Her eyes dilated and riveted to his, sliding a knife into him when her answer came without hesitation: "No."

Then her brows furrowed and she pulled out of his arms.

The past fell away with her, and Caiden couldn't hold on.

She was real. Alive. And he meant nothing to her.

"Nine," Abriss said tenderly, but even gentler was an order, "come away."

Leta treaded over to the group while hugging her arms. Her body was beginning to overload as it used to, in signs familiar to Caiden, but she had new protectors now. *Six* of them. The big Proxy with scrolled silver armor swept to her and asked one word, to which she nodded, and he wrapped an arm around her with his white cloak in his fist, cocooning her out of sight.

The Prime asked, "Was he so hard to stop? It would have been less cruel,

Nine, for him to believe you were a lie." She sighed. "Winn, I apologize that you made it this far, I did not intend your suffering."

Sound spiraled out of Caiden's ears, swaddling her words into muffles. He looked down at his empty hands. Sweetgrass twirled in his nose, the scent of hope, all in his head. She was *alive*—after years of nightmares where she wasn't.

"—enough to go yourself?" the Prime was asking someone.

"Yes," Leta replied. "The vessel's below."

Leta's voice. It really was her voice, except now a Dynast accent twisted it up. She was theirs, through and through, made into the Dynast's creature like Caiden had been made the Casthen's. When they were children, he'd intercepted the adult influences over her, but this time he was ten years too late.

"Good," Abriss said. "Take One and Six with you to retrieve it."

The voices washed through Caiden's awareness. Everything Leta had said to him had been a lie, and he'd bought it all, urgently.

The *Azura*.

Losing the *Azura* negated the entire miserable decade he'd spent on the run to keep her out of enemy hands. He'd sacrificed family and comfort and sanity for nothing.

Little boy... Abriss might be noble enough to spare En, but the nophek's gloss was maturing. Even nascent gloss was worth palaces.

Caiden's bloodstream raged loud in his skull as he rose to his feet. He made fists, squeezing the resistance of the gravity pockets.

The six Proxies fanned out like wings on either side of their Prime.

Tightly, Caiden said, "You and Threi are after my ship."

"I am afraid so." The Prime's dress of constellations shifted, twinkling in the dark. *Stars.* Caiden had been a fool to think anything he did in Unity went unseen. She continued, "Graven technology belongs to the Dynast family. Thank you for being its custodian. I will not keep you detained for long. You won't be harmed."

Her voice cooled his fire and unmade every knot of tension. The Graven part of him resisted, tingling all over, but as she closed the distance between them by just one meter, harmony shriveled up his dreadful rage.

The shattered quartz-skinned Proxy laughed. "Let him join the Dynast. He is a delightful fighter."

Another Proxy scowled. "He is a desperate fighter, spurred by jagged hate."

"That is delightful to me."

Abriss raised a hand, and the two hushed.

"Enough," said the beetle-black Proxy. "The abomination belongs in a cccccccell." The final word sizzled out the cracks of her helmet. She marched toward Caiden, her stride lopsided. A gaping hole remained in her abdomen where he'd impaled her.

Caiden planted his foot and gathered all that jagged hate, white-hot and terrible. He stilled as the Proxy neared, then rammed a sudden punch of clotted gravity toward the hole in her torso. Materials snapped as his fist twisted inside her rib cage. Force torqued through her lungs and ripped apart her wail.

"*Stop!*" Abriss shouted while Leta shrieked, "*Tayen!*" at the same time.

Leta's cry slapped Caiden cold more than Abriss's Graven command.

Two Proxies rushed to lock his arms and skull, then strip the node-generator packs off his body.

Tayen's Proxy crumpled to the ground, and fifth in the row of plates a hovering body woke with a start. Abriss raced over to ease the Grave down to the floor. "Get him out of here." Cradling Tayen, she speared Caiden with a look, and for a moment he was startled by the *hurt* on her face. Diamond wasn't supposed to crack. "Winn," she ordered, "*go peaceably.*"

His mind tried to reject the command, wrestling between the longing to please this serene Graven creature and the animal instinct that he was headed into danger. The two Proxies hauled him from the room. He went peaceably. His last sight was of Leta as she scrambled to Tayen's side.

The girl he knew really had died on RM28. This Leta was happy here as a Dynast drone.

The quartz Proxy on his right arm said, "Do not worry. Nine never knew or cared about you. Never mentioned you once, before this."

The other Proxy—the black-haired one from the lift—gripped Caiden's augmented arm so hard the sensors glitched offline. "You're not part of her world. If you're lucky, we'll toss you back to yours."

Caiden stumbled between his captors. His thinking cleared the farther he drew out of proximity of the Prime's gravitas. If it was Leta stealing the *Azura* in-Proxy, he could only hope En caught on to the betrayal fast enough to fly away first.

They reached a military wing of the Hold, where soldiers bowed at the Proxies' passing. Caiden drew their attention, too, not because they recognized the bounty but because of his freckle mutations, which meant two things here: Dynast family or Graves.

One Proxy unceremoniously stripped off Caiden's Dynast surcoat and shirt. Chill whisked across his skin as the other shoved him down a series of corridors and barracks into a small cell. Darts of sunlight bled through the perforated ceiling into the perforated floor in perfect stripes. The door folded seamlessly shut behind him.

Caiden remained on his knees until the ringing in his ears stopped. He crawled to a frigid metal wall and sat against it, his bare shoulders seared. He cradled his head, but his fingers trembled when they buried in the braids En had made.

This was exactly why he hadn't involved family. He should have kept on alone, counting the days until malnutrition or something finally killed off Threi in his universe prison so that Caiden could be free.

A familiar numbness echoed into him. He had run through the vacant desert of RM28 having lost his whole world. He'd shed tears and memories until he was empty and the one thing that filled him up again had been finding the *Azura*.

Caiden clawed fingernails into his scalp to focus his mind with pain. "Options…"

If he could engineer a chance to actually *converse* with the Prime, he might sway her against her brother. Threi used secrets as armor, and Caiden knew a fair share. Slim chance of an audience at all, but Caiden had nothing to do except line up his mental ammunition and trust En and C to defend the ship.

"Leta." Caiden banged his skull against the wall, sloshing the pain around until it consumed the thought of how he'd let his craving for forgiveness get the better of him.

This is good. It finally pried out a barb that had stuck in and scabbed over. I can move on.

The whole encounter had forced him to reconnect with his family, a step he might've never had the bravery for otherwise.

Leta—my past—has driven enough of my life. I have my answer. She's dead.

CHAPTER 12

PRIZED

Leta led the group through the Hold's subterranean passages. She tried not to worry over the possibility that Endirion might've flown the ship out of the storage cavern already.

"If we're fast enough," she explained, "Endirion won't activate the ship's universe. The nophek would be destroyed by the rind without time to give it the right injections. We can apprehend them before anyone's injured." *There's been enough damage already.*

Aohm One made a deep humming tone, a habit from their real yraga body, which was nonverbal and telepathic. Their Proxy towered over the group and moved the slowest, their smokelike cloak billowing into all the empty spaces of the hallway.

One spoke, delayed, "Are they stronger than Winn?"

Leta shook her head, hesitating. "I don't actually know Endirion's skill."

"I know it," Dian said, too eager. *"Not enough."*

Six was pent up and angry about the damage to Tayen's Proxy, which Abriss was toiling to repair. He would be vicious. Aohm was formidable, their pale carapace able to absorb most energies. And the group included four sentinels and a cluster of brawny trainees carrying a variety of devices.

Passages and lifts took them to the vast cavern where the *Azura* rested. Relief drooped Leta's tense shoulders. Still there.

Gentle light from the floor and ceiling flooded the vessel's translucent Glasliq. The metallic gills and ribs inside grew visible as candescence cast through, and the ship's spine—the treasure Abriss was after—had a biolu-minescence all its own, filling the liquid glass with an opaline glow.

Leta recognized the Glasliq shell of it as *Threi*'s starship, though his had been a flatter shape. Her frayed memories of Threi had weaved back together along with the ones of Caiden. She'd been hiding in the reek of the transport box. Its front lay open, blaring light, but that intensity seemed just as wrong as the dark, so she stayed still. Post-massacre, the sight turned claylike and unreal. Lumpy flesh spotted pools of blood so black it might've been water, except she recognized the clots and the stench.

The brilliance curved around a silhouette. Threi Cetre strode inside.

How did you survive, little thing?

A Graven voice. When he said, *Come out with me*, she took his hand without hesitation. He cupped her face in his palms, turning her head one way, then the other. His fingers were elegant and cold. He brushed tear-damp hair off her cheeks. She felt healed by the touch.

No, she's not one of them, he said. *That I would be so lucky.*

Threi took her anyway. He gave her sedatives—a wonderful gift—then lifted her in his arms and headed to a vessel like a great bird made of glass: her last sight before unconsciousness had taken her.

Then her life with the Dynast had begun.

Leta's group marched for the *Azura*.

Hearing their noise, Endirion strolled out the ship's open back. "Proxy? Where's—" He assessed the group instantly and raised a heavy glave. Milky aerogel-stuff bloomed in geometries atop layered, lens-shaped pockets on the weapon's barrel.

Leta recognized just as he fired—"*Snap rifle!*"

No time to shove the humans aside.

A split-second blast of sound energy emitted at blistering volume.

Aohm One stepped in front, their clawed fist closing. A silent boom cracked from the Dynast tech built into One's muscles. Scalar gravity welled to form a shield in front of them, deflecting the sonic click.

Leta's Proxy's eardrums closed off, but weird buffets still crossed her body as the two similar forces clashed. If they hadn't been shielded, the humans' eardrums would have burst if they weren't killed or paralyzed outright.

"Behind Aohm!" Leta yelled. Weaponry modeled after organic mechanisms was an interest of hers, or she wouldn't have recognized Endirion's rare B1S-Mark. The blasts were focused and not rapid-fire, he would wait to take aim.

"*C! Savage!*" Endirion commanded.

The nophek came tearing out of the ship. Its pupils dilated to huge disks of shining white, and Leta froze as memories surged up. Those same eyes. Same monsters. They'd haunted her ten-year-old self until the Graven treatments finally erased it all. She'd been *grateful* for that.

More of Endirion's blasts ripped the air. Aohm One blocked shots while Dian Six sprinted to Endirion to kill the weapon's range. Leta stood riveted as her past bled into the present: the sentinels and trainees corralled the nophek into the open while dodging its snapping jaws. The roars, too familiar.

Aohm swept off to help deal with the nophek. Endirion was holding his own against Dian. He'd abandoned the rifle for a slim glave that was defense and offense in one, flipping shape like a switchblade as he danced around Dian's attacks. Repairing Leta had given Endirion a sense of the Proxies' weakest joints and vital points.

But Dian was impatient and didn't care about damage. His ceramic-looking skin was neither fragile nor just aesthetic. Energy particles sprayed molten from each strike of Endirion's new glave but left no mark.

Six didn't fight well with others, so Leta kept her distance, but her hand hovered over her lash glave's hilt between her shoulders.

Aohm wrestled with the nophek, trying to keep hold of its head. Teeth knifed holes into their white carapace, down to the scarlet tissues beneath. Aohm sacrificed that forearm to position the beast.

Conventional sedatives didn't work on nophek, but scalar gravity choke-holders would.

The rest of the group fired a salvo of flower-shaped bolts into the nophek's muscular neck and shoulders. It squealed as the bolts barbed down. The sound twisted Leta's heart with fresh anguish and old trauma.

"Now!" someone shouted, and the four sentinels encircling the beast activated their chokeholders at once. The nodes bolted into the nophek's body repelled a strong force against the devices in the sentinels' hands, keeping the beast at a distance. It took their combined strength to help hold its thrashing, its long tail whipping, its teeth nipping the unlucky. Blood sprayed, its jaws red, a vision of terror in the darkness. Leta's heart rocketed in her chest, but this time her memories of slaughter mashed up with more recent ones of tender Caiden cradling this monster while untangling its mane. She stalled, her brain unsure which memory to follow.

Aohm restrained the pup until its fight waned. Half its collar vials were smashed and dribbling. Aohm drew away as the sentinels handled the sluggish beast. "Let us help Six. He is 'not enough.'"

Leta nodded, but a fog was taking her over. *These means to the end are wrong. Even if we fix it later.*

She picked up the discarded B1S-Mark and hefted it onto her shoulder. Air-light gel unfolded to form a chamber over top, brushing her hair back. Target and stat holosplays glittered in front of her face. Aimed at Endirion.

Aohm was two and a half meters of force and consumed all Endirion's focus dodging scalar weapons. Dian found an opening and slapped both hands against Endirion's back, spreading his palms apart rapidly to smear a stripe of gel-encased tech along Endirion's spine.

"Wha—" Endirion's word clipped off as he dropped. Nervous system jammed, he twitched in a heap. A weakness, that he was so much like them.

Dian Six stepped back breathless, his respiratory system making a sandpaper sound.

"Strong," One commented before they lumbered back to the struggling humans. They took over the lot of chokeholder devices, singly strong enough to restrain the weakened nophek. Growls rolled out of the pup's nostrils.

Leta set down the rifle and crouched by Endirion to strip off his other weapons. She dialed down the output on the jammer strip. Endirion relaxed, lungs drawing in more oxygen.

Leta brushed back his disheveled hair and refitted the clips. "Apologies that this was...messy."

"Who are you?" His gray eyes brimmed with violence, as sharp as a chipped blade. "Harvested precious memories from a dead girl in the lumi-niferity, did you?"

"I am the girl he knew."

"Ah. A Dynast slave, then."

"You'll be dropped off outside Unity, unharmed. Winn will be released soon, please just wait for him."

"Soon?" Endirion gave a brittle laugh. "Don't tell him that."

Leta cocked her head, not understanding. "He won't be harmed either. We only need the *Azura* returned to the Dynast, to which all Graven remnants belong."

The formal phrasing irked her as it usually didn't. Sisorro's words sneered in her mind: *That will be nice for your conscience.*

"Graven remnants," Endirion drawled. "Winn is part Graven. How long until your Prime decides he belongs to her too? Oh, wait—he'll have no choice because everything in the Prime's presence belongs to her. I should have known you were no exception, whether you're really that girl or not."

He exhaled and winced as the jammer squeezed his chest. He peered over at the nophek whimpering in the dark and his face creased up. Almost too low to hear, he said, "I should have stopped Winn even if that drove him further away. I should have broken you."

Leta's jaw clenched. "My intention was not to hurt him, only deceive him."

"You don't get it. Still a kid, fresh from the slaughter, he wanted to die, too, because he was so ashamed of running and living. Now he's never stopped running but he's stopped living, and the *hope* of you... that's the first thing to pull him out of it."

Dian made a nasal sound and bent to hit the jammer but Leta raised a hand. "Wait, Six."

Endirion's words sharpened all the edges of the discomfiting feelings bundled up in her. She said, "He *is* pulled out of it now. Unharmed."

"Unharmed? You've harmed him more than anything could. You're stealing everything from him: his keenest memory, his *Azura*, his pet, his ten years, his purpose. It'll be a miracle if he chooses to keep living after losing everything *a second time*."

A miracle.

All this was hooking into the same strange feeling Leta had when she'd allowed Caiden to reach her real body. When it had seemed meant to be.

An answer to a question slowly surfacing.

Locking eyes with Endirion, she thought over her deeds, Abriss's astrology, and Unity always moving events toward the most harmony, ensuring that even Caiden's best future was still ahead. "He's not losing everything. He still has you and the rest of his family."

And I have mine.

She nodded at Dian. He punched up the power on the jammer. Endirion's nervous system shorted out and he lost consciousness.

The nophek squealed, weak and wheezy. Aohm One walked over to Leta, drawing the beast with them on the leashes. "Shed your doubt, Nine. You have brought us salvation."

With new treatments developed from the *Azura*'s Graven energy, complementary to the Dynast strain, the Graves would live. The cost was only emotional; Caiden would heal from it, just how he'd been able to let Leta go from his mind once he considered her dead. He could handle loss a second time.

Dian added, "As the Prime said, sometimes a thing needs to break." There was a fire in his eyes as he massaged his injured joints. He clapped Leta on the shoulder. "The prize is yours to deliver to the research hangar."

These events may break Winn into the future he's meant for…

Leta remembered Caiden's boyish grin when he'd smashed a finger, his temper when something he'd fixed had busted again. He wouldn't break this time—he'd just become stronger.

Six lifted Endirion over one shoulder. Aohm hauled the sluggish nophek along while the trainees trailed at a distance. The uniformed sentinels gathered behind Leta as she stared at the *Azura*.

Moments passed after the others had left, and one sentinel ventured, "Mistress?"

"Stay out here, I'll take it alone." Leta walked toward the *Azura*, slowing as she passed the glitter of the nophek's smashed vials. Among splashed chems effervescing on the floor, she spotted two halves of a tiny, distinctive purple-blue flower. Chicory, fashioned out of glass. A blue string trailed from one piece, where it had been tied to the nophek's collar.

Leta picked it up. She used to make crowns of chicory or leave one on his doorstep, a languageless thank-you for saving her life...not once but in tiny ways all the time.

She squeezed the shards in her fist and crept inside Caiden's Glasliq ship. The crystalline mass embedded in the ceiling bathed her with a luminiferous radiance, many spectra layered beyond what a human could perceive. Bright particles and shadowy streamers moved inside the complex manifolds, reminding Leta of an organ, a brain. This enharmonic force...

"You're home, *Azura*. Whatever you are, you belong with the Dynast, our complementary half."

Leta waited in-Proxy outside of the research hangar's entrance while the Prime approached. She should have felt like a victor bringing a treasure home, but flying the *Azura* in had been an unwelcome feeling: her an imposter in Caiden's seat, and the ship's tones long and blue.

Atop that discomfort, she hadn't been back in her real body since Caiden reached it, and while she was still within a safe amount of time in-Proxy before it became more challenging to reintegrate into her real body...for once she *wanted* to return. Unity had pushed her so strongly toward that contact with Caiden, she wondered if something fundamental about her might have changed.

Her Proxy's pragmatic functioning dulled her guilt at betraying him, but she also wondered if that guilt lingered back in her real body, ready to saturate her when she finally returned.

Does it matter who I was?

Leta's Proxy was perfectly balanced on tiptoe blades. The slim muscular bundles of her legs were flexible after the quick repairs Abriss had done. Hips freed, shoulder joints de-clogged. This was the instrument that brought the best of her into the world. Powerful, capable, independent. Within this shell, Leta was all those things too.

Doll, *Caiden said... What does a word matter? This Proxy is beautiful and strong and made just for me. This is who I am.*

The Prime's presence in the Hold was palpable from a distance as she wended her way to the research wing. The glassiness of the towers and the open design and long walkways made activity more visible in general, but beyond that, Unity aligned for Abriss Cetre. Dynast sentinels, scientists, and scholars fell into orbit around her. She happened to encounter the exact people she'd wanted to speak to, and those she didn't were guided in other directions or interrupted on their way. Lifts arrived before she reached them. Birds flew by windows as Abriss passed, soaring in sync with her. The sun parted clouds when she exited a room. Reality conspired to bring her a beautiful world.

This is who I serve.

Abriss strode up, energized, and Leta swore the light took on more color and tessellated around the woman. A breeze snuck strands of hair out of her loose braid. Leta's synthetic heart did a flutter.

"I can't wait to see it," Abriss said, a little out of breath.

Leta smiled and invited her into the hangar. The *Azura* perched in the middle, its Glasliq preened back to reveal the crystalline spine running its length and most of its breadth. Machines had been carted into the ship's bay. Silken wires trailed from its ceiling to measurement devices that then arced through the vast hangar to distant machines. Holosplay data spiced the air all around. The *Azura* was strung up in a web of study.

And this *is what I've done. There was purpose in it.*

The affirmation made her lighter, and if that wasn't enough, then the look of joy on Abriss's face was worth the world.

The woman laughed and every head in the room turned at once. She folded her hands over her chest as she walked to the starship. The whole vessel glittered with bluish bioluminescence that snagged on the copper stars of Abriss's raiment and lit her eyes. The two things—Dynast heir and mysterious crystal—appeared destined to be together.

"Magnificent is a dull word for it," she said, voice trembling. "My stars spoke of this, but the real thing...the *music* of it. Nine, can you feel? Even more than I, surely."

Leta did, but something changed while Abriss approached it. The spine resonated in spectra outside of human perception, growing stronger and more detailed in her presence. It contained a luminiferous energy, a latent vortex scattering the structure of reality in the opposite way that Leta sensed Abriss drawing the world into alignment.

"What is it?" Leta asked.

Abriss entered the ship's bay while staring up at the translucent mass. Under its light, her freckles glistened, her eyes teared up, and a soft aura condensed around her. *Azura* versus Dynast, a matched pair. The two forces meeting seemed to peel a skin off the universe. Solid matter appeared fleecy and vibrating.

"A Graven chrysalis," Abriss answered, delayed.

Leta thought of a butterfly, the most she knew of chrysalides. Much of the spine's interior was filled with near-invisible tissue structures and metallic iridescence, but there was no distinct form inside. There was lightseep in it: not the imitation material of Leta's Proxy bones or Tayen's sword, but the *real* core of something whose vibrations had been stiffened by the coarseness of the perceivable universe.

Leta said, "It looks like gloss."

"There is a theory," Abriss began in her lecture tone, "that the parasites in nophek brains are not the clarient species but instead are sparks of fragmented Graven spirit. The crystallization of the gloss, then, is a rudimentary means of growing a physical chrysalis around these sparks and encouraging more to collect. There are non-nophek examples as well."

"Is this *your* theory?"

Abriss smirked. "This sight does make me wonder if it's not a large example of that same action. Nophek have, historically, been harvested before they reach true old age. Even the mega gloss I obtained from the Casthen to start working on you Graves was from a nophek in its prime. Who's to say how large gloss might become, whether it would eventually outgrow the brain and destroy such a creature, reaching a size like this?"

Leta puzzled those pieces. "You used stored energy from gloss to modify our biology. Is that how we've become 'more Graven,' by absorbing shreds of spirit?"

"I can't tell if your phrasing is grim or romantic, Nine. But yes, in a way, the microstructure of the gloss particles infused into your bodies amplified the biophotonic treatments."

Abriss stepped onto a set of blocks to reach the ceiling and stretched up her hand.

The entire hangar fell silent. Pressure vibrated Leta's bones and odd whispers echoed through her skin.

Two Graven opposites met.

Rising, slow and gut-turning, a soundless thunder belted the air, braiding across space. Oxygen punched out of Leta's lungs. Time hiccupped. A swarm of force amassed around the chrysalis.

Abriss merely sighed as subtle energies collided in her body, invisible to senses less keen than a Proxy's. Her bioelectricity shifted, her spirit expanded. All around, scientists and mechanics dropped to their knees in unison, felled by Abriss's loosed gravitas.

Leta rushed forward. "Prime?"

"I'm safe." Abriss drew her hand away and the pressures unbraided slowly, strings of space smoothing out. "Fascinating."

Leta flinched as more sensations grazed her up close, all in the shape of phrases like inaudible voices or echoes layering up. Familiar yet surreal. *The Graven?*

Abriss wore a look Leta had never seen from her: awe and fright combined. A teardrop escaped down her freckled cheek. "It's real. The other half of the Graven equation, the enharmonic balance to match my harmonic genetics. The true nature of it is locked inside this chrysalis, but I can both try to extract it and try to copy its strain so we can emit it through other devices."

Leta couldn't take her gaze off the two. Light caught on strange eddies of space, bending, prizing up shadows that didn't fit anywhere. Subtle energies leached from the luminiferity into only this spot in the universe, for perhaps the first time in millennia.

"This will heal us?"

"I promised. This will work. Your Dynast Graven bodies filled with the *Azura's* unique energy will make existence comfortable for you again in this physical dimension. No more dissociation. It will give your consciousnesses the anchor they need to participate even more fully in the luminiferity. To draw from ages of knowledge and—" She caught her tangent and swirled around, brandishing her smile.

Leta's heart filled, and she laughed.

Abriss concluded, "It gets us one step closer to realizing what the Graven really were and were capable *of*." She did sound excited and *happy*, even, despite the sorrow in that little word "us."

Leta matched *us* with *we*. "Don't work yourself to death. We need you."

Abriss strode to a holosplay and began combing through the test data already collected. "I can't imagine resting now. This confirms the Graven were able to manipulate physics not only on a quantum level but also a luminiferous one. It might even yield a means of correcting the multiversal fractures once and for all. Can you imagine?" She scraped the lingering tear off her cheek with the heel of her hand. "Countless lives and events aligned to bring this here. Your efforts most of all, Nine, from the day you were saved and brought to me. Thank you."

Leta's Proxy nullified gravitas, but Abriss's focused affection and praise was still... a lot. She nodded and dropped her gaze, even as she wished the moment would linger.

"Unity conspired this?" Leta asked. "So Caiden. Winn. He's existed to bring you the *Azura*?"

"Do not worry. I only need answers from him, then he can be cast back to his own course. He's played a part in a much bigger pattern. The Graven are still listening and guiding us. Even if I am the very last link to their will, the only one listening in return, I'm one link that's not yet broken."

Us.

Of all the Graves, Leta had expanded the farthest in the luminiferity without dying. The universe was a tapestry of misunderstood parts all trying to align, and it was shared omniscience that would merge them. An indomitable unity: the world Abriss was one step closer to manifesting, because Leta had become a betrayer.

CHAPTER 13

BROTHER OF A SISTER

"The Prime has questions," said Caiden's Proxy guard from outside the cell.

A chance at last.

Several days had passed, according to soreness and scabs. Over the years and across universes, that had become his measure: time and space changed, but the general healing rate of his body was a constant. Caiden counted time by wounds.

His mind's rotation—the *Azura*, C, En, the empty years—had scraped out all his words. He breathed vigorously, flooding his brain with oxygen. He wouldn't let this chance go unused.

The Proxy opened the door. "Walk peaceably, aser im." His voice was throaty and slightly muffled, emanating from behind a featureless mesh helmet. Caiden didn't understand the ursgen words, but they usually elaborated emotional intent. The Proxy clarified in Shihl anyway: "The only harm that will come to you is that which you create by provocation."

Caiden had heard this tall Proxy called "Eight." A white cloak and cowl draped Eight's head-to-toe armoring, which was delicately engraved. He'd been the slow and patient one during the fight.

The Graves are just numbers to Abriss. So many will die, why think of them with names?

Two more Proxies waited farther down the hall. The first was unfamiliar and faceless in a different way, with straight, floor-length opaline hair, elegant musculature, and webbed tattoos. Why did so many Proxies have no facial features? Another way Abriss kept them impersonal? The other Proxy was Six, with vitrified ceramic skin scored with sacred geometries. Crinkled black hair. He did have a face, all snarled up and hard-lined.

Caiden followed, tousling out the knots in his own hair and straightening the unfamiliar cut of the shirt and jacket he'd been given. Not having his morphcoat made him feel more unanchored.

No escape routes. No gravitas-susceptible groups in sight. If his future actions were writ in celestial alignments, Abriss could be shaping Unity to cut off every future where Caiden took the *Azura* back, if the vessel was even still in one piece. His only chance was to try to turn her against her brother.

Eight pushed on a wide door that phased open to the Prime's orrery. A spherical holosplay of luminous lines and glyphs over nine meters tall painted a map of the universe. Galaxies spiraled, stars jetted out, and rings of language looped around planets. Faint lines of relationship joined every part, peppered with symbols and numbers. Abriss stood at the center, with three figures at the edges.

Leta's tall Proxy was one, half of her glazed in light. Chained stars and streaks of orbital arc reflected across polished parts of her body. She turned her head to him, staring with bright, amber-colored eyes.

Leta had died. This person was someone else. Someone Abriss had purchased and reshaped. *Nine.*

The Proxies shepherded Caiden inside. Machines muscled the walls in the darkness, calculating storms of data while wheezing heat into the room, shredding the chill off him.

"Passager Winn," the Prime greeted him without looking. Her face was tilted up, eyes bright with reflections. The filmy celestial dress of starspun silk over her dark uniform glittered with metallic embroidery as she moved, and the freckles in her skin seemed to glisten. If someone had whispered to Caiden that this being was the very heart of the multiverse, he would have believed it.

Speak carefully. Resist gently. Caiden gathered his own gravitas, armored himself in it, fought off the wrongness of using it. "What have you done with my ship?" *Gently, idiot.*

"It's being studied."

"My nophek."

"Being studied."

"And En? Studied?"

"Escorted safely out of Unity, as I intend to do for you."

Caiden's relief was fraught; En would be constructing a plan and might rush back into a very bad situation.

Abriss added, "Winn, you seem to think I'm the same as Threi: chasing down and bashing open."

"Instead you lure and dissect?"

"If I had given you an invitation to share your ship, would you have ever come?" She finally pivoted to face him.

His tension unlaced. A serene sensation replaced it, filling cracks he hadn't realized were there, filling the hollow where his violence slept. Butterflies swarmed in his stomach. His thoughts ran in all directions and his brain redefined her flaws as perfections: ordinary became beautiful, mysterious turned compelling. He would have accepted her invitation had it been in person with all these modes of gravitas working against his better judgment.

The Prime continued, "I have questions about the *Azura* and your origins."

"Want to study me too?"

"Yes, as a matter of fact. But we've detained you enough. If you cooperate, I'll release your nophek with you. Winn, I have no intention of harming the things you care for."

Little boy. Caiden felt his way through brambles of gravitas while he stepped onto the orrery platform and knelt, playing nice. Abriss could force his cooperation easily, but she was allowing him agency for now. He needed to keep that courtesy.

She said, "First, there are some bigger matters to deal with."

"Bigger...I suppose there's nothing bigger than Threi's ego. All this to release—"

"This isn't about Threi." She crouched in front of Caiden, took his hand off the floor, and held it in hers. Tingles raced up his arm, every anxious knot in him melted, thoughts dissolved, feelings aligned, and if the world had struck him dead now, he would have died happily.

Abriss whispered, "Where did you find your ship?"

"The desert of planet RM28. Half-buried."

She rose and drew him up with her. His body felt afloat. Her hand was soft but not pampered like he'd expected. Calluses and nicks lay among the freckles. Paper cuts: a very specific wound. These were hands that used tools, wielded weapons, flew ships. A creator's hands.

Caiden tried to reject the respect that warmed through him. Why was the viciousness in him asleep now? He needed sharpness. Violence. Instead his mind spiraled down in senseless details like her copper fingernails until her voice drew him back up.

"And *how* did you find it?"

"I ran from the nophek until I saw it, jutting up. There was no other shelter anywhere."

Abriss smiled. "That sounds unlikely."

The long-haired Proxy chuckled. "Coincidence? Your favorite, Prime."

She beamed at the Proxy, then dropped Caiden's hand. Chills puckered across his skin as her warmth left. His head cleared somewhat. *Crimes, I'm powerless.*

Threi's obsession with his sister's death made more sense. Simply holding Caiden's hand had aligned his cells and twisted his will to cherish her—how powerfully would an *embrace* have moved him? A whisper by his ear? A plea? A kiss?

Ten years ago, Threi, with his gravitas temporarily enhanced by a bizarre vial of chemicals he'd consumed, had issued a Graven order: *Die. Die as fast as you can.* Instantaneously, hundreds of gathered had obeyed. Mass suicide. Was Abriss powerful enough to ask the whole universe to do the same?

"Your survival may seem miraculous to you...Happening upon the ship for shelter. Happening upon the crew you needed. Happening to encounter Threi in a Cartographer Den. But everything happens for a reason: even when it seems miraculous, it is manifested by collective will."

"Co-creation," Caiden said.

She blinked, eyes widening. So Abriss Cetre *could* be surprised.

"You're a reader, too, then? You had my brother's least favorite book among your things." Abriss gestured to a Proxy, who handed her Threi's volume, *Graven Intention of Prima Luminiferia*. Her nose wrinkled a little as she thumbed along the edge of dog-eared pages. "What is the *Azura* to you?"

"Home." The *Azura* was more than that, but he didn't have a word for it. Their neural bond had grown over the years, tangling body and nerves together.

Caiden straightened, attempting to gather his gravitas as resistance. "What is she to *you*?"

Abriss's eyebrow raised. "She."

"You're right: the *Azura* and I were united for a reason. We belong together." He deployed the Dynast's precious word again: "Co-creation. Let's collaborate. I know why Threi is so eager to be released. He's devoted years of training and research to finding a way to murder you."

Without much change of expression, Abriss closed the book. Her gaze saccaded across the stars. "Has he? I suppose we'll find out, since as Unity wills, they're early."

While Caiden tried to work out her meaning, the Proxies all moved at the same time. Six and Eight headed to the door while the long-haired one and Nine flanked the orrery platform. Caiden caught Nine watching him, but his only goal now was to get Abriss on his side.

The doorway phased open and Caiden turned to face the people he'd run from for ten years.

Seven Casthen entered, three of them wearing Cartographer gray and purple, striped with a specific shade of Casthen blue burned into Caiden's mind. He recognized a tall, black-skinned saisn with two glaves crossed at his back: Maul, a former Cartographer Disciplinarian. And Jet, a rough-skinned and stocky chketin hybrid—one of Threi's old crew.

Maul stared at Caiden as if looking upon a ghost. Caiden was the wisp slipping through Casthen grasp, outwitting every snare. It was partly Maul's work that had driven him to Unity in the first place in search of sayro for C's smashed chems.

Fight instinct ignited in Caiden, but the moment he coiled up, Nine stepped to block his path and Abriss cut in, "Stand quietly, Winn. This isn't about you yet."

Caiden's motion locked up in compliance. Nine had an odd look on her face, and whispered, "Don't make this worse," before she returned to the sidelines.

Abriss said, "Emissaries of Casthen Prime and Dynast Heir Threi Cetre. Stand here and be silent for a moment."

Instant adorants, the group obeyed. Abriss wasn't skimping on her gravitas with them as she had with Caiden. He hoped it meant she didn't trust or like them.

She pulled up new data, specific transit points illuminating in the orrery, which she observed at length. "You are here early because there's something I need to hear that will change my decisions…And you're here to take the ship once I've spoken to my brother. You have the keys to call him?"

"I am honored to oblige, Prime." Maul bowed deeply in the Cartographer way, then walked to a curious console at the far end of the platform. Whatever connection could reach across the multiverse to the Casthen Harvest and into Threi's universe for instantaneous communication could only be a Graven device, something the Dynast had salvaged. It was technology the Cartographers had been lusting after for ages, and Maul navigated it with reverence.

Meanwhile, tension strung every which way in the room. The comm linked. The orrery light sizzled away around a viewing window in the holosplay.

Behind a milky universe rind stood Threi, life-size and vague, with lean, angry muscle stringing his athletic frame. He now had a short, rough-cut beard that didn't suit him, and long dark hair that did.

It felt like all the years Caiden had been running jammed up in the space between him and Threi's projection, as if they'd never parted ways. The man had been figuratively right on his heels since their last exchange, but it was altogether different to meet face-to-face across galaxies.

Abriss's expression was wistful for a long moment, then dulled. "Brother, how have you been?"

"Besides violently bored, I'm well." Threi's voice came through rich and breathy. The sound of it transported Caiden back in time to when they'd plotted the Casthen Prime Çydanza's murder together. Threi said, "I see it didn't take you long to catch him."

"You didn't expect any less of me, surely."

"Efficient as ever, illustrious sister."

There was something off about their sibling terms for each other.

Still jarred by the voice, Caiden recalled Threi's fiction, the man's fingers around Abriss's simulated throat, and his order: *Scream louder.* Caiden had watched him suffocate the life from that vishkant-copy of Abriss. Caiden was the sole person in the room who had seen Threi's true motives.

"Prime," Caiden ventured, braving a step forward. Abriss's magnetism was easier to flow against when his intent was her well-being. "Threi really does mean to kill you."

Abriss gazed at him, expression neutral again. Caiden's mind masked her face in a memory: those same features contorting with horror as Threi's fingernails crimped her scream off. His murder-lust words, *This has to happen for the multiverse to survive. I have to be able to do this.*

"Kill me . . ." She turned back to Threi. "Again?"

All four Proxies shifted.

Threi grinned. "But I didn't kill you, did I? Just locked you away, snug and asleep."

"Ironic, don't you think? Imprisoned so long—wasn't it about ten years as well? I suppose you and I are perfectly even now." Abriss laughed as Threi's face creased in irritation. She shot Caiden a loving look. "Thank you for that, Winn."

Caiden's knees weakened.

Threi fixed his snarl into another smile. "I won't emerge quite as luminiferously enlightened as you did when you got free."

"No," Caiden interrupted, his thoughts all jumbled. "You'll emerge just the same."

Both Dynast heirs looked at him.

Like when he'd been fourteen years old, Caiden had witnessed something no one else had. He had no luxury of a memory jog machine here, but Abriss could easily verify his knowledge by ordering the truth. The wretched, bewitching, heavenly feelings he had for her would not let him lie. Truth would foster doubt, and doubt would turn her from Threi's side.

"Abriss," he implored. The name shocked him to say, and it seemed to rattle everyone else too. Her attention riveted on him, and he hesitated, wondering when anyone had last called her by name and treated her like a person rather than a Prime.

He continued delicately, "Threi practiced your murder on a vishkant who imitated you exactly. I watched him rip apart your throat." The memory inflamed him, coiled him back in time to a moment he never wished to relive. "I know you mean to release him by sending the *Azura*, but he's spent decades orchestrating the means to kill you. I've paid ten years to keep him locked up so he wouldn't. Believe me."

For several heartbeats the Graven magnetism between them aligned into something more neutral, and Abriss looked different. He hesitated to call it vulnerable. Her lips frowned, her fingers crawled down the braid over her shoulder, and her eyes glazed with memory.

"Truly?" she asked, taking a firm step toward him.

The universe shifted, his paltry resistance shattered, and her gravitas swelled over him. The truthful answer, "*Yes*," slid off his tongue.

Dismay flattened any surprise Abriss's face might've shown.

Threi chuckled. "Don't get your hopes up that he's as resistant as me. He is fun to play with but look at him, he *adores* you. Truly."

"Adorants cannot lie, which means you did as he claims."

Threi shrugged. "His truth is ten years old. I had an ugly grudge back then. Time reshaped us both, and I have my own domain now. Sister...I'd ask for your forgiveness."

Threi's voice had turned husky and nervous. A performance—he would never beg and didn't know what it was to forgive. He couldn't have changed that much. But Abriss's proud shoulders did cave a little.

He said, "Winn is right, I haven't stopped worrying about you, about the Dynast legacy weighing on your shoulders alone. How everything starts to feel unreal. When was the last moment in your life that felt like co-creation rather than control? You miss me."

Caiden was pleased to see that Abriss's expression remained flat, not buying Threi's act, but her chest shook as she breathed. She was pinching her fingernails against the pad of her thumb. Was her brother calling out history between them? Or maybe, like Leta had, she experienced a wealth of emotion that barely showed outwardly and Caiden wouldn't be able to gauge.

Threi continued, "The Cartographers, passagers, and Casthen are all on my side, ready to bend to the Dynast. Think what we could accomplish if we worked together. Besides..." He bowed elegantly and laughed: a silvery sound that Caiden had hoped to never hear again. "I'll never have control over you. The day you deposed and exiled me proved it, and I've grown since then—ready to stand by you."

Deadly words, delivered handsomely. Caiden's chance would vanish if Abriss believed Threi was being genuine.

His brain ached. Words grew skittish. Bloodstream hammered his skull. He blurted the first secret that assembled, "Threi told me there was one thing in the Casthen Harvest that the Dynast should never see."

That made Abriss pivot to Caiden again. He had her. Threi's secrets were chinks in his armor. Caiden would share them all if it bought her trust. Her gravitas weighted everything he said with truthfulness. "My Graven genetics aren't from a Dynast source. It's from something different that the Casthen call the Dominant strain. Whatever it is, it's hidden in the Harvest's subterra. He—"

"The Dominant?" Abriss expelled her held breath in the word.

Caiden's thoughts jammed up at the sight of her awe. He knew nothing more about the Dominant, and now his mouth was dry, a desert of words.

Threi chuckled. "Ah, Winn. I *did* desperately want that kept secret from the Dynast, ten years ago, but I've changed. I'm more than happy to share now. Darling sister, I have a present for you. Winn spoiled the surprise. It's a deal, actually, but also a present."

Abriss sniped, "You never did give anything for free."

"I know you abhor the multiverse, but I've found wonderful treasures in it. I don't need to tell you what the Dominant is, do I? You have the *Azura* now—*you're welcome*—and your own Dynast genes. That's the enharmonic and harmonic pair. But I have the third piece of the Graven trinity.

It's real. Tangible. Send the *Azura* here so I can get free. Once I'm out, we'll exchange knowledge and both have a complete trinity. Everything you always wanted."

"Or I keep you in there and come gather the Dominant strain myself."

Threi grinned. "I would love your visit. But the Dominant's nature and location are known only by me, and my sharing mood is contingent on getting out of this hole." He kicked sand below the projection frame.

"It's bait," Caiden warned Abriss. "You're right, you don't need him with the trinity."

Threi stepped closer to the frame, long hair veiling half his face. The icy hue of his eye ghosted through and he looked just like the man Caiden remembered. "You know what I want, darling Prime? New deal. Send Winn along when you send the *Azura*. His mosaic genes are built around the Dominant strain. I have a use for him that will add more layers to the research you'll receive once I'm freed."

"No," Abriss said immediately, and Caiden's heart swelled. "I said I would let him go."

"After the trouble he's given you? You've seen his unpredictable astrology. He has gravitas of his own and he's no weakling—*I* trained him, after all. He was willing to spend all of himself on revenge. He hasn't wavered keeping ahead of me and hasn't slipped up once. Do you really want to cut him loose and hope he *forgives* you for stealing his ship? Come now, be a little ruthless for once."

Abriss's eyes unfocused as she watched the orrery. She made small turns of her head. Listening?

Caiden wrestled slippery thoughts, wanting some way to keep his ship—a counter-deal, but what?

Threi couldn't stand one beat of silence. How easily his smiles turned nasty. "Here, let me be ruthless for you: send both the *Azura* and Winn, in exchange for both my research on the Dominant and *access* to it."

Caiden cut in fast, "Abriss, you don't—"

"Winn," she whispered. Her glazed look had a hint of fright in it. She scraped her fingernail across a luminous arc between planets in motion, then glanced first at Leta, then at Caiden. "You need to go with them."

"What?" All his slippery thoughts got loose. "Wait!"

Threi bowed again. "The Casthen flagship has a cell made just for monsters like Winn. Maul—escort our guest to his cozy room. Cart him back to the Harvest when you bring the *Azura*, and don't fly the two close together."

The seven Casthen advanced. Abriss motioned for Six to help and the Proxy was beside Caiden in a flash. He snatched Caiden's arms and wrenched them behind him while shoving forward.

Caiden opened his mouth to shout, but Nine beat him to it: "Prime!"

He hissed a swear and twisted through the pain for a final look, wishing to glimpse doubt left in Abriss's face. Doubt or some other seed that might grow to his advantage.

Abriss snapped her fingers and the orrery holosplay shut off, stars winking out of existence. Only the glow from Threi's projection remained, his form life-size and light-wrought beside Abriss. Murderer and would-be victim.

CHAPTER 14

LIVING GRAVE

The Casthen left and Threi's communication link ended.

Leta had analyzed Threi's microexpressions and inflections of speech while Abriss's attention volleyed between the two men. Threi had so many secrets, his body language couldn't hide them all—as if a true form might burst through his skin if he couldn't wrestle it down and wrap it in that lustrous silver voice and so many smiles.

When he set his claim on Caiden, that smile had sheathed a blade of retribution, ten years impatient.

Formalities over, Leta strode to the middle of the orrery platform. "Prime, you said—"

Eyes wet, hands trembling, Abriss gripped fistfuls of her overdress.

"Prime?"

"The whole trinity," Abriss whispered. "I was overjoyed to obtain the enharmonic, the *Azura*. But there really is a third, separate piece already emerged? I can't express its value. It would complete a scientific understanding that's been building over lifetimes. There is coincidence still at work, a Graven will guiding events. I'd foolishly thought Winn's only part to play was bringing the *Azura* here, but his presence forced Threi to reveal his biggest secret."

Leta pinched her lip between her teeth. "Shouldn't that be rewarded rather than punished? Losing his ship is enough. I justified my actions on your promise that Winn would be released."

"He will." Abriss looked at Leta but unfocused, her mind caught in itself, her face soft with hope. "Just not by me. My stars revealed that the Casthen won't be keeping hold of Winn, he's in no danger from them."

That reassurance didn't solve Leta's ache. She felt petulant, but she couldn't let this go without something more concrete. "Why not release him *now*?"

"I want everything that Threi is offering." Abriss wiped at her eyes and straightened her clothes. "The easiest way to get all of it is to keep him in a sharing mood. Winn is incidental to that and has been avoiding the Casthen Harvest for years, but his future is there. It's the only course in which he has a chance to live. I—I apologize that I can't explain all the pieces I see or how they will come about. The universe bends events around that man in unpredictable ways. But trust the outcome. Please. Trust me."

Leta wished to. It was hard to trust vague futures and not fixate on the *path* to them, but these things weren't vague to Abriss—she just couldn't articulate them. Abriss was always earnest, and she cared about Leta's worry. *I'm being petulant. Caiden has confused all my feelings.*

After so many complicated and unexpected events had brought her to this very moment, it was naïve to expect it to all disentangle neatly now.

"Ol, Nine." Dejin Eight crossed his big arms, silver armor flashing. "The Casthen Prime was correct. Winn is a threat. Better that he's contained while we still need the *Azura*."

Having seen what Caiden was capable of, Leta had a hard time denying the threat of him. However—"Prime, do you trust your brother and this deal?"

"I don't need to trust him." Abriss strode out of the orrery room into blazing daylight. "He's not as powerful as I am. Even the hybrids and other xenids among the Casthen and Cartographers are susceptible to my gravitas. I can't be harmed. The deal he's offering is genuine, we each have what the other needs, and if I were to balk at this path now...I really can't describe what that looks like..." She paused in the sunlight, gaze flicking across gardens and sky as she sought the language for her strange knowings.

Isme Two helped her along by saying, "During the meeting, you had that distant look that you get when you're...listening. More Graven echoes?"

Leta had heard her mention this in small hints, as if she hesitated to give it definition. Whispers layering up into presences. Echoes aligning from the past. Could things echo from the future too?

Abriss nodded. "All my theories of chaos tell me to trust inklings like this, a sketched pathway to a specific end. It's like...a claircognizance... a voice that forms in my head but sounds like my voice, made up of my thoughts. It assembles the celestial alignments that I see into grand totalities my brain is too limited to fully comprehend, but I get enough to perceive outcomes and the actions required to reach them." Out of air, she sighed the last bit of speech.

Events lining up through coincidence...through guided creation... Leta and Caiden brought together...crossing paths for tiny moments in the scope of eternity, to change the world's course forever...

Dejin rumbled, "What if the payoff of this guidance is beyond your lifetime?"

Abriss closed her eyes, going somewhere in her mind. "Then I am just a momentary co-creator of others' better future. That's all right with me. It's enough to see everything come together so beautifully after centuries of design." She smiled at them, but it was a lonely smile again. "Shall we go? I'd like the three of you and Tayen Five to assist with my examination of the *Azura*. You can perceive what my human senses cannot."

Dejin and Abriss walked ahead while Leta followed slowly, her feet heavy. Isme matched her stride.

Listening to Graven echoes. Where are they echoing from?

"What is it, Treasure?" Always prying.

It spilled from Leta: "The idea of a Dominant Graven strain and the trinity is so precious to Abriss, she'll never entertain the option of it being a lie—bait, like Winn said. What if her need is strong enough to create a blind spot? Everyone thinks she's infallible and omniscient but she's mortal. We have to see what she can't."

Isme crossed his arms behind his back as he strolled. Leta admired that he was always willing to listen. "She may be missing things amidst rash decisions. But equally, she may still be the *only* person seeing clearly."

"I know." Leta pulled her hands through the thick waves of her hair, gripping bunches to put soothing pressure on her scalp. She wanted to take action and pick a way to lean. She'd never vacillated so much as she had since meeting Caiden again.

I want us healed. I want the Prime to be safe, and I wish to serve. Her mind scratched at the patina of those statements. She said them so often, they felt old and worn. There was something showing through beneath. *What if saving us means thinking differently? Seeing something no one else can...*

Isme said, "Our Prime is passionate, but she's also intelligent and cautious. If she sees no threat in the cosmos, there is none."

"She doesn't know Casthen stars." Leta echoed something Caiden had said. "I can't help wondering if we've created a fiction of all this. The lies I told Winn were a different side of the truth. The treatments, the promises, the pain and loss. We want this next round to be the end so we can all be comfortable and happy, but Abriss doesn't know for sure, does she? She knows the ends, but are the means still guesses? If desperation is narrowing her view, I...I can't allow Winn to be a casualty of Abriss's haste to save us."

Isme bumped her shoulder with his as they walked. "I understand. You always feel deeply and think in directions no one else does. But let's see what our Prime can do with the *Azura*, first. It's what all this has been about, after all."

By the time Leta and the others finished assisting Abriss and had been released from duty, she was aching to return to her real body. That was still a strange want. Her confused feelings about Caiden during their fake rescue mission had straightened out, but she still wondered if the imprint of his touch had left something on her real mind. An answer to these new uncertainties.

She gazed up at her real body suspended over her Away station.

Her grave.

Ermin Three, shortly before perishing, had said to the group, *We are not named after the Graven, but because our bodies are living graves for our spirits, which will die inside of our vessels during our trials.*

Leta surveyed her own asymmetrical face: squished nose, cheeks and chin cleaved too hard, full lips that she liked but they were fixed in a frown. Her features were from here and there, her hybridization too tangled to pick apart and so mixed as to make origin invisible. Sisorro teased that her traits smudged together into something bland. Isme had deployed a more charitable word: mysterious. Her skin tone responded to seasons, but Solthar's shifted so frequently, it maintained a dull golden shade. It was mostly freckles in swirled patterns now anyway.

Strands of wavy brown hair spilled over her cheeks, which were dusted in spots like something left lying near fire. The sort of creature a spirit might die within.

My grave.

Leta turned her back on it and sat on her heels in front of the plate.

Dian Six and Aohm One were the only others still hovering above theirs: One was in-Proxy watching over the Prime while Six guarded Caiden's cell on the Casthen flagship.

Leta let her awareness unknot from her Proxy's brain, let her spirit slither from its fake lightseep marrow. Her awareness fuzzed up through the sensory details of the room as the luminiferity tried to expand her, but her real body was so close she slipped right inside.

Spirit soaked back into her cells, neurons, all the energy dynamics of her—and everything instantly became too much. Disintegration began and her body fought to process everything she'd been doing in-Proxy.

Leta scrapped her initial eagerness to return.

She opened her eyes and sighed out stale oxygen while her body lowered. Soles flattened, pains rocketed up her calves. Wishing she had the temperament for roaring and cursing, as Dian did, she instead wobbled and rubbed crust from her eyes and stretched a spine curled too long. Shivers turned to spasms as her thermoregulation kicked out of balance. That problem was specific to her and not due to being a Grave. Convulsions exploded through her chest.

"Slow yourself," warned an ashy voice. Leta startled as Isme flung a weighted thermal cloak around her from behind. "Consent?"

She nodded and let him hug her to squash the tremors with a broad pressure, something Caiden had known once too.

"Now what are you worrying about?" Isme pulled away to study her expression, and she was sad for the extra heat that left with him.

Leta answered, "What did he think when he saw me? I told him we'd been tortured, and he believed me. Do I—does my body—look that way?"

Isme chuckled. Yellow sparks burst inside his snowy lungs and he winced. "You look fairer than I, but we've all been half-finished for years, Treasure." His eyes were rosy jewels in translucent alabaster, his jaw and teeth were crystal, his hair curled and silvered by sweat. Leta could no longer picture what he'd looked like not diaphanous or Graven. He finished, "We'll be whole soon, thanks to your actions. All that's left is to test the Prime's design."

Abriss had finished building devices that could infuse the *Azura*'s enharmonic energy into the Graves' Dynast harmonic biology, like pouring liquid into a vessel.

It was time to send the *Azura* off with the Casthen.

Caiden with it.

In a matter of hours...

"Your catch is delightful," Sisorro Seven chorused about Caiden as they glided over from an adjoining alcove, having finished their radiant treatments already. Fuzzy tissues wafted around their spindly frame, bending light into curious shapes inside them. Their voice echoed, "Too bad he cannot stay. Pent up. Delightful to me."

"I did not *catch* him, I betrayed him."

Sisorro's head twitched. "He had fun fighting. He chose to come."

Isme added, "Treasure, you can't *betray* without having a relationship to break."

"I..." Leta hesitated and quested through her worries while she followed Isme to the alcove of radiation caskets. "The years apart didn't make our connection any less a connection. What if Abriss is wrong and he doesn't escape and the Casthen kill him?"

A big splash announced Tayen Five emerging from one of the baths ahead. Lavender steam billowed off her as the liquids touched air. She punched her collar to signal the morphfabric suit to spread over her naked body. Agreeing with Isme, she said, "Connection not real, don't mind don mine do mi." The parasite stole her syllables.

"His reaction confirmed I'm real and...meaningful." Leta probed her fingertips over the ropy lines of the brand on the nape of her neck. The way Caiden had looked at her when he felt it, with his eyes tearing up...raw and terrified and vulnerable.

Until meeting him again, she'd never felt unreal or incomplete, despite so many pieces of her having been erased. Those missing pieces existed in him.

Leta chose a radiation casket from the row of ten and stared at it. Needle resonators packed into its clear construction while wires braided down into the floor. Glossy fluid suspended particles that were arranged in fractal patterns by the vibrations filling the box. Genetic information was carried by coherent beams within, and faint acoustical waves made the box emit a low, muzzy sound.

This fluid had bleached memories and dissolved the impurities of the Graves' past lives. This light had erased Caiden for years.

Leta was happy with the Dynast and had rolled Abriss's reassurances around in her mind for days, but once the Casthen whisked Caiden away, Threi would murder him. Threi Cetre would smash the last piece of Leta's real past.

Tayen Five squinted at Leta while scrubbing her fingers across her scalp. "I don't care for men but dddddd"—she clenched her jaw as the word jammed up, then continued—"do you? Fancy him anc im ani an?"

It took Leta a moment to process Tayen's meaning. Then she laughed and felt a blush creep around her ears because she'd crushed on *Tayen* many years ago, before realizing it for what it was: admiration for someone stronger and more interesting than herself. A brief obsession. Leta had kept it to herself until it faded, and Tayen never knew.

"No, Tay. I never thought of him like that before, and I don't know him now." Leta's fascination with and worry over Caiden was muddled by how differently the intervening years had gone for them.

Isme chuckled and slipped into his own bath, all but disappearing in the watery light. Dejin was already folded tightly in another, long limbs and tail wrapped together.

Tayen leaned on the alcove's archway and crossed her thick arms, looking stern, which didn't take much effort. "What was Winn to you back thhhhhen, that he's stttttttt—stirred you up the moment he's moment he's mmmoment he's back in your life?"

"He saved my life," Leta blurted. The admission surprised her, then more memories took shape and she felt it clearly. "All the moments I thought I couldn't go on, couldn't find anything worthwhile to continue for, couldn't find anyone who listened and understood. He was present."

And she'd repaid it by taking everything away from him, including herself.

If Abriss really had gotten all she needed from the ship, Leta could break Caiden out and the Graves would still be saved—and perhaps Abriss as well.

Tayen snorted. "Don't reward him for im fo mor…" She cracked her neck angrily, then picked speech up. "For minimum kindness."

"Minimum." Leta huffed, dropped her thermal cloak, and stepped into the bath's seething light. Her morphfabric garments dissolved to bare skin on contact. "No, he always overdid everything."

She submerged. All sense of her body dissolved to weightlessness and warmth. She was supposed to meditate or sleep and let her body recalibrate, but agitation spurred her away. Joining the rhythm of the light, she let her consciousness bleed out of her body into the luminiferity.

Space cocooned her. It stretched infinitely while time made spiral octaves. She coiled into a memory of Caiden. During the lights' down cycle—their planet's version of night—the gray vapor sky became the color of five-year-old Leta's newest bruises. She shivered in the chill air after the ice bath she'd been shoved in to diminish the swelling and hide the signs. Not many others would care, if they knew. Defective children happened sometimes, they would agree.

Leta hugged the huge bunches of her tunic three sizes too large. The bovine nestled sleepily in their pastures on either side of the avenue, all soft rustles and gentle breaths in the dark. She limped over to Caiden's dwelling block and used the rhythm of her bare feet to keep steady. She'd forgotten her shoes when she snuck out.

Leta hadn't known Caiden long, hadn't accepted his friendship yet. She skirted the door and found the outside wall nearest Caiden's sleeping nook and sat down with her back against the metal. Chill soaked through her skin, coated the pain, and fatigue colonized her to the bone as she wept in secret. She balled up until the whole world evened out to a numb and manageable blur.

She could pass out until someone found her at lights-up and struck her more for running out. But Caiden emerged from the dwelling and swore loudly, rushing over. He didn't know yet to be slower and gentler, so he wrapped her in his arms and hit all the bruises—but she didn't mind.

Her world was fuzzy and lightless as he carried her inside and set her on a warm bed pad, then nested pillows and blankets around her until she was squished up tight and her shivering stopped. She saw only the top of his messy blond head as he sat nearby and held vigil that very first night she'd ever slept soundly.

Cai. I survived because of you.

Leta focused her awareness, in the present, as if seeking her Proxy, but this time she sought Caiden through the luminiferity. She visualized the western plateau where the *Sessrun*, the Casthen flagship, perched with Caiden interned somewhere inside. She imagined his metallic scent, the way sunlight soaked his hair, the places the shadows found his face, the freckles whispering across his nose. She filled her mind up with the real, current him, and let time and space align.

She found Caiden curled up asleep in his cell. Loud rhythms of him took shape in the luminiferity as she became mired in his slumbering energy, tangling up in his dream until she shared it.

The reek of blood. Teeth and tearing. Pounding feet and ragged breath. This wasn't either of their memories, this was pure nightmare, and she couldn't pull away. Scarlet and desert and nophek tore him apart. Echoes of other times smeared across her mind, mixing images, off-shooting recurrent events with previous ones.

Her awareness ricocheted through his memories, out of order: Caiden lying in a coffin of dreams, soaked through with savagery. Caiden huddled in the *Azura* as a child while the sky above caught fire. Caiden hugging Leta in the utter darkness of the transport when her mind and voice shut down and all the horrible things in the world disappeared as long as she wasn't alone. His shoulder had contorted to form a soft place to rest her head while his fuel-doused fragrance blotted the human stench from her nose.

You're hurting yourself, she said.

I don't mind, he answered.

He'd bundled her up in the corner of the transport and promised, *I'll come back for you.*

Then nophek devoured everything. Caiden ran, then flew, and he never came back for her. But he kept hurting himself.

I'll come back. He had buried that festering promise.

Leta finally understood the look on his face when he'd found her. That fragile smile.

These past days, Leta had been meeting Caiden anew, with years of a different life between her childhood and their reunion, but to him…she had been living in his mind ever since.

He'd risked everything and suffered his old wounds reopened with the teeth of truth. Part of him that had been hurting forever was healed for one heartbeat before she'd rejected him.

He saved my life. I can't look away and let his end. Leta focused on Caiden again, this time pillowing a soft energy about his presence in the Casthen cell. She let luminiferous energies tide in around her and dissolve good and bad, hoping it might soothe his nightmares.

You can't hear me, but I'm sorry. She tried to impress better memories onto his sleeping mind: her crowning him in chicory flowers after he'd won their race; cool grass soothing her bruises; the ocean's humidity that had frizzed her hair so much he'd teased her; the hive they'd found, where he'd gotten stung seven times, but honey tastes sweet even with a swollen cheek.

If every event aligned for a reason, she would fix what she'd ruined and the heavens would dictate the rest. She would be punished either way, but if that punishment was death, perhaps she wasn't supposed to have survived the desert after all.

Leta drew herself away, leaving Caiden with sweeter dreams, and sought nearby for Dian's Proxy.

CHAPTER 15

WRONGDOING

Navigating the luminiferity was nothing like moving linearly through space. Leta's consciousness sifted through the buzz of preparations in the Casthen flagship: Maul would head to the *Azura* and fly it on a separate route back to the Harvest while the *Sessrun* would transport Caiden and the rest of their business to rendezvous with more security.

If freeing Caiden is not meant to be, Unity will conspire to stop me.

Dian Six was guarding the cell. To navigate there, Leta conjured up familiar feelings about him: their years of missions together, the sixteen times he had almost died, the day they were told about Proxies and discussed what theirs would look like. "Art," he had said. "I will inhabit whatever art Prime Abriss Cetre makes for me."

Leta wrapped her mind around the vitrified ceramic of Dian's Proxy's skin and the painted tree of geometric paths growing up it. Inside was organic machine, and her awareness flinched at the complexity of it. Easier to imagine the Proxy was armor and Six's real body lay within.

I can do this gently, feel my way, accept Graven guidance.

No matter how gentle she was, Dian would fight her selfish desire and vague justification, trying to set her right. He might hurt her for this.

Gingerly she inhabited the same space as him. She wrapped her thoughts into his scars and freckles and mottling, all a tapestry of the trials he'd endured. She crept into his wry intellect and the harsh edges of his affection.

Nine?

His awareness turned to her like a puzzle box rotating and snapped the two of them together.

Leta replied, *I need you to release him.*

Because you can't handle remorse?

Because I was cowardly to use deceit before I had understood what my actions meant. His life shouldn't be expendable. Help me.

Dian's contempt flared, febrile and spiky around her. He never had worked well with others. He needed free rein, a straight path, and lots of room. Leta crowded his mind.

His tetchy thoughts carved around her as if she were a splinter to pry out. *Winn is a Graven abomination, not worth how the Prime will punish you for interfering with her design. I won't allow you to get hurt because you are deluded.*

For once I think I see clearly.

Leta's own Proxy was designed to call her in: she was music that had strayed from its instrument, and the strings welcomed her back. Its gentle magnetism sucked her into bones and muscle, settling her spirit at the reins of body. Dian's magnetism faced the wrong way, pushing against her as she probed whether she could share it.

What are you doing? Dian's alarm bristled across their joined mind.

I have to fix how I erred. I can't be a person who would deceive, betray, and bereave. I need to give him back the chance he gave me once. Can you understand?

Spiced carbon, coolants, actuators tinkling, tendons taut. She wriggled around the contours of him. *Help me, Dian.*

You aren't strong enough to force me. Go whine to the Prime again!

He did something that slammed her with a white-hot wall of force. Her senses hashed with nonsense colors and textures. Time bent, confusing the moment between others when the ship wasn't there at all or a different one was.

Leta clawed her consciousness back to him. She struggled to be gentle as they battled wills for control of his machine. Gale against firestorm. This wouldn't damage Dian—it'd just displace and disorient and piss him off. She hoped to jar his consciousness out so he'd wake in his real body.

She forced her thoughts toward joining him in the pilot's seat of the brain—a nest of lightning—then aligned to his resistance, matched his motion, swallowed up his effort. She tried to impress a soothing energy, but he was right: she wasn't strong enough.

This wasn't supposed to be possible.

He wrestled to hang on as she rooted her awareness in his tendons and nerves, overrode him, opened his eyes. The Proxy was already doubled against the cell door, twitching as control volleyed between them. Caiden shot to his feet at the commotion.

Six's mind had the access codes. Leta sought them in his skull, a sensation like digging in hot coals. Dian wrenched control back. His right arm flew up and slammed the cell door, sending Caiden jumping away.

"*Help* me do right," Leta pleaded, a yell, at the same time Dian growled, and a monstrous conflict of sound raked up the Proxy's throat. His thought roared in their shared skull: *Fight for it*.

Leta seized the codes and launched off her knees toward the control pad nearby. The Proxy's iron-stiff muscles made the motion laborious, like she held the reins of a hobbled, enraged bull.

Input. Energy ward down. Door opening—

Dian bellowed in her mind. Not hurt, just furious at losing. The Proxy seized, going blind, while Leta clawed around the doorway.

In a slam of blunt rage, Dian Six bucked her out.

No! Void devoured her shriek. Time decrystalized, turned fluid. Leta clung to Dian's spirit in the luminiferity.

Back, back. She slipstreamed his consciousness back to the Casthen ship. Her awareness tumbled inside again as the Proxy grappled Caiden into a hold. Leta plowed through Dian's nervous system and forced his arms to slacken just as Caiden's augmented fist barreled the side of the Proxy's skull. Long hair sprayed around his face. Cranial plates chipped.

"Run," Leta garbled against the floor, struggling to shape Dian's voice. "I'll h-hold him."

She shook with effort as Dian's will kicked inside the Proxy they shared. His fury crackled against her shame.

"Leta?"

The sound of Caiden speaking her name wavered her attention enough to black her out. Dian snatched control and sprang up to clamp Caiden by the neck.

Oh stars, he'll kill Caiden to prove his point. Leta resurfaced, horrified, and fought to relax Dian's fingers. Ratcheting tendons—why did he have those installed? Leta whimpered while her mind sifted through an inferno of nerve signals. Caiden's face started turning blue.

With his aug hand he snapped one of Six's fingers, which jarred control back to Leta. She released the rest and stumbled backward, clutching Six's face in one palm through torrents of black hair.

Shakily, she pointed out the door while trying to jam a smile on Six's lips. "I wasn't lying when I said this before, Cai, it just took me some time to believe myself. I remember you like there's no time between us. I care. I never meant for you to be collateral."

Dian Six's willpower smothered her like a tidal wave, crushing her spirit against the shores of his body, trying to wash her out. Her senses mushed into salt sweat, metal hums, ringing, and she hoped those were Caiden's pounding feet she heard receding.

Aohm One was guarding the *Azura*. Leta hoped Caiden fled to safety; if he tried to steal his ship back instead, he'd have to get through Aohm. Leta didn't have the strength to take over another Proxy and couldn't bear to. Shame blazed through her no matter how much she could say this had been like a sparring match, like any other tussle.

Leta had corrected the betrayal she'd committed. What happened next was Caiden's own agency. She was soothed a little by a new thought...that the futures those Graven echoes had whispered to Abriss had been right: Caiden *would* escape the Casthen. Because Leta released him.

She sustained Dian's tempesting for as long as she could to buy Caiden time. The Proxy heaved in her embrace, hard limbs cracking against the floor, fraying Leta's spirit until he could cast her out. Something else plucked her instantly from the luminiferity and hauled her back into her real body.

Leta's eyes snapped open. Fingernails dug into her arm and tore her from the casket bath. Dian. He was on all fours and weak, disoriented, pulling her until her body scraped over the rim. She tumbled onto the floor beside him. He spasmed, losing grip, pouring out curses that mashed up in Leta's ringing ears. The shadows behind him fretted and shouted.

"You faithless wraith." His voice filed against her raw skin. *"He's not worth you!"*

Leta blinked at Dian much too close, and her muzzy brain stalled, thinking she was looking at herself, still entangled, still a tempest; his billows of hair, tongue lashing with swears, skin sweating. Fury and protectiveness clashed inside him. He never knew how to deal except through meanness.

Someone pried Dian Six away. He pushed them off and crumpled to a sitting position, catching his breath while fixing Leta with a conflicted stare.

Leta curled up, completely spent. In the periphery of her vision she caught horrified looks from the other Graves, who didn't understand what had happened.

She planted her forehead against the floor and let the darkness chew her away. She clung to the knowledge that she had acted on her own for another's sake, not because she was ordered to, but because her heart needed it. It didn't matter that Caiden would want nothing to do with her now. If he was fast, he would be safe. Leta had reversed her betrayal, setting the universe aright.

———

Caiden shook the blood off his fists as he stalked through the biomedical wing of the Dynast Hold. Lights blared, alarms wailed, and armed personnel coursed into the facility's veins. Caiden had stolen a fresh Dynast surcoat, courtesy of a bruised sentinel, and through a mix of stealth, acting, and violence, with a minimum of Graven coercion, he made it into the labs.

"Little boy." Caiden burst with relief. He rushed inside, where his nophek stood alone in the center, whining. Caiden had wondered how the Dynast caught him, with tranquilization not an option. Scalar chokeholders worked, especially with three of C's collar vials smashed and the others depleted, he must've been weak and brain-fogged enough to catch.

Caiden wrapped his arms around the beast's head, murmured sweet words, and scritched fingers under C's collar until whines turned to purrs. C's eyes moved slow. His breath rattled wetly against Caiden's skin. "I'm here."

If his bio cultures and other components—the damned sayro that started all of this—weren't still on the *Azura*, he wouldn't be able to save the pup. Caiden kissed between C's ears, then lurched to his feet and to the array of machines, pouring all his hacking skills into disengaging the gravity nodes.

The nophek's rigid muscles relaxed. He shook from head to tail, then pinned back his ears and wagged in a weak greeting.

Caiden hugged C fiercely. His fur smelled of sweat and blood and hunger. He huffed and nuzzled Caiden's ear. "Strong enough to walk and bite? Let's go get home."

Don't think about the meds yet. Azura next.

The stars of Unity weren't on his side, but anger always had been.

He whisked over to a research terminal and paired a floor map with his memory of the schematic Leta had given him before.

Leta. Caiden pinched the bridge of his nose and shook that thought off. *Step by step.*

He found confirmation that En had been escorted out of Unity as promised. Now the *Azura*—she wasn't far.

Caiden raced from the lab, but his speed suffered as C lumbered behind. The corridors here were set at hard angles, making it easier to ambush groups and flow onward. He had a shock glaive he'd nicked, knew pressure points, and could disable—escape like this was nothing after so many years spent running.

The Dynast Hold itself slowed him most. The orbital lightseep field interfering with holographic reality on Solthar's surface also cast into the lightseep of the Hold. Energy refracted according to ethereal rules, bending reality. Some research annexes were nighttime, others day, different weathers, and Caiden, running, passed from one mode to the other fast enough to trip up his dehydrated brain. Time shifted as if he'd been running for days.

Finally he reached the long windowless hallway in front of the *Azura's* hangar. A score of researchers poured out of the doorway, saw Caiden, and hurried the other way. Behind them, a figure glided out and filled the entire height and breadth of the space.

Caiden stumbled to a halt and threw his arms out to either side, stopping C behind him. He hadn't fought this Proxy earlier.

Their body had a clustered carapace of thick bone plates and crimson connective tissues over their torso, arms, skull—vaguely humanoid but unsettlingly not, as if the carapace disguised something wholly inhuman beneath. A cape-like film of smoke draped from their middle, stuck to the walls, curled against the floor, taking up the space around them that their sheer bulk did not.

They said, "I am One."

C growled, and Caiden backed up a step to wrap an arm over his neck. "One. Does that mean you were the first Grave?"

"No. Most died. Remaining ten seemed promising. We were renumbered. Ten is the number of hope."

The last sentence sounded rehearsed, and was cast in the same accent of every Dynast creature—Leta included—as if everything was litany, assured and filled with energy. Maybe it was easy to feel validated in a universe shaped just for you.

Caiden said, "Doesn't seem like hope's served you well, with seven left."

One lifted their hands to either side, palms open, four beefy fingers tipped in claws. Glints of a shiny venous tech laced through their muscles, and a muted thunder teased Caiden's ears.

Unclipping the shock glave, Caiden regretted not taking time to track down an armory. The Proxy stalked forward, bringing one hand high and one low, fingers splayed. The smoky tatters of their cloak snagged in a spiral around their palms. Caiden's eyes widened as he realized—too late.

One lunged. Caiden dived forward to slip past, plunging his glave at the Proxy's spine on the way. Their open hand speared at him and something invisible stabbed the meat of his calf. His momentum hauled backward while his glave slapped futilely against the Proxy's carapace.

The invisible needle that impaled him was a scalar gravity field tightened down to a point. Before he could rip himself out of it, One's palm snapped closed into a fist and the field expanded, tearing Caiden's flesh apart with it.

He roared and scrambled away. His leg spasmed, gushing blood.

Scalar gravity hadn't been developed into weapons in the outer multi-verse. Unity's physics apparently made it possible to manipulate nodes of space into blades.

C barreled in and clawed lethargically at the Proxy's arm. He was thrown down the hall, narrowly avoiding colliding with Caiden.

The Proxy's cloak plumed a spiral around their hand again, revealing how space warped. Caiden swore and rolled just in time to dodge a punch of condensed pressures. One's fist struck the floor instead, but they had withdrawn the scalar field before impact: expert control and perfect force if not range. They felt no pain, had no need to breathe. No easy vital points. Abriss wasn't designing bodies, she was designing *weapons*.

Caiden shuffled lopsided to his feet and signaled C to await command.

The hangar door was *so close*.

C quivered, blinks slow. Internal corrosion had started. Caiden whimpered a curse—which was pause enough for the coiled Proxy to strike. Caiden rammed into a wall to dodge the cleaving sweep of a gravity-built ax.

One's bulk bent forward with the heft of the strike.

"Set!" From behind Caiden, the nophek jumped and bit One's shoulder whole, carrying their body backward to slam the floor. C continued bounding past with a chunk of bony plating in his jaws. Scarlet flesh and porous metal rods lay beneath. Caiden darted in and jammed the shock glaive straight into the wound.

Plasma arced through thick red muscle. One jerked and their huge arm crashed Caiden backward. An armor plate glanced off his temple. Sparks exploded behind his eyes. He was spun then reeled against the wall, blinking at a dark square. A door. *It's* right *through there. Fight smarter.*

There was barely half a meter's clearance anywhere around the Proxy.

Caiden forced his panting into a rhythm, triggering tranquil neurochemicals. Some of the pain in his calf ebbed.

The Proxy clawed up a blade of space that protruded from their palm. Caiden parried the blow but it peeled the glaive from his grasp and sent it bouncing down the hall. He cursed. *Smarter!*

A subtle rumble itched Caiden's inner ear as One's fingers curled to narrow and lengthen the blade. They heaved it at Caiden.

He whistled frantically. C loped, paws slipping, but he was close enough to bite One's hip from behind, torquing the Proxy so the scalar blade snagged an inch from Caiden's face.

Caiden sidestepped, squatting, and palm-struck the back of One's hand with all his augmented strength. The momentum of their blade hand redirected at themself and flew up at an awful speed, spearing straight through their skull and out the other side.

Fluid sprayed the ceiling. A nasty hole remained in One's head. Their arm fell limp to their side as they wobbled.

C snarled and clamped down on One's other forearm, but they twirled and grabbed the nophek's jaw.

Not enough. Caiden raced past to snatch his glave where it had fallen down the hall.

C jerked side to side, shredding the Proxy's arm. Glints of the scalar tech dangled among lightseep bone and dribbles of glossy fluid.

"Back!" Caiden yelled, wanting C safe. The Proxy pivoted to Caiden charging in. He aimed for their perforated skull—two and a half meters high.

One's arm flew up. Caiden's blow struck a solid scalar shield that jarred him backward, lanced with pain. He switched the glave to his aug arm and struck every opening, but weird gravity didn't yield to electricity. Sheer force beat Caiden to his knees.

One tensed their fingers to turn shield to blade: the air thickened, space bunching into a deadly edge.

C leaped from behind and clawed into the Proxy's clavicles. His nails screeched over carapace until they prized between plates. One's arm flew up with a shield to block C's teeth inches from their head.

Now. Caiden scrambled up, planted a foot on C's hip, hand on his shoulder, vaulted up high to plow the shock glave into the hole through One's skull.

Electricity detonated, iridescent and wet. It spidered down One's spine and thunder-clapped against C and Caiden, toppling them backward. Caiden smacked the floor and heaved an empty stomach. He barely curled away to miss C's landing.

The nophek tumbled hard. His full weight smashed Caiden's ankle, but that was the least of the pain as waves of agony glitched through Caiden's machine arm. He clutched it and gritted his teeth to pinch off a scream.

The Proxy was a wreck. White plates bulged out as red flesh distended. The head had blown open, the interior dazzling like a fractured gem.

"Void with this," Caiden groaned between clenched teeth. He rocked to his feet, punched a rhythm on his augmented shoulder to signal it to reset, and helped C up.

The nophek huffed, his retinas flashing in the dark. He pinned himself against Caiden's side as support for the busted leg. This was a familiar scenario to them both.

"Yeah. Good boy. Best boy. Let's hurry."

He dash-limped through the doorway. There would be more Proxies inbound, and if he ran into the Prime herself, she would tell him to stop, and he wouldn't be able to disobey.

The luminous warehouse lights phased on all at once as he entered, and the sight of the *Azura* tripped him in place.

CHAPTER 16

SACRIFICE

Caiden's neural link with the *Azura* sunned over his mind. It cleared dross from his gray matter, washed his pain away with warmth, and threaded his body with wings. Hope had a bright taste.

He recalled his younger words: *If I have to endure horror every time I dream, for the rest of my life, at least I have you. I can survive it if I have you.*

The ship's Glasliq had been completely demagnetized into a shimmering cloud of liquid and particles hanging above her folded black skeleton. The crystalline spine was exposed and hooked up to strange Graven devices. It had changed: the inner angles and the bioluminescent veins were responding to what the machines had done or were doing, and Caiden couldn't help but visualize a being laid open on an operating table, plugged with wires and bent by forceps.

The Casthen had ripped her apart, pre-Glasliq. Abriss had gingerly probed and questioned.

"Az." Caiden limped over and laid his hand and one cheek against a folded vane. Soft sensations lapped through their link. "You're all right, beautiful. It won't happen again. I should never have left you."

He hobbled inside. C lumbered in, too, and collapsed on the bay floor, nestling his head between folded paws.

Caiden's personal effects looked to be untouched. He yanked out the medical drawer and sank in relief. Everything was as he'd left it. Abriss had been careful and respectful. Caiden thanked her damn stars for that and whipped up a fresh vial for C. He hastily applied healing agent and sealing spray on his own bleeding calf, then limped over to C with a bouquet of medicines.

He stroked the nophek's soft face. "Sorry, little boy, gotta put you out for a while. You deserve a rest anyway."

C puffed into Caiden's palm, flicked his ears, and closed his eyes.

Caiden hurried to the cockpit. The lines hooked up to the *Azura* were two-way, easy enough to hack the room's control systems. He remagnetized the Glasliq cloud onto the ship's avian scaffold. Liquid streamed all around the ship, congealed and adhered, then solidified into layers of crisp, translucent glass.

Checks streamed on the holosplay. Engines looked sound. Settings unchanged. Abriss really had been delicate, as if the ship were an animal to tame rather than a specimen to dissect.

Caiden fired the engines. Sweet tones weaved through his mind. He melted into the seat and his awareness expanded to take up the musculature of the ship. Turbines whispered and phase shifts sang.

"I don't know what they did to you or learned, but we'll figure it out later. We're together." He relished a few heartbeats of relaxation, eyes closed. The *Azura*'s sunny resonance filled him. "Let's go."

Maps: one charted the holographic elements of Solthar, another imaged its lightseep obsidian, while more tracked seasons, population distribution, traffic. He zoomed out to get a sense of the lightseep passages like the ones he'd flown in through. Once inside those bones, he could travel them like rivers and pop out above the planet's crust at any of hundreds of natural outlets where the lightseep jutted aboveground. The Dynast wouldn't be able to guess where.

Security chatter streamed in. The Hold was locking down, patrol ships circling. The Prime's sentinel guardians were nervous about the Graves. The dissident one was being hauled to an audience with the Prime in the upper court.

Leta.

Caiden kept the lines open as he hacked passcodes to drop the hangar walls. He flew cautiously into empty, ornate caverns beyond. Sure enough, one had a lightseep floor, connected to solid, labyrinthine underground channels.

More speculation rebounded in the chatter. *Termination*, they agreed. The Grave was too risky if she would disobey *and* had the ability to inhabit vessels able to kill the Prime. That was a risk no one could abide. Better to terminate her now. There were still six others.

"All damned," Caiden swore. He zoomed the map out. Upper court—that was surrounded by open air, visible from everywhere.

Get out, then think. He grazed the crystalline florescer over his head. The *Azura*'s universe bloomed. Light purled outward, space simmered, and effervescence settled in the wake. The vibrations quieted to a perfect chorus, ethereal and whisper-sleek.

"Ready, gorgeous?"

Hums petted Caiden's nervous system in response. He raised his hands into the luminous drive guides and pulled down gently, palms up. The ship descended. The rind sank into the lightseep, then the *Azura*'s belly cut in like a glass blade through water. Caiden could *feel* the obsidian stuff around the ship's body, but for all intents and purposes there was no solid matter in their way. He allowed himself a smile and powered forward.

The "lake" of the cavern's bottom tapered to slim canyons and fissures cutting through the planetary rock crust. The Glasliq material reshaped to fit tight spaces. Her thrusters bullied through pockets of bizarre air and fluid. Caiden skimmed easily beneath the Hold past aboveground flight patrols and outskirts. The ship was a splinter zipping through the bloodstream of the planet.

He pulled her up out of the earth many kilometers away, where a rock canyon heaved open to expose the lightseep underground.

Covered by a web of giant trees and projections of fiery rainfall, Caiden disengaged the universe bubble. He hovered the ship facing the palace of the Hold. Its majesty struck him again. Chiseled out of space and time, the world warped across its clear obsidian planes. In one of the spires was the court where Leta would face the Prime and be terminated for having helped Caiden escape.

His sweat cooled in rivulets. Pulse relaxed.

He was free, he had his ship. His nophek was asleep, gloss intact. Galaxies away, Threi was still imprisoned, and both the Dynast Prime and the multiverse were safe. Caiden held the only key and could fly away with it right now. He'd be back in the outer multiverse in no time, becoming a ghost once again.

The only thing that leaving would cost him was Leta.

Caiden closed his eyes. Leta had had no choice but to end up where she was now, Graven-influenced, and even if she was a pampered weapon—even if she loved it—it wasn't *her* choice. She wasn't shaping her own life. Ignorance and lack of choice were the same prison they had both grown up in. A myopic worldview, impoverished imagination, stunted desires.

Leta lived trapped in Abriss's loving web, yet her feelings about Caiden had been strong enough to overcome that Graven loyalty and set him free. She'd proven she wanted a connection, however small, and now she might be killed for that gesture.

Caiden could restore the *choice* she lacked, by tearing her away from Abriss's web.

Gathering up resolve, he scrawled a message to En and Taitn that would reach the *Wintra*: *I'm free. Have the* Azura *and C.*

He hesitated. If he mentioned what he wanted to do next, they would definitely not listen to any plea to stay away.

Instead, he jotted a maybe-lie: *I'll contact you again soon.*

Soon...

Fool. This was beyond foolish.

He walked over to the drawer with the culture tank of C's meds. Way in the back, buried under containers, he pulled out a small biosecurity case.

Chills needled up his spine. The Graven thing in him prickled his nerves at the very consideration.

Caiden flicked the latches open, which felt very much like the clips on a leash. He pulled out a lone nonagonal glass vial that fit his palm, filled with a pearly liquid. A Graven enhancer.

He hadn't looked at it since he'd stolen it from Threi's possessions, along with all the man's Graven research. This included hints about a Dominant Graven strain and Caiden's engineered brood.

Decade-old memories surged up. Broken vials littering the Harvest's polar plateau. Threi Cetre, all but sparkling with Graven appeal. His altered voice: silver-smooth, thick, and sonorous. Caiden hadn't been able to resist loving that monster, even when Threi asked the gathered hundreds to die for him. Instantly they obeyed. Even Caiden's hand had reached for a blade.

The sound of mass suicide thundered in the air for ten arcseconds. The vision of it haunted Caiden to this day.

The enhancer's effect had worn off on Threi after a while.

How long? That's important.

The whole event was a blur. The chase and struggle and murder of Çydanza were both an eternity of detail in his memory and a flash of brutality. Less than forty arcminutes, all in all, but Threi had ingested more than one vial and started before Caiden had arrived.

Besides that, Caiden wasn't the same kind of Graven as Threi and Abriss, so Threi's experience was a poor model. Caiden had no Dynast genetics and was nothing like the *Azura*. He was made from this third thing, his genes fashioned as a scaffold for the Graven Dominant plus more hybrid nonsense to fill the huge gaps. He was a shot in the dark, a hope that maybe *this* design would be a viable host.

Feeling nauseous, he crawled back into the pilot seat and rolled the vial in his palm. The luminous liquid whispered nacre colors as it swirled. It reminded him of substances that the *Azura*'s engine generated: mesophase fluids, glossy and gorgeous. Its look hadn't changed and composition hadn't decayed in all these years, like an immortal fluid, which unnerved him even more.

He didn't know what the fluid was made from and hadn't tested ingesting a single drop, too intent on keeping the Graven part of himself leashed. At best, it could temporarily enhance his Graven energy, making him more equal to Abriss and able to resist her influence. Her Proxies were gravitas-immune—no upper hand against them.

At worst, this will kill or impair me.

Caiden couldn't combat the stars, couldn't know in what level of detail she had already predicted his escape and what came next. The future in Unity belonged to her.

"I promised I'd come back for Leta, I can't run again." He squeezed the cool vial and flicked the cap off. His hand shook.

He would have to be fast. Very fast.

In the distance, the Dynast Hold glittered sapphire as eclipsed light sank to the horizon.

"Just have to do it." He drummed up courage and licked his lips. More chills quivered across his skin, and the *Azura*'s warm vibrations increased in response. "Is that a yes?"

The enhancer fluid sparkled like melted pearls. *Take half? All of it?*

"To void with this."

He tipped it to his lips and drank the whole thing.

Quicksilver down his gullet, blade-cold.

His cells caught fire. Veins raged with starlight. His flesh was built of specks of time from countless ages held together by the magnetism of a dead idea. His bones were fractured planes of space and his marrow became crystalline, built of infinite fractals. Body was a nova, then nothing, a cloud of potentials. His awareness slathered across a dimension that was empty and limitless at the same time. Eternity in each speck yet each stretched endlessly. The luminiferity.

Caiden.

He tried to recover himself but each sound of the name spiraled into the infinite, echoed by every time the same sounds had ever been made by anything. His spirit became a different shape that didn't fit him but instead fit to eons of memory, countless bodies, lifetimes spent finding and losing oneself. The Graven in him.

Different echoes emerged, voices built up one frequency at a time, layering across the ages until perceivable. One voice was his but not. Another was a voice he loved that carried through every memory, singing in every landscape imaginable, always the same song with different languages braided together. A new language added from every lifetime.

Singing—the universe was singing.

Ghost of Azura.

Dying.

Willing.

Graven.

Save me . . .

A melody called bits of him together like instruments invited to join, playing their part, weaving a richness of timbre that made him up. The singing quenched him—it was the *Azura* singing—and his consciousness condensed back in his mortal skull. He returned to a body that wasn't starflame and memories that weren't boundless.

Where?

Thrumming engine pulses within the fuselage coursed over Caiden. He lay sprawled on the floor. His body was all tingles and pressure and ice-fire. His sensory systems were beyond inebriated dizzy.

The *Azura* tried to sing him together again with a flow of vibrations. Caiden whimpered and mouthed the words, *Thank you.*

Eventually, finally, paralysis cleared. He shivered, his flesh heavy and feeling…not his. More of something else like a density of suggestions from some past form he'd forgotten. His face was wet from tears he didn't remember shedding, throat sandy from screams he couldn't recall.

The ship's ambient temperature ticked up and the floor warmed beneath him. He rose to his feet and the room spun. He hit the wall and doubled over the console. Stars detonated under his skin.

"Wh—" His Graven voice was built of flame. He hit the floor again as an inferno of energy bucked in his chest.

That was half a word. Caiden gulped breaths and clawed his way up what he hoped was the pilot seat swaying between darkness and light. Whatever had happened to him wasn't good, but Leta was facing execution and he had to hope his spirit would reconnect to his body in time to save her.

He raised his hands in the air, where the light guides seared around them.

Help me, he pleaded of the *Azura*, and drove his hands forward to accelerate.

CHAPTER 17

RUPTURE

The other Graves had wanted an explanation that Leta was too shut down to give. Without speech, she stumbled as she was hauled to the Prime for judgment. Her short stature and weak knees poorly matched Tayen Five marching on her left and Dejin Eight lumbering on her right, both in-Proxy.

Tayen's glossy black armor reflected the spaces they passed through, whole vistas bending across her. Dejin's ornate silver mask faced ahead, stride brisk, white cloak and hood billowing with light. It didn't matter that they didn't have faces to scowl or snarl at her with, their silence was plenty.

Leta would stand up for her decision to release Caiden, but she was drowning in the shame of a repercussion she hadn't expected: how badly Caiden had impaired Aohm One's Proxy's brain. Their yraga body had erupted in scarlet blooms and weepy veins. They curled up tightly in the levitation, interpathic communication closed off. Their vital signs were reassuring, but the disintegration of their real body was a ticking clock toward death without their Proxy to swap into. Abriss had raced to repair their Proxy and coax them back in.

Naïve of Leta to hope Caiden would simply run away. Wasn't he supposed to be good at running? She should have remembered his separation anxiety and anticipated his violence.

Dian Six had unleashed a tirade of her faults before he'd finally exhausted himself and refused to speak to her.

Isme Two had tried to understand her but said, *We have nothing in the world but Abriss Cetre and one another. So what happens if we can't trust one another?*

His disappointment burst cracks through her heart.

Leta had been trying to trust *herself*, for once.

Five and Eight pushed Leta into the audience court, a space as tall as it was wide—perhaps half a kilometer—completely empty. The walls were lightseep obsidian except for one end open to the sky. Solthar's clouds warped across every surface. Why bring her here?

The Dynast Prime stood in the middle of the court. She held her mini orrery over one hand, building a small heaven around her from light motes and candescent arcs.

When Leta approached, Abriss turned, her overdress rippling molten. Instant harmony washed through Leta. The world tuned into alignment near Abriss, and the air lay thick with something foreign: echoes of energy, whispering away.

"Go help the others," Abriss called to Five and Eight. They left without hesitation since Leta was no threat in this body.

Silence steeped the empty space while Abriss gazed at stars. Tiny suns orbited through wisps of hair that had escaped her loose braid. She looked harrowed and weary after hastening to save Aohm and she'd not rested a moment since acquiring the *Azura*.

"Forgive me," Leta whispered. "I couldn't—"

"Do not worry," Abriss said lightly. At this proximity, Leta's worries evaporated on command.

Abriss closed her orrery and started to affix a strange harnessing over her own hands, like butterflies wrapping her knuckles, joining circuits that sank into her freckled skin, and tiny crystals on every fingertip.

"You won't be terminated, Nine. How could we possibly lose you?" Abriss stepped close and asked, "Consent?" to which Leta was so startled and starved she nodded before a yes reached her tongue. Abriss smiled cautiously and took Leta's head in her hands, fingers folding through her hair, moonbeam-soft and deeply calming. The delicate tech caught the light and glowed, warping the air along petal-like distortions.

"You've done the impossible and proven that the Graves can connect with structures that aren't designed to accommodate them. Although my council is trying to warn me, for my safety, that my Graves become more dangerous each day—"

"We would never hurt you," Leta cut in.

"I know. You've been perfect, Nine. Since my meeting with Threi, I've designed these events. Neither Caiden nor the *Azura* are truly freed yet. Love is a chain, and it's tugging both of them back here." Abriss released Leta and pivoted to a wall. "From the south. What happens next will be his doing. And he might surprise us yet."

————

The *Azura* streaked out of Solthar's lightseep obsidian marrow and rocketed vertically against the towering mass of the Hold. Brilliant air leached through Caiden's messed-up vision. He dared not blink. His pupils were stuck dilated. Nervous system compromised. He was a lot of lightning in a tiny bottle.

Patrol ships clotted up behind him, but he had only enough function for one focus now. The stars would align or they wouldn't. Leta had broken him free despite years of loyalty layered up in her—if she could do something so impossible, it gave him a chance, not to snatch her away but to break her free of coerced loyalty so she could think for herself.

"Be fast, *Azura*." He swallowed sparks of adrenaline. The *Azura* had never sung so loud. The Glasliq blazed with sunlight. She was armor and wings, and he was heart, and they could do this impossible thing together.

Twenty stories up, Caiden peeled from the lightseep wall and stalled horizontal, facing the audience hall. The *Azura*'s universe swirled colors through her glass wings, which flattened out and solidified as the mini thrusters engaged, hovering the vessel. He'd expected to have to plow through the lightseep wall, but the court's far end was a wide opening with a landing zone big enough for a flagship.

Leta and Abriss stood alone in the cavernous court.

No guards? No Proxies. Leta was alive. He'd been swift enough, and the bizarre fire of the temporary enhancer was still in him, turning his veins into lightning strands and his flesh into cloud. He looked solid and normal enough to his own eyes, yet false at the same time. New white freckles dazzled on his skin and made it seem all the more like a fallacy, a human disguise draped over a Graven monster of energy. The same monster he'd been trying to leash for so long. The thing he'd felt echoing into his body from distant eons when the enhancer almost ended him.

Caiden curled his fingers in the guides and spun the *Azura*. He pushed out of his chair and used neural link control to set her tail on the court's floor while two-thirds of the ship still hovered over the cliff drop. He would need only a moment: that's all he would last.

He charged through the rind's iridescence and blinked away foggy vision on the other side.

The Dynast Prime's heeled boots clapped the floor, amplified by the vast space. She had no weapon, but she was armed to the teeth with words.

The sight of Leta, real and awake, stalled him in place. Her posture was firm, but her sleeveless suit pinched around a skinny frame, hands clawed around her upper arms. A breeze snatched up waves of her hair. Her eyes, wide and worried. Caiden's brain knew only nightmare, imposing the vision of ten-year-old Leta with the same expression looking up as a transport descended from the vapor of their world.

Focus. Resist. As Abriss walked near, adoration didn't rile up in him like it had before. The space between them ratcheted tight and electric with gravitas.

She cocked her head. Could she sense any change in him? To Caiden, a veil was lifted off her. Features his mind had willfully ignored before were more obvious, like the human faults of her face, the red flecks on her lips where she'd bitten them, and how the galaxy of freckles on her left cheekbone was thicker than the right.

The enhancer had given him *time*. Processing time to gather up the nuances that had washed together before, like a swift bird's wingbeats slowed down for the human eye, revealing the mechanism behind their flight. He noticed the tendons tight in her neck, the constriction of her pupils, the angle of her feet: all the microexpressions and body language that he'd been blind to before. Divine veils peeled off and revealed her as human.

Caiden stood breathless, whipped by wind, the *Azura* humming behind him. Leta was mere strides away. He could grab her and run. But it had to be her choice: he would create this one moment where his enhanced Graven force counteracted Abriss's into a neutral space where Leta might choose of her own will, as she hadn't been able to before. A moment of clarity.

He extended his hand and tried to infuse his speech with all the intensified storm burning inside him. *"Leta! I'm here. Think about what you've been through. You can come with me."*

Strands of hair caught in Leta's sudden tears. "Why did you return?"

That lyrical Dynast accent again. She took a step toward him—

"Stay," the Prime interrupted. Leta's tension sagged as Abriss's web struck her. "He came for *you*, but the *universe* brought him here for me."

Calm. Abriss was too calm. She'd predicted this. But how much of it?

"Leta," Caiden tried again, "I know you remember us. When—"

"I am sorry, Winn." Abriss's eyes flashed amber and something changed in her face, something even his humanized view of her couldn't catch. "She's precious, and you have proven you cannot protect precious things. Won't you step aside?"

Her request filled up ravines in him. His body listed sideways. He pinched his aug fingers into his bicep until pain shot up to his neck and rang in his skull, smashing her request.

A landscape of Graven pressures lay between them. Quantum potentials snapping in flurries as their willpowers warred. Abriss could win in an instant. Why didn't she crush him? Whether it was complacency or compassion, he would leverage it while it lasted.

Caiden's extended hand shook. He pulled again on the connection he'd rekindled with Leta, as fresh and fragile as it was. "Please. You need to be free of this."

"Cai…" Leta drifted forward, but Abriss gently grasped the girl's wrist and spun her in place so they faced each other. Caiden saw a spider wrapping prey.

Then within the nuanced time that the enhancer had granted him, he recognized Abriss's expression. Beneath her serenity he saw the feeling he knew so well: loathing of one's own Graven sway. She didn't *want* to force him.

"You hate it too?" he asked, dazed.

Abriss's brows drew together, mouth open, but she didn't speak. She dropped her guard at his acknowledgment, and her Graven focus diminished.

Now. Do something.

He closed the distance, snatched Leta's hand, and yanked her to him, folded his arms around her and coiled up every ounce of strength to step backward against the tide of Abriss's power as she said Gravenly, "Stop before you hurt yourself. This doesn't have to end in loss. She doesn't want to go. I need you to—"

"You don't get to decide that," Caiden argued, the words sour on his tongue, but he managed to say them.

Every step backward toward the *Azura* was a battle. With Leta in his Graven embrace and his soft voice by her ear—*"Come with me?"*—he hoped his enhanced will was enough to neutralize the Prime's magnetism and allow Leta to make a decision of her own.

Another step. He watched for Leta's confirmation. She looked up at him confused and dreamy, still moving with him. This was a lot to ask her to process so fast. The *Azura's* rind washed sounds away as they stepped through it but he thought he heard her say, "Yes."

Ease melted through Caiden on the other side, and Abriss's draw lessened. The ship's ramp knocked the back of Caiden's heel, and he stepped up inside. Leta jarred from his arms.

Abriss approached them, one step for each of his, unhurried. Curiosity brightened her up.

Get inside. Signal doors.

He staggered back, clear of the ramp. Grabbed Leta's sleeve.

Abriss raised her hands netted in complex jewelries. No—*devices.* She spread her arms and laid both palms on the fluxing surface tension of the rind. It illuminated her beautiful, eager face.

Leta is bait.

Caiden's resolve withered. How easily he'd raced into the same trap.

"Thank you for coming back. I still needed a world to test this on."

Abriss closed her eyes.

She took a breath.

The *Azura*'s universe split apart.

Feral colors rippled through the rind, then tears shredded across it like a punctured bubble slow enough to see. Brilliant beads scattered off in a cascade from Abriss's hands all the way back to the nose of the ship.

A shock wave bowled Caiden over as the universe dissolved and the physics inside converted to Unity's. He was hurled onto his back, and in a slam of light to his skull, his neural link seized up, senses snuffed out. The air was sucked from his lungs.

The engines stopped. All sense of the *Azura*'s structure dissolved in his mind, a spreading void. Agony filled him, filled his ship, his *Azura*. His skull rolled and he looked on through the open back of the ship: Abriss was emblazoned on the universe in manifolds of light. She grabbed Leta's arm, pulling the girl onto solid ground, then stepping as if she might reach for Caiden, too, but the *Azura* toppled backward into sky.

Caiden's scream cut off as his back slammed the dropping floor. He slid until his hip struck the pilot's seat, almost horizontal. The nophek's unconscious body tumbled over, and Caiden twisted to clutch him. He braced on the seat and stared up at the ceiling. Mangled sounds tore out of his mouth.

A crack fissured down the *Azura*'s crystal spine.

The ship plummeted. Glasliq melted off its frame. Air shrieked as wind tore ribbons of liquid glass away. Caiden had no control. He hooked his arm through C's collar and another around the seat. The light guides were gone, console blank. Vapor howled against the cockpit windows, flickering up a view of the ground kilometers away.

In layers the ship's body let go of itself: glass wings tattered, the scaffolding tore off, metal disjointed from muscle, and fluids sparkled away.

"Azura!" Caiden roared as everything disintegrated around them. The sky swallowed his cry. The floor gave way, the engine modules fractured apart. Caiden gulped wind and clung to C.

A bone-shaking vibration separated into high and low chords as more fissures ricocheted across the *Azura*'s spine. Jagged energy screamed within. Caiden panicked, reached inside it, hand lacerated and burned by wrenching crystal and liquid that boiled into a wheeze of light.

Then thunder cracked.

The entire spine shattered. Wind blasted out and stole Caiden's desperate shriek.

He flailed his hand, couldn't grab the fog of light that escaped her. His skin was severed by shards twinkling out of sight against the sky alongside teardrops the wind ripped from his face.

A gale tumbled Caiden and C in free fall. They slapped against wreckage while debris zipped all around. Sliced and pummeled, blood spinning in streaks, Caiden screamed a raw sound shaping *Azura*'s name. He hugged C tighter and turned his back to the ground and prayed to all the stars that had betrayed him.

CHAPTER 18

WORLD'S END

Caiden plummeted with the *Azura*'s shards, clutching C, losing sense of speed. Metal debris tried to tear him from the nophek. The ship's fragmented spine refracted space.

Through tears, Caiden watched a quicksilver aurora race through the shattered Glasliq's waves, like wind made visible. Wisps of light snagged his limbs, pillowed under him, and sent him spinning, tumbling, momentum stalled.

The ground roared up at them. Caiden squeezed his eyes shut and caged an arm around his skull.

Smack! Breath punched out of his chest. His head hammered. Half of him landed across C before the two of them rolled apart. Caiden curled up while rubble, glass, and splashes of liquid crystal rained across the plateau.

The clanging and tinkling rain settled. Caiden couldn't feel much at all except cold. Consciousness ebbed and delirium flowed.

Azura. He forced himself to sit upright but tipped over, hacking blood. Pain in familiar kinds, all over.

Ruin littered the lightseep plateau. Nothing was left that could be called a ship. Hunks of metal and Glasliq, long ribs, small shards. Sparkling dust filled the air, the remainder of the *Azura*'s crystalline spine. It made reality shimmer. Tears prickled in Caiden's eyes and distorted the sight. A wretched scream snagged in his throat, and the sharp sound cut him silent.

The *Azura*'s last exhalation of energy had broken their fall. She'd saved him one last time.

"Little boy?" Caiden choked. He twisted to face the red-black mound of fur nearby.

C roused, uncurling. His pupils filled with reflected light and contracted to slits. He whined.

"A-all right?"

The nophek flicked one ear, then sniffed the air and limped over. Caiden raised his throbbing arms to gather C's head as the nophek leaned into him. He tangled his fingers in thick mane and hugged tight, letting soundless sobs empty him while C's big heartbeat filled him up.

After a time, he untangled to inspect the nophek. Hardy pup, nothing fractured.

Caiden carried through the familiar routine of probing his own injuries. It felt absurd to care at all, but the monotony of his motions and the bluntness of pain helped steady him. He plucked shards of glass from his bloody scalp and repurposed tattered clothes into bandages and a sling. He removed his torn boots and dumped blood from them.

All in all, he was in miraculously decent shape, just fractures and sprains beyond myriad surface wounds. The released energy pressure and C's thick body had helped break his fall.

C licked his wounds. Occasionally he licked Caiden's, too, the spiny tongue possibly doing more damage than good.

The universe. Abriss popped it, just like that...

The enhancer hadn't rendered him resistant enough against her gravitas, and Caiden's desperation hadn't circumvented the knowledge she'd gained from her heavens.

He wiped his face, smeared blood. More grim thoughts bobbed through. The little lab and the sayro, destroyed. Collar smashed in the fall. C's condition would decline unless Caiden could somehow replace the meds.

He stared at the lightseep ground while muddiness cleared from his ears. The shrapnel pinged as it cooled, sounding like rain. C leaned against Caiden's wet back and his guttural breathing swelled into purrs.

Tingles flicked through Caiden's body and eddied around injuries. There was a heat that wasn't part of the pain, and a weave of pressures that permeated his shape.

Crimes, the enhancer hasn't worn off yet. That monstrous Graven energy still coursed through his body. He swore some freckles were new, bright-white flecks deep in his tissues. They didn't seem to move with the other cells, like they weren't part of him—pinpricks in a backlit canvas.

Caiden watched them in his palms, but they didn't burn out or burrow away.

He'd paid some permanent cost.

Wind raked across his shoulders. The blood began to crust. The Graven enhancer filled in his emptiness, colonized his body, and corroded the edges of his senses, chewing holes in time. Ships were coming for him, then not. Pockets of the world changed form and weather. It must've been Solthar's orbital projections shifting. He didn't want to think it was his mind.

C whined, all twitching muscles and stress-panting. If C died too—

Caiden twisted around, and the sparkles within the humming air moved *with* him, the wind snagging. C curled and laid his head in Caiden's lap. Caiden threaded his arms around C's neck, bent into soft fur, and closed his eyes. He was done.

―――――――――

Dead. He's dead. Death was painless expansion toward complete dissolution, Leta knew that—but the word of it tasted flat and chalky. Caiden had fallen among the sparkling wreckage, a sight as surreal as something from one of Abriss's storybooks. The fall of a mythic creature with broken wings, the fall of a spirit leaving a body.

Leta understood something new about him. The unease in her heart now was what Caiden had felt about her for years, the *doubt*: if she did not see his remains, did he really die?

She crept to the edge of the hall to look over the drop. The air appeared ruffled from the explosion of energy. The luminiferous dimensions remained disturbed enough for Leta to sense it without traveling there fully: the fabric of everything undone, the strings of space snapped and whipping. It distorted the view of the plateau far below. Specks. Sunlight scattered through larger crystalline remains. The red streaks, those were—

She turned away fast.

Unity had judged her choice by taking away everything she'd tried to correct. She should have trusted Abriss.

Leta took a numb step forward, but her body wasn't going to oblige. She folded down to one knee, then the other. Her eyes unhooked their focus. Bits of crystalline debris glistered across the floor among dust that had settled in rings of force. Calm and pretty. Destruction wasn't supposed to be pretty.

"Nine." Abriss swept over and crouched. Her voice swaddled Leta in a cozy feeling that harshly mismatched. A pretty feeling. "You're all right."

I don't want to be.

"You've done nothing wrong. Your feelings were correct." When Leta didn't respond, a look of grievance passed over Abriss's face like a shadow. Then she lightened her voice and asked, "Will you consent to touch?"

The request came as a shock. *Yes, a thousand times.*

Leta nodded and Abriss's hands wrapped her shoulders and pulled her into an embrace. The world became the softest nova, an intersection of sunbeams. Her numbness lost mass and she felt downy, adrift from what had happened. Fraught lines of thinking suddenly aligned into harmonies.

Did Abriss really hate her gravitas, even though she used it to heal?

"If I can erase any guilt from you," Abriss said, "I wish to. If the others are angry or resentful of the part you played, I'll palliate them too. I apologize for using you as bait a second time. The push you kept feeling, the wrongness of his imprisonment—that drove you to release him, which reversed his view of you and in turn drove him to return here instead of fleeing."

Clutched against Abriss's shoulder, Leta felt calm enough to speak. "You *meant* for me to disobey you?"

"Delicately. Extracting the *Azura* robs my brother of a working universe generator...but if it became Winn's fault that it happened at all, an accident...Threi's deal remains intact. He needs me."

"Extract?"

Abriss still wore the lattice meridian gloves, the device that had destroyed the *Azura*'s world. Aurasever, she'd called it. The name gave Leta a chill.

She released Leta and rose to her feet. Heaviness resettled with the removal of her touch. "Without a universe to test on, my calculations were off. I expected the physics rupture to force the Graven energy or spiritual thing out of its chrysalis so that this—" She snapped her fingers.

All around the hall, small devices blasted online to reveal a plethora of measurement fields and energy-capture structures: thread-thin laser lines latticed the air along with feathery veils of light, sonic vibrations outside of human hearing spectra, and other etheric emitters.

"So that this could capture it. I didn't anticipate the chrysalis itself to shatter since nothing can crack matter of that type, but it seems there's an added destructive force as the rind equalizes, physics itself rupturing in a flux…" She was caught up in her own mind.

Leta disconnected again as Abriss spoke.

If she hadn't known the chrysalis would shatter, what else was a surprise?

Abriss snapped her other fingers, and countless holosplays sprang into the air to report what she'd captured. The data was displayed in a variety of language forms that didn't make sense to Leta. Abriss glided around the information field to peer at it from other angles, overlaying one with the other, even looking at passages reversed in the lightseep's reflection.

Quietly she said, "He was meant to stay on solid ground. I could have pulled him to safety as well. I hadn't foreseen…the casualty of him, and I'm sorry to you both. I regret being gentle and letting him act on his own." A ragged sigh fluttered out of her at that complicated thought.

The casualty of him.

Leta squeezed her eyes shut. She didn't have the energy to scream or rage and had never been the type.

Because Caiden had, in my stead, when we were small.

Caiden could have flown away but he'd come back for her, selfishly, wielding his Graven influence to tear her away from her life. Her memories were real, and she'd cared for him still, but the ten years of angst he'd built up—and the symbol he'd made of her—let him think he had to bash his way to everything he wanted, thinking he had the right to choose what was good for her.

She'd read him wrong. That was her only fault. The rest had been his own choice. And Unity had allowed it.

Reasoning didn't make the sight sting much less.

Leta looked over the holosplays and tried to feel whatever invisible spiritual thing was hanging in the space of the hall. The data meant nothing to her, but she recognized the increasing dismay on the Prime's face.

There's nothing. Events engineered, a life lost, and—

Leta's skin prickled into bumps. "What was it meant to be? A creature? A spirit?"

"I'm honestly unsure. We're dealing with Graven elements the world hasn't seen in millennia, and past the point where the old books have any insight. The thing inside that chrysalis might've been immature, or so luminiferous that measurements fall short." Abriss's voice came delicate and reverent, as if something really could be lingering and she might disturb or offend it. Cloaked in stars and galaxies and hope, the Dynast Prime looked fragile. She teetered a little, despite the solid obsidian of her palace right beneath her feet.

"There's nothing here, is there?" Leta stood with effort. Wind grazed her back from the open wall. Her bare foot hit one of the bluish shards that had scattered on the floor before the ship fell. She picked the piece up and quested, "Does this mean the Graves' new treatments won't work?"

That was why Leta had done all of this: the *Azura* would fix them, the last seven of twenty-two failures' worth of effort.

Abriss turned back to Leta and her worried look dissolved, her momentary fragility vanished—she was diamond again. "Dear stars, don't be alarmed. I should have more than I need to heal you. The Aurasever functions. There is data here from the rupture. And captured spirit or not, you know what we do with gloss."

Leta turned the translucent shard in her hand. Freckles deformed in her skin behind. "Melt it."

"Precisely. Any matter that has encapsulated such a powerful energy like the *Azura* for so long will have that energy's nature impressed upon it. I'm not worried that it cracked apart, though I can guarantee my brother will be."

Abriss clapped her hands to shut off both measurements and holosplays. The sudden removal of so much sensory information struck Leta like a blow. With all the hums in the space gone, her shoulders sagged. The world grew foggy, underwater-slow, but she had one last quest: "The Graven willpower you sense so often..." She was unsure whether to call it a will, a presence, or just a force. "Did it guide you to this outcome?"

"*The Graven will*...If you mean the pressure I feel toward one future over another, yes—I believe this outcome is a Graven will, or a collection of them operating within Unity. Please trust us, too, Nine."

Us. Trust. Silky words, like *hope*. It slid easily on the tongue.

Abriss lifted the shard of chrysalis from Leta's hand. The Aurasever reflected strangely through those glossy inner faults. Bands of shadow wriggled beneath Abriss's skin around the device. She closed her eyes, focusing as she had done to sunder the *Azura*'s universe. Thunder of intent filled up space again, echoing from the luminiferity...

The shard splashed into liquid in Abriss's hand.

She yelped. Silvery rainbow dribbled over her forearm. "Well. This enharmonic force will take some practice. More...more hours of work to get it applicable for you Graves. Meanwhile, you deserve a rest. You've done so much."

What have I done? Leta felt strung along on a course she couldn't see. The choices had still been hers, which meant the guilt was too. The shards and the blood were her doing.

CHAPTER 19

CHRYSALIS

Metallic shrieking tore the air in the distance. Caiden roused and released a pain-thin breath.

A small Casthen ship was inbound, banking around the Dynast Hold's glittering flank. It leveled out. Thrusters burst. The dark wedge of it blasted straight for the plateau.

Staring, Caiden laid a hand on C's back. "Assist." The nophek groaned and stood, pulling Caiden up with him.

The Casthen ship tossed mist in curls.

The *Azura* was gone. What could they want?

This ship wasn't discharging any weaponry, so they either wanted him alive or wanted the wreckage intact. It was slightly larger than the *Azura* had been, big enough to hold ten or fifteen soldiers.

Caiden buried his hand in C's windswept mane as he watched their approach.

No scrambling for a weapon. No racing for cover.

He'd spent too long running from the Casthen.

He would show them what their years of chase had created. He was a Graven abomination filled with darkness and violence. And the Casthen system had long ago taught him he could bridle despair with rage and take it into battle.

The taut, ridged muscles of C's neck vibrated when he growled.

"Hungry, aren't you?"

C yowled and shook again, kicking a back leg at his tummy.

Caiden picked up a severed metal rib of the *Azura*'s wing, bent and sheared into part club, part blade. The oxidized exotic metal was exceptionally hard to deform, but apparently the rupture of an entire universe would do it.

"C, let's pretend this is the end of the world."

The Casthen ship kept up speed as if it intended to plow right into Caiden and C, or else fry them with the rear jets, or toss them off the cliff in the slipstream.

Caiden gripped a fistful of C's mane as they stood their ground. Mist whipped across the Casthen hull as it cleaved toward them, jets roaring. A beat before impact, C leaped, three bounds, clearing the nose of the ship and landing on one wing. Caiden, pulled along, kicked off C's knee and settled astride him. The ship's wing pitched hard into the ground with their weight. C jumped over the spine to the other wing, slamming it down before he bounded off again.

The ship's nose plowed into the unbreakable lightseep. Alloys buckled, and the unbalanced vessel cracked side to side like a flopping fish.

C landed beyond it, Caiden astride, loping easily to a stop to watch the fools wreck.

The ship yawed hard into crags that tore up its thrusters. Small explosions peppered the ship's side as it skidded into a forest bordering the plateau. Nine Casthen poured out fast.

Caiden brandished his makeshift club in his augmented hand and held on to C's mane with the other. They loped back into the middle of the *Azura*'s ruin.

The Casthen group met them. Maul scowled and held up a hand. "Surrender peaceably."

"Turn around and leave," Caiden countered, but his Graven voice was hoarse, barbed on his tongue, and didn't cross the distance. It would've been an order if he'd had enough energy to force it out. They might've turned tail and fled, saved themselves.

He shifted his muscular tension, cueing C to run.

The Casthen opened fire. Energy beams striped toward them while smaller glave bolts tunneled through the air. C dodged some and took the brunt of others, the energy snapping harmlessly off his hide.

Caiden slid to the ground while the nophek sailed into the group as a savage mass of muscle, teeth, and hunger. His roar devoured the Casthen's screams as he plowed through them, smashing into blasts of glave fire. Armor-tearing claws opened the soldiers.

Caiden stalked forward. The familiar sounds threaded holes in his brain and cinched him tight.

Maul drew two short, sticklike glaves off his back. One he twisted, baring blades on either end, which he tossed high in the air. It spun like a saw blade in a field of unusual magnetism. As it started to fall, Maul swiped the paired glave in his hand, directing the first to fly at Caiden, a blur of cutting edges. Caiden parried with his club as it glanced by, air shearing past his cheek.

Toys. Caiden had enough of the Casthen's toys. He advanced, peripheral vision filling with the nophek's havoc.

Maul swept his baton to the side. Behind Caiden, the spinning weapon curved back at him. Caiden poised his club high over one shoulder while piling charge into his aug arm. The sawlike disk whirred toward his neck. He timed it by sound. Last arcsecond, he ducked, struck his club into the thing with explosive force, and sent it hurtling back at Maul faster than the saisn anticipated. Maul deflected with his baton, which shattered on impact. Magnetism lost, the spinning half soared off at nothing.

Caiden wasn't here to play.

He sprinted, bare feet slapping lightseep that felt molten under his soles. The air didn't seem cold, but he steamed, and he might not have thought it a Graven fire except for the bleak look on Maul's face as the distance closed between them.

The saisn drew a long knife and adopted an elegant fighting stance that promised precision, but Caiden's heart wasn't in the fight. He wanted them all to stop moving, he wanted to be alone with his sorrow—couldn't Unity give him something so simple?

In smoothly powerful, minimal motions he hacked at Maul, chaining together a necklace of momentum, each snap of bone and gush of blood a jewel leading him to the next movement.

Maul matched stoic fury with precision and bent sections of Caiden's club with his special blade. Caiden threw the beat-up haft aside and launched in, hand-to-hand, into panting and pressure and the joyless rip of tendon and split skin.

Maul's blade missed a neck artery and plunged into Caiden's shoulder. Inferno ate up the pain before it registered. He wrenched Maul's wrist away, curled his left hand into a fist, and rammed at Maul's skull, cracking him hard to the ground.

The saisn didn't stir, but still breathed, blood foam fluttering at his mouth.

Caiden turned to where C had tangled with Jet, the chketin, over two meters tall and all rough-skinned brawn—a decent match for the nophek. Except Caiden had trained him to know where soft spots were, where sweet veins lay, and where one puncture could sever a joint.

The last Casthen soldier bellowed and ran at Caiden with a spear glave brandished.

The Graven enhancer *still* sizzled through Caiden's bloodstream. He was a thing of flame. Illusions throbbed in his vision. It warped the Casthen grunt, dimpling air around them, as if the musculature of space itself were visible and Caiden could flex it as he pleased.

"*Stop*," he said, voice cleaving the wind this time.

The soldier obeyed, staggering in place and falling to their knees. The tip of their paralytic spear spat electric filaments a meter from Caiden's face. He gripped the shaft and tore it from their grasp. Plunged it into their chest. Shock ripped through and dumped their body on the ground.

C finished with a few meals.

A breeze combed over the battlefield, the quiet masses, and the cooling blood. It snagged twirls of steam from Caiden's body and he finally felt a chill. Maybe the enhancer was wearing off at last.

He dropped the glave and ambled back to where he'd first fallen. Bits of glassy shrapnel carved into his soles. He pulled out the knife in his shoulder, chucked it aside, and let the wound bleed.

C padded over with Casthen blood dribbling from his fur. He huffed and lay down to lick his paws.

Caiden sat on his heels, nauseous and bleeding and empty. Who cared, at the end of the world? Shadows taunted him deep in the lightseep with echoes of falling wings and bright aurorae. He laid his palms against the surface. Scintillating particles jittered around his imprint: the last dust of the *Azura*.

He scraped up a handful. It dissolved on his skin, whatever it was, like tiny ice diamonds contacting an inferno.

The whistle gale of a warship stuffed Caiden's ears. He didn't bother to look over. If it was more Casthen, he would tell them to jump off the cliff, and if his bloodstream's fire was any indication of the continued Graven enhancement, they would do it. They would do it lovingly.

The vessel hovered nearby, threshing up mist and dust. C perked up sharp.

Hungry. Hungry little boy.

The ship howled in descent. Engines shut off but the rumble continued, echoing down into the lightseep. The nophek surged upright, and Caiden tumbled onto his side without the prop. Grit mashed into his cheek. He stayed there, blinking at the ground where some of the *Azura*'s dust had settled in spirals.

In front of him, vapor twined around the indigo mass of the parked *Wintra*, Taitn's Maltaean warship. Reflected cirrus clouds lazed across its skin.

Caiden righted himself.

The side hatch opened, and three figures stumbled out, rushing at first, then slowing as they saw him and took in the wreckage.

C curved his haunches protectively around Caiden.

"Winn?" The breeze had to carry Taitn's gentle voice over.

Caiden let his spine bend. With him the sparkles shifted, the wind tugged backward at his clothes, and the dust vibrated. Why was the world moving with him? The enhancer was still screwing up his eyes and his sense of everything. Why couldn't it just burn him up—

"*Caiden*," En said with force. Her voice pealed out, hooked in. He turned his head.

What happened? Taitn's lips formed the words, but air currents snatched the sound. The shock on his face spelled the same question.

En said, "We have to load and leave fast. Ships coming."

The third figure was Ksiñe. Medic. Surgeon. Distantly, Caiden's mind sparked—*yes, need*—but his body wasn't connected. Frigid, burning, his shivers melted into the vibrations of lightseep and sky and *the* Azura *was gone* and Leta was bound by a spider and a few meters away, the three of his family stopped and Taitn whispered, "No," as he realized exactly what the wreckage was.

Caiden had no words for them, and for a fractured moment he understood something about Leta that he hadn't before: this feeling of knowing but not having words that were enough, knowing the shape of the silence while the right words lay there even though his mind couldn't churn them into speech.

En crouched, looped an arm through his, hoisted him to his feet. He pushed at her, but all his injuries raged at the sudden motion. A sound clogged in his throat. Pain collapsed him into En's arms. She grunted as she caught him. "Ksiñe. He's..."

The Andalvian glided over. The chromatophores of his skin all agitated purple and his face scowled dark green as he looked over Caiden's wounds, donned a medical glove, and started palpating Caiden's skull.

C growled deep. Caiden gave him a "stand down" signal.

En said, "Don't worry, Ksiñe whipped up a batch of your pup's meds. Something new, even better than before."

Caiden sagged in relief.

Ksiñe's whipkin pet uncoiled her long furry body from around his neck and squeaked when she spotted Caiden. She leaped to him, her webbed body catching a bit of air before she struck his sternum and promptly wriggled down into his shirt. She was soft and warm as a heater, flattening her body against his chest with her clawed paws gripping his shoulders. Caiden hugged her against him.

Words still refused to form in his mind. Taitn's boots lay in his field of view, dust swirling around the tread. The pilot's hands were fists, shaking.

Ksiñe sprayed and stapled temporary fixes over Caiden's worst injuries, having to prod the whipkin aside to reach his ribs.

En hauled the Casthen remains somewhere.

Taitn laid Caiden's morphcoat on his shoulders. The material ruffed up into black feathers around his neck. Between that and the whipkin, fresh heat started to win over the chill.

"The *Azura*..." Taitn started, but a sort of sob cut off the rest. "We tried to get here sooner."

Caiden shook his head weakly. The words *I'm just happy you're safe* flipped over in his mind.

Bent near his head, Ksiñe muttered, "Biochem is off..."

Caiden looked into the Andalvian's pupils, the deep eyeshine metallic red. Still Gravenly enhanced, Caiden earned a response that would have required flexing, before. The dark lines in Ksiñe's skin bubbled across his cheeks and away, his whole face paling as affection overcame him. In a hushed voice, Ksiñe asked, "What did you do?"

Taitn's hand squeezed Caiden's shoulder. "Is he all right?"

En returned, windblown hair striping across the concern on her face. "Should I carry him?"

The softness of his family's care was the enhancer's fault. They should have been shouting at him, incredulous: How could he fly back when he'd been free and clear? How could he risk everything for someone who didn't want him anymore? What Graven bastard was he that he would storm in and snatch away the will of a girl who had a happy life?

Threi. Threi's elixir brought out the worst in me. The vision reared again of hundreds obeying the man's command to die. The whole universe had aligned to him. Caiden had wanted that power for himself to never feel helpless again. His hubris had cost everything.

"Come on then," En said, hooking Caiden's augmented arm around her neck and lifting him up again. The air eddied as he moved. Glisters danced in his vision, winking like diamond dust. That wasn't normal.

Taitn took Caiden's other arm.

He put one bare foot in front of the other, his dead weight feeling deader by the moment. The wind bent to snag his limbs, his hips. Sparks danced in and out of the skin of space.

Caiden hobbled onto the *Wintra*'s gangway. Once inside, Taitn dashed into the pilot position and got the ship moving. Ksiñe fussed with a lab case and a spread of tools to analyze Caiden further. He whistled for the whipkin, who crawled out of Caiden's shirt and leaped over, darting among supplies to fetch things.

En said, "After you're patched up, fed, and rested, we'll rendezvous with Laythan and Panca. We'll discuss what's next, together. All right? All right."

That idea dribbled through the holes in Caiden's mind, returning him to empty.

Wind had entered the ship with him, bogging at his legs and dizzying the walls. Did the others feel it? They were busy fretting. It must have been Graven pressures braiding so intensely into space it warped things. Odd tones populated the air. The sizzle of his nervous system...*Ah, the enhancer is going to kill me. It didn't dissolve from my biochemistry because it is* dissolving *my biochemistry—is that it?*

Taitn initiated the pilot's chair to split into two separate seats side by side. En deposited Caiden into one, and Taitn crowned Caiden with a neural halo, a thread-thin ring of light that riveted at forehead-height around his brain's implant.

"Here," Taitn said, featherlight, "let's get wings under you again. You'll feel more secure even if you aren't piloting. S-solid again." He swallowed hard and tried a friendlier, "We never got a chance to fly tandem before, huh? Maybe later."

Caiden *did* feel more stable with a sense of the *Wintra*'s dense mass around him and steady functioning within, but it was more bitter than sweet. No glass star, this.

A map showed the Casthen ships behind them starting to fan out and stop nearby vessels. Taitn swore and flew faster while En bent to scroll through escape routes. "This one's our best shot. If they comm, let me talk."

Ksiñe glided over to Caiden, skirts swirling and belts laden with tools. The whipkin clung around his waist. He gently took hold of Caiden's jaw, applying a scanner field to his skull. With a thumb he scraped a nearby tear off Caiden's cheek and muttered, "What fool thing did you do now? Body is rewriting itself." He pulled back the scan and looked at the readings, temples swarming with irritated teal stripes as he trudged off grumbling, "Impossible."

Caiden tried to chuckle. If there was one thing he seemed good at, it was doing the impossible.

The engine surged. The cockpit filled with blankets of holographic light, no way to tell real from projection as Solthar shifted like a restless dreamer. Weather slid past, twisting in and out of types.

The injections and tinctures soothed Caiden's stiffness but left him feeling even more insubstantial. C filled Caiden's lap with his head, increasing the pressure.

"Shit!" Taitn barked. "Casthen on us. Scan requests sent to everyone."

The *Wintra* wasn't going slow by any means.

Taitn punched the thrusters harder and weaved into a high-altitude traffic stream. Wind still screamed in Caiden's head from the free fall. The warship had a tone, and the two sounds melted between his ears into something that resembled the *Azura*'s singing: the vibration of eldritch components, resonated by her spiritual wind. The crystal, bright and pure.

Taitn focused on an evasion route. The pursuing ships threaded up behind them. En and Ksiñe argued while En pawed at the map.

Sour feelings tumbled into Caiden's stomach. *I have to pull myself together for them, they don't deserve my misery. It's all I ever seem to give them.*

He straightened and slid his fingers into the soft fur around C's ears, but as the ship sped on, lifting into clouds, Caiden couldn't bring himself to help pilot through this.

Taitn expertly skirted surveillance zones and extra patrol vessels but swore steadily under his breath at the Casthen's sticky pursuit. They kept pinging for answers.

En clung to the back of the seat. "Need me to take over with words?"

"Not yet," Taitn said through gritted teeth.

Turbulence surged up. Something pitched around the wings—Caiden could feel a shape to it through the link.

En lost balance and rammed against a wall. "Crimes, turn up the scalar grav if you can't handle some wind."

The pilot shot her a glare. "The sky's smooth as glass. New Casthen defensive tech?"

"Abriss could have seen us in her precious stars. Let me talk to the slods."

The *Wintra* shook, pitching nose up then tail, metal groaning. Whatever was trying to snag them bent through even the Maltaean armor.

Caiden straightened, swaying, and eyed the tandem controls. He wasn't well enough to pilot, but if he tried his best, they could get through weird defenses working together.

He still wished to believe anything was possible together.

Caiden tried to raise his hands for the controls to help, but the nervous signals blipped before they reached his limbs. The neural connection blurred his world into a rush of pressure around the vessel. Caiden's head lolled, his hair lifted by his cheek. Why? The ship was level.

"All damned, we're—" Taitn bit his words off. The force surrounding the warship threaded impossibly through even the finest shielding gaps. Stall warnings popped up in the holosplay. "Something's getting in the systems. Controls are shutting down."

"Get them back!" En yelled.

Caiden blinked, too numb to make sense of the shouting and frantic motions, but he could make some sense of the ship's mechanics, and whatever was taking it over was creeping into every inch.

They were going to crash. He'd crashed before. At least his last memories would be of the *Azura*. He owed her his life for saving him in the desert of death. It was fitting that he should die once she did.

Taitn tried to claw back command of the ship. En grabbed a glaive—what for?—perhaps to feel like she had some kind of control too. Ksiñe braced. His whipkin chittered, stuffing herself into his dress coat. C planted a giant paw on Caiden's lap, pinning him back in the seat.

In the chaos, Caiden was transported back to the fall. He heard the *Azura*'s doleful singing, felt her weight in his hands. Reins, bands of vibration permeating solid matter at a frequency too high for the coarseness of human senses.

It seemed so real.

The warship yawed while it nosed down, and the scalar gravity blipped on and off, tumbling Caiden's inner ear.

Confused, Taitn stopped moving, his hands hovering in the drive guides. He swiveled his head all around, then riveted on Caiden. "W-Winn, are you feeling this? The *shape* of it."

Caiden frowned at the man's perplexed expression and drew himself up.

Long blue tones laced through the fuselage of the ship, resonating inside, just like the *Azura*'s sound and feel.

He wasn't just *remembering* her. The others sensed it too. This was real.

Caiden closed his eyes and strained to perceive the vessel through the halo link, sensing the skin and bones of it, the zapping nerve lines and clunky brain. It was transforming as more energies seeped into it, and it felt *familiar*.

Something spiritual was infiltrating the ship.

CHAPTER 20

SPIRITSWARM

Substances dewed inside the *Wintra*'s fuselage, engine, and thrusters. Biominerals crystallized, creeping like a frost while nerves bloomed and hijacked digital systems. Caiden sensed each physical change through his link as the vessel plumped out with new muscle and plating.

The thrusters erupted to life, the ship hurtled, and Caiden staggered right into C. The nophek yipped and pressed against Caiden's trembling legs.

"It's all right," he whispered. Tears blurred his vision as he looked around, though the ship didn't appear different on the surface. *Inside*, it transformed, reanimated—was freshly inhabited. "It's *Azura*."

The ship leveled out and hushed, cruising through puffs of cloud faster than should have been possible. The pursuit on their tail was torched so fast it fell off the holosplay map.

Taitn's eyes glistened as he held a shaking hand over his mouth.

En and Ksiñe didn't have a neural halo to link their senses to the ship, so they hadn't felt its transformation or the spiritual force wending inside its construct. Ksiñe's blanched skin and wide eyes said he knew, while a confused En ventured, "Is this what I think it is? *How?* How in all the worlds?"

Caiden grazed his mind over the new shape of the energies within the ship. Somewhere burrowed deep in the skull of it, nestled in newly formed, gauzy neural matter, lay the florescer just as it had been in the Glasliq version. It activated at his thought: in a rush, the *Azura*'s universe bubbled outward. Sugar sweated over Caiden's tongue, his body grew buoyant, every cell fired up, and his sorrow scoured away.

His knees gave out and he slumped against C. With sudden terror, he clutched the nophek, whose blood wasn't compatible with the crossover—but C was just fine, and licked Caiden's face.

"That's changed too? How?" He squeezed the pup tight and closed his eyes so he could soak in the *Azura*'s song. Her world *did* feel differently tuned now, the air ionized and bright.

The others were shocked speechless, except Ksiñe, who waved a testing device in the universe's air and said, "Impossible, again."

"Chrysalis." Caiden exhaled the word.

Ksiñe nodded. "She is not Graven *technology*. She is Graven *being*. Maybe not whole or mature... but more than what vessel houses her."

Azura hadn't died when her spine cracked. It had released her. The strange wind he'd felt tugging at him... the cry of the air... the unnatural pressures and sparkles following his motions. She'd stayed with him the whole time.

Exhausted beyond measure, Caiden flopped to the floor, hugging his nophek's warm body.

Thank you.

Whatever *Azura* was—some spacetime creature, a spirit of dimensions, a thing locked in a chrysalis—her presence relieved and awed and made him *whole* again.

The warship cruised on, quieter than before, engaging the wind in a new way. A projected lightning storm filled the sky of Solthar, muffled and faded, surreal. It concealed them from the patrols and small cities below.

"All right," Taitn said. "Well. Let's... let's fly?" His eyes glistened as he raised his fingers into the drive guides, twined with light, and *Azura* purred in his hands. He glanced at Caiden and smiled in disbelief. Caiden managed a slow blink and a smile in response.

Taitn powered the ship in ascent, and it was undeniably *Azura*'s energy buoying them out of atmosphere. The thunderstorms peeled away into silence. At the planet's orbital shield of lightseep shards, the *Wintra* sailed through, encapsulated in its own universe—the shards didn't exist in *Azura*'s world—and they were free in open space, undetected.

Taitn murmured, "Wait until Panca sees this."

En strolled over and lifted the neural halo off Caiden's head. His deep sensations of the ship ebbed away.

"Come on, let's have a better look at you." She shepherded him toward a mat Ksiñe had prepared. As he lowered onto his back, relief sank in and *Azura*'s song petted his mind as he drifted on the edge of passing out.

Ksiñe rushed around him muttering dire things about his physiology "resetting." The whipkin cuddled in the crook of Caiden's neck. C plopped down and started to groom, licking a paw to rub over his own face.

Sedatives took effect and Caiden drifted in the interstices of *Azura*'s melodic energy. He missed his bed on the old ship, the woodsmoke scent of the coverlet, his own possessions, and the tiny but familiar layout of it all. Her vibrations coursed into his spine through the *Wintra*'s floor, and as he cuddled against C's giant paw, he could imagine this was the same, his little unit of three complete again.

Caiden woke in a cold sweat from a nightmare he didn't remember. C licked the side of his head, snuffling meaty breaths against his ear. "I'm all right, little boy," he said, voice roughening it to a lie.

Fresh vials clinked on C's repaired collar. Caiden was used to the distinct chime of the glass chicory flower that used to be strapped there. Gone now. Another sign that it was time to let go. He was never getting the girl he knew back—she'd become something else. He'd fought for a moment of Graven neutrality so she could make her choice about him, and she had.

The cost was this Graven intensity that still hadn't extinguished. It felt fire bright, like it bubbled his bloodstream, rippled heat and chill through him in swirls. Perhaps his cells were dying and rebirthing at frightening speed to remake him into something else. The new white freckling deep in his tissues hadn't faded.

"How long was I asleep?"

En walked onto the bridge with hands pitched on her hips, and said, "Not long enough, by the look of you."

Taitn glanced over his shoulder from the pilot's seat. "We're trying to track down Laythan and set up a rendezvous. Then we talk."

Talk. Caiden expected a loving punch or two.

En said, "I've got networks back in Unity looking into what's going on with the Dynast and the Casthen. We'll know more by the time we rendezvous and can sort everything out, but for now, you get cleaned up and fed."

Sort everything…

Abriss possessed a device, reverse engineered from the *Azura*, which could collapse a whole universe. She could let Threi out.

Caiden pushed to his feet, assisted by C. Crusty blood tugged across his skin. Remnants of clothing were clingy with sweat. He shrugged off his morphcoat and En squinted in disgust. Caiden rolled his eyes at her and headed for the scour.

"Catch," En called, and tossed a bundle.

Caiden caught it—fresh clothes—and trundled to the ship's branching atrium. Delicious scents wafted from somewhere and prickled his stomach. Ksiñe's cooking. His mouth watered at the thought.

Keep things simple. Scour. Eat. Heal.

He crashed into the scour chamber, let it whip through him, then emerged feeling peeled and not altogether human. Veins burning, skin chilled. The frantic events of the last days lumped into him like a hot coal, and beyond that, the Graven energy smoldered still. Too strong for all his leashes now, would it lash out? Control him? Ksiñe would know.

Caiden dressed in the clothing En had picked out: loose sikkel leather trousers with a webbed sheen. A tall-necked, sleeveless gray shirt that fell over his hips, and a ribbed sort of vest in indigo with armor tech within the boning. Separate sleeves were held on with cinches, black and warm, covering his hands. Windy swirls embroidered the fabric. All flattering seams and well tailored—he expected no less from En.

Caiden grew sad as he wondered… how long had his family been expecting him back? Was this a "one day" outfit she'd bought long ago, or something new scrounged from the ship's supplies?

"Come here, C."

Caiden coaxed the nophek into a curled shape inside the cylindrical scour chamber, this one just big enough. C roared inside as it initiated, but the process finished in a flash. He emerged fuzzy and bewildered, with the scaly patches of skin on his legs and tail glistening black, and the reddish undercoat brighter in his shiny fur.

"You smell better too." Caiden couldn't stop chuckling as they both trudged back to the bridge.

En called, "Nine crimes, it's good to hear you laugh." He surveyed Caiden with approval this time. "That outfit looks…just as I'd hoped. You've gotten leaner, though."

"An unfair comparison," Caiden said. En's current male physique was perfectly proportioned and bulked up.

Ksiñe clicked his tongue on his teeth. "This will remedy. Sit."

The Andalvian fussed at one side of the bridge, tossing down floor cushions and setting a food case in front for a table. His whipkin was draped over his shoulders and perked up after spotting Caiden, her whiskers springing on her dark muzzle.

C padded over to sniff the case first, then the whipkin, who arched out of reach and gave a warning peep. His ears flicked and his tail smashed back and forth.

"Tail," Caiden chided. C settled but it quivered, drumming the floor. "Be nice to the little girl."

When Caiden sat, the whipkin jumped to his shoulder, then crept down to his lap to curl into a ball. Extra skin flattened over her tucked limbs, showing the black-and-white marbling in her fur. C inched closer with sniffs, but she hissed to warn him off. He grumbled and settled back on his paws.

Caiden chuckled and petted her while inhaling the amazing scents of the meal.

Ksiñe's chromatophoric skin strobed wisps of happy peach hues as he dished gourmet items onto baskets and painted plates. Dark volcanically baked bread slices dolloped with a spicy-scented glaze. Eight tambuya: steaming balls of thrice-fried three-egg mixture, filled with soft grains and a center of velvety meat. Tiny succulent fronds and red flowers in a salad glistening with oils.

Caiden bit into a slice of spongy bread that was the perfect balance of spicy and sweet. It was plenty of distraction as Ksiñe intruded in his space with a medical glove and measurement devices, collecting fresh readings.

Ksiñe muttered to himself about horizontal gene transfer and frayed stitching in foreign repair genes. He asked again, "What did you *do*?"

"Remember... the vial of Graven enhancer that Threi consumed, that day he gave orders to the entire Casthen Harvest? And the spare I stole from his room?"

Disgusted blue flicked through the Andalvian's spotted complexion. He raked a frustrated hand through the fine spines over his scalp.

Caiden winced. "I meant for you to study it directly, but... Did you learn much more from Threi's research I sent you, long ago?"

"Winn." The medic shoved a palmful of data in front of him. Figures hovered on a grid of dimpled air over his fingers. It reported Caiden's current state, and there was a whole lot of red change in the readings. "Stable since we picked you up."

"So it might not wear off at all." Caiden let that idea sink in. He wiped his fingers on a damp, hot cloth, then took up an earthen bowl of steaming liquid. The special Andalvian clay between his hands lent a smoky scent to the caqeña's nutty, roasted flavor. He sipped while gathering his thoughts.

The "thing in the subterra" was all he'd heard his origin called. Caiden's brood's genetic records named it the "Dominant." Threi had confirmed that to Abriss during their meeting.

"My genetic makeup is a different Graven type than Threi's Dynast strain. Is that why it faded in him but hasn't in me? If he's synthesizing the enhancers from the same source as the Graven part of me, a Dominant Graven, maybe that's why it's more stable in me, like it's adding more of what I'm made of rather than balancing something different..."

Ksiñe nodded. "Dissipates from Threi's Dynast system because incompatible. I could not discover what Dominant was. He erased evidence. Silye hacked some research, not enough."

"So we don't know how the enhancer is made, or whether the source of it is in code, genetic material, an actual being?"

"Hold up." En strode over from the cockpit, plopped down on pillows, and snatched some food. "You're saying the Graven thing you're descended from is a *person*?"

Caiden waved his hand. "We don't know that the Graven were people at all, just that they participated in the physical world at one point."

"You don't know anything new, then. Two important things: can Threi make more of this, and how do *you* feel?"

"Safest to assume he can," Caiden said, "but until we know if it's a finite source or not, we can't be sure of anything."

"And you?"

Caiden probed his Graven force carefully. The mass of it was stronger now, yet the heft felt easier to flex. Compared to what he'd sensed when Threi had taken the enhancer, Caiden had a cloak to gather up in his arms while Threi'd had a fabric that stretched hundreds of meters out across space, with hearts sewn up in it. A concentrated gravity, affecting not matter but minds.

Was that Abriss's idle state of being?

Threi's old words seared in him: *Welcome to a life of lies.*

Caiden took a gulp of caqeña. The heat settled in his belly among the butterflies. En waited patiently and Ksiñe packed up the empty dishes. Caiden didn't feel like explaining all this and wasn't used to sharing anymore. That, or he didn't want to name some of these things, in case admitting them made them more real.

Like the presence he'd heard or felt after that first dose of enhancer, as if something else had doubled up around him. Echoed into his space.

En said, "Ah, you're still worried about coercing others. You should be. But—"

Caiden interjected, "My gravitas has changed over time. Harder to control, sometimes an outburst—"

Ksiñe made a nasal sound. "You bottle up temper too. Bottled things under pressure burst. What about giving in?"

"No," Caiden replied so sharply it woke C, whose head perked up and pupils dilated.

"Learning control?" En offered.

Caiden looked at his reflection in the bowl between his hands. "I don't want to become irreverent with it, like Threi or Abriss. Threi sees only the means to his end, and Abriss sees only the end to her means."

With more permanent enhancer, he could easily outmatch both Dynast heirs and change the multiverse for the better, rather than picking away with small valiant deeds here and there, struggling to make a difference with limited reach. But he would never get back to being himself. En had been right: he wasn't living yet, and he'd have no chance to if he threw it all out to serve a multiverse he hadn't come to love yet.

"You are scared." Ksiñe's spots thinned to pensive stripes.

"Yes," Caiden admitted. "I'm scared of it. I should be."

"I don't think it's so bad." En stretched his arms over his head and leaned back. "And not because I'm mildly resistant and I like you anyway. I mean that I can't imagine you using your Gravenness to harm or exploit. Look at you now—you're so stuck in your head worried about a misstep, you're tense as a rock."

Caiden forced his shoulders to relax. He stroked the whipkin in his lap. "I've studied about the Graven. Apocryphal history tumbled by myth and folklore. The ideas are smooth as river stones now, and half of them still just speculation. What were the edges they used to have? What could the Graven have done that no one alive would think ill of while coerced?"

The Dynast clung to the idea of the Graven, inflating the concept of them, whetting words into stronger blades. But hadn't Caiden done the same with Leta? After her death, he'd clung to and emphasized her meaning to him, desperately needing an emblem of his guilt so he could keep taking responsibility for what had happened.

"Ah, I see." En shook his head and flopped backward onto the floor. "Rid the universe of Graven beings entirely, level the playing field, is that your standard? Does that include you? Does *Azura* count? Should she be destroyed?"

"Of course not. I just don't trust the idea of the Graven yet. Not even in myself."

Those whispers, echoing through me…

En reached up to punch a gentle fist against Caiden's chest. "Cool it, hero. Let's see what I learn when intel comes back, what Panca analyzes about *Azura*, and what Laythan thinks of all this. You've been running so long you want to rush right on to the next thing, but we're here to slow ya down finally." En withdrew his fist.

Ksiñe refilled Caiden's drink. Caiden paused halfway through a sip because En's side-eye hadn't moved off him. "What else?" he said into the bowl.

"The thing you haven't said a word about yet. Your girl."

"Leta's not mine, and never was. She's grown now. She chose to stay."

"And that's it?"

Caiden found his reflection again on the dark liquid's surface. "That's it."

CHAPTER 21

VOWS KEPT

The west lab's entrance was framed in a sculpture carved from a porous mineral like frozen ocean foam. Ghostly figures tangled in the billows, somewhat humanoid and xenid but blended with beams of light and plants and shreds of weather: the artist's interpretation of the Graven.

Standing between Dian Six and Tayen Five, both in real bodies too, Leta peered up at the art, waiting for others to arrive before they entered.

Did the interpretation mean the Graven could shift their form? Or did it suggest they were purely luminiferous and emerged into the physical world periodically: as a person or a plant, a ray of light, a rainstorm? It sounded nice.

"Nine," Dian said, "get out of your head."

"I like my head."

Leta could measure his forgiveness by how close he stood to her. Half a meter now: his pique hadn't quite returned to protectiveness, but after Abriss had explained how events were engineered, it almost seemed like his resentment switched to Abriss instead of Leta. She didn't like that much better.

Tayen Five rapped her fist against her thigh repeatedly. The last time the Graves had undergone a dramatic new treatment like this, one of the dead had been someone dear to Tayen. Sometimes it seemed like she lived on out of spite, or an attempt to make Four's death worth something.

Sisorro Seven and Dejin Eight approached at last. Dejin's big body was scrunched, his small eyes bright but ears pinned back. Sisorro blurred between times.

Leta asked eagerly, "What did you see?"

They'd been part of the team investigating the wreckage.

"Chunks of the crystal," Dejin reported. "Lots of blood, some meat."

"Paw prints!" Sisorro chimed. "Cute."

"The nophek survived and attacked the Casthen there."

"No whole bodies left. Delicious."

No bodies. Just meat. Of course, only a nophek would survive such a fall, hardy and tough-skinned as they were. Where was the beast now?

Dejin sidled very close to her, looking guilty, with his tail looped around one ankle. He didn't want to say that Caiden was meat sprayed across the ruins of the *Azura*. He didn't have to say it.

"Consent?" he asked, fidgeting.

"No, Dej. Not now." Comfort would crack something in her now.

The ursgen wilted a half meter of height, wringing his hands.

Leta's mood sank and the doors opened. An assistant bowed them in.

The lab resembled a larger version of Abriss's personal workroom: the edges hulked with strange Graven technology, rare matter, clouds of exotic electricity, and all manner of tools, books, and holosplays. Both side walls were glass, with jungle gardens growing behind and open windows beyond, spilling sunbeams through the green. The salvaged chunks of the *Azura*'s shattered spine had been piled all around and added bluish bows of light across the room.

Isme Two was already present, out of Proxy.

And Aohm One. The yraga's body was as tense as a closed-up bud, nestled inside a new feature of the lab: one of the Graves' bioradiation caskets. This one had been lined with all the smaller fragments of the *Azura*'s chrysalis. The bristling tub held a liquid in which plasma arcs tasted the edges of One's skin.

Abriss knelt at the front, moving with enervated slowness. She'd repaired One's Proxy, made Aurasever adjustments, and finished investigations into the *Azura*'s chrysalis matter, among all her other duties as Prime. The weight of a universe showed in the droop of her shoulders, the purple rimming her eyes, the strands of hair slipping from starburst clips: Abriss had absorbed the burden she'd worked to relieve.

"Come see," she greeted them happily as she spread her hands around the yraga's flowery cartilage skull. "I may not have captured a Graven spirit from the chrysalis, but I have enough understanding of the enharmonic strain now. Some of the same energy remained in the shards as I hoped, and the Aurasever is designed to generate a copy of the ship's power to microtune dimensions."

Abriss's voice lost volume with weariness. She closed her eyes and continued, stronger, "I can now infuse your harmonic Dynast biology with the *Azura*'s enharmonic current. Balanced, as you're meant to be."

She held a breath.

Leta sensed the Prime's intention thundering softly into the luminiferity, pressuring reality to conform. Was this like gravitas on a more fundamental level?

A glow festered in the crystals. Bluish biophotonic rays knotted around Aohm and smoldered through the spectra of their body. New freckling whorled in and out of their flesh, sparkling into the air like wildfire rain.

In moments, One's body healed. They looked aglow and mesmerizing as they unfurled from the cramped casket. Air dimpled around their boundaries, bending light.

Leta gaped. In ten years, she had never seen them so *revitalized*.

Holosplays measured Aohm's vitalities and reported a now exact balance of the two strains. Their Dynast Graven vessel was filled with the promised energy of the *Azura*.

Abriss wilted over the casket edge while gazing up in triumph.

Aohm curled a tendril arm under her waist and drew her to her feet. Opalescent plasma arced out of their skin and snagged around the edges of Abriss.

You have done it, Aohm's thoughts extended.

"Describe it to me?"

I show. Aohm One extended a limb to a large chunk of crystal.

Leta couldn't stop her awed grin or the flutters in her belly as she witnessed the miraculous: the crystalline matrix melted and levitated, streaming together into a shape between the yraga's frond hands. Rivulets coalesced, fangs dripped down, and they'd fashioned a crown that solidified suddenly. Dust sprouted into tiny flower tendrils wrapping around and draping like a veil. Light motes gathered into rays.

It so resembled the artist's rendering on the doorway outside of impossible realities colliding.

Aohm placed this bizarre crown on Abriss's head. She laughed and covered her mouth with her palms, stifling her gush, "Incredible."

Aohm thought at her, *You did not know this?*

She gingerly stroked one of the rays of light. "I did not, except to read of it. Unity conspires to surprise even me."

Abriss removed the crown to inspect it, mussing her hair in the process but not noticing. As she held it, Aohm wafted a hand over top, and the whole construct tumbled apart into petals of some gelatinous glowing matter. Abriss laughed again, the sound filling the room, and Leta couldn't recall a day that had ever been so lively. *Hope.*

"Nine? Come next."

Leta's heart crashed around. She gazed at stunning Aohm as she treaded to the casket and shoved away memories of their previous treatments, which—she was ready to admit—had been as horrendous as she'd described to Caiden.

Leta's morphfabric suit thinned and loosened its weave as she lowered herself in. The fluid was heated, softened, barely sensed. The shards might as well have been fluffed wool, almost intangible. She relaxed while Abriss's fingers caged her skull. More doubts crowded in, recollections of the way the *Azura*'s universe had burst at Abriss's touch.

Be fixed. Be fixed, all the stars forfend, let this be the last of our treatments.

The crystalline nodes of the Aurasever heated, equalizing with Leta's skin until she lost sense of where her bone ended and Abriss's fingertips began. Leta meditated and breathed, her mind expanded past her skin, consumed the room and the Hold, Solthar, the heavens, and the ineffable border of Unity. She contained the whole, which contained all of time in a flow that coursed both directions at once, and all of it was singing a more perfect music than anything earthly. Without beginning or end, the luminiferity could not be expended, only transformed, and Leta cast her wish that she would be transformed too.

Subjective eternities passed by. Leta roused when Abriss's touch shifted.

Her awareness rooted in her body again, but her physical shape felt smoke-built—all strings and phantom pulses. Abriss was smiling down at her. Her hands cradled Leta's head, seeming to hold together the expanse of Leta's consciousness, allowing it, impossibly, to fit within a human skull.

Leta gasped deep and slow while sitting upright. Liquid tumbled off her—no, steam, then effervescence, then sparks wriggling into nothing. Every pain had ironed out. Every chord in her tuned. Her sensitive nervous system fuzzed at the edges like the pages of the most-read books, velveted from a history of touch.

The lab became luscious with new detail, from the vhisilin-mined silver that leafed the spines of wood-bound books to the blades that bit the quarry for the stone columns to the luminescent nectar of the overhead lights that haloed Abriss's head and turned her brown hair golden, and through—

"Better?" the Prime asked.

Leta nodded, robbed of words.

Her own body didn't jab her. The Graves' shuffling sounds were fleece-lined instead of abrasive, and she had some control over where and how much her senses extended into the world. All the nuances of her experience were intact but, yes—better.

Abriss had kept her promise. The Graven tales Leta had grown up on, which seemed too miraculous, were real. *This* was Leta's intended form. She wasn't going to die in the grave of her body. Everything about her life—her childhood with Caiden, which had looped him back here with the *Azura*—was for this purpose: the power to create worlds.

Abriss invited Isme Two over and began his alignment next.

Leta picked up a book from a stack nearby. Without opening it, she knew its content, the construction, the meaning infused into it, and all the deleted passages that lived on in dimensions unwritten.

Her mind devoured every word, lapping up the ink of it backward and forward, along with every moment of the thirteen times Abriss had read this romantic tragedy. She felt the impression of all the hands that had held it. The tree gall the ink came from, the flowers pulped and pressed to make up its pages, the sinew of the running animal threading it. The years-old salt of Abriss's tears on the final pages.

As her concentration devoured the book's history and makeup, it physically disassembled in her hands. The stitching and fibers let go, strings slithered through her fingers, and paper crumbled. It lost the physical form that gave it the name "book."

When Leta realized her hands were empty, she squeaked, "I'm sorry."

Abriss's eyes flew wide with amazement. "I . . . really hadn't imagined the scope of these abilities. Popping a universe may seem immense to some, but the *detail* workings that you and One have done astounds me."

Leta could tune states of matter and energy. Quantum potentials fixed by participation. She thought of music: changing keys, shifting notes, the length of strings, material and timbre. She had never felt so perfectly fit to the world, nor so much in command.

Leta looked again at the perfect balance in the holosplays that monitored Aohm One's state.

Degrading.

The enharmonic strain that Abriss had conditioned into One's body was now disintegrating faster than the Dynast strain *ever* had. This balance wasn't going to last.

"Aohm!" Leta yelled and swiveled to face them.

The space around One began seizing up in great spasms. The air malformed, their body contorted, shriveling, and Leta was slammed with memories of past failures. Dead Graves. All the things she'd told Caiden were true fears rearing up now: bones splitting from skin, spirit leaking out veins.

Abriss shouted something and rushed to wrap Aohm in her hands. The Aurasever ignited light in the air and pulled it around them, bursting starry specks beneath their skin.

The other Graves hesitated in half motion, unsure how to help.

Abriss looked like she wrestled with a shadow inside Aohm's pale tissues as she retuned their nervous system before worse happened. She quaked with concentration and wheezed pained sounds as she scraped the dredges of exhaustion for more strength. She kept the pattern of the *Azura*'s energy measured as it fell out of Aohm's Dynast makeup, like amplitude attenuated rather than suddenly dropped. Aohm was all right in moments that also felt like an eternity. They uncurled while catching Abriss, who collapsed in their arms.

"Your"—her ragged breathing cut up her words—"yraga physiology… is more complex than…"

Leta's hearing began to mush sounds into strange echoes. Light in the room wriggled away from her retinas. It wasn't just yraga physiology.

The balance the *Azura* had given her was temporary.

The promise was a lovely lie.

She was next.

Leta's mental gears stopped one by one, function fled. The room and everyone in it sank into a murk of layered time all in one location, all the matter ready to shift, everything malleable. The luminiferity swamped in around her.

Abriss's science hadn't been wrong, and neither had her expectations or hopes or heart, but this was new territory with unpredictable variables. Like all the treatment rounds before.

At least one of them had always died.

Not me. Leta wrestled her spirit's tattered edges out of the luminiferous chaos and focused on her body, intent on shoving lightning back into cloud. Space contracted, time seized, and she gasped as she opened her eyes.

Freezing, tearing, bones ringing. Abriss clamped Leta's skull in two palms with the Aurasever. Sounds mashed against her eardrums. Solidity slammed back into the features of the room, all too crisp and light-harsh.

"Isme." The thought and name spilled from her at the same time. He'd be next. "Isme!" Leta screeched as she pulled from Abriss and scrambled for him.

He startled, but otherwise sat on the casket bath edge fine and looking *striking*. The *Azura*'s energy had filled his translucence and brought out features hidden before. Leta almost froze at the sight but she could see space around him starting to buckle like an aura inverting. Her own body disobeyed, tripping her, spinning the room. She collided with Isme at the same time his perfect balance started its reversal too. His skin split into gold. A cry pierced out of his lungs.

"Not you," Leta whimpered through gritted teeth as she pushed him back into the casket bath, half of her falling in too. Isme was the strongest of the Graves in-Proxy but the most fragile in his real body. She wasn't going to let him die.

Aohm One looked all right in the corner, if "all right" could be a term for their normal, aching, curled-up state. Dejin and Tayen crouched at their side.

Abriss had nothing left in her, she could barely crawl. Dian Six scooped her up to bring her over.

Leta dived into the casket, inhaled light, pressed her forehead against Isme's shoulder, and refused to believe his body was a grave for his dying spirit. She let her consciousness bleed out into the luminiferity.

This was her best skill: drawing another's spirit back together. She'd saved one, almost two, of the Graves this way before, and she hadn't been as skilled then.

The vast enveloped her, abuzz with lifestreams of consciousness: not individual minds but one collective mist that individuals dispersed into. While grasping tightly to her own self so she wouldn't dissolve, she called up everything she knew and loved about Isme Two, in the hopes of calling him together in this point of space and time.

She thought of the heartbeat of pause before anything he said, proving he gave everything thought. The quiet patience of him, the knowing looks, the way his smile didn't change when he was in pain. That he used names, not numbers. His brilliant empathy and willingness to listen. The accent he had, the shape of his questions, the colors of his name. The nuance of him that would remain strong in the luminiferity.

Leta?

Yes. Her heart soared. She hooked into his spirit, hauled herself back with him in tow, imagining them both as waves crashing back to the same point.

Isme fought for air. Both of them convulsed—he with shock and she with the enormous effort. Dian Six pulled her from the casket and for a moment she wrestled him, feverish to hold Isme together, but *she* was hardly together. Dian wrapped her in something plush and locked her firmly in his arms until she regained her senses.

Her vision was sideways and fogged. She saw Aohm, curled. Dejin held their shoulders and mediated, forehead-to-forehead.

Isme shrank into the casket. Glossy gold speckles swarmed his flesh as they used to. The translucence was back, layered textures of organs and tissues that the casket's rays started to heal. Tayen cradled his face in shaking hands and tried to say things to him, but the parasite in her wouldn't let her have the words. This was nearly the tragedy with Four, all over again.

Everyone fell still, breathing loud.

Abriss slumped over the end of the casket. Face wet and eyes staring. Mind calculating.

When everything calmed, it was clear that they were back where they'd started. Imperfect and counting time.

Aohm, Leta, and Isme would need more healing but weren't in worse shape than they'd been after previous failures. While that was a grim thought, Leta accepted it eagerly: she hadn't lost either of them, after all. Everyone in the room seemed to be processing the same...the somber idea that this was in fact a victory.

Dian released Leta, then swaddled her tighter in the thermal cloak, brusque but caring. All the protectiveness was back in him. His anger retargeted at Abriss, but in her presence his feelings diminished to quick glances and flared nostrils. If Leta had been stronger, she'd have chastised him because Abriss was doing beyond her best.

Tayen was quaking, fighting flashbacks of losing her partner. She pushed into motion to fetch a thermal cloak for Isme, then gathered him and crowded him between her and Leta, leaning against the casket side. She wrapped a firm arm around them both.

Isme's head flopped onto Leta's shoulder. Her breath rustled his damp hair. She didn't dare touch him. He looked more like glass than ever.

Abriss, at the limit of her resilience, checked over Aohm One with special devices. Yraga biology wasn't straightforward to see.

"Healthy." She collapsed to a seated position, then carried on mumbling, "The enharmonic force does work. It doesn't *last*. Is the energy I copied too incomplete, larval? Too soon from the chrysalis? Or is the balance too powerfully tenuous on its own? Stars strike me, we need—"

"The stabilizing force," Leta finished. "A Dominant Graven strain."

"Yes." Abriss's response came out so ragged and weary, Leta regretted speaking. This failure hurt Abriss more than all of them combined. "The Dynast's harmonic strain and the *Azura*'s enharmonic naturally balance each other and should have remained balanced within each of you. It *worked* on a smaller scale, the combination was stable and perpetuating, there was no reason you . . . You're—" Her voice was almost gone. "You're far more complex than small-scale tests and simulated models. If we had the third strain, it would bind the other two in place, sealing the energy in your bodies so it doesn't evaporate back into the luminiferity."

"You prommmmise," Tayen muttered, squeezing Leta's and Isme's shoulders.

This time . . . we have all we need . . . Abriss has said that every time.

A promise behind a promise.

Threi had the third piece they needed.

"I *do* promise," Abriss said, pushing herself up. Tears shined across her eyelashes. There was nothing left in her, but she stood with Aohm's help. Like Leta, she was desperate to not lose any more Graves. If she didn't hurry to save them, some would die. If she hurried and failed, some would die.

Leta sympathized with that impossible choice, but right now it couldn't balm her heart's hurt. She cuddled her temple against Isme's.

Dear Aohm rose with Abriss and spoke in everyone's minds, *She gives all for us. We become miraculous, piece by piece.*

Having tasted success, Aohm One would trust that more of it would come. They always had. Even pain couldn't break Aohm's trust. Leta wished hers was that resilient.

Abriss said, "I wasn't intending to release my brother. He only had what I wanted, not what I needed. But now I do *need* the Graven Dominant from him."

Leta filled the unsaid: "You're leaving Unity."

"Now that I know for sure what we're missing, we can rush straight to it. If Threi won't give it up nicely, I'll make him."

Tayen said, "His deal, his claim to have to ave ove e . . . thhhe Dominant could be a lie."

"More risk," Dian agreed. Anxiety finally drove him up to pace the room. He still had a few tetchy glances for Abriss when he drew out of proximity.

"A risk I'll take for you. I won't leave you two-thirds finished now that we *do* have the two strains and we've witnessed what it can make of you." She stroked Aohm's arm once and gave Leta a knowing look. "It will be a safe exchange. My brother succeeds in manipulating others because he's Graven, not because he's as clever as he likes to believe. He's not used to opposition. I won't force any of you, but I would ask you to accompany me in-Proxy."

Sisorro shivered in time. "I wanted what One and Nine had. Looked fun. How long will the trip take? Three and Ten died on return last time we were in-Proxy for too long."

Dejin shuffled and sobbed a low sound at that. Tayen squeezed shoulders again.

Aohm One thought, *This power. This clarity. This all-oneness we are accomplishing in the luminiferity. If even a single of us survives, we will have made a path to perfect physical being for all. It is worth us. We are worth it.*

"I am aware—" Abriss fell to her knees, still held awkwardly by Aohm with an arm raised. Dejin hovered at her other side, tail swishing with worry. "Aware that it all sounds too immeasurable. Comprehending all eternity... and trying to bring eternity back to something simple. The Dominant is the third and final Graven piece of this puzzle I've made of you all. I am here for you. We'll keep working, together."

We.

Isme roused to shake his head weakly, hair bouncing around his face and Leta's cheek. He curled his cold, glassy fingers around hers and squeezed. Golden nerves flared up his wrist. "Let us go alone for you, Prime."

"Only I can wield the Aurasever in its current state to sunder his universe." She managed a smile. "Do not worry. As One said, you are worth it and I will spend everything for you. The risk is minor. Harmony is my Dynast nature, and Threi's. That's why he—intentionally or not—has unified the three large factions within the outer multiverse. The two of us together will only propel the worlds on a course for further reunion."

Leta sighed and squeezed Isme's hand back. She wanted to do something for Abriss but had no more to give except to be heartened by the thought that only one last hurdle remained.

"Please," Abriss whispered as she tried to straighten but failed. "I'm so sorry it came to this again—please seat in your Proxies so your bodies can heal, and prepare for our departure."

Pleases and apologies—bright as diamond.

"Nine," Abriss added, "your real body will need to come with us."

CHAPTER 22

TOGETHER

Laythan's ship—a huge freighter—plunged into view through the *Wintra*'s cockpit window wrap. It descended out of sight to prepare the standard coupling to Taitn's security-class warship.

Reunion time. Again.

The sight distracted Caiden from his sparring game with En, who pulled a punch an inch from Caiden's face, then patted his cheek instead.

"Aw, you're worried," En exclaimed. "Don't worry. Laythan's age is starting to show, he's softened, slowed down, hooked up. And Panca misses having another mechanic to talk to." En mopped at sweat, then twirled his messy hair into a complicated knot that a worn-out magnetic spray helped keep in place.

Caiden tucked a few sweaty flyaways behind his ears. "It's not them, just...haven't been sitting still in space for this long in a while."

"No Casthen in sight, kid. And none of my early intel suggests that anyone suspects the *Azura* is still...alive. Do we drop 'the' now? Just Azura?"

"Panca will be able to tell." Caiden turned at C's growl, a precursor to boarding sounds in the *Wintra*'s hallways. "C, stay. They're more friends."

Laythan and Panca entered the bridge.

Caiden was sure he witnessed the instant effect of his Graven energy. The softening of their strides, Laythan's look of affection where there should have been a scowl, Panca's animation where she would have been timid. Part of him wanted to say he was overreacting, or that it didn't matter whether their attachment was real if he wasn't using it to harm.

Laythan halted at the sight of Caiden.

Slim, elegant Panca kept approaching. Saisn existed in a sense-sea, which would clothe Caiden plainly in all his hidden emotions. The faceted core embedded in her forehead refracted the room's glow as she moved while bright limbal rings in her completely black eyes flicked up and down, sensing the unseen. Ridged musculature in her face relaxed and she swept toward Caiden to slip straight into a hug.

"Panca." He curled his arms around her, something cracking at the familiarity. "Nine crimes, I've missed you most."

"Ouch," En muttered. Caiden laughed.

Panca craned her neck up and back, gazing at the ceiling, then all around. Her lips rarely smiled, but the dark grayish-purple skin around her eyes crinkled like velvet. "She's changed."

"The spine...the whole spine shattered. The Glasliq and fuselage ripped apart. I thought I'd lost her."

"Not at all," Panca said, her voice's timbre airy and familiar.

"Check out the engine now?" he suggested. "A bunch of things have transformed...I've been too tired to look it over."

Panca paused to wrap a slender hand around his jaw. She fixed him with a deep look filled with a recognition of everything he couldn't talk about.

Crimes, I can't take this yet. He cleared his throat and leaned his cheek into her palm, smiling. She nodded and headed to the engine room.

Caiden straightened in front of his next judge.

Laythan Paraïa's arms were crossed, and all two meters of his height were not bent an inch by the years. A storm of marbled gray-and-white hair crowned him—gone were the remnants of dark brown. A thick beard the same color framed his pensive scowl. Like cracked leather, his wrinkles had multiplied in his rich-toned skin. The decade had sharply hewn the muscles of his broad build, giving him a tight-strung presence honed all the more by a finely cut pilot's coat.

Caiden wasn't sure which way this reunion would go, but he would stand by his prior choice to carry his burdens alone. He was thirty years old by ephemeris reckoning and had flown through uncharted depths of the multiverse. He hadn't needed help to keep safe or stay on his toes. He wasn't a child they needed to talk sense into.

Laythan's prosthetic eyes narrowed in a twitch. Faint chevron weave glinted.

Finally Caiden said, "My left cheekbone isn't as bruised, if you want to punch there."

Laythan cocked his head aside and massaged his knuckles. Cracked a couple.

Caiden braced.

Laythan's face creased, then he guffawed loudly. "Getting too old to haul your ass out of a mess this heated, boy."

The big man marched forward and smashed Caiden in an embrace, squeezing the air right out of him. Caiden grunted, then inhaled the captain's familiar smoky, leathery scent, and instantly felt put together by the solidity of this fortress of a man whom he was happy to call—never to his face—a father.

When Laythan let go, Caiden said, "I'll haul myself out, just—"

"No, you won't." Laythan planted his hands on Caiden's shoulders and held him for a long look.

Caiden couldn't tell if the pinched brows and shivering eyelashes were signs of a Graven-cued feeling or if Caiden really looked so much worse than what the man had expected.

Instead of a reproach, Laythan said gently, "Go spend time with Panca. We'll talk after. If you haven't forgotten how to talk out your problems."

"I haven't. C's a good listener."

Laythan raised an eyebrow at the nophek, who was lying obediently, licking between his four-inch claws while giving the newcomer a slitted side-eye.

"Stay," Caiden said to the pup, and left the bridge. Behind him, Laythan called out to Taitn. Endirion hummed while working at the communication array. More of Ksiñe's cooking spices wafted in. It felt homey. The *Wintra* wasn't anything like the old vessel Azura had inhabited, but with her spirit thrumming behind every surface, Caiden had everything he needed.

Leta hadn't been part of this family of his. It was easier to give up something that had never happened, since it didn't feel *missing*.

He crept into the *Wintra*'s engine rooms. The lighter-than-air jelly streaks of Andalvian lighting outlined different parts of the big modular engine. Panca drifted around with palms and fingers touching surfaces, learning more through touch and her sense-sea than most mechanics would with a collection of tools and instruments. Her eyes' limbal rings were especially bright in the dimness and showed her watching invisible currents in the air.

Caiden swore Azura's tones grew more complex as he approached, chorusing through modified alloys and whispery organic manifolds. "What do you think? It felt like she converted materials inside, like how the old vessel had changed when her universe was active; things shapeshifting, grown biological networks and fluid systems…"

Panca made a sound of agreement as she settled her hand atop the housing of the stellerling core. "Machine spaces're filled up with hybrid of plant, virus, phantom structures."

Caiden placed his hand on the core next to hers. There was a breathing rhythm beneath and a mass like something jammed too densely in the chamber. "Taitn says she's entangled in the ship's nervous system but not altering data or present in the digital interface."

"You're sad?"

Caiden chuckled. "I'm curious, I guess. She doesn't have a voice, has never used language inside the ship's systems. I've always understood her without that, and she seems to be aware of my thoughts, neural link or not. But I still can't tell if she's an intelligence or just an energy structure responding to input."

"The shape of her's changed. More coherent. Before's one slow thing, now feels split up, quicker, many hands at work. A frozen river thawed 'n' rushing."

New burbles coursed beneath the metal under Caiden's palm in answer. "Is this permanent, or can she leave the *Wintra*?"

Panca laughed, an airy flutter. It took Caiden a moment to realize she was laughing at his jealousy that Taitn might have Azura as part of his ship now. Caiden snorted and said, "Yeah, well, she likes him too."

"The engine modules could revert safely."

He leaned his forehead against it. Steady thundering filled his skull. "A spirit in a vessel…"

He imagined Leta's spirit peeled out of her body and then shoved into a Proxy machine doll. In the luminiferous dimension between, would she have been able to interact with Azura? By that logic, was Azura a conscious entity without a body? A collection of entities?

When he pulled away, Panca cocked her head at him.

"Azura's reaching in one direction, down from the luminiferity into physical things to cause change. The Dynast is doing the opposite, seeking enlightenment, seeking upward. The Prime reverse engineered Azura's energy into a device and is trying to meet halfway."

Caiden raised his fingers to the Andalvian lighting hovering above the module. The light candled through his hand, revealing freckles not unlike Leta's. He hadn't been created with any higher purpose in mind—Çydanza just wanted soldiers with gravitas.

Panca read his feelings and said, "You can't make a moral judgment 'bout Gravenness in you without judging Graven as a whole. That includes Azura. Give yourselves time." Panca exited the room, adding, "You're both very young."

Caiden laughed and followed her back to the bridge. Saisn were long-lived, making Panca young, too, by that measure.

They joined the others at a low table with a variety of drink ingredients on top. Ksiñe was cutting hair-thin peels from a tiny fruit with a molecular scalpel, En assembled a complicated beverage with layers of fizzing ice, and Taitn scratched C's chin as the nophek waited for scraps.

Panca bent to give Taitn's shoulders a warm hug, and obliged En's proffered cheek with a graze of a kiss, then sat between the two.

"Sit," Laythan said to Caiden. "I want to hear what mess you've created that's ten years in the making."

En passed Caiden the fancy drink. "I played up your heroics."

"Thanks? They didn't do enough, in the bigger picture." Caiden took a sip: crisp and sharp with citrus, effervescent like tiny blades of heat on his tongue.

En said, "You just didn't stop to look at how your deeds rippled in your wake. I'm impressed your altruistic side kept blazing. Save a galaxy here and there while zooming away like it's no big deal."

Unaccustomed to praise, Caiden flushed a little. But the good he'd done felt like bailing water out of a sea. Only Threi and Abriss had the potential reach to change the multiverse, but Threi focused on himself while Abriss focused on Unity.

Caiden took a few sips for courage, then dived into his explanation, covering everything that had happened from the sayro to Solthar and the destruction of his ship and Abriss's fearsome new weapon. En filled in bits of the last section, including them scheming to break Caiden free.

The summarization highlighted all the unlikely odds and circumstances.

Everything happens for a reason... "*manifested by collective will.*" *Whose will?*

Laythan reclined and nursed his drink as he mulled things over. Caiden waited patiently for the captain's conclusion. The whipkin had meanwhile crawled into Caiden's lap and draped over his thigh, while the drowsy nophek managed to inch so close his nose was almost touching hers—and she allowed it. Smirking, Caiden stroked her long back.

"Intel's back," En called from the cockpit, where he'd wandered. "The Casthen flagship, the *Sessrun*, took off from the Dynast Hold. Word is the Prime's boarded with all seven Proxies. Including your not-quite-betrayer, who was carrying an unconscious young woman."

"Her own body, must be." Caiden sighed and refilled his drink with something new, a pink sunset in a glass. "Why?"

"Test subject," Ksifie said, and at the same time Panca offered, "Sensory informant."

Caiden grimaced. Neither sounded good. Anyway, Leta wasn't his concern. "Abriss is headed to release her brother. I've been struggling to prevent that for ten miserable years. There may still be a chance. En, is it possible to get a message to the *Sessrun*?"

"Not the way they're traveling, and not if we want to beat them to the Harvest."

Caiden swore and sipped his drink at the same time, then coughed as the combination fired into his lungs.

Taitn patted him on the back. "The Dynast Prime is too Graven to stop. What's your plan?"

"More enhancement," Ksiñe suggested.

"No! No." Caiden had a sudden, better idea. "Threi's universe prison is enclosed by a structure, and there's a safety protocol that will lock it down from the inside. Even Abriss wouldn't be able to order her way in."

"Sounds temporary," Panca said. "Easier to let her release Threi, then kill 'im fast?"

"Threi will be gunning for a dose of enhancer and he'll murder Abriss the moment he has fangs. She's exactly as strong as Threi tried to tell me before—he won't hesitate."

"And if he *doesn't* attack?" En asked, twisting in his chair to face backward.

Caiden gave that heavy question the consideration it deserved. Seeing Leta in person had affected Caiden so much. Would Threi meeting Abriss be just as powerful? A brother fulfilled by a missing sister? If Threi had a change of heart, if he didn't murder her and instead fell under her gravitas, the pair united was an even more frightening thought.

Laythan grunted agreement with En. "Time has passed. He's done about as much good as you. The Casthen rehabilitate species, reverse extinction, supply accommodations. You haven't stopped to look at who he's become because your heart needed to keep seeing him as a villain to justify your foolhardy runnin'."

When Caiden didn't respond, Laythan knocked his drink back and said, "Threi and I talked, ten years ago, during the Çydanza business. I was involved in his mother's death. Laureli Cetrin—she was murdered because she wanted to abolish the Dynast and share resources and power with the multiversal factions, breaking down borders and the like. Threi claimed to hold that same goal. He cares about things out there."

Caiden buried his fingers in C's short mane beside him—a soothing habit. His other hand rested on the whipkin, a warm ball in his lap, and rose and fell with her breathing. "None of you spent time with Threi. You didn't see him with his secrets shed off. You didn't look through his room or read his books. He doesn't care about anyone but himself. But say they do join forces; Threi will be wrapped right up in Abriss's aim, which definitely isn't abolishing the Dynast. Her new technology collapses universes. Guess what—the Dynast has always fantasized about 'correcting' the multiverse and returning it all to Unity's physics like it was originally."

Caiden had been avoiding the vision of Azura's world sundered, and avoiding the idea of the multiverse being dismantled, every world converted to Unity's predictable physical laws. His brain hurt at the scale of that impossibility.

Laythan slapped a hand on his thigh, understanding. "No one could stop her from popping every bubble out here."

Caiden added, "I'm not saying that's what she intends to do, especially since she's put years of effort into careful immigration. But the technology suggests it's possible, and I'd rather worry about the worst thing that could happen."

"Crimes," Taitn swore, "don't make her death sound like the right outcome."

"It's not. Threi kills Abriss, takes up that universe-collapsing tech, becomes the Dynast Prime, the Casthen Prime, the Cartographers' darling, and he has most passagers' respect now, doesn't he? He's arrogant and self-serving. Abriss at least can be reasoned with."

From his brief interaction with her, he didn't think her aim was malign. Misguided or desperate, perhaps. He'd glimpsed her with her light peeled back. She was human.

"Winn," Laythan said with an intense gaze. "We don't have the time, forces, or firepower to charge into the Harvest and stop the two strongest Primes in their tracks."

En added, "Not our job, either, as fun as it sounds."

Caiden worried his fingers through his hair hard enough to sting his scalp. "At least...first I want to stop both of their capability to enhance their Graven influence, or worse, somehow make more Graven soldiers like I was meant to be. If I can't stop their meeting, it will preoccupy them while I get to the Dominant. Whatever that is has all the answers I need about what...what I was made from."

Ksiñe ventured, "Maybe not your fight."

"Then whose is it?"

Laythan rapped a fist on the table. "Why do you always try to fight the biggest thing you can find, eh? You're like those weird little skyfish from Galkern, except those do it in *groups*."

Caiden sighed as fatigue piled on. "I'm thinking too far ahead anyway. En, can you even get me to the Harvest before the *Sessrun*?"

En narrowed his eyes. "*Me* or us?"

Caiden couldn't see a way to do this himself. Twenty years old, freshly accelerated in age, he'd rushed to the Casthen Harvest alone—with Threi, but that didn't count—to throw himself at something too big. This time he would try taking everyone with him. He could finish the one fight he'd left undone. Yes, like one of those weird Galkern skyfish.

Grateful but grudging, he answered, "Us."

En beamed at him. "The Casthen have a special route to get home fast, chaining through stellar egresses to skip all the way there. I've yet to charm that secret out of anyone. Commander Artensi, you wanna help me out? It'll take some military-grade egression knowledge to pull this off."

Taitn scoffed and brought his drink with him as he joined. "You just want my company, admit it."

"Always."

CHAPTER 23

DEUNIFIED

On the bridge of the *Sessrun*, Leta in-Proxy hugged her real body tight. Paired up, it was stark how much more petite she was than her brawny hybrid machine body. She cradled her own head against her shoulder, metallic fingers spread through her hair.

What a weak thing to have so much spiritual power. *Skinny*, Sisorro had said. She palpated down her ribs. Caiden had felt her ribs too, and instantly clutched guilt tight, taking responsibility for her frailty and all her ten years he'd been gone. What a flaw that was—to have become a sponge for the misery of others.

Leta looked over at Abriss, whose features, seen in-Proxy, were quite unremarkable besides the thickness of her freckles. She was tired as ever, braid loose and shoulders sagging. She'd banished all the Casthen and kept her Dynast Safeguard pilot on-course to the Harvest.

The pilot turned the vessel, and the Proxies all pivoted as one, staring down Unity's rind: a wall of interknit streamers of energy where space was made and unmade, where physical laws clashed.

Before leaving Solthar, Abriss had augmented each Proxy with multiverse-friendly materials. She'd added a crystalline fix built from glossalith and the *Azura*'s shards, which would avoid the ghastly crossover Leta had experienced in-Proxy before and would keep their consciousnesses tethered to their Proxies. The matter glittered in all their spines. Their fake lightseep bones smoldered faintly, tendrils of opalescent light snaking outward into the biological parts like it had when Leta, Isme, and Aohm had been filled with the *Azura*'s energy.

Unity's rind drew near—the moment of truth.

Abriss had guaranteed that their consciousnesses wouldn't be slapped out of their Proxies, but her assurances sounded flatter now. Dian Six and Tayen Five in particular still acted slighted.

Leta slithered her awareness out of Proxy and back into her real body, just in case, then wriggled from her Proxy's heavy arms.

Everyone tensed as billows of rind light swept through the cockpit. Shadows rippled off surfaces. Leta closed her eyes tight and hugged her arms as the rind passed through her. The new universe invaded, unbraiding her quantum makeup and whisking her energy across space. Then *snap*! She was whole, different, lightweight—she hit the floor and her awareness fuzzed. Sounds and sights returned like the swash of waves up a beach.

Leta groaned as Tayen Five lifted her up in this leaner gravity. She clung gratefully to the Proxy's armored waist while she got her bearings, feeling not just lightweight but…smoother? No pockets of soreness or stripes of ache. She didn't sense her tendons tugging on her bones, or her nerves threaded through her flesh—her body fleeced together whole.

"Is this how other people feel?" Leta murmured, perplexed. This wasn't as wonderfully fixed as her body had felt after the brief conditioning with the *Azura*'s strain, but she'd never felt so put-together before.

Tayen's grip tightened around Leta's middle. Reflections skated over her glossy black helmet as she peered down and cocked her head.

"I feel *better*, Tay," she whispered, and pulled away to feel the fluidity of movement, the gravity as gentle as bobbing in an ocean.

The Proxies were muttering. They'd all remained conscious as promised, and the new mesophase materials had endured the transformation of laws well: none of them disintegrated like Leta's had before. But outside of Unity…in this new universe's parameters…it was *better*. For how long? Was this an unusually lovely universe? Such things *existed*?

Dian snarled and turned to the Prime. "You never told us."

Abriss frowned at them. "Are the components—"

"Did you know?" His volume dropped, the words tightly reined.

"Ah, you feel changed. Each universe we enter is unique and will affect each of you differently. Unpredictability is the flaw of deunified space. I can tweak the Proxies' new alignment points when—"

"No," Tayen Five said. "The problem wasn't our bodies, all this time. It was *Unity*. Unity hurting us, Unity that was difficult. But I'm here, and *it's* here, and we're...I'm..." She quavered and trailed off, astonished by her own speech.

Tayen's words weren't being clipped up by the parasite tangled with her consciousness.

Dejin Eight made a startled sound and requested consent before he grabbed her skull and turned it as if he could see the two things inside instead of one. "Ase sam sistrai, you are untangled here?"

Dian marched over and put a hand on her forehead. "Tay?"

Her helmet *shushed* against his ceramic fingers as she trembled and looked at him. "I remember everything *in order*, Six. The detours in my mind are gone."

Leta pivoted to the remaining two. "Aohm?"

Their huge Proxy sat folded in on itself, emitting tiny chittering sounds like metal edges vibrating against one another. New microperforations in their carapace had let the material adjust safely, but they looked wrinkled and unwell. "Better, but not for all."

On the other side of the bridge, Isme's fingers were twitching. He cradled his faceless mask in one hand. "Worse nerves, for me," he muttered.

"Isme." Leta frowned, roughened by the idea that she could feel so much better at the cost of others. The problem wasn't Unity, as Tayen thought, but neither was the problem their bodies. A mismatch...

Sisorro twirled to face Leta. "What do you feel?"

She inhaled. Her lungs inflated so gently here, she realized how much Unity had felt like breathing underwater. *"Manageable..."*

She struggled for a word to convey it. In Unity, her spirit had been embroidered into spacetime's fabric with too-tight stitches. Atop that, the sheer quantity of the information content of the universe had burdened her constantly, filling up every bit of her awareness she gave it. But here...that was lessened a hundredfold.

She'd always imagined that the Graven's original singular universe—all of known space—had been broken like a pane of glass in one cataclysmic event, cracks bursting through, turning one whole into a puzzle of fit-together shards. The multiverse. She just hadn't imagined how *different* each universe could be.

Leta glanced at her slumped Proxy. "It's not just the new laws of this universe, but the *size*. Like our Proxy shells help us process our expanded senses by containing them, this tiny universe, like a shell, contains the breadth of possible content. It's so much less complex than Unity. *That's* why it feels better to me."

Sisorro grumbled, "Prime, all this time, you did not predict *better*?"

Dian paced. Leta read the hurt in the set of his shoulders. "She *didn't look*."

"You're deceived." The sad Graven edge in Abriss's voice made Leta's heartbeat palpitate but glanced ineffectively across the Proxies. "Compart-mentalization is a flaw. The foreshortening of potential that is inherent in a smaller world is not a boon. Yes, Unity *has* been hard on you as you've evolved and your biology changed, but with the Graven trinity complete, you will have this 'better' while within Unity. Think of this as a taste of what you will become. This and the reality-augmenting powers that One, Two, and Nine had before."

Sisorro perked up. *Looked fun*, they'd said before, not seeming to grasp the cost of those powers.

Dian continued pacing, with threat in the weight of his steps. Dark hair veiled his features. For a flicker, Leta's visual of the seven arrayed around Abriss looked like nothing more than weapons pointed toward her.

Tayen, swordless, instead smashed her armored fist against her sternum in soothing rhythm and hissed quietly inside her smooth black skull. "You didn't consider anything outside of Unity, even if it would have solved our pain. Have we been suffering for nothing all along? You say the Dominant will save us, but what other universes might've sa—"

A riot of light whipped through the *Sessrun* as it flew into another universe.

"—avvvvvvv." Tayen snagged on the end of her sentence. She cut off and stood very still, breathing heavily but bereft of words.

The parasite was well and tangled in this universe. Five's arms fell slack at her sides.

Leta started to ache all over in this new world.

Aohm One straightened and made a long, easy sound. Isme relaxed. Dejin buckled to one knee and slammed the heel of his hand against his helmet a few times before he straightened and fixed his cowl.

Abriss looked over them sorrowfully and said, "It's not stable out here, Five. And for everything that's better in one universe, there is something else that's worse." She shut her orrery off and stood, but hesitated. She was a natural comforter, but unaccustomed to dissension.

"Unity's inhabitants have worked for centuries to create safe, infallible science for all compatible species. The reason we only lost twenty-two Graves was because you were in Unity. Yes, I did gather technology and material from the outer multiverse but brought those parts *into* our world. Anything unstable in Unity is unfit to be used."

"Everything gets sanitized through Unity's rind, then?" Dian said. "What about Five and her alerid parasite? Are they unfit because they're unstable?"

"That's not what I meant." She sighed, visibly hurt by his mistrust. "Unity gives us the understanding to—"

"Out here you lose your stars and that dear Graven voice that echoes to you. Unity is predictable, but you didn't predict the *Azura*'s chrysalis to be empty or the Aurasever treatment to not be enough."

Tayen rapped her sternum harder, faster.

Abriss replied, "Yes, the Graven presence I sense is only clear in Unity, and I can't put into words everything I understand...but I've sensed the ineffable and I know we're being protected and guided. Please trust me."

Dian's trust seemed planed so thin it might snap.

Isme stepped into the middle of the tension with a diffusive elegance. "Trust," he pleaded too. "We have been out of Unity for less than three arc-minutes. In five, we'll be on to yet another new universe. No one wise ever judged so fast or reflexively. Be patient."

Aohm added, "We are here to protect and to learn."

Abriss gave the two a loving look, then turned to Dian earnestly. "Six, we are at the edge of what anyone knows of the Graven. Unity used to be all of known space before it split, with a large-scale structural coherence that allowed miraculous things. The Graven were so knitted into the function of the cosmos, death was just a shift in dimensions, a change of circumstances, easily reversible. When Unity splintered, it broke that coherence and the state of being the Graven had attained. The luminiferity became invisible, impenetrable, scarred over. I am trying to *fix everything*." Her bone-weary sigh added an unsaid word: *alone*.

The pilot flew the *Sessrun* through the bright portal of a stellar egress. Leta felt slathered across space, the luminiferity skinned bare for a heartbeat of time. Then they were through and Leta was back together. In this new universe her skin tingled, and her pupils must have dilated because the light all around took on a soft bloom.

Dejin Eight clutched his head again while Sisorro Seven made irritated noises and shook all over, colorful clothing rustling and fair curls springing.

Leta backed up until she hit her Proxy and sat in its lap again. She settled her consciousness back inside it, where the ache left but new buzzes inhabited her Proxy's joints.

The shift made everyone quiet and glum, nursing their disagreements. Abriss tended to a few Proxies before returning to the cockpit, disheartened by their stress.

Leta hugged her real body again and let her disturbed thoughts settle. She tried to categorize all the crossover changes as the *Sessrun* threaded universes like a needle. Some were cold and biting, others dry and brittle, still others with velvet gravity and ghosts in the air. But in every universe— magnitudes smaller than Unity—Leta sensed the whole shape of it in an unburdened way, as if entering a room and for once being able to see the walls and everything inside.

The constant changes lost novelty fast.

Dian, Tayen, and Dejin resorted to movement and did training drills. Aohm meditated. Isme was restless, too, but hid it well and read a book. His long hair spilled over his crossed knees and the bench, filled with smoldering light from the *Azura*-derived crystal fittings on his spine.

Sisorro sidled over to Leta and plopped down next to her. Colorful textiles spilled around them. They smiled at her unconscious real body and ruffled her hair, then met her in-Proxy gaze.

"Dreams," they said. "Seeing them is my specialty. Some people watch media. Boring! Dreams are stranger. I figured out One's ability: they can see memories instead, if the person is thinking of them. Even more fun, since those are secrets. I'll show you?"

Leta blinked at them for a moment. Seven was both refreshingly direct and frustratingly obtuse. "Yes?"

Sisorro grinned, then nodded at Abriss sitting near the cockpit, her eyes closed. "Too anxious to sleep. She is thinking of something. What is it? Let's go see!"

As if it were that simple, Sisorro tilted their head back and was gone from their Proxy, which slumped onto Leta's shoulder. They were always both endearing and baffling.

Leta followed them—she needed the distraction.

Eyes closed, consciousness away. The luminiferity in this random universe was no different from Unity, except that the scope of it was leagues more manageable.

Sisorro?

There. She homed in on their presence hovering around Abriss like an excitable cloud. Leta joined cautiously. Seven was right: Abriss's mind held a memory. Leta let her consciousness sink into it, an impartial observer while the timeless luminiferity fleshed out the holes in Abriss's recollection with vivid detail, joining the past to the present.

Abriss was remembering Threi. She looked to be in the middle of adolescence, and he in early adulthood. They sat on a padded bench at the foot of her bed in a massive room. One wall opened to Solthar's morning sky. A Dynast-blue blanket scrunched between her and Threi. His skin, before paling through accelerated aging, was only a touch lighter than Abriss's tawny shade, and spiced with just as many freckles. They looked nearly twins.

Abriss breathed in gentle morning sunbeams. She forced her hands to not shake. The luminiferity patched up Leta's understanding: Abriss grieved the loss of her father, Veren. But Abriss Cetre wasn't allowed to simply grieve. She had learned her feelings shouldn't take up space. Her grief was tinged with gravitas that engulfed everyone around her in it, so she forced herself to be soft and featherlight, and drifted above the sea of her sorrow.

Threi had murdered Veren in gruesome self-defense. His hands rested palms-up on his lap, burned skinless, gloved in pearlescent bandages. Strict orders: touch nothing.

A medical blindfold of silvery satin cinched over his eye sockets as the organs rebuilt beneath. Threi had cut his own eyes.

Abriss raised a pottery mug to his lips, which were crackled from embers. A balm glistened over the rips of red skin. She tipped slowly and watched for his reaction.

The blindfold's ribbon ends swayed as he tilted his head, dark snarls of hair flaming around the fabric. He swallowed, wincing. Skin creased around the lacerations peeking onto his cheekbones.

"I can taste it," he whispered, voice as delicate as ash. Abriss leaned in to hear. "Vanilla?"

The girl beamed. "Yeah."

She'd mixed it herself. Medicinal and creamy. She'd checked the temperature twice, so it was warm but wouldn't scald his raw throat. He'd already tasted coals.

She set the mug down—

Leta's awareness was kicked away as Abriss shook that memory off. But another one sprang up, and Leta crept back in to observe, wrapped up in this vulnerability she'd never seen from the woman before.

In this memory, Abriss's young self stood in one of the Dynast Hold's high gardens.

The fresh air would be good for him, she thought. Threi liked to brood, and Abriss took it on herself to pull him out of it. He trailed his fingers on the fluted stone of the terrace railing to find his way. The blindfold ribbons flashed in the breeze. He tracked her from the sound of her shoes.

"Check if you can smell." Abriss folded over the railing to snatch a long bobbing stem. She arced the bloom over toward Threi. It smacked him in the face first, and he dodged backward, bewildered, and Abriss stifled a laugh.

She cupped the flower beneath his nose. The curled petals were so voluminous they formed a perfect sphere, the color of a sun.

She waited.

"Just smoke," he said. "Everything is smoke and burned flesh. Please stop."

Abriss brought the bloom to her nose and inhaled the strong, spicy citrus of it. She released and it whipped back on its stem, springing toward the sky. "Let's—"

"Riss." Pain abraded his voice. "You need to stop—"

"Caring? Don't you want to know that it's genuine care? It's just us in this family now, with Veren gone. The two of us."

"And whose fault is that?" he whispered.

Her grief twisted up, tight around her ribs. "I don't blame you. I—We only have each other now."

Abriss snapped alert, and Leta's consciousness was tossed out of the woman's currents. Sisorro too.

Leta roused in her real body, blinking. Next to her, Sisorro tilted their head side to side, birdlike, then concluded, "Boring memories. Are they lonely or happy? Don't know." Sisorro shoved to their feet and jogged over to the others.

Leta looked to the cockpit and struggled to fit the hopeful expression of Abriss's younger self onto her mature face. For all the woman's talk of having perfect control over Threi and understanding his nature, of using him to get what she wanted...did her memories betray a desire to revive a real companionship? More important, did Threi feel the same?

The *Sessrun* finally cruised past long queues of ship traffic and through a stellar egress that was the singular entry and exit point to the Casthen's otherwise un-enterable universe, the reason their bastion had remained secret for so long.

On the other side, within an indescribably vast structure of barely there lightseep, lay the Casthen Harvest: a knobby planet, tidally locked, with a sunny side and a dark one. It was encrusted with megastructure, like a planetary armor of interconnected buildings and decks. A skin of city. Tiny universes blistered its surface while some hovered above, poked by catwalks. Nearly Leta's whole life had been spent in one universe. To see a place *teeming* with them was unnerving somehow.

As the *Sessrun* began its descent, increasingly larger and stranger waves of bass pulsation buffeted over Leta's body from something on the planet. A presence, permeating space, swashing into her senses not quite like an intelligence but a living thing, whatever it was, immensely complex. It emanated both from deep in the planet and from the luminiferity, swaddled up in dimensions, inhuman.

Leta closed her eyes and sought it out. That's why her real body had been brought, after all, to survey luminiferous threat. She carefully slipped her spirit halfway into the luminiferity, like cupping an ear or peeking into a room.

Its pulse slicked around their ship and eddied about Abriss Cetre, swirling invisible particles. A Graven force, but different from her and more coherent than the *Azura*.

Leta followed its intensity farther toward the planet. It was alluring in the way that only Graven energies were. It hummed then sang, ruffled tones then smooth, echoing itself, and reminded Leta of a dreaming creature. She tried to tune into who or what it was, as she'd done to observe Abriss's memory and how Sisorro spied on dreams.

A voice? A structure scattered in little bits across time... but if she lined herself up so they were all in a sort of row... echoing into a fuller image...

Suddenly Leta was aware of her body heating, each Graven freckle in her flesh like a barb strung up with connections to the thing, and it *reeled her in*, swamped her in pressures. It wanted so badly for a vessel.

Her awareness tumbled past the megastructure shell where the facility cored down into the crust. She passed through metals, through flowers, into water, wrapped in vines of searing energy, and she was drowning in a garden of pain and desire. Time unwound—then suddenly Leta was gagging on the *Sessrun*'s floor while many hands seized her.

Aohm and Dejin pulled her back, safe, whole—right? They held her arms while she convulsed and panted in a jerking rhythm that matched the pulsating *thing* she'd just dived to try to find.

Abriss knelt in front of her, holding her jaw in fingers laced with the Aurasever. "Come back slowly. We have you."

"A Graven energy," Leta whispered. Abriss's touch started to clear her daze. "Down there somewhere. But it's not Dynast like us and not like the *Azura*."

"The Dominant?" Abriss suggested, then called behind her, "Stop the ship."

Propulsion torched from the ship's belly to hover it in place over the megastructure.

Dian Six growled. "It's aggressive?"

"Asleep?" Leta replied with effort. "That's the only way I can characterize it. I didn't comprehend its true form. Is the Dominant a...could it be a being?"

The Proxies exchanged alarmed glances. Sisorro said, "A thing so strong we can feel it from orbit...and it is *sleeping*. Delightful—what is it like awake?"

They all turned to Abriss and grew quiet.

"This is, at least, confirmation that Threi wasn't lying about the Graven Dominant." Abriss gestured for the pilot to continue descent. "Nine, could you pinpoint a location?"

Leta wasn't keen to look again. A chill raced through her. Dejin squeezed her sideways in response. She said, "If I were closer. It's too deep and too spread out in the facility."

Six was watching Abriss's expression. "You crafted our bodies and our Proxies from Graven secrets. We are weapons. What weapons could Threi have made with his own Graven secret?"

The *Sessrun* touched down on a massive landing pad.

"You're not weapons, Six, you're family."

"What do you know about family?" he quipped. He wouldn't realize all the layers of hurt in that statement, but Leta did.

Abriss flinched and something in her eyes shuttered for a moment. "Threi is my family, and I know exactly how much power I have over him. He's used secrets as a currency since we were children—he knows I'm here for an exchange and that it's in his best interest to be tame. I feel safe entrusted to your care, my Graves. We don't have the luxury of time, since you can't stay in-Proxy forever, but in every other sense we have the advantage."

Dian Six didn't respond, but Leta knew his shadowed look: he was wondering what Threi was capable of to *help* the Graves.

Abriss tugged the celestial dress straighter over her fitted suit, then spread an arm to invite Leta. "Nine, let's find a safe room for you while you join us in-Proxy."

Leta willfully ignored her continued sense of the Graven Dominant's energy and was happy at the thought of returning to her Proxy shell to dampen it.

In the corridors of the flagship, Casthen staff became snared in gravitas, reverent and eager to serve. Abriss doled out requests and briefly met emissaries, a vortex of purpose rippling through the space.

Leta relaxed. The entire Harvest could be wrapped up in Abriss's will in an instant if she wished. Loyalty would be the Dynast's strongest armor.

CHAPTER 24

GARDENS

Caiden snuggled against claws and teeth, stuffed into a smuggling compartment with C. A giant paw curled around his thigh. Rancid breaths pumped into air pockets as the nophek panted, overheating. Caiden's ear rested against C's rib cage, pounded by a heartbeat that drowned out the sounds of the Casthen's inspection of the docked *Wintra*.

En's bribes and charm had gained both vessels clearance to the Harvest. They hadn't arrived as quickly as Caiden had hoped, but to make it at all, so cleanly, was something he couldn't have managed on his own.

The compartment cracked open. Caiden tumbled out. C trampled him, then did a whole-body shake.

En said, "Covered in shed fur, smelling monstrous, hair plastered sideways—not a bad look on you, that last one, but yeah—go scour. We need to slip out while the place is bustling."

Caiden scowled at En and trundled into the scour. When he rejoined her in the armory, she had weapons and clothes laid out. She was already outfitted in Cartographer light gray and purple and had changed her augmented build—long-bodied like a swimmer—and her androgynous face, broad and stern, nose crooked, pigment dark and cool-toned. Her eyes were still gray and glittering, and Caiden chuckled at the grain of truth in some fringe worlds' folklore: that shapeshifters' eyes couldn't change.

She weaved her hair back. "Are you eager to look like a Casthen again?"

"At least it's not the old armor." He threw the thick, pleated Casthen coat over his other clothes. The skirt panels caught in his legs as he tested a few fighting motions.

"No, but the old armor had a mask, and your face has been burned into the mind of every Casthen officer for years. Come here."

En opened a case of materials, sprayed foam in her palm, then mussed it around in Caiden's hair before slicking it all back. "Auburn clashes quite nice with your eyes." En wiped her hands clean, then seized his chin.

He gave her a crabby look.

"Stop wrinkling." She smoothed something over his skin with a small sponge, covering the freckles.

Disguise or not, his latent gravitas would draw attention, even if it was useful backup in a pinch. He would have to work harder to mitigate proximity, sight, and sound.

Caiden grumbled, "I thought you said Ksiñe had been adapting nareid research to find a way to mask faces."

"I didn't say he was finished."

Caiden endured as she flamecombed his stubble off, fussed with his cheekbones, did something to his eyebrows. When her crimpy smile became too much, he tore free. "Now you're just having fun at my expense. Are we ready?"

"You look fantastic."

"We're ready." Caiden rolled his eyes.

He gestured for C. A purr clicked in the nophek's throat as Caiden wrapped his arms around the beast's big neck and got a head-butt in the chest. "You can't come." C's tail battered the walls in irritation. "The floor tracks our steps, and four paws will raise suspicion. That and the rest of you."

En said, "I know you didn't point this out to the others... But the new surfacewrap security doesn't just track steps, it interprets intention from speed and route. The upgraded biotech interfaces throughout the facility are un-hackable. The retinal bug Panca gave me will help, but we're moving in too fast to adapt to Casthen technologies we don't know the extent of."

That was Threi's style: on the surface he'd opened the Casthen facility and made operations more transparent, but the security was tighter than ever, the secrets more secreted away.

"Years might've passed," Caiden said, "but I know the rhythms of the Casthen Harvest." His body remembered the site of each attack, every corridor where he'd had to keep glancing over his shoulder. This was the last place he'd ever wanted to return to. "It really might be faster if I do this—"

"Alone? Nope. Come on." En slapped his back as she swept out the door toward the *Wintra*'s side hatch.

"Stay, little boy, and listen to Ksiñe," Caiden commanded C before joining En at the aperture. To her he thought aloud, "If we don't make it to the viewing platform before Abriss, we gauge the situation: how many Proxies, how much of the Harvest is tied into her gravitas."

"You've gotten more calculative," En said cheerily.

"It's how I'm still alive." Caiden took the first step off the ship. His boot pressed on Casthen ground, and just like that the timer was going, his every move tracked. "Threi never did catch me, in the end."

A sudden pressure tugged his body. Bands of solid wind wrapped around him—he recognized this from the plateau after the crash.

"A-Azura?"

Mass pinched his legs and hips as he carefully pivoted to face the *Wintra*, his mouth hanging open. Even without wearing a neural crown, he sensed Azura slither from the warship the same way she'd infiltrated it. Energy shifted inside. Faint hums fell out of chords and died away. Metal popped and strange sounds gushed inside the hull as the components that Azura had grown or changed reverted back to their original design in her absence.

Taitn stumbled out of the ship. He wore a neural halo and was able to feel—"Azura's leaving. Is she—"

Caiden's awed expression must've shut him up. Azura flowed out of the ship and into the air—or space itself—around Caiden. He swore the tips of his hair lifted. His breathing felt buoyant. There was a catch of emotion in his voice as he said, "I guess Azura is coming too."

Space seemed to ruffle its feathers around him, getting cozy. When he stood still, he sensed nothing, but as soon as he moved, the pressures bunched around him again, as warm and twitchy as the air before a storm.

Taitn's eyes were bugged wide. "Is she *attached* to you? Or sentient and making choices?"

"W-we'll see, I guess."

En tsked. "We don't have time to gawk. Let's move feet."

A patrol bobbed around the concourse, about to swing in their direction.

Caiden saluted to Taitn before catching up with En striding across the busy dock. A ruddy twilight seeped through the open ceiling, and various ships streamed in from a cloudless atmosphere. Smaller bubble universes blistered around platforms labeled to describe what xenids that universe was hospitable to. The Casthen had courtesy now.

Caiden wrinkled his nose at a rainy, metallic fragrance that he remembered, not fondly. The walls of the gigantic space were a dark-gray metal in familiar styling, same as his childhood world. These spaces were branded into him.

I was born here.

The thought intruded.

Somewhere here my "birthing pod" was housed and my "little egg hatched." Threi's phrasing—even worse, he could visualize it as something literal.

Caiden and En blended in as a Casthen researcher and a Cartographer Domineer. They threaded through the crowds to a wall terminal beside a facility door.

En raised a hand to the interface. Her eyes flicked rapidly, and she blinked often, the retinal tech helping her see the back end of the admittance protocols.

Caiden propped a forearm on the wall and caught a hazy reflection: smoky pigment swooped over his eyelids and temples, meeting across the bridge of his nose. En had done something to make his cheekbones sharper. Caiden snorted and went back to surveying the room in his peripheral vision.

"En."

She shushed him. Her fingers whisked through commands, but the admittance markers were still negative.

Caiden swore as he spotted four Casthen approaching for their turn at the terminal. "Hurry."

"Not helping."

"Then let me help." He pivoted and bumped her arm out of the way, plunging his fingers into the milky, layered holosplay to start diving through code.

Within a heartbeat, before he'd input anything, the system sparked with positive admission markers all over. Cleared for entry, at the highest level. The door's locks liquefied inside the wall.

Caiden stalled in shock. He hadn't even touched the code.

En gaped, staring at whatever her retinal mods let her see in the deeper bio-code.

They both dithered in front of the terminal, which happily displayed "move along" affirmations, and the Casthen group behind them barked, "You done?"

Caiden nodded stiffly and herded En through the door. She hissed at him, "When did you get miraculous fingers?"

"I didn't." He swept into the lead, past facility guests and staff.

Bumps prickled his skin at the thought that the Harvest might still recognize his genetics, recognize its Enforcer coming home.

He stopped himself at the first tiny holosplay that wanted access codes for a warehouse of sensitive goods. Not where they needed to go, but he needed to test. He raised his hand and gathered his intention, dipping one fingertip into the holosplay data.

It blipped merrily: GRANTED.

The door locks disengaged.

This time, Caiden had felt it: the incongruous *action* coupled to his will, and a ruffle in the feathers of space.

"It's Azura," he whispered, and stood stricken before remembering he was in a public hall and his movements were being tracked. He marched into the warehouse and skirted along a wall, pausing to feign business with the shelves.

En kept stride. "You mean she can infiltrate more than ships?" She blew out a breath that ended in a whistle. "Well. That makes this easier. Can you control it?"

"Not sure." Caiden exited into familiar avenues, with nostalgic scents and sights, and his stomach curled the lingering shock into knots. "Do you think...we could erase our foot tracking too?"

"You tell me, gallant."

Azura had the power to manipulate space, to generate a bubble of unique physical laws. She could infiltrate large-scale neuromachinery in starships. She could—apparently—invade the digital systems of a facility in a localized area. It wasn't a leap to think she might be able to erase his footsteps from the ground.

He carried on toward their target while Azura's spirit raced alongside, the facility as her vessel. He began to recognize her presence in shifts of light, sounds in the wall, blinks on terminals. It felt as if he walked atop a sea while a massive creature swam just beneath, barely rippling the surface tension.

Even if Azura wasn't the manifestation of his will, if she was sentient to whatever degree, she was listening to him enough that he felt they could do the impossible together.

With new vigor, he strode through the Casthen Harvest like he owned the place—not like he'd been designed and incubated here, not like he'd returned to murder the Casthen Prime, and not like he remembered every trauma this place had branded into him.

En huffed loudly. "You two are frightening. Nophek also. Never imagined this from you when we found you in the desert."

"Neither did I."

"Although you really were prepared to knife up old Laythan." En snorted a laugh.

They entered a vast atrium open to the twilight through a domed ceiling. Bubble universes hung inside, from two to five meters in diameter, while Cartographer horticulturists puttered between them. They sowed seeds in frozen vapor matrices, where the seedlings germinated in happy physics. These were plucked and planted in a fountain in the center of the room. Little fishes pruned rapid-growing roots. The hard-skinned fruits were picked and tossed into a tiny bluish universe, where rogue physics split them inside out, baring juicy purple innards that attendants scraped into centrifuges.

"Lifesaving medicine, that," En said. "Used to only be able to extract it with mandible acid from tricten, till they went extinct. Then the Casthen revived them too."

"There may be good people here, but you won't convince me that Threi is one of them."

"Who do you think developed this operation? Who thought of trans-universal serotiny in the first place?"

"Through here." Caiden veered on a less-traveled route to an outdoor area.

En needled, "He has a sharp mind—should, after accelerating as many years as you say he did—and he's funneled his boredom into solving problems."

They stepped into a universe that domed out of the planet, brushstroke sunset orange. Bumps prickled across Caiden's skin on the other side. Some of the Casthen staff morphed completely as they crossed over. A Maltaean xenid cruised through the rind on spidery legs, but their body broke up on the other side into a swarm of sticklike creatures bristling in a cloud. A good-natured pallyin quadruped howled with laughter as they passed through and all the fur on their body prickled with static charge.

"How about this." En gestured at a building labeled ASSISTIVE SERVICES. Through the glass front of it, Caiden spotted temporids fitted with time-riveting gear and mauya trying out levitation prosthetics. "A lotta technology and sciences developed to allow more species to participate safely in the multiverse. The Cartographers—"

"I've heard about it." Caiden talked over her.

"—which facilitated about a thirty percent increase in passager diversity. The Casthen're also encouraging economic niche matchmaking, pairing species with a trade that they naturally—"

"I said I've heard it. I've been on the move, not shoving my head in a hole." He flicked his hand through a gate protocol and watched it chime approval as Azura rushed through the floor.

"You've heard but you haven't listened. You still hate this place and everything the Casthen represent. All I'm saying is, look around and you might not see the old Harvest—you might see the garden that Threi's made of it."

Rust crackled off an old anger in Caiden. He picked up his pace and realized he was grinding his teeth. En was right.

She fell silent for a while.

The viewing platform of Threi's universe prison was in the Enforcers' sector. Heavy security clotted around the sector's entrance. Caiden kept up his pace, raked the checkpoint holosplay with his fingers on the way by—GRANTED—and said through gritted teeth, "*Let me through.*"

The Graven enhancement raced through him, tickling his throat and adding extra dimensions to his voice.

The guards folded away, wills bent, bodies bowing.

En clicked her teeth. "Between your Graven genes and Azura, the whole world's lining up. Easy."

"*This* is what Threi's life has been like. With the privilege of living on an easy setting all the time, no wonder he turned into an entitled ass."

En threw her head back in exasperation. "You and him. I don't get what tangled you two this tightly."

"And I don't get why you all seem to *like him* so much now."

They passed squads of Casthen soldiers, all exuding a happy camaraderie that Caiden had never seen when he'd lived here before. Çydanza had ruled by shearing dissension and ambition with a scythe of fear and sorrow, cutting memories into jagged collars.

Seeing Caiden's expression, En added, "Maybe being imprisoned and having his Graven willpower diminished for so long has been good for Threi. Time and lack might've brought him perspective."

Her sentence hung as if there were more to it, like *as much as it's stunted yours.*

Caiden wasn't ready to believe Threi had changed. "We'll be face-to-face soon. Then see."

He would lock down the platform room from the inside and be trapped with the very man he'd been running from for so long. Abriss would have no influence and would be forced to listen. If he convinced her of Threi's treachery, she could wrest control of the entire Harvest away from him in an instant.

Security protocols increased the farther they went, but Azura opened doors and machine barriers in front of him each time . . . unlocked database access . . . cut alarms . . . erased surveillance. Caiden flushed with warmth at the support. He struggled to criticize it being *easy* as they speed-walked down a long, empty causeway that stretched atop busy open spaces below. Two courts over were Threi's domain and a lift down.

En gave a mock sigh and said, "Well, this is no fun. I was hoping we'd warm our fists up at least."

Caiden said, "I'll show you where to warm up, when this is all over. Plenty of fighting to be found in the—"

Abruptly he halted and En ran into his back. He looked wide-eyed on a sight right beneath them. Sparse crowds clotted up like leaves caught in rapids.

Amidst the disturbance walked the Dynast Prime and seven Proxies.

CHAPTER 25

AURASEVER

Crimes," Caiden swore, "that's all of them."

Abriss Cetre and her entourage of Proxies strode down the avenue beneath the causeway. Leta Nine was there in-Proxy, her real body absent. Viewed from above, the group did seem like something that could take down even Threi Cetre in his own domain. They had a sharp, purposeful energy, with a handful of Casthen officials trailing behind, coiled up in Abriss's gravitas. The crowds flustered around her and a strange, windy sound rose up as they muttered at once.

Caiden spotted the delicate tech webbing her hands and wrists, and a cold dread bloomed through his core. "We need to race," he said, and lunged forward, but En's arm caught him in the chest.

"It's too late."

"If—"

"She's thirty meters from his door, Winn!"

Caiden tore himself free and backed up. He could sprint to the door first, but one shout from Abriss and he'd stop in his tracks. He swore a stream of the worst saisn curses he knew.

"Hey now, save those for when we're really fouled. Let's think."

Caiden thought. "If she'd listen, if we can convince her that Threi not only means harm but has been developing a substance that enhances gravitas—"

"Without proof?" En interjected.

"—and get her to..." Caiden growled more curses before he caught himself. "Talking will go the same way as her audience with Threi and me did before, when she insisted on hearing both sides. She's fair and calculative, not vicious, which is a problem right now."

The door to Threi's universe viewing platform opened. A familiar old dread riled up in Caiden at the sight. He squeezed the causeway railing with white knuckles.

The Dynast disappeared into the room with her phalanx of Graven-immune Proxies.

"They'll be enough. If Threi makes his move, seven of them will be enough. He can't harm her unless he's equal, can't be equal without enhancers. They're too organic and complex to pass through the rind of that world, so he won't have any on hand."

En suggested, "Find his enhancer stash and the Dominant thing and smash it all?"

"I don't know where to start looking. If any vials get to Threi, Abriss will be dead by the time we find the rest."

His pulse hammered him and his mind grasped shreds of logic. The moments counted down to Threi's release and Abriss's death.

"So what's our *imminent* plan?" En asked.

A thought jolted chills through him. "Leta."

"What? You want to rescue her while everything goes to rubbish?"

"No. No, she doesn't want rescuing. But Abriss will listen to one of her Proxies." Caiden forced himself to pivot to En, turning his back on the door. This plan could work. "Her real body wasn't with the group. They must've left her on the *Sessrun*. We find her, I tell her about the threat and have her relay it in-Proxy to Abriss. At best, we'll stop Abriss from rupturing his universe at all, and at worst, she'll be suspicious of Threi and able to control him before he gets out of hand. That will buy us time to get to the Dominant first and see what it is and where we stand."

Leta would help if she understood Abriss was in danger. If she didn't, Caiden could guarantee her help with a Graven order. Nothing repulsed him more than the thought of inflicting that on her, but this was the only safe way to influence events: indirectly.

En said, "Abriss or Threi could bring the whole Harvest on our heads the moment we trigger an alarm or snag anyone's interest."

Caiden mashed a hand across his brow before remembering the concealer. He rubbed the tackiness off on his trousers. "Yeah. They can. You start figuring out where Leta's body is held and plan a way there. I'll figure out what to say to convince her in the shortest time possible."

And use her like a doll, like a weapon, like Abriss has all these years.

There was no way to convince himself that was all right, but he saw no other choice.

─────────

While the megastructure of the Casthen Harvest wasn't anything like Solthar, the energy inside was much the same as the Dynast: intrepid thinkers discussed theory in huddled groups while scientists buzzed between rooms and universes, their thoughts and fingers playing with the laws of physics itself. Excitement hummed thickly and felt a bit like home.

Leta's Proxy senses—not well calibrated for this Casthen universe— didn't pick up as much of the slumbering pulse of the Dominant...thing... deep inside the planet. It disappeared under the rush of the community's energy.

Abriss had taken her time, asked the Casthen staff about it, and poked into databases. They weren't able to lie to her. Threi really had hidden both knowledge of and access to the Dominant so securely, only he was the path to it.

Their Casthen escort filed them into a room cramped with machines and displays, then down steps to a large platform hugging the edge of a bubble universe: the world where Caiden had trapped a man and then flown off with the key.

The entire universe and viewing space were encapsulated by a dome ceiling. The only light emanated off the rind itself. Opalescent cerulean and pink arced across the air. From the rind's curvature, Leta guessed the universe was a kilometer or two in circumference: a small place to be imprisoned alone for a decade. Inside lay pallid sand and occasional pools of liquid. No structures or furnishings except for several desks of a glossy white material, which shot out of the ground and projected holosplays. So—he got to watch the outside world happen without him, to make choices and commands but never feel their effects.

Abriss's Casthen guide jogged aside toward an array of control devices linked to a portal frame built into the rind.

Abriss stood in front of it, aglow, while the Proxies formed a crescent behind her at the back of the platform. The embroidered stars in her celestial dress glittered, and her galaxies of freckles seemed starker. She'd let her hair down in waves that looked honeyed in the light, and her liquid eyes turned amber. To Leta, she resembled the younger woman in the memories she'd glimpsed, bright with anticipation.

Abriss clasped her hands over her breastbone. No one but the Proxies realized the power she held in those filigree gloves of the Aurasever, able to wreck this universe with a touch.

The rind's milkiness started to resolve within the frame. Threi Cetre's dark silhouette grew sharp-edged as he neared the rind's illumination. The sight transported Leta ten years into the past, when he'd treaded into the Casthen transport box and crouched before her. He had been her savior.

The light revealed him in layers. Pigment-drained skin was thick with even whiter freckles. No one would mark him as one of the Dynast family until they were close enough to see and too close to maintain a will of their own.

His smile bloomed, slow and mesmerizing. Malnutrition from a forced mono diet had planed his handsome face, making a ridge of his cheekbones, while the years lacerated wrinkles around his ice-blue eyes. Long, dark hair swept to one side and over his shoulder, and a short beard scragged off his jaw. His soft black shirt was worn down so much by time it was a film of shadow clinging to his athletic frame as he sauntered up and stood glazed by the pink iridescence of the rind.

Even in-Proxy, Leta couldn't help being as mystified as she'd been that day as a girl.

Abriss stepped forward to mirror him, highlighting the family resemblance. An almost imperceptible quivering of her shoulders made the stars on her clothing shimmer. "Hello, brother."

"Sister." Razor edges on these sibling terms they used with each other.

Leta wondered when it had started. Threi said, "I never dreamed you'd really come to see me."

Oh stars, his voice. Even siphoned through the rind and its amplifying machines, his voice was silken and lyrically measured, with a deep, rich purr beneath it. More memories rushed back to Leta of that Graven timbre: *How did you survive, little thing?*

Abriss looked pensive. "Your prison appears a deal more spacious than the chamber you stuffed me in."

Threi winced. "I have apologized for that."

Leta struggled to read him. Either his microexpressions and energy states were expertly controlled, or the universe rind interfered with all her senses. Or both.

The other Proxies looked uneasy too. Not least because the Casthen soldiers prickled with nervousness behind them on the steps, the only exit. It was a Graven-induced nervousness for sure, but it felt different from what Leta was used to sensing from the Dynast citizens. Was that because the Casthen were mixes and xenids?

Sisorro Seven looked intrigued, head cocked to one side and a grin stretching their face. Tayen Five quietly rapped her thumb against her armored thigh.

Abriss ignored her smiling brother to look over the turbulent, luminous rind. It would destroy most matter that touched it, they'd been warned multiple times. Ironic that Abriss's own touch could destroy *it*, but her hands were still clasped together. The coppery bands of the Aurasever glistened, so tight they dimpled her skin. Threi hadn't so much as glanced at his sister's pretty gloves.

When Abriss returned her gaze to Threi's, a tiny, ragged sigh escaped her. "Our mutual gravitas is quite lessened by this particular rind."

"Ah, was that your whole reason for coming? You crave opposition, however small. That's why you like me."

"I don't like you at all," Abriss replied, and though her tone was flat, Leta thought back to the memories she'd glimpsed. Those two young heirs, alone, with no one genuine left in their world except each other.

"Did you ever?" he asked. "You don't like me. You *love* me because we're family. Ten years apart is long enough to have forgotten what a somewhat-equal felt like. Let me out and we'll see."

Abriss clenched her hands, crystalline pieces glistering. "Is that taunt or bait?"

He grinned.

In Leta's years as Abriss's bodyguard, she'd never once witnessed opposition. Threi's playful arrogance disguised the power gap, and until the rind was down, she wouldn't get a sense of whether he was a threat or not.

"You claimed to have a way to release me without the *Azura*. Show me. I know you're itching to order me to kneel faithfully again."

"Did it needle you that much last time?"

He shrugged. The handsome smile was matched by an intelligent sparkle in his eyes, and Leta hated how hard it was to dislike. "You'll find I'm more mature now. I would kneel willingly...but I would much rather stand at your side." On this last line his speech crept into a new language, an archaic Dynast tongue of raveled melodies. Leta's brain's translation came as a lagged echo.

Abriss lowered her hands to her sides, and all the Proxies fidgeted, knowing the power her web-wrapped fingers held. Threi noticed at last. Lines crinkled around his eyes.

Matching his language, she said, "One thing I was never able to figure out...Did you murder our father because he robbed you of the succession you craved, or did you murder Veren because he was the last person alive able to love me for me, being more Graven than I?"

"Ah, this is a test."

"It's a question," Abriss said.

"And I taught you that all questions are tests. You think I killed him to rob you of love forever. Why do you care about a measure like *genuine*, creature who can have anything she desires? I really never understood."

"Because you've never felt the difference." The brambles of her language grew thorns. "You don't like me, but what I need to know is if you hate me. Enough to chew hot coals again to dull your tongue? To drink the smoke, burn your sinuses raw? Would you cut up your own eyes again to rob yourself of the sight of me and gain a sliver of resistance? It did work well enough to resist Veren."

Leta jerked at that, recalling the woman's memories. Threi's injuries. Her hands crept closer to her weapons as the space between Threi and Abriss narrowed, the energy intensified, and their language danced away from their meaning. Isme and Sisorro likewise had blades and glaves at the ready.

Abriss squeezed her hands into fists, then opened them. The Aurasever was too tight to make a sound, but the Proxies noticed.

Threi gave a courteous bow. "I don't hate you. I might even grow to like you. But we'll never know until you pop this bubble, weigh our gravitas, and get the reassurance you need."

"And—"

"And then a trade: knowledge of and access to the Graven Dominant for what you've learned and made of the *Azura*. We work together. So let me free?" Threi took the last step dangerously close to the rind and gave Abriss a look that poured out his heart and almost melted even Leta's knees, paired with the silk of his voice. "Unless you're lying about having the means—"

Abriss laughed. "Maybe I just enjoy seeing you helpless."

Threi smiled and dragged his hand up through his hair, where it stuck in tangles. "Your ragged, helpless brother is at your mercy, for your amusement." His gaze flicked across the Proxies. "You surely can't be worried about me with this many Graven-immune soldiers behind you."

"I have never been worried about you. Step back."

He cocked his head at her, brows drawn together. Then he stepped backward several meters and gave another dramatic bow.

The future pivoted on this moment. Leta widened her stance, ready for anything, but *hoping* these two powerful creatures would finally spiral together, joining forces that unified the multiverse.

The fine netting of the Aurasever reflected swirls of pearlescent color as Abriss raised her hands. Threi startled as she settled her palms harmlessly against the bright surface tension of the rind, which dimpled into throes of color at her touch.

She closed her eyes. Expanded her will.

The universe of Threi's prison shattered.

Radiance sawed through the membrane from her fingertips outward.

Space shredded into scarlet fire while searing beads sputtered backward in a wave as the bubble popped.

The pressure dropped everyone except Abriss to their knees. The interior of Threi's universe was devoured by new physics. Pools of water roared and boiled into mist. The sand melted into briars of glass that then whipped up and levitated. Threi, in the midst of it, covered his face with his arms. The ground scabbed indigo and pitched him stumbling as soil was heaved up by masses of fast-growing lichen. In moments it laced across the ground and flowered vigorously, fresh as snow.

Thunder settled. The transformations tuned into an abruptly peaceful environment. Chemical luminescence flooded the space. Lightflies hatched and took flight, reflecting across the sand-born glass still levitating overhead. The holosplays had winked out and electricity shorted across the consoles.

Threi uncurled and gaped at the sight.

Leta craned her neck to take in the vitreous aurorae, the vaporized pools, and new plants. She imagined even larger worlds, with even more variety, completely transmogrified in a snap.

Abriss huffed an elated breath and looked over Threi, who stood a meter away with no rind separating them anymore. Fresh magnetism crackled between. She whispered, "*Now* it feels real."

An inner battle played out on Threi's stunned face.

Leta didn't loosen her grip on her glave hilt. Neither did the other Proxies. Dejin surveyed a new team of Casthen that crept in to inspect the space and harvest data from the busted consoles.

"Bad?" Aohm whispered.

"Trust," Isme replied.

"I admit," Abriss said to Threi, "there was a chance the rind's flux might've killed you as it swept past. I knew you'd tell me to do it anyway."

"Correct." Threi marveled at where the walls of his prison had been. Voice husky with emotion, he drawled, "After all this time..."

Abriss laughed. She swiped lightflies away from her face, but they caught in her loose hair, pulsing like stars.

Threi took a hesitant step closer, crushing bright ruffles of lichen beneath his feet. His gaze riveted on the Aurasever lacing her hands. "What have you done?"

Abriss closed the space between them to smash her startled brother in an embrace.

He raised his hands, quaking, then something rough washed out of his face. He shut his eyes and closed his arms around her fiercely.

Gravitas.

Leta was almost jealous. At that proximity, Threi's senses would be overwhelmed by Abriss's warmth and scent, the sight and feel, the energy of her spirit. No one alive could resist loving her so close.

Leta released her weapon's grip. Dian Six grunted in relief.

"She has control," Leta whispered.

Tayen's tapping rhythm didn't ease. "Don't interrupt. We'll miss sssssssigns."

Leta didn't read any resistance in Threi's face. He had no weapon, was in no rush, and seemed disarmed by emotion. The moment appeared crafted from one of Abriss's storybooks, with the soft glow surrounding them. This wasn't Unity, where reality fit her whims, but it was hard to believe Abriss hadn't manifested this exact scene.

Threi laid a brotherly kiss on the top of Abriss's head, then pulled away and held her shoulders. "You saved me."

Even as Leta melted at those words, her trance ebbed and the majesty of the scene cleared away. More useful senses flooded her: a burnt yet damp scent, a stiffness in Threi's fingers dimpling the fabric of the Prime's coat, and the way his spine curved like a rearing snake. Was this normal resistance or misread emotion—how could she notice if he was pretending?

Sisorro Seven drew their glaive first, pulling the slim rail from against their calf with an audible *snick!* The sound whipped Leta, who reflexively flicked out the ribbon blade from against her spine. Dejin and Tayen followed, and in a rush the whole room polarized, Casthen took defensive postures and Proxies stood on edge.

Threi retreated from the embrace and raised his hands, placating.

Abriss swirled around. "Ah, stand down, my Graves. He wouldn't."

Unconvinced, the Proxies didn't shift. Abriss looked between them before shaking her head. She leaned toward Threi to demonstrate.

"*Step back*," she said in a light-but-firm Graven voice. It might as well have been a thunderclap.

Flinching hard, Threi stepped backward.

It hadn't been full volume. She hadn't even touched him.

He tilted his chin down, face flooded by shadows. "Has that demonstration soothed your suspicions, darling sister?"

"Yes. See?" she said to the group, voice trembling.

The spell between her and Threi broke. Leta watched it break in Abriss's eyes and stiffen the soft, human bearing she'd had a moment ago. She fixed a regal posture back into her spine. Their tenderness was a lie. They weren't truly equals, and Abriss couldn't pretend otherwise.

Don't let it stop your alliance, Prime. Leta re-sheathed her weapon first.

Abriss and Threi weren't equals, but it was the closest Abriss would get.

The woman composed herself and gave her brother a flat, apologetic smile. Vulnerability glimmered in Threi's wintry eyes as he rushed on to business, waving in a Casthen team and barking orders: reboot the consoles that had been compromised in the physics change, salvage the data, have the monitoring teams report if there was any backlash elsewhere when the universe popped.

Sisorro circled among them, sussing out prey. They wanted a game. The colorful drapery they wore swished around their legs and churned up light-flies from the flowers. Five of the other Proxies took up a relaxed cage formation around Abriss.

An aide scurried over to Threi. She passed off a bundle of supplies that looked to be new clothing, a flamecomb, a pack of water, and a cluster of medicines. The Casthen Prime accepted it with obvious relief and scratched his beard as he chose a smile from his arsenal. "Recovery will take time," he explained. "My gut's been destroyed for years, and I've missed luxuries like baths and feasts, and I've seen the same damn sight for years. But to void with it—the beard needs to go first."

CHAPTER 26

US

Both Taitn's ship and Laythan's freighter, the *Second Wind*, had to leave the docking concourse and station in orbit. Caiden told himself they were safe and standing by.

The Harvest's intelligence network didn't have anything to report about Threi or his universe—Caiden was almost sure that Abriss had ordered the entire area to either vacate or keep quiet and give her a private audience. If that meant she was going slow and being cautious, all the better, but the lack of information felt like it took the floor out from under Caiden's feet.

"Hey." En shouldered him into a hallway alcove and transformed: a clean-lined and scholarly face, muscles deflating and bones shortening. A softer En. "Now you," he said, spritzing something into his hands, then mussing it around in Caiden's hair before making a severe part and raking the locks to one side. "Fetching in blue too."

Caiden wrinkled his nose. "You're having too much fun."

"Always."

"At my expense."

"You're an easy target."

Caiden pushed off the wall and shook the tension out of his arms. "This is serious. One chance, no traces."

"You're too serious."

They both donned sober expressions and fake conversation as they walked briskly through a glass-roofed atrium full of soldiers and Enforcers.

Rough-looking chketin guards stood on either side of the flagship docking pad's massive doors. In the center hovered a luminous biosecurity holosplay.

En's plan involved knocking out an Enforcer who had clearance. He nudged an elbow in Caiden's side to turn him away from the door, but Caiden was feeling impatient and "less serious."

He gathered up his Graven energy and marched right up without a glance at the chketin guards. *Be with me, Azura.*

Caiden plunged his hand into the biosecurity glyph, which threaded around his fingers, taking his print and pulse. Pressure burgeoned in the metal beneath his feet and a subtle bass vibration arced up into the door. Azura's strange wind tickled around his neck.

The seal twinkled away with the word GRANTED.

A thrill surged up him. *Oh, you're fantastic.*

Emboldened, he gestured En to follow and strode in as the huge doors slid apart.

Occupying the entire hangar stood the *Sessrun*. Its hollow cylindrical middle was sharp with fluting that looked like teeth from the back.

Smaller vessels parked nearby. Scores of soldiers streamed under commanders' watchful eyes.

"With purpose," Caiden said, fitting that warning into his fake conversation with En while carrying on like they had a mission. Caiden faked a moral disagreement to keep En from getting bored and picked a straight route that was as far from anyone as possible.

With glances and murmurs brewing up behind them, they made it to the *Sessrun*'s hatch.

It opened instantly. Knots unwound in Caiden's shoulders. Azura surged past him. Her invisible force soaked into the vessel's thick construct, eighty meters longer than the *Wintra* and two decks thicker. She pulsed through the meat of it before regathering in the deck ceiling over Caiden's head. Palpable, like too much electric charge.

En patted a wall. "Lots of jobs I would've liked having her along for."

"Me too." Caiden led the way toward the bridge at a strange pace between sneaking and rushing. Peak attention. Instinct primed.

Not a sound anywhere. Empty halls.

A sinking feeling settled in his gut as he found the bridge empty. He whooshed over to the consoles to bring up thermal and biodata signatures. A beat before he got there, Azura was ahead of him: the whole room exploded with status holosplays. It took his eyes a moment to parse it out.

"The ship's empty. You said she was here!"

En folded his arms. "No record of her carried out. Abriss's doing?"

"But it *was* her body that her Proxy carried to the flagship, on Solthar?"

"Absolutely."

"Shit. Are we too late?"

He threw his head back and cradled his neck in both hands as he turned in circles, thinking, then threw his plea to the ether. "Azura, if you can understand me or anything as specific as this: I need you to help me find Leta."

In the span of one vigorous arcminute, Threi had shaved his face clean with the flamecomb and hacked off his long hair into short, messy snarls that his fingers could run through without snagging.

Leta watched him while the other Proxies surveyed the staff's activities.

Threi guzzled water and nutrients and protein bombs that must have been better than anything the Casthen had designed to pass through the rind before. Beyond all that, the mere fact of being released seemed to inject him with vitality, transforming gauntness into intimidating poise. Time had cut away everything extraneous from his body, leaving keen musculature and a hunger for more than food.

Perhaps it was an effect of the universe shift: as sand had become glass and soil became lichen, Threi became a bright, upright creature.

He wet his hands and tousled his fresh-cut hair again, then roared with elation and laughed as if his voice had been freed too. "I knew the *Azura* was special, but this is beyond what I'd imagined."

Abriss chuckled. "You're thinking, *My sister's foolish research is finally interesting.*"

"Your words." He smiled. "I would never call any research foolish."

His aides furnished him with a regal, calf-length Casthen coat. Its fitted cut combined Casthen black and red with Cartographer cloud-gray and purple.

Put together and energized, he turned to face Abriss.

Now they looked like two Primes.

Tayen's knuckles drummed her shell to the rhythm of anxiety. Sisorro hadn't put away their weapon, still seeing two sides of a scale that might yet tip.

Threi had been keeping careful watch on all the Proxies and caught Leta's stare for a flicker of a moment. His brilliant smile was even in his eyes. Universe veil removed, he looked more like the person Leta remembered striding in from the light as she huddled in darkness and despair. Radiance clinging to his back. Something had imprinted on her in that moment. Honestly, how could it not?

She was very aware of the girlishness of her reactions, the irrationality of childhood patterns. She wouldn't let one striking memory of Threi color her perception of him, but at the same time she didn't detect a splinter of malice. Just that playful arrogance she found disgustingly charming and hard to read.

Maybe charm enough to make Abriss forget the disappointment that they weren't Graven equals. Enough to bring down her political armor, bare the humanness of her, make her playful in return. Leta yearned to see more of *that* Abriss Cetre.

Tayen Five asked low, "What do you see?"

"Nothing," Leta admitted, relieved. "Just powerful siblings who haven't seen each other in a decade. Their reconnection won't be perfect at first. Give him a chance."

Tayen's black facade had no expression, but her shoulders tightened and the lightseep blade creaked in her grasp.

Isme Two said, "The Prime herself is our measure. Watch *her*. She knows him best."

Dejin Eight huffed. "He is no threat. Resistant enough for snark, but look: he is as enchanted as any."

Threi extended both hands, palms up, to Abriss, inviting hers.

She considered him for a moment, then obliged, placing her palms atop his. The light caught on crystalline threads and ruffled into petals of distortion. She said, "Aurasever, I named it."

He raised an eyebrow at that.

Abriss seemed to blush. Or wince? Leta couldn't interpret these signs anymore, wasn't familiar with them.

Threi's eyes crinkled with a smile, but his hands trembled and he couldn't hide it. Was he trying to? Maybe Isme was right—Leta didn't know the man enough to pick out incongruities. The whole sight made her realize how infrequently she'd seen Abriss let anyone touch her—for their sakes, most likely, so her gravitas wouldn't rob them of all autonomy. Maybe the rareness of touch could bring the spell back again.

"It wasn't the vessel that was special." Excitement rushed Abriss's words. "It was the chrysalis melded into it. I merely copied the enharmonic strain's energy and reverse engineered a method of discharging it. The power to disrupt and reorganize space."

Was it *her* hands quivering?

She actually looked shy. All the delight she'd never been able to fully share was more equally shared with Threi, but now that she had him, she seemed cautious. The spell of equals had broken once. It could break again.

Threi squeezed her freckled fingers and turned them over, examining the Aurasever across her palms.

Nervous waves emanated off him. Leta examined the pitch of his shoulders, rising like hackles, his neck curving forward again. Being around a superior was a rare experience for him too.

Dejin fidgeted. Aohm, towering behind Abriss a couple paces away, folded their huge arms and drew Threi's glance for a moment.

Dian leaned to mutter to Isme, "Have you ever seen her happy like this?"

"Yes," Isme replied, and both Five and Six looked over at him too. He nodded at Leta, who understood. "I have seen many of the Prime's memories. When she's tired, she goes back to him in her mind."

"I saw one!" Sisorro chimed, trying to rein their volume. "Boring memory. They just talked, like this."

"Something happened when they were young that pushed Abriss toward her current ideals. Not one event but a chain of them, from the first death in their family. Threi's played some part in it, which I haven't fully seen, but this knot between them needs undoing before they'll agree to the research exchange. Let them sort it out with words."

Leta recalled the young woman watching her brother's blindfolded face intently, hoping he would appreciate her concern. He was the one person who could be most genuine with her, whose esteem she'd truly cared about.

Abriss blinked slowly, aligning her thoughts in whatever special way activated the Aurasever. She closed her hands into fists, then opened them. The space around her palms crimped in lacy lines, refracting the world into liquid condensations, a hint of rindlike iridescence.

Leta would never forget wielding those same powers herself, albeit briefly. The *feel* of the world yielding to her intention.

Threi's eyes widened, and a lump bobbed in his throat. "What will you do with it?"

Abriss's knowing smile sent a visible shudder through him. She let one heartbeat stretch to two without answering, and it was clear they both knew what she would do with the Aurasever.

Then she laughed at his deepening frown. "Oh, it's not as dire as you're imagining. In truth, my technology still needs many more tests and iterations. I thought you'd be pleased to think I rushed here to let you out as soon as I had the means. Really, I admit to wanting your expertise about the nature of different rinds. And..." Her voice softened. "I had hoped it wouldn't be what *I* will do with this, but what *we* will do."

That word. That shard of a sound that Leta had seen tumbling around in Abriss's heart for as long as she'd known the woman. It was a word that broke hearts, always and forever.

Abriss finished, "I'm not the last of the Dynast family, I acknowledge that. You're still alive. Against all odds, perhaps."

Threi gazed at her hands, distracted, thoughts working on something. Then he said, "The trinity."

"Complete. Once you hold up your end of our bargain."

"Nothing good comes from rushing."

"So something *good* came from your time confined?"

"A few things. I recognized why I was cruel to you in the past." He squeezed her hands before letting them drop. "And my time confined is exactly why you'll have to wait for the third piece of your trinity. Allow a starving man to find some food, some drink, a scour, steam soak, sex, some fresh damned air, and to see sights that aren't through a holosplay." Threi rolled his shoulders as he started toward the exit.

Abriss followed and said, "I'm afraid I'm in a hurry. Enjoy yourself later. You can get air and see sights as we talk."

"Happy to see you didn't lose your love of talking," Threi teased. He snapped his fingers at an aide, who scurried over to hand him more water and vials of liquid nutrients. He downed one, a greenish fluid, his face scrunching against a foul taste.

Abriss did love talking. Leta had always tried to listen but never deployed engaging responses fast enough, so Abriss would curb herself and fall inward. Threi, surely, could keep up. Even rivalrous energy had sizzle. It gave Leta a strange joy to think Abriss finally had a better match—not just Gravely, but politically and intellectually. It lifted visible burdens.

More practically, these Primes could do amazing things. Reshape the exchange system of cultures, combine nonstandardized communication methods across the multiverse, create better pathways between ecology and economy.

Isme nudged her with an elbow. "Nice to see."

He'd been thinking the same thing. "Finally."

Dian made a strange sound, half intrigue but not of a sort Leta liked. His brows pulled into a V-shape of wrinkles that reminded her of an animal before it bit.

Threi was saying to his aide, "Prioritize restoring communication networks from the wrecked consoles. The two-way vocal lines specifically. You had the demonstration holosplays loaded on the higher deck?"

At their nod, he sent them on their way, then sucked in a dramatic breath, tasting the outside air. He led the way out of the viewing room.

The Proxies fell back to split duties. Six and Seven would watch the Casthen staff. Five would monitor the wider Harvest activity. One and Eight would guard Abriss. Two would tune his senses to the luminiferity. Leta volunteered to watch Threi.

Dian, on his way past, sniped Leta with an accusatory, "Don't fall for him too."

Leta scowled. "Compelling, that's all."

"I was watching your face glow."

"Our faces don't have that kind of function."

Threi doled out more orders to Casthen eager for his input, and he grew more animated as he saw the expanded effect of his gravitas. Maybe it felt as good as a muscle stretch or joint pop, after being Gravenly cramped for so long. A fleeting famished look he gave some of his attendants would have made Leta blush if her Proxy had been able.

Dian snorted at her and she scowled at him again.

Threi had an infectious charisma that was so much different from Abriss. Leta realized just how docile Abriss was with her gravitas: she handled others like they were made of glass, while Threi looked like he danced with a reckless energy, picking up and dropping partners on a whim.

What occupied Leta's mind more was how both Caiden and Threi tangled together and how she had fallen into it. Caiden, lost on RM28. Threi, flying there to find him but instead finding Leta. Then handing her over to his sister. Years later, Threi suggested Leta as bait. Caiden flew to Solthar to find her and—*dies, dies . . . he's dead.*

She swallowed and blinked hard to focus on Threi.

Events had thrust her back into his proximity. How many perfect events had come together, lives strung like ribbons in a corset that was beginning— ever so slowly—to cinch tight? What would it look like, complete?

Everything for a reason.

He led the way up curving steps and said, "The universe implosion had a more destructive effect than a mere physics swap."

"You noticed." Abriss sounded happy. "That extra energy discharge was what shattered the *Azura*'s chrysalis and dismantled the ship."

Threi side-eyed his sister. "You shattered it on purpose," he guessed. "I would be furious, except you did come get me anyway."

Abriss hesitated only enough that the Proxies would notice. She hadn't anticipated the shatter. "You flatter yourself. I came for our exchange."

"This'd be a private discussion between friends, if you'd come for me."

He pivoted to look over the Proxies and continued walking backward up the stairs. His pale gaze lingered on Leta for a beat.

Sisorro Seven sidled over to her. "This hallway is wide," they whispered, lolling their head near her ear, "but it feels like a blade edge."

"It's called banter."

"If they become allies," Seven mused, "will half of us stay here with him? Will he come to Solthar? He seems delightful. Whe—"

"Sis," Leta chided.

They smiled and swayed away.

The flight of stairs ended at a freight lift. Threi's Casthen assistants stayed behind while Abriss with her entourage trundled inside with Threi. Was shedding his protection a conscious gesture? Him paving a bridge over any lingering suspicions of threat?

The freight lift rose to the very roof of the megastructure. Abriss and several Proxies—Leta included—went wide-eyed at the sight.

CHAPTER 27

WE

The lift stopped flush with the rooftop: a flat, empty rectangular deck, half a kilometer long. No walls or ceiling except the pale-peach film of a universe rind encapsulating most of it. A smaller opaque indigo rind attached on one side at an angle, and a little pink sphere was nearly contained all the way by one corner.

Leta gaped at the surrounding vista. Countless universes of all sizes foamed across the surface of the Harvest. The megastructure itself was a complex architecture of deep pits and arching scaffold, looking more like a grown shell than a built structure. Gardens were encapsulated by it or spilled from it, along with rivers and chaliced lakes. A dim bronze twilight bathed it from the horizon.

Far past the atmosphere lay the fractured spacetime planes of the vast lightseep obsidian structure encompassing the little planet and its sun. It spread immeasurable kilometers, strung on crystalline vertices of light that resonated together. Space itself seemed to harden into a labyrinth jewel of light-bending angles.

Threi gulped outside oxygen as he peered up.

Abriss picked at the Aurasever's threads while she also gazed at that Graven sky. "Trapped."

He looked over quizzically.

"When Unity shattered or bubbled off," she elaborated, "these rinds would have split it up like walls, making rooms out of one gigantic space. It trapped these wonderful Graven things inside and changed them."

Leta caught the subtext in Abriss's sideways glance. Both she and Threi knew what it was like to be trapped. He wore a pinched expression that Leta wanted to translate as guilt or regret—at least, it resembled how those emotions had looked on Caiden. Guilt meant redress.

"If this world was returned to Unity," Abriss said, "would this lightseep husk turn back into a city, galaxies wide? A creature that sprouts wings and soars the cosmos? A flowing river of cosmic energy?"

"Ever the romantic idealist, Riss," Threi said. The nickname slipped from him easily, but Abriss missed a step.

She cleared her throat. "If a structure this magnificent can exist out here in these broken worlds, think what it would be if Unity's laws were everywhere again. Grand-scale structures would be revealed and transformed. The Graven's world would surface from hidden dimensions, just like this."

Leta was caught up in Abriss's familiar excitement, her imagination fleshing the massive structure in scales and wings and a ferocious pulse, like something from one of Abriss's storybooks.

Threi strode to the middle of the rectangular deck. "It's not quite the shard field of Solthar, but it'll do."

"Reminds you of home?"

He laughed. "Depends if home is a place you were born or the place you love most."

Abriss glanced back at the Proxies. "Home is where you're most comfortable. Sometimes that's among certain people."

Threi stopped walking. "Then I would say *welcome home*, but you're only here for an exchange."

Time hasn't done these two any favors. He's as defensive as Caiden was, driven by a deeper desire to reconnect. He's just ill equipped to achieve it.

The *hope* in Abriss, by contrast, was so palpable, her wishing to share excitement with someone genuine, unable to abide a forced version. Caiden had also imagined that no feelings or actions created through influence could be real or trusted. What lonely thinking.

This is why that echoed Graven presence within Unity appeals to her, faint as it is. A thousand crimes, Abriss, you don't need abstract inklings—your chance for camaraderie is right here in the flesh!

It was maddening, the two of them so close but playing dance partners with denials. Leta had never understood political creatures. Being only a guardian, she had to stand back and simmer.

Threi spread his arms and snapped fingers on both hands. Transparent holosplays bubbled online all around them, as tall and broad as the side of a building. Light vined across the fields of dimpled air and congealed into scientific archives in countless languages. In subtle gestures Threi navigated the data.

Abriss stood near him, and Leta's mind superimposed the memory of them sitting on the bench, him blindfolded, her hopeful. Leta found it reassuring and rare to see two things: Abriss not flexing her gravitas at all—perhaps careful *not* to—and her composure dropping in genuine ways.

Beside Leta, Isme chuckled silently. He must've thought the same.

Aohm One had stayed by the lift, while white-cloaked Dejin was Abriss's snowy shadow. Tayen fidgeted in place. Dian paced and rapidly read the holosplays. Sisorro was distracted by the view.

Abriss smoothed her hair over one shoulder. "If what I wanted lay in a database, I could have hacked it myself and left you where you were. You haven't yet told me what the Dominant strain is or how Çydanza came upon it."

"Embarrassed to admit," Threi said, "I feared you would back out on our deal and not come if I didn't have enough to offer. I don't actually know how Çydanza acquired the Graven Dominant, and all that's left from her misguided experimentation is a shred of genetic fragments."

Leta straightened. *What I sensed earlier was from mere* fragments?

"Oh, brother," Abriss joked with that barbed term, "you are hopeless without me."

"I would never compare my humble self to the greatest Graven scholar alive."

"Humble?"

He laughed, voice rich yet soft, and Leta hated the way the sound drew her in. "And you already have a plan for the Dominant, I'm sure."

Abriss lit up, and Leta internally cheered for her. Someone was speaking Abriss's language. "The Graves, once trinitied, will have full and easy access to the luminiferity and its accumulation of millennia of collective knowledge. Quantum control of the physical world. Time... We might even control *time*, Threi. I don't want to hoard these gifts. With the outer universes returned to Unity, everyone and everything will at last be true and equal."

A brittle chuckle rattled out of Threi's chest. He had stopped browsing and turned to face her, the luminous data striping half his face and filling one pale iris. "The Dynast litany. You do realize that the Graven lived out here in the multiverse after its creation—or *catastrophe*, sorry. The Casthen and Cartographers have been studying the multiverse for centuries. Signs of the Graven's participation are everywhere. Why, if they despised it and thought it imperfect? Why would they create egresses to travel the multiverse?"

Signs, not proof.

Threi's tone became lively, full of lazy gravitas. "Has nothing about your luminiferity suggested that the Graven might have created the multiverse on purpose in response to the nature of their evolving spiritual intelligence? Your Graves don't feel it harder to enjoy physical being? They don't feel stretched to their limit?"

Every Proxy shifted at that.

"They do," Abriss enunciated carefully, "and that's precisely why I'm here. As complete beings, the Graves will be privy to the dimensions the Graven lived in, and there will be no more debate about what the Graven's intentions or attitudes were regarding the multiverse. Now, you promised—"

"Remind me how many Graves tried to expand themselves to encompass all of Unity, only to shatter? Yet you would make Unity *even vaster*."

"You promised *access* to—"

"Let him speak," Dian Six interrupted. "I want to hear it."

Leta startled. The Graves were Abriss's guardians, not political equals who could interject into this discussion. Their concerns would be aired later in private.

Tayen Five stepped forward too. She tapped her obsidian sword against her greaves. "I wish to hear hea er," Five said, the parasite alive and well in this universe.

Threi surveyed the Proxies. "Have you been feeding them the same drivel?"

"I don't have to tell them anything. They're witnessing luminiferity for themselves. They experience remnants of the Graven, they sense the shape of palaces and creatures ghosted into the world as it used to be. They've tasted what control of this physical dimension is like."

Threi stopped in front of Sisorro Seven but spoke over his shoulder to Abriss, "What if the unpredictable messiness that you've been conditioned to hate about the multiverse is *the entire point*? Limitations give us creativity and room for growth, otherwise everything would be uniform entropy. Existence is a continual movement of creation and destruction: the very two polar points of the Graven trinity you revere. There is no final harmony, no grand unity."

Leta realized she was quaking, and she cued a command that flushed the tension from her body. *What's turned so quickly? The smallest trigger...*

Seven swayed in place, drapery shuffling. "The Graven *made* the multiverse?"

An absurd idea, that they would have willingly generated suffering. But Dian Six was already primed to mistrust Abriss, like a beast with its hackles up. He said, "So the outer universes are not incidentally better, they are *intentional*." His fingertip traced across the sacred geometries painting his skin.

Dejin Eight caught on slower. "Smaller universes constrain information, make it palatable, as Nine said...I can believe the Graven, expansive like us, would have wanted that."

Stars forfend, those were my words when we crossed over out of Unity.

Each universe had felt like stepping into a manageable room, walls visible, contents perceivable, even if other parts of its physics irked her.

Threi bowed gracefully. "So I believe. You've been built to evolve into the Graven, yet you're suffering in a universe as vast as Unity, and I promise you, any more trinity conditioning will only exacerbate that, as will any more expansion of Unity. This is why my sister contained you in Proxies. Wouldn't the ancient Graven have done the same? Except they had the means to contain themselves in *entire universes*."

Threi continued a slow pacing.

Abriss stood still and said calmly, "Why would perfect beings in perfect order ever wish to break their own world and make it less accessible? It holds no reason."

"*Who* said the Graven were perfect, or that perfection is not absolutely boring? Why is universal entropy cited as perfection? There are unlimited ways to grow and engage in life out here. Why couldn't the Graven have meant the expansion of the multiverse to be the true goal? Think how much better you Graves might be in one of these many worlds, able to achieve your potential without constantly struggling to keep your cracks together."

Better. That word snapped Tayen Five to attention. Her sword-tapping tempo increased, sound ratcheting the tension across the deck.

Abriss stepped forward, but Leta cut in first, "However angered by discovering we've been suffering in Unity and function better in other worlds, remember it's only because we're unfinished. Unity *is* perfectly harmonious to the other citizens. There is no safer or better universe. The Dynast means to share that with others. What is malicious about that goal?"

Isme joined her defense. "Unity is harmonious already, while the war and disruption the multiverse causes between cultures and species is well known. None of us can judge Unity against the multiverse *until* we have experienced Unity's full future potential. You wouldn't compare us, incomplete, to fully manifest Graven, no more than you would judge a child against an adult."

Threi ignored them and said to Abriss, "You're coddling them and you're still—like when we were young—bending myth into the justifications you need for a selfish hope that someone can stand you without being forced to."

A cold laugh punched out of Abriss. Leta was jarred at the sound—she'd never heard Abriss angered. It was a nasty lie Threi had slung, and now the armor was back on Abriss, the glow of hope shuttered up. She watched her brother while his footfalls and Tayen's tapping fell out of sync, then she said, thick with force, "*Stop your pacing and face me.*"

Threi halted, tendons and veins betraying his fight against her gravitas. Words mumbled off his lips. An apology?

Abriss reined her tone in. "How is it selfish to wish to unite the world, cure all illness, give individuals the ability to manifest their own desires and co-create reality with others? The proof of this potential is already in Unity.

Did you really find it so boring to live in a realm free of war, disease, and unrest?"

"Isn't it lonely at the top?" He stepped toward her but caught himself midstride as the proximity intensified her effect. Leta could feel the subtle shift in dimensions, the compression of energies flowing around them. Polarity had changed, no longer drawing them together.

Dejin Eight stiffened and angled himself to step between them in one stride, but Abriss had complete control over her brother: it was a courtesy to let him debate this much.

Emotions flurried across Threi's face before he stood his ground. "In a unified world where everyone is equal because everyone's Graven, you won't be alone. You dress your own desolation in nobility. But you don't need to level the playing field to have peers."

Threi braved a step toward her, as if stepping back to the tenderness they'd had moments ago, but his hungry gaze was on the Aurasever.

Abriss strode at him with force, and he stumbled back to keep space between them. She stopped, pained, and said, "It's lonely at the top, when you insist on wallowing at the bottom. If you really can't stand to be around me—"

"We still can't stand *each other*."

The air all but crackled with electricity. Abriss laughed hard once, a hammer force smashing her last hopes. "You forgot, didn't you? I cared. I healed you. I saw you struggling back then and offered to fight with you. I've done nothing but invite you to participate. *You* have always been the one with the cold shoulder. I guess time can't solve jealousy."

Buried deep in their argument was a subtext of war. These were Primes, not just siblings, and Dynast Unity at war against the Casthen–Cartographer multiverse was a vicious shadow cast by all their fiery words.

He shot her a snarl-smile, then whirled back to the Proxies to stir them. "What happens if the barriers the Graven built get removed? Our illustrious Dynast Prime has the technology to do that now. She'll create a singular world, and I guarantee you all will become equal and equally powerful, but have you stopped to think of what that world would actually *feel* like?"

"Just *stop*," Abriss called. Her Graven bluntness shut his mouth. He blinked rapidly as her force impressed. His back curled, hands shoved in his coat pockets. "I said nothing about wrecking the multiverse so callously."

Leta's lungs were hyperventilating to the rhythm of Five's clinking sword. Her awareness folded time back to memories: young Threi telling Abriss, *You need to stop—*

Dian couldn't contain himself any longer. He paced forward and broke the space between the Primes, snarling at Abriss, "It looks easy to be right, when you can stop debate with a single command."

Behind Dian, Tayen said, "Pettishhhhhh."

Sisorro's slender fingers probed their skull through curls. "Is that what she's done to us? We are immune to Graven influence in-Proxy. But our Proxies are driven by hearts Abriss shaped. What shape are we really?"

Stars forfend, how do I stop this? Threi was turning Dian and Tayen's cynical minds, while playful Sisorro leaned toward anything novel. Dejin hated conflict and dithered, while Isme and Aohm would take Leta's side but weren't as aggressive as the others.

"If we aren't here to discuss alliance," Leta began, lacing in that tender word, *we*, "then we should refocus on the exchange, which needs no alliance. Shared knowledge to reach an *informed* conclusion about the multiverse and the Graven."

That solution was so close. They simply had to put the past behind them.

Threi chuckled. "Compromise is only possible between equals."

"Our Prime," Dian agreed, "will get her outcome through gravitas either way, Nine. It's why we've never failed her."

Isme stepped closer, rapping Leta on the shoulder on his way. She followed him to Aohm's side while a web of tension strung tight between the seven Proxies and the two Primes. Even faceless, Dejin's and Aohm's doubt showed in their postures, feet ready to spring. Dian, Tayen, and Sisorro appeared ready to snap. *Three and three.*

Leta included, that was four on Abriss's side. She didn't fault the others' doubt, but she wasn't about to cave to silver words without proof. Life with the Dynast had involved pain, but also care in equal measure, and they were *so close* to true answers about the Graven.

Tayen stopped tapping her sword, removing the metronome of dissension. To Abriss, Tayen said, "I trusted usted ste yyyyou."

"Isme," Leta whispered, tightening her grip on her lash.

"Be sharp," he replied. "We're past words now."

Threi closed his eyes. "Darling Graves, out here in the wilder worlds, you're free to think for yourselves. And sister...if only *you* would listen."

He pulled his hand from a pocket and thumbed the caps off two vials of pearlescent white fluid. In one draught he slammed them both back.

His energy shifted instantly. The magnetism between him and Abriss ratcheted up, thick as cords of gale. Force invaded the mass of him from marrow to sinew, vibrating like a plucked string.

Leta realized first, but too late. Threi was already in motion.

CHAPTER 28

CONVERGENCE

Isolated. Elevator locked flush with the ground. Nowhere to run. No comms. No one to hear a scream.

Threi's whistle cut across the open deck. There were no hatches or walls... but a score of Casthen soldiers spilled from where they'd hidden inside the opaque universe that bifurcated part of the deck. They wore tight strips of something around the middle of their heads over eyes, ears, nose— sensory veils?

Abriss shrieked Threi's name as he lunged at her. Without a flinch, he smashed her in his arms, his bicep curling around her skull, fingers digging into her temple—about to snap her neck.

Leta dashed in. She folded her knuckles in a flat wedge and punched at the artery in his neck. A gurgle exploded out of him and he buckled over. Leta jammed her fingertips into pressure points to loosen his arm and tear him off.

She shoved Abriss toward Dejin, who swept in to catch her, white cloak swirling. He bundled her safely behind him.

"*Stand down*," Abriss called to Threi and the soldiers gathering into range.

The group did hesitate, but the command wafted off Threi, who regained his poise and massaged his throat. His eyes were glassy, the tenderness frozen over. Whatever he'd consumed had made him gravitas-resistant. *How?*

"Graves!" Threi shouted. "Choose! Be free from Dynast subjection and decide your own path. No more promises. Only results."

Even Leta's spirit roused at the implications stitched into those words. She took up a flexible stance, her muscles filling with charge, grip tight on her ribbon blade. *The snake promises there will be no promises.*

Threi thumped his fists against the front of his shoulders, activating hidden webbing inside his Casthen coat. It plumped out, armor hardening. Outer layers firmed around vitals, gloved his hands and neck. Leta wouldn't get a second cheap shot.

Threi called to his soldiers, "Six meters away from her!"

He pulled a cluster of purple seedlings from a pocket and smashed them between his palms. They squished and caught some form of fire, the fluid spreading down his fingers and gauntlets, giving him fists of flame. He cracked his wrists together, then scraped them apart, igniting a line of brilliant heat that hung in the air, sparkling like thermite before it winked out. Casthen toys.

His attempt to reconcile with his sister had felt genuine to Leta, but he'd still planned this option *thoroughly.*

Chaos erupted. Aohm mowed into the Casthen soldiers. Dian and Tayen fought on the Casthen's side. Sisorro—Leta couldn't tell. Isme faced them down, trying reasoning first.

Cursing, Leta left Abriss's protection to Dejin and advanced on Threi.

———

"Guest chambers, twelfth room," the xenid wheezed, sagging in En's vise grip. Bruises blossomed in their face from the "persuasion."

En kissed their cheek. "Isn't cooperation better?"

Caiden yanked En's sleeve and started moving. "We're not here to have fun."

While they sought out Leta's body, Threi could already have been let out, Abriss already dead.

En jogged beside him. "That's your problem. *Fun* is a state of being concurrent with other situati—hey!"

Caiden pulled him from the common spaces to a less-traveled corridor shortcut. Nostalgia bristled up as they ran past Caiden's old room.

En said, "You enjoy how Azura opens doors and manipulates code, but you won't flex your Graven whatever to get information and assistance. What's the difference?"

Caiden whisked around another corner and nearly slammed into a trio of soldiers. Their glaves raised. On instinct, Caiden hammered his attacker's forehead into a rising knee. Blood sprayed from a split tongue. En elbowed another's skull into the metal wall.

The third guard's glave tip sparked.

"*Stop.*" Caiden bludgeoned with his Graven will. The woman hesitated and lowered her weapon. "Just stop."

En bolted past with augmented speed, folded her against him, and held her neck stretched out. "Would you please?"

Scowling, Caiden strode over and plucked a chem pack from a set Ksiñe had given him. He delivered a sedative, having to look away as her expression was overcome with affection at the proximity. The enhancer still fevered through him.

It's not the "enhancer" anymore. It's me. This is me forever.

He straightened and found Leta's numbered door. Pulse throttled his neck, fanning the embers of that Graven fire.

"Time's ticking," En muttered behind him.

"Leta isn't just anyone, to use her like a tool..." *Like Abriss does.*

"If you do have to coerce her to make this happen, she'll forgive you if it saves her beloved Prime's life, eh? Don't you worry. When has your heart led you astray?"

Caiden's jaw snapped tight, and he rounded on En. "Every time! My heart's led me astray every damn time! That's—" The admission caught in his throat. "Why I stopped listening to it."

En was resistant to Graven effect but not immune, and Caiden saw how his outburst had singed, much more than it would have before the enhancement.

He turned back to the door, scrubbing his bloody knuckles on his Casthen coat. The gap of years compressed again, like he'd never left this place. Like he'd never peeled out of his Casthen skin and the blood hadn't ever stopped flowing.

Very gingerly, En said, "Give your heart a chance to prove you wrong."

"It's had too many chances."

Caiden lifted a hand for the security pad, but Azura was ahead of his intentions. The door opened.

It was a tiny room, little more than a bed shelf overflowing with blankets. Leta lay unconscious on the pile. A skinny arm crumpled by her neck while the other sprawled. A long creamy thermal coat covered her morphfabric suit, tangled up in her legs. Light-brown hair splashed around her head.

Azura slipped into the walls and ceiling, cocooning the room in power. Caiden sent a silent wish that Azura would disable any protection that lay around this Grave as he crept to her bedside, waiting for a trap to spring.

The air hung quiet enough to hear her breathing, with a slight hum in her nose, like when they were kids.

This is wrong.

He lined up his words and prepared to unshackle that Graven thing curled in him and let it fill up his voice if needed. Once he touched her, she would be drawn out of Proxy, her consciousness jarred back to its source. The Proxy would drop, interrupt whatever the Primes were doing, and Caiden would tell Leta the danger and send her back to her Proxy to deliver it. Abriss would listen.

Caiden shuddered a sigh and knelt. He had important words for her and he had to ignore his heart to say them. There would be no second chance.

"Leta...I'm here."

He's fast. Leta flicked her ribbon blade at weak points to test Threi's reflexes. Dilatant armor gave him freedom of movement until pressure struck and it hardened.

She aimed her lash for his face. It wasn't armored in smiles anymore.

He blocked with a rising wrist. The purple spore-fire lit with the friction. Grasping the ribbon's tip, he yanked Leta toward him, straight into the burning line hanging in the air.

Her tissues charred, fake lightseep bones white-hot. The pain was too intense to suppress. A scream reaction cinched up in her jaw. This fight was going to *hurt*.

She flicked at his ankle, nicking his boot as he dodged and then charged in, closing the range, deceived into thinking Leta's weapon was meant for distance.

Hyperextending, she whipped to encircle his torso and dashed behind him while pulling. The ribbon sawed through his coat. Smartly he ducked *toward* her, loosening the coils before they sliced flesh. He sparked fire in front of her face, flooding her thermal sensors, carrying that raging line past her sword arm to force her to turn.

He calculates. She retargeted, slashing along his ribs and tearing down to bone. He howled, clapped his hands to summon flame, then grabbed her neck. Her organic skin burned, but with more than plain fire: this was a chemical vitriol, viral, an infestation. Her hybrid materials blistered apart and sloughed off. His searing fingers pushed into the frame of her windpipe and cervical vertebrae.

Pain exploded in her mind as he shoveled down into nerve bundles. She choked on her own burning flesh. Half-blind, Leta barreled a fist into his groin.

Abriss darted in from behind him, snatched Leta's ribbon sword from the ground, and whip-coiled it around Threi's neck. She kicked off his back, sawing the lash through his armor with all her weight. Material shredded. The ribbon bit skin. Threi roared and grappled at it, ruining his gloves in order to burn it apart with a final *snap*.

Freed, he whirled on Abriss.

Leta lunged to catch Threi's arms behind him. "Do it!" she shrieked.

Abriss pulled a spike from her boot and arced it for Threi's jugular. He twisted hard and the spike sank into his clavicle instead. Bellowing, he drove his elbow into Leta's skull behind him.

Light blasted through her retinas. Visual blips swarmed and mushed his silhouette. Leta toppled to the ground on unresponsive limbs.

No! Recalibrate!

Threi locked Abriss up against him, grasped her head with one hand and dug his thumb into her right eye. Purple fire poured into the socket. Her screams striped through Leta's faulty vision, darkness then light bloom, the sound distorting.

Abriss tore her arms free and buried her fingers into Threi's hair, pulled his forehead against hers—at point-blank range she pleaded, "*Stop this!*" Her volume was raw with sobs. She forced the rest in a whisper, "I still care. You're just hurting. You've always been hurting."

Valiant, sweet Abriss.

Her fingers quaked. The force drained from Threi. His features still snarled, but teardrops pearled on his lashes.

Abriss wriggled away. Half her face smoldered with chemical flame. The closed eye wept sizzling blood where Threi's thumb had dug deep. She sobbed and choked at the same time as she looked frantically for her Proxies, for a weapon. Dejin swept toward her, heading off Casthen soldiers incoming.

Leta wobbled on numbed limbs, materials recovering faster than her mind. Sensations were wiped: the scene was a mess of incorrect amplitudes of sensory signals.

No exit. The elevator. Impossible to even see where it lay in the floor.

"Kill her!" Threi roared, recovering. Tears streaked down his cheeks and blood down his chest where the spike Abriss had driven into his collarbone still protruded.

Leta rushed him. He ignited curtains of flame across the air, but she barreled through, snatched the spike from Threi's torso, then jabbed it between his ribs, puncturing a lung, missing his heart. Screeching, he stumbled back and fell to a knee.

Leta toppled, too, suppression functions failing, agony seeping through. Strips of burnt flesh curled off her. Alloy bits shattered. Her brain screamed and struggled to piece together the chaos.

Medical officers mobbed around Threi. More pearly vials?

Abriss—with Dejin, good.

Dejin was ruthless and large enough to shield Abriss as he fended off Sisorro Seven. Abriss commandeered a handful of unmasked Casthen to her side.

Leta staggered upright.

Her shoulder exploded. Tayen's lightseep blade cleaved it from behind. Pain signals splintered through buffers as her arm tore off completely. Her mouth gaped open, the wail locked up in tremors.

Tayen bent over her, as dark as a shadow ripped from a pit. She grabbed Leta's wrist, planted a foot on her hip, and stretched her torso out to sever it in half with the sword.

Leta wriggled—no leverage. "Tay," she moaned. "No."

"You won't die. Just the doll th ol thllll…" Tayen's blade rippled space as she raised it.

Isme tackled Tayen, tearing her off Leta. He pinned her on the ground and flipped her as his fingers turned surgical, bending at inhuman angles to pry open her spinal plating. It separated wetly, like a beetle's shell, exposing the *Azura*'s crystal beneath: the modification that allowed the Graves' consciousnesses to be in Proxies out of Unity.

"Here!" Isme wailed.

Abriss rushed to him, stumbling to a kneeling position.

"Do it now." He pinched Tayen's flailing arms with his knees.

Abriss dug her shaking fingers around the crystalline mass and closed her good eye, tears streaming. She focused with the Aurasever, reality ruffled around her fingers, and the mass ruptured into liquid. Tayen's flailing cut off and she slumped into dead, silent weight.

Leta stared at the body, sensing the pressure, like a shriek without a sound, as Tayen's consciousness unraveled. Energy drained from circuitry and biology. *Tayen will awaken in the Dynast Hold. She'll be home. She's all right. She'll forgive us and we'll forgive her.*

Isme slid off her Proxy. "Up, Leta, we're running. Together."

Abriss rose too and picked up Tayen's lightseep sword. Misery wrenched through her face before it sheeted in calm. "There is nowhere to run."

The edge of the deck behind them was a sixty-meter drop to the roof of the structure below.

Leta stood shaking, one-armed. Dejin fought his way to their side. Aohm One battled the pair of Dian and Sisorro, tripping one and catching the other's neck in an arm lock. Leta recognized Dian's look: lost in his own vigor, the momentum of the fight chaining him up, locking out reason.

Aohm bellowed to Leta's group, "We are expendable! She is not."

"We kill Threi." Dejin shed his sullied white cloak and planted his feet.

Leta ripped the dangling tendons from the remains of her hacked shoulder. Her body crackled with force as she stepped to Eight's side. "This is why we're here."

Isme reached into a pocket and tossed up a handful of pebble-sized drones that hovered around him. The starry things snapped electric links among one another, forming a deadly constellation that shifted with the movements of his raised fingers. "Prime," he said, voice sweet. "We are your shield."

Abriss balanced Five's big sword on her shoulder and placed a reassuring hand on Dejin's arm as she took position next to him. "I am sorry, my Graves, I failed you again. But I'll see us through."

Threi limped to the front of the Casthen mob. A quick-seal foam dribbled from the holes in his torso. Sweat curled his hair. His eyes were sharp and wild, and the Graven enhancement had turned him ethereal, too pale and almost aglow, aureated in power that Leta's senses felt dimpling the air, ripening the very fabric of space with his desperation. Decades of precision lay in this predator's movements, as if he'd dreamed this day over and over.

Soldiers poured around Leta's group at the cliff's edge while Threi yelled, "*Capture the Dynast Prime!*"

Abriss shouted a counter-order, "*Casthen! Protect us!*"

They hesitated, sheltered by their special wrap masks and sensory veils, but the Prime was now a *sight*. Her tattered gown flourished copper stars. One eye wept tears and the other blood, and the sight of injury would ignite a protective instinct in anyone who saw her.

The vision seared across Leta's mind too. A new emotion occupied Abriss's features, something Leta was terrified to name.

The Casthen crowd unraveled and the battle shifted, but it was unclear which order carried more weight. Proximity effect, pre-invested loyalties, and their sensory-deprivation masks made a mayhem. Aohm One was swamped in the thickest Casthen bunch. Sisorro appeared to switch sides on a whim.

Leta said, "I take Threi first."

Isme huffed. "You are missing an arm, Treasure."

Her lips twitched a smile. She extended her good hand to Eight. "Spare something for a girl's only arm, Dej?"

He grunted and took off one power gauntlet, strapping it to her forearm. The knuckle portion fit too large, but she could still make a fist, and the force gathered up.

Abriss swept the sword in an arc in front of her, a rippled wave of cleaved spacetime. She'd forged it herself, years ago, and the weight lay well in her hands.

"Dian Six and Sisorro Seven," Abriss called, voice pain-raw, as the two emerged from the fray. She had named and forged both of them too. "Whatever your grievances, I would hear them without bloodshed. I have never once lied to you or concealed my aim. My brother armors himself in lies and hooks hearts by weaponizing others' greed."

Threi strode forward. "You aren't among the faithful anymore. Let them be greedy. Let them want and take."

Sisorro, light on their feet and smiling too wide, could have been thinking this was all great fun. Dejin crooked his finger at them. They grinned, easily taunted.

Abriss intercepted Dian Six. Isme's floater drones zipped in constellations between the Casthen soldiers and precisely blasted their special masks off, freeing all their senses to absorb Abriss Cetre rushing into battle and shouting, "*Fight with me!*"

Leta stalked toward Threi. She smashed all her notions of him as the dashing savior of her ten-year-old self. She owed her childhood survival to Caiden, and everything else to Abriss. It was time to repay.

Threi had restored his chemical-fire gloves. Close-range risk. She charged in and feinted, made him open, then slammed her force-gauntlet into one of the ribs she'd stabbed before. A curse crumpled out of him as he hurtled backward.

Leta stomped after him. Her Proxy filtered her dying senses to the essentials. Threi's center of balance. Breathing. Injuries. She whipped in, hooked his leg to trip him onto his back, then hammered her fist down at his face.

Threi jerked away and smacked his wrists together, sparking bio-flame that clung to his fist as it barreled at Leta's head. She snapped her neck aside to dodge but missed his follow-up palm strike to her stomach. Fire chewed into her flesh and corroded abdominal plates. Invading cells wriggled toward her organs.

Static vision. His face below. She pulled back for another punch, bracing so her exoskeleton could mine energy to flow into her strike.

Leta plowed her charged fist at his head.

Threi was faking the opening. His knee—he'd snuck it between them. He spun her viciously sideways. She yelped and her fist pummeled the floor instead of his skull. Metal dented.

Threi climbed over her and caught her wrist, plowing fiery fingers into the gauntlet's lattice to crush it, not just mashing the nerve lines but caging her one good hand in deformed steel.

He pinned her on her stomach. His fingertips pried around the edges of her spinal plates. The residual flames on his hands burned her nerves as he probed for a seam. *He saw what happened to Tayen.*

Pain signals detonated, distancing her consciousness from its frame, trying to tell her it was better to give up.

Arm. Nerves sputtered in a dead hunk of muscle.

His fingernails caught a plate joint and dug in, blasting sparks through Leta's warning system.

Spacetime roared apart in an arc cutting toward him. Tayen's lightseep blade.

Abriss slammed it at Threi, and he rolled too late. It grazed his shoulder, exploding through fabric and flesh. She followed immediately with a stab at his chest. The blade bit the floor as he rolled away and kicked Abriss off balance. She landed on her back, the air crashing out of her. He snatched her ankle and yanked her toward him.

No! Leta lurched up and wrapped her arm around Threi's neck from behind, carrying him backward with her flailing weight.

Abriss kicked free and pinned him down with knees and elbows driving into his wounds. Threi howled, bucking. Abriss averted her gaze as she pressed harder. Panting, she buried her face against his arm, unable to look, and wailed: *"Do it!"*

Leta forced her mangled hand around the haft of Tayen's blade and raised it. Air billowed in its wake. She heaved it over her head, her whole body contorting to put muscle behind the one-armed motion. She would cleave his neck.

Threi gazed up with wide, wet eyes.

Leta gathered the cresting force at its peak and drove it *down*.

At that same time a sensation rammed her.

Spirit, grazed.

A tidal sense of *need*.

Her real body was calling her back.

The mechanics of her Proxy locked up, and her awareness began to slither off, uprooting from the exoskeleton. The call became razor-sharp, yanking at her consciousness to return.

Oh crimes, no.

Her grip on the sword softened. She clamped down, desperate to stay and do this *one thing*.

Leta started toppling backward instead. Spirit draining fast.

No! Fingers loosened. She willed her body to arc forward, to fall *with* the blade, right on Threi's neck.

Static chewed up her sight. Walled her cry. She fell back, dead weight, but with the last of her willpower she heaved the sword in front of her and down. Down. Half a meter.

The killing blow—

CHAPTER 29

ELSEWHERE

Caiden dug one arm into the blankets, looping beneath Leta's shoulders. Speaking alone hadn't woken her. He didn't like the idea of restraint, but he needed her to be still while he deployed the swiftest explanation he could all at once.

Her weight was so slight, her face frowning—Caiden fought off long-buried memories that tried to match up. She'd fallen out of the oak tree and fractured a rib. She wasn't crying but he'd stayed with her until she could focus, then helped her home.

"Leta."

She stirred, blinking sleepily. Consciousness filled her hazel eyes softly.

Then her pupils snapped to points. She gasped and wrenched from his arms, tumbled against the base of the bed shelf, slamming her shoulder with a *crack*. She yelped and scrabbled at the floor, opening and closing her hand like she meant to hold something that wasn't there. Her gaze dashed around the room and she quaked, not even registering him.

"L-Leta? Leta, you're safe. I have to—"

"Caiden?" Her gaze riveted on him. Frantic energy spilled out of her, chattering her fingernails against the floor as she braced.

Caiden raised placating hands. "I need you to listen. Th—"

"No."

The little word kicked him like the rejection she'd given him the first time.

"No, oh stars, no," she whimpered, staring through him. "No, no, no."

She grasped the blanket and squeezed until her knuckles were white. Shut her eyes, face blanking with sudden calm.

"Leta, what's happened?"

En made a frustrated sound from the doorway. "If she won't listen, we need to *go*. Use your Graven whatever. Security's forming unusual perimeters around this sector."

Caiden straightened, his heart burning with the rejection. He coiled his Graven will, readying his voice to do the unforgivable and force her to hear him.

"*Thhh—*" The sound whispered past her lips as her slitted eyes went glassy. She started to shut down, consciousness leaving. Her body toppled sideways. Caiden swooped down and caught her. He cradled her skull before it hit the floor, and he was close enough to hear her finish the word. "*Threi.*"

"Shit," Caiden barked. In one motion he scooped Leta up entirely and swiveled to En. "The meeting's already soured. We have to go."

"Been tellin' you," En grumbled as they swept into the hall, blasting a path through security forces flooding in.

Leta clawed across space and time toward her Proxy, dim and damaged. She sharpened her focus, cutting away from the sense of her real body jostling in Caiden's arms and instead clutched the panic of who she would find dead at her feet: Threi or Abriss.

She dived into her Proxy. Snatches of bright sensory information bubbled in the murk of space. Pain bludgeoned in tempo with her pulse. Her bloodstream *hissing*—that had to be a bad sound.

Threi towered over Abriss, haloed in light. Very much alive.

He pressed down with a shard of knife.

A sound: a scream stretched as thin as a thread.

Abriss. Her hands shuddered, sawing wounds into her fingers wrapped around the blade as she desperately tried to push away. The ragged edge tore across her jaw, opened into her windpipe slowly as Threi levered down. The scream was hers, drowned by her blood.

Leta shrieked Abriss's name and pushed herself up to barrel into Threi's side. The knife pulled with him and another gargled scream ripped from Abriss's throat.

Sensory input clipped off. Leta's Proxy smacked the ground and her awareness jarred loose, her spirit uprooting. Visual data gave way to scents. Metallic blood and murder lust.

Threi straightened.

No! Leta pressed into her Proxy until the world smoldered back into shape. Light exploded around a chaos of figures. Dejin Eight dived in, a shield wall, blocking her view of Threi. Leta scrambled off the floor. Arms hoisted her from one side, and she flinched before realizing it was Isme. Frantic, he said, "This way."

He pulled her over to Abriss, who lay curled, clutching her neck. Her violent shaking pumped more blood out of the ugly fissure. Isme clamped a palm over the wounds as he lifted her up.

Dejin dealt Threi a charged blow that sent him flying back into his soldiers. While Dejin tangled with them, Leta snatched the lightseep sword and pleaded to Isme, "Get behind us and keep her safe!"

Leta intercepted Sisorro. They wore an amused grin, their curls swaying as they advanced, fingers wiggling and ready to snap pressure points and disable joints.

Leta hefted the blade. "Don't do this."

"Do what?" They moved playfully, layers of bright cloth flashing. "You saw the Prime wreck Tayen."

"To protect us!"

"Who is *us*?" Sisorro launched. Leta swung but they ducked beneath, knifed their fingers into her hip plate, hooked a nerve bundle within. Leta yelped as her middle gave out, pitching her to the ground. Alarms exploded in her head.

She heaved upright using the sword, then readied it while Sisorro rocked calmly.

"What happened to family?" Leta stumbled, planting the sword again to stop her wobble. "This is *real*. This isn't like sparring."

Seven's smile crumpled. They dropped their deadly hands in a huff. "Us. You *really* want to go back?"

"Sis, we need you. Please."

Sisorro blew out a breath and made a show of shrugging, face still creased in worry. "'Us' *is* all I have, but—"

Behind them—

"*Sisorro!*" Leta shrieked.

Dian plowed a broken glave haft between Sisorro's shoulders from behind. A snapping sound cracked through their vertebrae, electricity dancing across bluish crystal that showered in sparks. The playful light left Seven's eyes. Their hands fumbled with the exit wound before dropping.

Leta screamed raw and she forced the words, "They are *family*, Dian!"

Six yanked his weapon free. "They'll return to their real body like Five did. When we wake up, the Prime won't be around to control us. Don't you get it?"

Hurt laced his words and contempt creased his face, but Leta remembered what it looked like when he laughed, and the times he'd picked her up off the training-room floor with a grin, and how he'd bolstered her confidence on the hardest days with the perfect pithy words.

She pleaded, "We *need* Abriss. We'll die before long without our Proxies. Five and Seven—"

"*That's* the lie! Now you grasp it. The Casthen will take us in. Threi has the Graven Dominant, the last piece to heal our Dynast biology. Or perhaps there's a universe among these billions where we wouldn't need Proxies anyway because we would have been … just … *fine*." The final words sieved through his teeth as his jaw clenched more and more.

"Dian, please…"

"We are numbers because there are an infinite amount of us. We are family because it is convenient. Power structures are designed to control lessers—and what is the biggest structure of all? *The Dynast*."

He hefted a pair of glaves and fired, but a mass swelled at Leta from the side: *Aohm One*. Snips of energy glanced off their carapace, shielding her.

"Six!" Aohm bellowed. "The man has given you nothing!"

"He is giving me *choice*," Dian growled, and fired another flurry. Aohm's armor swallowed the energy bolts and shattered the material ones.

Dejin Eight came in to scoop a big arm around Leta's waist and haul her away. She found her feet despite the bad hip.

Isme and Abriss were already running. Threi was lost in a tangle of Casthen, trying to roar orders, but whatever he'd done to enhance his gravitas ebbed away. In the mass of the crowd he looked meek, doubled over with ugly injuries.

Abriss's group reached the deck's edge while glave fire rained on their backs.

"*Go!*" roared Aohm as they staggered to join up. "We are expendable!"

"Go?" Isme echoed.

Then Leta understood. "Now we jump."

There wasn't time. She peered down the sixty-meter drop of metallic wall and hard landing.

Aohm barreled toward Abriss with their remaining strength. They picked her up and cradled her body as they hurtled straight off the deck's edge.

Leta gaped after them. She'd been ready for the idea but not the execution. They plummeted, a mass of white carapace and shadowy cloak. Too many heartbeats later they slammed the floor with a resounding *crack!* Abriss's fall was broken full-force in their embrace.

Dejin strung together ursgen swears and slung himself over the side of the cliff, using his gauntlet and feet to dig a huge gouge in the wall and slow his descent.

Isme muttered a rare curse. His Proxy's bones cracked and joints sizzled, switching to shock-absorption construct. He glanced at Leta for her to nod she would be all right. Reassured, he leaped off the side.

Leta jammed her mangled grip around the sword and relished a glimpse of Threi's startled face as she stepped backward off the edge too. She skewered the fake lightseep blade into the wall and rode its screeching cut downward. She lost grip, was jarred off, and picked up speed.

Leta struck the ground and bounced. Matter around sensitive points puffed temporarily to absorb the shock. Dejin rushed to her side to inspect her damage.

Isme gently extracted Abriss from Aohm One's limp Proxy.

One. Leta blinked at them, eyes not focusing. Her pain shorted out on blunt pathways, creating patches of numbness.

She craned her neck back to look upward but couldn't see activity on the deck. Threi and his group would be headed down and calling for reinforcements.

"Ai pwan." Dejin confirmed her wellness as he cracked her joints back into place and used her severed tendons to cinch up loose skeleton. He gathered her to her feet. "Where now?"

Leta groaned several crude swears in one noise. "We need medical for—"

Abriss gagged on blood, a terrible sound. Isme whipped his belts off and ripped strips from his skirt, cinching around her neck wound as best he could. His fingertips brushed the puffy, blood-covered socket of her eye. She flinched hard.

"Let's move." Leta picked up Tayen's sword where it had fallen. "Nothing matters if they catch us."

They had landed on a proper roof. Leta spotted a utility pathway at the far end. Her brain flickered between too many things, body suffused with hormones and strange melodies. Her thoughts raked over Caiden and her real body, vulnerable, and Six's belief that none of the Graves were free.

Seven, Five, and One were vulnerable back home. Would they fight? Or come to their senses?

Leta limped as fast as she could while surveying the facility from the height to plan their course. Dejin plowed ahead and Isme carried Abriss. Down the pathway, Dejin kicked in a door to an incubation warehouse. There was only minimal activity around, sounds sparse and echoing. Everything dim, light rationed. No pursuit yet. Thankfully the surfacewrap security didn't extend to these outskirts.

"This way." Leta steered them through a freight tunnel and narrow supply passages to an iris that opened into light. Fields stretched a kilometer square, hemmed in by megastructure on all sides but open to a dark sky above. A cluster of bright rinds arced out of the planet's skin. Each universe was a different biome, filled with gardens or machinery, staff milling around. Hazily peaceful after the battle they'd raced from.

They plunged through an indigo rind into a quiet universe. In the crossover, stripes of organic tissue melted off Leta's frame to bare more inner skeleton. Isme's long, bloodied hair lost weight and spiraled around him. Abriss breathed easier here.

Between stone pathways lay long troughs of black plantings with maroon flowers, glowing fungus, and streams filled with sparkling organisms. Veins of fog hung in the air with fits of lightning darting through.

The scientists around stopped their chatter and riveted on Abriss. She rolled her head against Isme's shoulder and said, barely audible, mostly whimper, "Help me."

The staff swept over, infused with a yearning to help. "Nine crimes," one swore, staring in horror for a beat before doling out orders to the others to grab medical kits.

This district was focused on biological medicine—thank the stars. Even here so far from Unity, coincidence still lined up to their advantage. Leta took quick stock of the group and relaxed when she spotted no particularly Graven-resistant xenids. She cradled this tiny hope that Graven Abriss, even robbed of a voice and halfway to death, could still pave their way with help. They could secure a ship to flee the planet if Abriss didn't recover enough to take over the Harvest.

Isme laid her down. Dejin knelt, fretting over her torn clothes with clumsy motions, and finally rose to his feet to survey. Isme calmly conveyed requests to the Casthen workers around them.

Leta's mind crowded her with delayed concerns, but one important detail riveted her: the Dynast Prime had a look in her eyes that wasn't pain, anger, or sadness, and it frightened Leta more than the woman's wounds. It was a broken, vanished look she'd never seen before on someone so strong.

"Prime," Leta whispered.

Isme's gaze flicked to Leta, acknowledgment sparking before he turned back to Abriss.

"We need you lucid and with us," he said, his ashy voice forced even softer.

Abriss blinked and nodded, as if there were some duty she was neglecting. Automatic, she fished in her pocket, hand shaking, and emerged with her mini-orrery, which glimmered to life over her palm. It wasn't what Isme meant, but foreign stars twinkled, wrapped in lines of relationships and numerals, and Abriss's tense shoulders drooped in relief.

"Thi—" Abriss choked. Lips quivering, she pointed instead. Her fingernail indicated one projected planet, swept its arc toward another celestial body, then settled on numbers indicating time to alignment. Six arcminutes. She formed the word "interception" with shaking fingers, plus the gesture for uncertainty.

"We hear you," Isme said, then frowned.

Her skin had paled from blood loss, the freckles starker. Several scientists returned carting medical supplies and small machines. The rest dithered in a strange orbit between adoration, shyness, despair. Leta scrutinized every-one who approached, running through mental checklists of threats. Dejin busied himself examining every item the group brought near.

Isme became serious and precise, directing who could touch what and where. He kept to the edict of "consent" at every step, checking with Abriss, who stared into enemy heavens and merely nodded.

Leta wriggled a finger in the socket of her missing arm. *Expendable.*

Dejin's silver armor was dented and riddled with the smoking gashes of glave blasts. Half of Isme's faceless mask was smashed apart, leaking metal-lic fluids out of the vitreous maze of his skull. His long, nacreous hair was plastered to his body with Abriss's blood.

The workers stitched then wrapped the gigantic slash through her jaw and neck. Then her scorched and thumb-gouged eye, though there wasn't much that could be done without advanced tools. They cleaned it and applied a seal. To Leta, Abriss's wounds looked all the worse with the knowledge that they'd been inflicted by family.

Abriss lost consciousness during the ministrations. Her hand fell slack and the orrery glitched. Isme curled her fist closed around it.

Leta shooed the staff away. Isme walked to a large holosplay field set up for research and switched it to a facility schematic.

Hushed, Dejin said, "Abriss was wrong."

He meant something very big by that word.

Leta replied carefully, "That doesn't mean Threi is right."

As bad as she was at deciphering faces, she wished Eight and Two had expressions she could read. Abriss's trust in her brother and confidence in her gravitas had been naïve, her desire for connection too blinding, and her philosophy too dogmatic, but who hadn't been a failure to themselves at some point? If Abriss's despondency was any clue, she wasn't letting this lesson go unweighed.

Jolting rod-straight, Dejin blurted, "Nine's body."

A beat passed while they each reached the same realization: Eight and Two's Proxies could be destroyed and their consciousnesses would return to their bodies in the Dynast Hold on Solthar. But Leta's real body was here. Detouring to save her was too risky.

Expendable. Leta said, "Caiden—Winn is alive, and he's here. That's why I was pulled away. He'll help us if he's still here."

She remembered only snippets of that frantic waking moment. It had been paved over by the chaos right after. Why had he come?

Dejin shook his head. "He'll help *you*. Remember what the Prime took from him."

"The world conspired before, across years, to bring the *Azura* to Abriss through him. What if synchronicity is lining up again to get her safe? What if that's why he's here, and—"

Terminals nearby exploded with activity, beaming in a report. Several languages stacked on top of one another and contained the same phrases: *Security sweep commencing. Tracking extended. Mandatory wait in place for all personnel and guests.*

Across the facility map, every door, aperture, and passage flickered red: shut and locked. Every door in the tall walls of their current location closed with a rumble. Reinforcements began to cluster around their sector of the megastructure, along with air support and digital surveillance.

Leta cursed. "It's possible we can hide, but we can't run. Escaping in a ship will be difficult since the stellar egress is the only gateway in or out of this universe. He'll have closed that off too."

Dejin offered, "If we find structure-wide comms, Abriss could command everyone."

Isme shook his head. "She's not conscious enough to manage."

"We don't know," Leta added, "what the Casthen Prime did to make himself more powerful. I saw it fading from him by the time we jumped, but he might have the means to do it again. In a tug-of-war between them, in her state—we'd lose."

"Ol. We hide." Dejin scooped Abriss up in his big arms, ready to carry on.

"Where?" Leta asked. "He'll turn this facility upside down to find her. We might hide long enough for her to heal, but what will *he* have done in the meantime?"

Isme gathered the orrery device and said, "We trust her. She gave us a way forward."

He paired the orrery to the holoplay console. Projected stars sprayed across the map, superimposing. The countdown to the exact conjunction she'd indicated still had a few arcminutes left.

Leta blinked. "She didn't mean the lockdown."

They watched the Casthen heavens shift. Long streams of tiny numbers glittered, calculating time and space. Leta's brain continued to sort through solutions, rejecting and reconsidering, flipping through them like a deck of cards.

"There!" Isme pointed in the facility map where a small trajectory of blue blipped through the locked-down red of it all. Doors opened, then jammed again. Lifts headed up, then down. Flickers.

"Threi?" Leta asked. The anomaly was moving closer, parallel to them.

"It's coming from the opposite direction," Isme said, a frown in his voice. "I trust it, if you both do. Let us be quick."

Dejin grunted but obliged, readjusting Abriss in his arms. Leta and Isme led a straight course to the side door nearest the anomaly's projected route.

In a universe garden of crystalline rootlets and raindrop leaves, the physics corroded some of Leta's nerves. The Proxies were more susceptible to physics shifts given the damage they'd already sustained. Dejin's scrolled armor oxidized, and his breaths wheezed. In the next universe, Leta's hybrid flesh caught actual fire, and she sprinted ahead to get out and have time to peel the melted bits away. Isme's mask contracted and stressed, throwing more cracks and exposing more brain behind.

By the time they made it to the door seven bubble universes away, they were far worse for wear. Leta dragged herself into the lead, roaring with effort, and ripped open the door's terminal panel, assessing the half-biological wiring within. Slow-going hacking, one-armed. Rushing didn't help but if they were too slow, the anomaly would pass by and the doors would lock in its wake.

"Moments left, Treasure." Isme watched the holosplay, where the blue indicator blipped through the facility like a rock skipping water.

Finally the big cargo door flew open, rods jammed back into the wall recess. Dejin growled in triumph and hustled through carrying Abriss. Isme led them into narrow passages, labs, then backtracked, chasing whatever thing was headed toward them on its own incomprehensible route. The closer they came to intercepting, the more Leta perceived a soundless roar all around, whipping and glittering at the edges of her senses.

"Through here." Isme charged under an archway and stopped so abruptly, Leta slammed into his side and clutched his arm to keep steady. Dejin planted his feet.

In front of them, two people sweeping through the hall stopped just as suddenly.

Caiden. Endirion.

And Leta's body, in Caiden's arms.

The visual was so jarring, and such a strange mirror—the two groups, each carrying something precious—Leta stalled in shock.

Caiden tensed up, cradling Leta's body closer, her head tucked against his neck. Leta lost herself in that image of time echoing: her at five, six, eight years old being carried in the same manner, taken away from trauma or overload or injury.

Regaining logic first, Leta stepped between the standoff, raising her one arm. Before she managed a word, Abriss whimpered and roused in Eight's arms.

As close as they were, and looking as vulnerable as she did, her gravitas was guaranteed. Her good eye rolled to take in the scene. She fixated on Caiden and in a Graven quaver pleaded, "*Save me.*"

CHAPTER 30

SAVIOR

Caiden froze, staring at the collar of bruises on Abriss Cetre's neck from Threi's fingers. His mind thrust him ten years back, into a field of flowers, with Threi grasping her skull, tearing the same wounds into her throat. It had been a vishkant that time, a practice run, illusory. Now the bastard really had tried to do it for real.

Caiden was infested with a need to help her. Buried in it was the satisfying idea that if he took Abriss, he was taking something invaluable away from Threi.

"Protect her," said the long-haired Proxy painted in insects and webs, "and we have no reason to harm you."

En swung his glave down, compelled into affection too. "Truce."

"Do you have a ship?" asked the brawny one in silver armor, Eight.

"This way," Caiden said, still dazed. He clutched Leta's real body tighter as he strode ahead, aiming for a rendezvous with the *Wintra* on an edge of the megastructure. Azura swept with him through the locked-down facility, creating a pocket of freedom by opening barricades and blockading personnel who might intercept them. Caiden veered through tunnels to one of the colossal warehouses, where they could sprint a straight distance.

Thick door plates shoved back. Caiden skidded to a halt.

His brain registered a Proxy approaching on the other side. It was the vicious one he'd almost fought before, Six, all ceramic painted in archaic diagrams, and long black hair in damp kinks.

Leta strode forward one-armed, brandishing a lightseep blade. Her eyes filled with fight.

Caiden hesitated. *This Proxy's an enemy now? Of course—that's how Threi got through Abriss's guard. He doesn't need gravitas to flip loyalties around.*

Caiden cut off Leta's trajectory and pressed into her, spilling her real body into her Proxy's arm. The awkward weight slumped her to the floor. She gazed up at him, startled.

"Keep safe." He grabbed her sword and hefted its strangely floaty weight as he strode toward Six in her stead. En jogged up beside Caiden, the two of them blocking Six from his quarry as he readied a spear glave and crouched for a launch, fixating on Abriss.

"Two!" Eight yelled.

"Right." The other Proxy strode to the fight while Eight and Leta dashed off.

A flock of tiny starry drones erupted off Two and constellated around Six before the other Proxy could bat them away. In a snap they magnetized onto his body and triggered a sustained electric shock. Six's limbs seized up and he bellowed, half-paralyzed, a distorted sound like shredding metal.

Two closed the distance with inhuman speed, jabbing brutally and precisely to dismantle armor plates. Six's spear was a blur of parries. With another roar, he dropped to a squat, then sprang, thrusting the spear glave up through Two's stomach.

The Proxy choked, then chuckled and twisted himself to wrench the spear and Six with it, toppling them both to the ground. Two pinned him, still impaled, and yelled, "Now!"

Caiden rushed in, swinging the sword down on Six's head. It cleaved space, bent light into ripples, bleeding shadows in the wake. The Proxy jerked so the blade crushed only half his skull into the floor, spraying fluids and shards.

"Not his head!" Two cried. "Rib ca—"

Six kicked him away, which broke the spear in half. The drones tinkled to the ground, snapping the shock field offline.

En rushed in, pinning Six again and ripping at his chest plating. The ceramic shattered, but the lightseep beneath didn't give. Something inside emitted a sickening vibration, bright blue under En's tearing fingers.

Caiden raised the sword with both hands to impale. "Move back—"

Six bucked first, flipping En off him. He snatched the glave haft and stabbed at En's neck. Caiden aimed a kick just in time to knock the spear sideways so it tore only flesh. He followed up with a sword blow, but Six danced back from it and stumbled, body twitching as bursts of fluid and air flushed out of his body. His half skull sat tilted. Bloody hair draped over his shattered torso and its mess of inner components.

Caiden helped En off the ground. Two groaned and yanked the other half of the spear from his middle. "Dian Six's brain center is in his chest. Otherwise, target the crystal mass under his spine."

"You both join the others," Caiden said. The group had pulled out of sight, running for the warehouse's far wall.

"And let you have all the fun?" En's gouged vocal folds vibrated in triplet.

He rolled his shoulders and spine in a full-body motion. Bones crackled and muscle filled out in a runner's physique. En's facial features became more feminine, her hair shortened to bluish curls, and some of her neck wound healed over with material from elsewhere. Caiden recognized her favorite combat physique. "*This* is the fight I was waiting for."

Caiden grunted. "If we don't stop him right here, it won't be a fight, it'll be a race."

He gestured to the colossal warehouse. Stacks of equipment and containers piled high on the floor. Platform islands hung overhead, up and up, maximizing vertical space—except the items on these islands were held on by small-range scalar gravity generators at the center of each block. Objects jutted sideways, at angles, or upside-down. Walkways connected the islands at angles while others had articulating lifts. All around, little universes bubbled the space.

It was either the best or worst place for a fight.

"Then let's start with the finisher." En snapped two fingers on her right hand—a signal Caiden recalled from training. He fell into synchrony with her: dive, foot planted, side by side, augmented arm winding back. He and En punched as one. Dian Six crossed his arms to block his exposed chest, but the two augmented uppercuts exploded force that hurtled him upward.

His body twirled as gravity nodes from an island overhead snagged his limbs. The force intensified with proximity, sucking him up toward the platform, which was a ceiling to Caiden and would be a floor to Six. The Proxy landed in a crouch with a boom that resonated through the scaffolding beneath him.

En craned her neck, looking wide-eyed up at the ceiling and their upside-down opponent. "Ah. I see what you mean now."

Something clanged farther off, where Leta and the others had fled. The Proxy, Two, held his stomach and stumbled into a run toward the sound.

Six noticed and sprinted that way across the maze of platforms above.

Caiden cursed and said to En, "Throw me, then catch up with the others."

"Reckless kid." En squatted and layered two palms as a foothold. Her muscles bulged with charge. Caiden planted his boot and En launched him full-strength upward.

He sailed, and as the force of the throw ebbed, the planet's gravity started to pull him back down—until a new gravity webbed him. He slowed to a stall at the apex, midair, hair and clothes lifting in the pull of the island's scalar field. Bumps cascaded across his skin. Force wafted over him in complex ripples.

The scalar gravity won and pulled him in. Up became down and he plummeted toward the island's grate flooring.

Caiden rolled, his stomach lurching at the reorientation. He stumbled up to his feet and spotted the Proxy sprinting ahead.

Dian vaulted off a platform's railing toward another island suspended seven meters away. His momentum waned halfway across before the next gravity field caught him. He landed awkwardly and now stood sideways from Caiden's perspective.

Caiden would never make the same leaps. He raced across a catwalk to a platform of flora that spilled out of canisters, the stems squiggling into the gravity's patterns. He batted vines and tried to keep sight of the Proxy running sideways on the island parallel to his.

Many meters below them both, En and Two rejoined Leta's group and kept running toward the farthest wall of the warehouse.

Dian clambered onto another railing and ran along it, flexible toes splayed. He got ahead of Leta's group and squatted, aiming his broken spear haft for a drop down that would precisely lance Abriss with his fall when she passed below.

Caiden couldn't leap seven meters across to the other island...but he was good at falling. As he peered up at a higher vantage point for a plummet, his platform suddenly engaged a lift, pitching him onto a small elevator that started to take him several islands higher. *Azura?*

The dizzy rumble he'd been feeling in his head must've been her as she joined him from platform to platform.

His insides churned around as a new gravity swirled through him, rearranging micro beads of force through his body. He groaned and righted on all fours. "This is going to get old."

Azura's vibration surged through his palms. He chuckled. "If I jump, you'll catch me again this time, right? Be my wings." Caiden aimed himself to fall from the extra height right onto Six below while the Proxy waited for Abriss to cross his path even farther down at ground level.

Caiden leaped across. Gravity shed off him. The lightseep sword wailed as he dragged it over his head, and a ribbon of space cleaved in its wake.

Four meters out, he started to fall. Bridges swooshed past him and gravity patterns flirted with his limbs but never grabbed him. Sweat flickered off his body.

As he arced toward Dian Six's island platform, its scalar field cushioned into him, sucking him downward with *too* much force. His aim zigzagged with air drag. His inner ear recalibrated. He struck the railing shin-first, toppled over the side, and had to jam his sword into the fencing to stop his fall. He dangled over the platform edge, swearing.

The startled Proxy was thrown back when the whole platform shook. He made his jump, diving past Caiden and down at Abriss, spear poised.

But he stalled midair like a snagged fish.

Thunder buffeted space as Azura reversed the nodes of the scalar gravity field *below* the Proxy. It repelled his fall, levitating him in a clumsy tumble. Leta's group hurried on below, veering to get to safety beneath other islands.

Azura, I love you. Caiden grinned and let himself drop from the railing.

The fields shifted pattern to propel him downward even faster. The lightseep blade sang in front of him in his white-knuckled grip. He barreled into Six midair. The sword impaled the Proxy's hip, nearly taking one leg clean off. It jarred against the bones and shattered in half. Shards hovered in the air, refracting space.

The scalar field changed again with a *crack* and dropped them both. Dian smacked the ground hard. The field morphed its pattern just in time beneath Caiden, keeling him softly around. Beads of nodal space frothed against his body to lower him gently the last four meters to ground level, right side up.

Caiden's adrenaline was winking out. Pain smeared with every motion. He dropped the broken nub of his weapon and blinked away black spots. Ahead of him, Dian scraped his mangled body off the floor.

Farther past, blurred by distance, En and Leta's group raced to an open doorway in the vast outer wall.

They were free and clear. Dian Six couldn't run to them fast enough on an injured leg.

"You," the Proxy bellowed, the sound distorted through his half skull as he rose monstrously, lips torn and bloodied. A black mane of hair slicked off his shoulders.

Caiden's spark of relief died out. This next part wouldn't be pretty. *His chest core or spine. Both are through the rib cage.*

They stalked around each other, out of strength. Caiden raised his hands, feinted, and took a blow to the hip that let him get close enough to lock Six's arm back.

Their pathetic efforts tumbled them both to the ground, a pile of agony. Caiden balled up charge in his aug fist and punched at the Proxy's chest, over and over. He clawed at whatever materials busted loose.

The Proxy's shoulder joint distended to let him slip from Caiden's hold. He twisted and stabbed upward with the jagged end of his humerus bone, straight into Caiden's soft middle.

A scream exploded out of him. Lancing pain weakened his grip, and the Proxy squirmed free while kicking him over. Dian's arm bone squelched out of Caiden's side.

Caiden clamped a hand over the gushing wound, cursing how useless his finely engineered Graven physiology was if he was still this squishy.

The Proxy suddenly wailed, a bestial sound that blared through his half-wrecked skull. Out of the darkness, a burly shadow engulfed Dian's torso in teeth.

"C!" Caiden toppled over with relief. "Crush him!"

The nophek roared with his mouth full, huge teeth spiking into Dian's ribs and breastbone. The Proxy vise-gripped C's nostrils, pinching his breath off to force release. Then he stabbed the nophek's neck with his broken arm, but C yowled and yanked the rest of the Proxy's shattered limb from its socket.

Caiden wobbled upright.

Energy shifted with him. Left. A sound grated the air.

Azura opened an iris in the ground, a pit to more storage levels below.

"I hear you," Caiden whimpered. Fire tore through his guts as he charged, tackled, shoved with the last of his strength and sheer body weight. They both toppled slippery to the floor in front of the hatch. Caiden skidded in his own blood while grappling and kicking to heave the Proxy into the open pit.

Dian toppled over the edge. Azura's force crested in the floor, spiraling the iris closed over top with a final *slam*.

Banging resonated through the sublevels, echoing with distance as the Proxy fell onto other platforms below. Faintly, Caiden sensed their gravity fields flickering offline: Azura was making sure Six fell a *long* way.

Caiden pushed shakily to all fours and stared at the floor. Sweat drops pattered the metal. His various pains evened out into one whole-body throbbing.

Azura returned to him as a faint thrum inside the floor. The rhythm started to match Caiden's pain, which made him laugh and twinged several more ribs. He flattened his palms and relished her purring, that same delicate presence he'd always adored about his ship, knowing there was a spirit to it, an intelligence merged with his.

"Thank you," he murmured.

C bounded over and licked the side of Caiden's face, bathing him in real purrs.

"And you."

He gripped C's mane and was lifted to his feet. Bruises settled in his body like a sack of rocks tumbling. He inspected the nophek first, grateful to find only a flesh wound in the fatty part of C's neck.

"I know I'm heavy," he wheezed, "but..." With a grunt he hoisted himself the rest of the way onto C's back, draping his soggy limbs over and clinging to C's mane. He cuddled his cheek into soft fur for the short distance it would take to reach the door and outside and the *Wintra*.

Azura followed them in the air and within the floor, his personal tidal wave of invisible force. This little family of his, at least, was safe and complete.

CHAPTER 31

WITHOUT WORDS

The nophek carried Caiden back to family, and while the state of him—bloody, pained, numb—had been his normal for years, he was self-conscious knowing that people who cared about him would see it. It didn't help that the Casthen surroundings returned him to the mental state of his younger time here: unsure whether his actions were doing good or bad, unaware of what it was costing.

Get it together. He righted himself with a groan. The stomach wound leaked beneath his palm.

Taitn's warship was expertly parked ahead in a place where a ship shouldn't be. This gigantic shelf cut into the megastructure was for incubation and storage, open to the atmosphere on one side. No personnel anywhere. Thick tube pillars of various size crowded the space from floor to ceiling, filled with aquatic creatures and plants, glowing pastel hues. The *Wintra* fit snugly between columns of flowering kelp.

Azura's movement became visible: bright schools of fish shivered in ripples, sea buds bloomed or closed, and pods of mammals swirled into frenzies as she passed. Her strange force flowed through the wiring in the walls, through the many eyes of surveillance and the unseen energy fields striping the air.

Caiden sighed and slid off C's back.

He had to be ready to see Abriss taking command of his loved ones.

C leaned into him and grunted a questioning sound.

"Keep alert in there. And don't... just don't scare Leta, all right? She has memories of nophek that weren't as nice as you." He scratched under C's chin and collar. "Stay in the atrium, out of the way."

Azura cracked open the *Wintra*'s side hatch and Caiden headed in. Her slow wind tugged at his legs and coat, kissed the back of his neck. He marveled all around as her force weaved into the walls of the vessel, infested its bones, gripped scaffolding, plucked nerves. A sweet sound like a waterfall behind ice babbled beneath the ship's skin as materials transformed. Biological components plumped into empty spaces. Chemical systems fizzed, carving fresh pathways through the hull as new physics imparted itself on the ship.

He sensed the potential of the universe florescer too. It was no longer a piece of tech with a trigger, but it felt more like an embodiment of Azura's willingness to follow his will. His awareness of it linked her to him, and through him to reality.

Caiden smiled, and when he entered the bridge, he saw the same awed expression on the others' faces. The three Proxies looked edgy and backed away from walls. Leta reached out to spread a shaking palm on the ground.

Ksiñe glided over. The Andalvian's skin shimmered with alarmed prismatic spots. He tackled Caiden's middle, slicing clothes up to expose the gnarly wound. Caiden grunted but kept still. Ksiñe's medical glove explored the injury while a holosplay above his other palm approximated a visual of Caiden's insides.

"Most frequent and hated patient," Ksiñe muttered, forehead strobing prickles of blue.

Caiden chuckled, which hurt a lot. "Love you too."

En limped over. "I was about to rush after you." The words trilled inside her half-repaired throat. Several bins of her tools and aug parts were strewn around the three Proxies, who were mid-repair as well.

"I can handle myself."

"*Can* and *should* are different things, kid." She clapped him on the back, giggled at his wince, then headed back to her repairs. Had Abriss ordered her to tend to the Proxies?

The Dynast Prime lay by one wall on a slab of padded medical gel, with Ksiñe's instruments and medicines surrounding her. The sight gusted

energy through Caiden. Bumps flocked down his skin. Enhanced Gravenness still fizzed in his veins, and while it made a difference in the idle state
of Abriss's gravitas, his resistance took focus, and he had only so much of
that left.

Did I make a mistake, saving her?

Abriss's long brown hair had been combed to one side and shaved
around a deep gash. More lacerations split down her cheek and neck. Her
burned eye was black, puffy, striated with fingernail half-moons. The
cleaned wounds glistened with a nacreous balm like liquid pearl poured in.
Freckles both white and dark teemed in her healing flesh; he could almost
see the motion of them, born then nova, a sparkling slowed to a visible rate.
Graven cells.

Ksiñe slathered something on Caiden's stomach. He choked on a sudden scream and looked down to confirm it was that terrible leech-heal stuff
from Andalvia: his tissues wriggled, plasma foaming inside the hole, and
something webbed over to close it temporarily. The pain forced him down
to a knee. *Bet Ksiñe didn't use this on Abriss. Crimes.*

The medic returned to the Prime. Soft lavender hues clouded across
his skin while his fingers flamed with a dark nervousness. Already part of
Abriss's web.

Leta's Proxy seemed only half-aware. One arm was missing and most of
her body damaged or melted off. She cradled her real body against her chest
and frowned down at her own face.

The big silver-armored Proxy stood straight. "I am Dejin Eight."

Caiden couldn't meet a gaze: these two masculine Proxies had only
masks, one scrolled metal mesh and the other half-shattered glass.

"Isme Two," said the second, but his muffled voice clipped off with a
wince. En started working on the hole in his impaled stomach. Long gossamer hair spilled down his damaged body, and his shattered mask was no
easier to read for its rainbow cracks.

Dejin asked Caiden, "Did you destroy Six's Proxy?"

A sinister tone? Before Caiden could answer, Leta in-Proxy startled to
attention. "He'd go back," she blurted. "Stars forfend, Proxyless he'd go
back to Solthar and he could murder you both."

Dejin nodded once, as if that precisely had been on his mind. Isme sighed.

"He fell," Caiden answered. "*Far.* I sealed the opening above him. He might've survived."

Isme said, "He can choose to return to his real body at any time, by his own will. A one-way trip. He won't be able to reconnect with his Proxy here again over such a distance, but in the Dynast Hold, he can kill us or wake our bodies when he pleases since Abriss isn't there."

"And who knows," Leta added quietly, "what's happening to the others already back there, if they've done nothing to you yet. Came to their senses or died or..." She trailed off and retreated to inner thoughts.

Caiden glanced at Abriss's injuries. "Threi will keep Six here as a weapon able to kill your Prime."

Leta hugged her real body and looked to the other two Proxies. "Get back to Solthar and find out what happened to Aohm, Tay, and Sis. Either seize Dian first or run. Tell the council everything if you can."

Dejin bristled. "We will not leave the Prime."

Isme reached out a mangled hand to pat Leta's armless shoulder. "It's not safe yet. You're stuck with us, Treasure."

The pet name scraped oddly across Caiden's ears. But he wasn't the hero sweeping her out of imprisonment to a better life this time. Her choices were her own and she had people who cared for her. He was happy to see it.

Caiden ran a hand through his hair, fingernails roughing his scalp. The real complication was the Dynast Prime. When they rendezvoused with Laythan and Panca, Abriss would harness up his whole family in her will, whether she meant to or not, like hounds snapped to a pulling line.

From the outer hall, Taitn entered, saying, "There's a room...for one of them." His volume dwindled as his attention snagged on Abriss and his face softened. Caiden went unnoticed for several moments before Taitn looked over with a smile. "Laythan is prepared to swap passengers once we pick a location."

En added, "I'm working with my smuggler contacts. There's a chance his ship can get clearance to leave the universe with delicate cargo."

"The security net's stiff," Taitn said. "Airspace won't be safe. Normal routes will be watched."

Caiden offered, "The dark side of the planet is the best place to meet with Laythan, away from notice and activity. There are—were—abandoned sections of megastructure there, out of rotational use. Check it out?"

En gave a little salute and jogged over to the cockpit. Taitn joined her and slipped into the pilot's seat.

Ksiñe finished applying a translucent membrane seal over half of Abriss's face and neck while the medicaments beneath worked on healing.

Caiden approached her. An earthy fragrance like rainfall and sage cut through the crispness of chemicals. It put hooks in him, but if he focused enough, he could think clearly—migraine notwithstanding.

Abriss's good eye focused slowly, the brown iris paling as the pupil contracted.

Her attention almost bowled him over. He fought for focus and saw something flat and resigned take over her face as she registered his expression. The same reaction Caiden wore often when recognizing his Graven effect.

He said, "You *do* hate it."

She frowned, perplexed.

"The coercion. Disingenuousness. Ambiguity. I can't imagine how bad it is for you." He knelt, mostly because he was getting too weary to stand.

Abriss was quiet for several moments, then said, "I remember a time, as a child, when I simply thought everyone liked me and was very kind." Her sigh came stuttered by pain.

Caiden was overwhelmed with a desire to soothe her. Even if it was just to acknowledge that she was a human deserving of genuine care. He tried to count the years, and compared her to Threi, and couldn't imagine how she'd turned out even this stable while wielding so much power, so isolated. Had she craved losing control, only to pay for it in injury?

Instead of fighting his engraved loyalty, he fit the words he wanted to say within it, bolstering them with believability. "I almost gave up once. You've stopped being able to see when people cherish you for you, or when it's just effect. Those people exist. Your Proxies. That's why you crafted them, isn't it? Poured your hope into them? How much of feeling alone is just you not learning to see what is genuine?"

That made her flinch. Her shoulders drew straighter in the same regal posture that Threi often assumed. Had they both been groomed from childhood to bear whole universes on those Dynast shoulders?

She replied, "I have had more ephemeris years than your entire life to learn what is genuine. To hope the universe might prove me wrong. Today proved to me it doesn't matter. I do not exist to contest being alone. I don't exist for myself. I exist to make everyone *all one*, to grasp the future with a creative hand. I exist for the whole, Caiden Winn. That includes you."

Her stance reminded him of his past vengeance against the Casthen: a single-minded aim, throwing himself at something too large, sacrificing for it, and believing that self-destruction was serving something greater. His desire hadn't been wrong, but it had made him blind to other things.

"You warned me that Threi would try to kill me. I didn't want to listen." The glassiness in her gaze reminded him of Threi again, whenever the man had reminisced on his Dynast past. Perhaps it was just the sibling resemblance that kept matching up memories that should've remained separate.

She ventured, "You used an identical substance to elevate your Graven resonance, didn't you? The vials he had..."

Caiden nodded slowly.

Abriss closed her eyes. "I can guess he synthesized it from the Dominant, and it augments his Dynast expression. Threi didn't share what form the Dominant takes, but Nine sensed it here, farther down in the planet."

An electric chill washed over Caiden. *It's real, not a taunt or a lure. It's here. And I'm here in this web of unlikely events.*

He intended to sort out his origin once and for all, even if he didn't like the answers. He could still eliminate the source of the enhancers and rob these two Graven heirs of a thing that would make them even more powerful. Just like he'd kept Azura from Threi—

A realization jolted him.

The technology Abriss had designed, with the power to destroy worlds. He gaped at her hands, where it *wasn't*. Just messy rings of razor-thin cuts around her fingers and wrists. Caiden's heart smashed against his ribs as Abriss raised both bare hands.

"Aurasever, I called it. Is that an overdramatic name?" She attempted a little smile, but it fell. Her hands quaked and she folded them over her chest. A few of the cuts beaded blood. "Threi took it."

Graven Threi, freshly released and dying to stretch his new freedom, possessed the most powerful tool the multiverse had ever known.

Abriss cocked her head at Caiden's expression. "Threi can't use it just by wearing it. Its function requires a meditative state that draws on the source energy of the luminiferity. Special training."

"But he's crafty."

She nodded. "He is crafty. He'll figure it out or twist it into something new, given time. We cannot let him gain that time, and I…" A vulnerable quaver broke up Abriss's careful enunciation. "I need to get home. Threi is no match for the entirety of Unity's heavens predicting his actions, and I can now discard the pretense that we could ever be equals."

Time. Time was always Caiden's enemy—either too compressed or too drawn out. Ten years of monotony, and now he had mere moments to decide what choice was best for the future of the multiverse *as an entire concept.*

"Caiden."

He fixated involuntarily on her as she spoke his name, her injured voice velvety. She labored to form words. "When Threi figures out how to use the Aurasever, he will collapse Unity entirely."

Imagery flooded Caiden's mind: Azura's universe splintering into light…the same happening to all of Unity, and everything inside transformed or destroyed as physics contorted to new rules. The very nature of being, upheaved, in the largest universe of all.

Abriss whispered, "You have to stop him. *Promise.*"

Caiden tripped over the order. Was it an order? He was determined to do this very thing either way—he'd decided it before even reaching the Harvest. Threi and the Dominant were his unfinished business here, and he would stay to deal with them once and for all.

But everything in his life since promising Leta he'd come back for her had been him paying for breaking that promise.

Please, Abriss's word ghosted as she trembled.

It might have been the gravitas carrying her feelings to him...but he sensed that something in her was fractured for good. Something that she'd patched over and over through the years.

"I promise," Caiden replied, but he heaved to his feet and didn't stay for an acknowledgment. He wasn't doing her bidding. He pushed through gravitas and migraine to head back to the Proxies.

Leta's had slumped unconscious, its function worn out or herself too exhausted, because her real body didn't wake either.

Caiden knelt at her side.

Isme Two cocked his head but didn't threaten. Dejin Eight took one looming step with his gauntleted fist clenched.

Caiden raised his hands in a soft gesture and said, "She's my sister too." His voice broke. He swallowed hard and waited until Dejin backed off. Then he gingerly untangled Leta's body from her Proxy. Silvery fingers vise-gripped her thermal robe. Caiden had to prize them loose. Her hair was caught on ragged edges of glassy chest pieces, and a line of tiny punctures crowned her brow.

Caiden's hands shook as he gathered her up in his arms. She was warm and alive, a strange reality that crammed itself against all his bad memories and nightmare visions of her dead.

He was relieved she wasn't conscious, because he didn't know what to say or do. The world had reshaped them both. Even if she had wanted to connect, how could two broken pieces fit together again?

C stalked over and gingerly sniffed at her toes. "Stay," Caiden whispered.

He carried Leta to one of the spare bedchambers Taitn had cleared out.

Azura's hum sulked into the metal beneath Caiden's feet. Pressure seeped up around him like thunder frozen in time, lifting the edges of his morph-coat and hair. "There you are. Don't like the Dynast Prime?"

Threi's presence in Azura's old ship body used to make the engines staticky and unsettled too. A mismatch of Graven opposites?

Azura filled the walls and made a cocoon of the little room as Caiden entered. Plush coverlets were already peeled back on the bed. He made sure Leta's limbs weren't smashed or crooked as he set her down, then drew the blankets up. He puzzled over the depth of swirled freckles in her flesh, the main feature that distanced her from the girl he remembered. She was otherwise the same on the surface: a young woman now, full of stories he didn't know.

Pain or painkillers started to wash him out—maybe both warring with each other. His need to function battled with fatigue. He sat on the edge of the bed and folded his hands in his lap...and wasn't sure what to do... except sit with the knowledge that this might be his last moment alone with her before Abriss wrapped her right up like a spider reclaiming its moth.

———

Leta awakened, leaden with exhaustion and agonies of familiar types. She was paying for overfunctioning while in-Proxy for so long. She had it easier than Dejin and Isme, who hadn't returned yet—they would pay the most when they did. But then Leta was lucky her body was safe at all. She owed that to Caiden.

She kept her eyes closed while arranging each sensation to rebuild her world at a manageable rate. On top of her lay blankets, too hot and not heavy enough. Beneath, a mossy bed with loamy give and a fleecy surface. Her thin morphfabric suit covered most of her skin and tried to be padded but she still felt every fold and seam in her thermal robe and the coverlets.

The world scratched and prodded her, but somehow it was always her fault, her body the thing that didn't fit. If her bones or her muscles or her skin were reshaped, maybe this or that crease wouldn't hurt. She wriggled, stacking her knees. The air smelled clean and recycled, faintly lilac, and something else: metallic and sharp—

Blood.

Leta opened her eyes. Her breath hitched as she registered Caiden, his frowning profile bathed in a glow. He'd removed his bloody coat, piled on the floor, but some of his cuts still bled. He stared at his bruised, lacerated hands in his lap.

Did he come all this way for me again? He'd interrupted her killing blow, inadvertently saving Threi's life. A bad coincidence—not his fault.

Leta appraised him while he still hadn't noticed she was awake. She couldn't speak even if she'd wanted to. Her thoughts matted around the hard edges of her exhaustion before her mind could construct them into words. And if she'd had those words, they would have stagnated there while the physical apparatus failed to respond. Something always died on its way to speech.

In the past, Caiden had understood her even without words. They'd created a language, a tiny vocabulary of eye movements and touches. She reached out, despite herself. The same gesture at identical speed, her fingers crooked the same way, knuckles brushing the outside of his sleeve.

Caiden flinched and turned her way. His eyes widened, a pretty color blue like Solthar's sky on a hazy day. As a child she'd thought it was a rare color, as not much else on their world had been blue, not even the sea. Perhaps she'd been right about its rarity—blue was a mutation, after all. *Blue as chicory with the purple taken out*, she'd said at six years old, hoping he would think she was clever.

The memory made her smile a bit, and Caiden blinked, that blue glistening. *I know that look.*

She clung to the imagery and tried to recast his scent as not the blood of a man of violence but the boy she knew who would smash his hand in the door to stop it hitting her as she moved too slow. The boy who collected the strikes meant for her, then smiled, crooked, as blood ran down his cheek. The boy who forced a laugh when a fence nail skewered his hand, just so she wouldn't cry for his sake.

Her curled fingers still hovered against his sleeve. He responded—remembered their language—correctly: he averted his gaze and reached up to hook his fingers around hers. *Like a chain, right?* he'd said the first time. *So you know I'm here. I won't let you fall.*

He smiled but the tears in his eyes looked about ready to spill.

She needed to ask why he came. What he intended.

Language required, to ask.

Seeing him now, it was harder to be angry that he'd intervened, since he *had* fought for the Prime and saved them in the end. And saved her body, which she had been ready to leave behind as an expendable thing.

Too tired to keep her arm up, Leta slumped backward, but forgot to unhook her fingers. Caiden stiffened around his wounds and made a hurt sound as he folded sideways, one elbow propped.

She wanted to apologize. Language required. Their proximity unspooled more old memories that had been erased by her Graven treatments. Time collided between them in the luminiferity, and she wished she couldn't feel it so clearly. She wished time would unwind entirely and everything else could disappear for a moment.

Leta folded her forehead against his chest with the lightest contact and let the plush cushions bury her cheek, let something else hold her body up for once. She wanted not to care what he thought, whether her feelings were Graven-coerced, or how much time she had before a duty hauled her back into her Proxy.

Leta sighed out those frustrations.

His heartbeat thudded against her forehead, too fast, out of sync with hers so tired.

He was shaking—at least half from the pain. "You're safe," he said.

I've always been safe with you.

Leta's words derailed and none of them said what she felt anyway, if she even knew what he meant or if this was a dream pressuring her with unresolved doubts.

Caiden gave in to his own fatigue from the fight, the chase, the anxiety. He folded onto his side next to her and murmured, "I apologize for... for manipulating your feelings."

Did he forget I did that very thing when I lured him to Solthar?

He added, "I want you to be free to choose what—"

She squeezed him tight enough to force the air out of his chest. *The fool of a boy has become a fool of a man.*

Caiden sighed and flinched and said nothing more.

Physical contact, slight as it was, grounded Leta as if she were an electric creature. It kept her together, blocked out the world, stopped her edges fraying. Exhaustion towed both of them toward sleep, but Leta sensed something would tear it away soon. She shut out the world and forced herself to enjoy this tiny moment of softness that the universe doled out so ungenerously.

Caiden's breathing started to slow.

A commotion on the ship shattered the peace. Already.

He jerked upright, then hissed as the injury in his side twinged. Shouts ricocheted down the hall. Leta parsed bits together: *security inbound... flagged noncompliant.* The ship's engines roared to life.

Caiden's body sagged and tensed at the same time. Leta pushed him off the bed and started to climb down. He swiveled to stop her. "Rest. You've done enough."

So have you. Like always, he threw himself in too much and admitted too little. But Leta nodded and let him go. Her Proxy was all hacked up anyway... What use was she without it?

CHAPTER 32

TANDEM

Caiden staggered onto the bridge. C piled behind him, quivering, hackles stiff. He'd been bottled up too long on cramped starships. He stuck to Caiden's legs, taking cues from the pressure—a pack instinct, in their tiny pack of two.

Through the cockpit view, a flock of unmanned Casthen security ships poured in from above. They were shaped like broadhead arrows with vicious angles that bent at high speed. Their pleochroic skins shifted color as the viewing angle changed. Thirty darts of a dangerous rainbow.

Taitn stood at the drive guide controls, light twining his hands and forearms as he barreled the *Wintra* out of the megastructure shelf. Weapon particles peppered the Maltaean armor and started to converge on concentrated points as the flock coordinated.

Caiden and C slid to the cockpit. He jammed his heels in and yelled, "Brace!"

C clawed for purchase in the floor seams until the *Wintra*'s scalar gravity switched to a battle pattern, the nodes finer and stronger. Weight returned to bones. Caiden started to lock himself into the tandem flight system beside Taitn.

"Winn!" Taitn shouted. "You're not healed."

"Ksiñe's patch'll work." Caiden secured his boots into the floor holds and initiated a mini gravity field that belted his waist to hold him in place. He jammed the thin, radiant ring of a neural halo over his head. "Azura's universe is our best cheat, and the Casthen don't know it still exists. You have no way of activating it, but I do. She's listening to me."

So I have to stay conscious. Get everyone safe.

He spared one thought for Leta, his heart full and confused. He'd expected her anger, or coldness at least.

The drive guides' viny light congealed and threaded around his fingers, infiltrating his nerves. Azura's ethereal singing immersed his senses. He could tell right away that not only were two pilots better than one, it would also take two to draw out the full potential of whatever Azura had reforged the *Wintra* into.

Taitn grunted exasperation, but his eyes were crinkled with a smile. In elegant motions he bunched then unfolded his arms at a precise rate and fingers flared just so, twirling the blade of the warship down, then thrusting sideways to cut straight between layers of megastructure to caverns beyond. Caiden, flying secondary, added variations to tow the ship's motion in, dodge facility gravity fields, or add a flick of power to clear a tight squeeze.

The flock scattered up behind them. Together, Caiden and Taitn weaved their hands up, knees locked, and skewered the ship though the Casthen mob. They powered forward into a kilometer-wide cavern, weaving the ship into the deep.

Keen as homing bolts, the tiny ships followed.

"En!" Taitn called.

"Got ya," En chirped. She dashed between them and slipped into a seat at the console, then slapped the weapon systems to life.

Caiden felt little turret ports bud across the *Wintra*'s back like a thousand eyes drowsily blinking. En swept her finger across the display, activating all twelve of the warship's weapon toys in a row. The *Wintra*'s insides contorted to ready the machinery, and Caiden would've stumbled at the mental busyness of it if his toes hadn't been locked down.

Taitn yelled, "Endirion! Not every—"

"Cool it, gallant. Sweet Azura might've changed some weapons. See! She reanimated the hulltaxers' chemicals. They look like they're *boiling* in there. Get me closer!"

Caiden and Taitn scooped their hands upward, pitching the ship toward the twilit sky. Megastructure swept past and the Casthen flock zoomed in pursuit. Caiden winced as the shield strikes peppered his brain.

A box of guidance light hovered around En's head to track her micromovements. Her bluish ringlets bobbed as she flinched. "Gotcha!"

Something that was tightly curled blasted out from the *Wintra*'s left side. A white-hot ball streaked toward the closest Casthen ship and unfurled as it went, becoming a riot of tentacled energy. It slammed into the side of the little vessel and wrapped around, half the size of the fuselage. The impact sent the ship spinning while the sticky plasma limbs of the hulltaxer corroded straight through the shell. Metal boiled into shrapnel that sprinkled toward the ground.

En whistled. "I'm calling them hullmelters now."

Caiden felt the mass of them in the warship's belly, hot as lava after Azura revived their biochemistry. "Use them up fast or they'll melt our hull too."

He nudged a thruster to put more of the flock in range. He and Taitn threaded through them while En, giggling, blasted hullmelters with abandon.

The streaks bloomed into whipping arms, slapping ships broadside and tearing straight through. She ran out of hullmelters fast, but the flock had whittled to four: not enough to peck at a warship of this caliber. They peeled off and Taitn steered away from the planet's belt of golden twilight. The dark side of the planet was where their rendezvous lay.

En let out a long, happy sigh and piled her curls up in her fingers, releasing them as long jet-black waves.

Far off, vessels of all kinds buzzed on the megastructure's surface, rustling out of prim traffic patterns as security ships harried through them.

"The Casthen will try to track us," Caiden warned.

"I hope so," En said.

Taitn kicked her shin.

She flopped her head back and grinned at him. "They're busy sorting through all the ships in airspace anyway, looking for Abriss." En disengaged weapons and stretched in her seat. She looped her hair up in a high tail. "The whole universe is in a frenzy. The Casthen are trying to net all the ships in orbit and stall everyone planetside while hiding the fact that Abriss was here at all. From what I gathered, Threi is tied up in a bow calming everyone down and shutting access to the stellar egress."

Caiden said, "If he can't just order everything he wants to happen, that means he's out of enhancers."

From the side of the bay, Dejin Eight boomed, "The Casthen Prime is badly injured. Treatment will slow him down."

Taitn looked over and his gaze caught on Abriss, eyes softening.

Caiden tensed to keep the ship level as it lilted in response. "Taitn," he whispered, pouring his own gravitas into the name. It was enough to snare his friend back.

Taitn winced and nodded guiltily. He trained his eyes ahead and looped his fingers back in the guides.

Caiden stole his own look at their unconscious passenger, half her face and neck still sealed with pearly film. His heart skipped some beats before he could tear his focus away. *There's no getting rid of her now. If saving her was a mistake, I already screwed up.*

Taitn cruised the *Wintra* to the dark side of the planet. Stars glittered above and ice crystals winked below, compressing the ship between heavens. Diamond dust peeled up in their slipstream. These sectors were even less inhabited than Caiden remembered, as if Threi had concentrated Casthen activities closer to his prison over the years.

The megastructure swept below: smooth black plateaus encrusted with rooms and translucent domes, buildings nestled in like knots in wood, and interconnected facilities housing small universes.

"Boring," En said as she curled out of the gunner seat and left the cockpit.

Taitn snorted, amused.

It was nice to see they were closer friends now. When Caiden had joined the crew as a child, their relationship had big, hidden wounds. Those still hadn't healed completely when Caiden left years ago, but he took credit for forcing their overdue reconciliation.

Frost grew mirrored by snow, and Taitn flew into a blizzard. Guidance holosplays fractured across the whiteout view. Thundersnow filled the cockpit in soft pressure booms while Taitn threaded the *Wintra* between lightning.

Caiden tried to fit one worry into the peaceful moment: "I really didn't want you caught up in—"

He cut off, sensing a jolt of presence. The view showed whorls in the cloud and distant blasts of thruster fire.

"Seven," Taitn counted. "Fighters this time, not swarm."

And not small. The monstrous ships cleaved through the storm on either side. Plasma fire striped from above, chewing through the hexagons of the *Wintra*'s armor.

"There's a massive lake ahead filling a hollow in the megastructure," Caiden blurted the moment he remembered. *I hope it's still there.* "The Casthen ships aren't aquatic."

The *Wintra* was. Caiden and Taitn plowed their hands forward at the same time, diving the ship down. Waves appeared through the snowstorm.

En stumbled in. "Need some f—"

The warship plunged underwater. En pitched headfirst into the floor, adroit enough to break her fall with a roll.

The world grew quiet and slow beneath the waves. Overhead, lightning flashes outlined the shadows of the ships coasting above the surface. Purple thruster streaks marked one closest, a big wedge-shaped vessel like a tailless bird in flight. Thin streamers flickered off its wings.

"Nine crimes!" Caiden exclaimed. "That's a—"

Pinch-missile fire volleyed down. Water detonated. The *Wintra*'s matter shields screamed as the impact directed to one wing, which spun the ship to expose its belly for a second hail.

Caiden's stomach dropped as the scalar gravity tried to hold the inversion so they weren't upside down inside the ship. C's claws screeched in the floor seams as his huge weight lifted. Caiden gritted his teeth and joined Taitn in jetting the ship forward and sideways against the stream of pinch beams. The *Wintra*'s energy shielding wouldn't engage in a fluid. The Casthen knew it.

"Where do we go?" Taitn said between panting breaths.

Caiden dug through all the Casthen knowledge he'd tried to raze out of his mind, wanting nothing to do with this place again. He *did* know the Harvest well from all his forced studies and lectures and Enforcer tasks. He hadn't ripped that part out of himself but just buried it like dirt poured on a grave.

En was zooming through maps. "Lake's big as a sea."

The destroyer overhead continued firing at their tail. And something else started up... tiny slashes chattering against the *Wintra*'s nose. Not a weapon. In the dark, it took too long to realize... "Ice," Taitn said in alarm. "The water's starting to freeze. En?"

She found a bright schematic overlay: sure enough, the vast ocean-lake froze toward its center, where they were headed.

Caiden groaned. "They're driving us into a solid ice wall on purpose, and if we pull out of the water now, they'll char us."

The *Wintra*'s nose shoved through bigger shards, taking successive damage. Volleys of pinch fire continued chasing them as they evaded. Taitn exchanged a grim look with Caiden. "Caught between fire and ice—which do you want?"

"Neither." Through the sound of the shattering ice, Caiden heard Azura's ethereal singing. "We change the world."

Caiden punched the drive guides for a blast of speed. Massive blades of ice crashed on the *Wintra*'s nose, thicker and more solid as the ship plowed straight in like the Casthen wanted. The cockpit fluttered with alarms, seconds until the ship started to shred. One or both Proxies bellowed behind them.

"You're—" Taitn fumbled the guides as his ship's skin was stripped off by ice.

Hey, Azura.

Caiden mentally reached for the crystalline structure of the florescer. A warm, organic matrix of energy lay in the *Wintra*'s brain. He lasered his awareness into it and his will for a new universe. The rind bloomed in resplendent waves and frothing space, encapsulating the warship. The battering ice dissolved into bubbles.

Their Casthen pursuit fell off radar, believing its quarry had been chewed apart by the frozen wastes. The *Wintra* cruised through kilometers of solid ice. The silent purple-black landscape was filled with captured white bubbles and streaks of old fault lines.

Taitn, wide-eyed, pulled one hand from the drive guides so he could slick the sweat off his forehead. "All right. Yeah, that works."

En slumped in her seat. "I missed this ridiculous kid."

Caiden stifled a whimper. The universe worked, but it webbed him up, drawing on all his attention to maintain. C shook, happier in this world, and licked Caiden's hand.

"Good boy," he said, but couldn't tear his attention away enough to pet the nophek. The universe was a heady weight in his consciousness, like it hadn't been previously, as if Azura was *too* anchored by his will now that she didn't have a chrysalis to fixate her. If he lost consciousness or wavered, she would let the universe dissolve with him.

"If the Casthen think we're destroyed," Caiden began wearily. Sweat trickled down his neck. "We can—"

Then everything *cracked*.

A fissure blew the ice thirty meters apart around them. Azura's universe melted the tumbling ice before it hit, but the warship was heaved around like a stick in rapids. More ice sheets calved off the mass, and water rushed in to fill the canyon. Caiden whiplashed forward. Pain exploded up his spine and down his leg, struck his brain, and winked out his focus.

He lost his grip on Azura's universe.

The rind sucked back to the ceiling. Caiden's senses flipped from smooth to serrated in an instant. His scream was eaten by the explosive cracks of the ice around them as pressures poured onto the unprotected ship.

Taitn piloted up through the chasm as walls of ice caved in. The Casthen's destroyer hovered up ahead, emitting pulses that fractured the mass.

The snowstorm had cleared completely. Taitn skated against the frozen ocean's surface, which stretched for kilometers to walls of megastructure on all sides. Spindly pillars of some ancient tech pierced up from the surface, sparking filaments of lightning between them: a great spider web of energy. Taitn stayed below the field while the silent destroyer gained height above them.

As they sped on, titanic frozen waves arced out of the ice plains like ancient monoliths, formed from water crashing the same way over and over.

"Where do we head?" Taitn asked.

Caiden fought to concentrate. His eyes were confused by the wild, wind-brushed ice shapes because they appeared filled with veils of light in constant motion. Tendrils unfurled and dissolved.

Then he recognized this sight from old reports of Casthen energy operations. "They're alerids," he said, awed. "This has to be the subtemp zone, incubating alerid species."

"They're harvesting *wraiths*?"

"Just the energy off them. Stay low."

The destroyer would have to be tracking them by sight.

Taitn gaped and weaved around more giant curls of ice, frozen tidal waves, an ancient storm paused in time. Inside, pulsating cerulean spiraled through a gossamer bioluminescence at massive scale.

Growing in height and complexity, the waves formed a mountain range of glassy purple with blue cracks. Each massif was a cocoon filled with maturing alerids that looked like smoldering suns entombed in winter. Gigantic conduits perforated in to channel their violent energy out, then snaked across the ocean's frozen surface and down into the abyss and the facility beneath.

"There, those," Caiden said, breathless, hardly believing his own suggestion, "the conduits are our way out. We can...we can fly into them."

"That energy will obliterate us. If you lose consciousness again and the universe drops—"

"Says the man who flew into a star." Caiden chuckled, but it burst needles in his chest, reminding him he really wasn't all right. "I'll hold on for a few kilometers. Once within a conduit, we can fly inside the facility and underneath the top plate. No one will track us."

The destroyer flickered red in their ravaged sensors. Taitn veered the warship into the frozen mountains' tight valleys, cutting off the enemy's visual.

Caiden's lungs burned and his stomach felt full of coals, but C nuzzled the back of his legs and Azura sang at the edges of his hearing. He wasn't alone.

Billows of light filled the ice cliffs. With the warship knifed into the mountain's narrow cracks, Caiden sought out one of the massive conduit pipes' atmosealed outlets.

Deep breath.

"All right. Go."

With a mental flick, he activated the universe around the ship and plunged into a river of raw power. Bands of void tangled with gemstone radiance, clawing around Azura's rind.

He hadn't actually been sure she'd keep them safe.

No time for relief—his nervous system screamed in every inch of him. Fever and fatigue gnawed his awareness to shreds as he kept up the link with Azura, all her force centered on his will to keep the universe active. "Straight," he murmured, "just go…away here."

Taitn, grimacing, sped inside the megastructure's veins of energy. The ship passed a junction beneath an ice mountain that cocooned one colossal alerid overhead. Translucent veils wrapped a ghost of unrefined energy. It waved tendrils of light or arms of force: unclear if it was a creature or an organic reactor. The radiance resembled tissues, layered and clouded, filled with veiny filaments.

Everyone on the bridge hushed at the sight. Taitn cruised onward and yawed down into another river of power surging away.

"Just ahead," Caiden said, more to himself. Energy whooshed past, splattering strange colors against the rind. Through the neural link it felt like a planer scraping his brain. He was losing his sense of Azura. "Right here…"

"Winn?" Taitn quavered.

Caiden sagged in the scalar hold, propped upright by C's flank.

Taitn accelerated to blinding speed and pierced out of the first atmoseal they passed. The maneuver yanked Caiden hard and Azura's universe shriveled away. En swept in from somewhere as Caiden pitched out of the tandem hold. She wrapped him up, muttering gentle words while she let him collapse in her lap.

The *Wintra* dipped beneath the top plate of the megastructure. *Safe.*

Guidance rays burst online in the dark, outlining the industrial features of the abandoned sector. Bioluminescent things crept in to overgrow the caverns and passageways. Fungus or maybe flowers, plus vines and fleshy lace.

Caiden's weary sigh squeaked. Ksiñe knelt at his side and started a frantic inspection. He peeled the membrane off Caiden's middle and made a hissing sound. Darts of fear striated his face.

En petted Caiden's hair back in a hypnotic rhythm. Analgesics ensured he didn't feel whatever Ksiñe was doing with the needles of an etheric surgery device, but he smiled when the Andalvian muttered, "Did not miss patching you so much."

Out the cockpit view, more of the biological mass overtook the megastructure. Most of it appeared inert: a dried-out fungus with small pockets of bioluminescent activity, like an organ still churning away or a dendritic network sparkling. Huge gashes had been lasered into the mass, plus craters like a giant's fist trying to dig it out: evidence of the Casthen's failed battle with whatever this overgrown thing was, before the whole sector had been decommissioned and the aggressor died out. So many secrets and so much history, this place.

Taitn slowed in an enormous cavern. He opened comms to Laythan and talked too quietly for Caiden to parse.

They'd made it. Safe for now, and completely hidden.

Caiden rolled his head to the side. Abriss lay asleep on the other side of the room. *"Safe." That depends...*

En straightened Caiden's head between her hands and peered down. "Winn, just black out already. You're so stubborn."

Caiden laughed at that, which exploded pain in his middle, and the blackness swallowed him as he cuddled his cheek into En's palm.

CHAPTER 33

TREASURED

Leta's awareness fumbled into her Proxy. Its wreckage vied for her attention: hardened joint fluids and overcrusted biolacing, depleted plasma, overtaxed organs. She slammed offline as much damage monitoring as she could to dampen the agony to a simmer.

The *Wintra*'s bridge smelled medical: blood and chems, fluid-sweet aug parts, crisp air flushing out fear sweat. Through the cockpit view lay a cavern of ancient megastructure covered in luminescent knobs of fungal growth and draping curtains of petals.

Voices stitched into Leta's awareness.

"Just wear the damn corset." Endirion's voice. There was a buzzy flaw in their consonants. "We don't want your guts spilling out or that flash-meld pack punctured."

Caiden was sitting cross-legged, getting dressed. Scarlet and mauve bruises covered him, the color meaning they'd bloomed again after a scour. Deep things. And so many scars.

Leta tried not to stare. Why did it matter if he'd chosen the path of scars?

He wore clean gray trousers and a sleeveless shirt fit tight, over which Endirion was plucking the cinches of organic corset webbing. Caiden's posture drooped tiredly. En fussed with armor patches before tugging Caiden's limbs through his morphcoat. It fuzzed into tiny black feathers.

En pulled fingers through Caiden's short, dirty-blond hair and frowned at the length.

These tiny gestures of closeness clearly illustrated how much Endirion had *missed* Caiden. The way one lock of Caiden's hair always curled the wrong way, the embarrassed inattention Caiden affected, his athletic shape that suggested he'd grown up so much.

In all the awful events that had transpired, could Leta take credit for and be happy that this was one of them? Caiden thrust back into the orbit of those who cared for him...

Leta wished, a bit, to creep into that orbit too. Back in time to that moment they'd shared before the ship chase.

Not she half machine and he half killer.

Instead, a girl and a boy in a field of wildflowers. Friends.

Caiden winced as Endirion tugged the bandages padding his abdomen. Then he noticed Leta was conscious in-Proxy. She rose to her feet with a wobble, and he walked over with a limp while fussing with the fit of his clothes. He looked over her in broken glances, making her even more aware that her Proxy—so useful for so much—was a thick mask between her and everything else. It shelled her off from connecting with him like they almost had before.

She still had questions for him and an apology to deploy.

Caiden stopped a couple meters away. He rubbed the back of his neck absently.

The brand. Leta still had hers. Caiden's was inscribed in diamond now. Why had he chosen to keep it? Why upside down? More questions.

"Thank you," she said.

The words crossed the space between them. Rope thrown across a gorge.

Caiden simply nodded.

Leta scratched along the nub of her missing arm, then the gashes in her cheek, chunks taken out. No wonder he cringed. Most of her facial nerves were shot, no chance of a smile.

Caiden finally met her eyes for a longer moment, and Leta puzzled over the strange new determination in his face. It was urgent and hurting, with an undertow of guilt.

What if their tender moment had actually been a dream while she slept? An ideal, another fiction. What if *this* was real: ten years of distance crammed in these two meters between them.

Or was the tension simply his insecurity about whether she was the Dynast's creature, bound to leave with the others? *Dear stars, we have to bridge this gap with words, don't we?*

"Winn!" the pilot shouted from outside.

Caiden startled. The roar of a new ship tore the air and pummeled the walls of the cavern. It was Caiden's friends' freighter, the *Second Wind*, arriving. He seemed grateful to leave, dropping his gaze and striding out, taking that grim determination with him.

"Nine?" Dejin called from the *Wintra's* atrium. He cradled Abriss in his arms.

Isme emerged from the room the Prime had been resting in. "The medicines will have her sleeping for a while, the medic said." Isme looked far worse for the ordeal than Leta remembered. Clotting foam, ill-fitting stopgaps, and cracks filled with a black matter that couldn't settle on one viscosity. He hobbled, the grace robbed from him.

Heart sore, Leta stepped to his side as the three of them exited the ship.

Dejin explained, "Even with the Prime unconscious, the crews will be compelled to help her. I have discussed our course with Taitn Maray Artensi and Kasiñae. The *Second Wind* will bear the four of us back to Unity. Her healing can continue during the voyage."

The freighter settled on the rough surface of the cavern floor, crushing plant life that glommed over the metals. Fronds waved along the walls, whispering together.

Taitn stood with his hands on his hips. Beside him Caiden waited impatiently, wringing his wrists in his hands. The freighter's auxiliary engines powered down. Insects croaked in the fresh silence, and wind skipped over apertures a half kilometer overhead, whirring with gossip.

The *Second Wind's* gangway extended, its door folded open, and Caiden jogged over with all the buoyant energy he hadn't mustered for Leta. An elderly human male and a dark-skinned saisn emerged from within.

"Let's go, then," Isme said, crossing over to the new ship. "Every moment we wait, things get worse here and at home."

At home . . .

Dejin grunted and followed, Leta behind him. The captain and the saisn dropped their conversation and pivoted to Abriss as she was carried into proximity.

"Captain," Eight rumbled.

"Laythan Paraïa," he said.

"You will transport us to Unity. Do you have a room for her?"

"Show them, Panca," Laythan said.

The saisn nodded and returned inside the *Second Wind*. The Proxies followed, and Leta caught half a glance of Caiden, which was all she could bear of his injured expression. He was biting his tongue. This was what his grim mood had been about, seeing his family whipped up in Graven purpose that had nothing to do with him.

Panca showed them to a large medical suite with an operating slab in the middle. Dejin laid Abriss down on this, which filled under pressure with candescent light and plumes of heat.

Isme let the saisn leave, then the three of them sat around their Prime in a stifling silence.

Words that had queued up somewhere in Leta spilled out: "We're so far from home."

"We will get there together." Isme's shattered mask couldn't show a smile, but Leta recognized the sound of it in his ashy voice.

We.

Three of seven was a sorrowful count.

He added, "But right now, I need to return to my body in the Hold. We still don't know what happened or is happening there."

Leta tried to read his masked face, the cracks throwing shards of rainbows across the room. Bloodied gossamer hair slithered off his shoulders as he tilted his head. She whispered, "Isme."

He chuckled bravely. "I'm no towering ursgen, but I can outsmart or pacify the others, and the councils are accustomed to listening to me. My consciousness returning transcends the limits of space and time, faster than any message we might send to Solthar."

Leta agreed with his logic but craved to deny it. After everything, the thought of one more person she cared about leaving—into unknown dangers—crushed all the fortitude she was building back up. Her gaze followed the fissures in his face, and she searched for a sense of whether his bravery was real. Her mind's eye imprinted his true face: eyes gemstone and gentle, his cheeks like melted glass with sparks scintillating within and golden nerve firing suspended like lace.

"Isme, once you leave, you won't be able to return to your Proxy until it's closer to Unity."

"It must be done. You suggested it yourself before—now you won't let me go? The Prime will still have you and Dejin."

"You've both been in-Proxy for long enough that..." She had to say it plainly. "You might die immediately upon return, unable to reintegrate. Like Three and Ten."

"Then Dejin is taking a bigger risk than I am by staying."

Leta picked up one of Isme's hands, crackling her wrecked fingers around his.

"Don't fret, Treasure. It's likely Dian survived the fight and is still in-Proxy here. If he'd returned to his real body, I suspect he would have killed or awoken us both already, to rob Abriss of her guardians while Threi tries to track her down. If Tayen was still dissenting, she would have done the same, correct? Perhaps Aohm or Sisorro have everything under control already."

Leta had a sudden thought. "I can seek Dian out. Scry remotely through the luminiferity, see if he's still in the Harvest and where. All this back and forth is making me stronger."

Isme cocked his head aside and squeezed her hand. "I'd be grateful for confirmation of at least that much of what I'm headed into."

"I'll check now." She would do anything to make this whole mess a little lighter.

Dejin scooted close on her other side and offered one brawny arm. "Consent, mae li sistra? I will prop you up."

Leta leaned her fleshless shoulder against his armor. She kept hold of Isme's hand, too, and thrust her awareness from her Proxy.

Her consciousness slithered off mechanical tendons, uprooted from smashed organs, and drained into the luminiferity, where she resisted the draw of her real body on the *Wintra*. Instead her spirit evaporated from droplet into field, a cloud in the vastness of space and time.

Leta stretched her awareness to inhabit the skeleton of the megastructure, the hidden universes it built around, and the warm pockets of its gardens. Internal rivers and air systems infiltrated the structure, which made it appear biological: endocrine, lymphatic, bloodstream, nerves.

Her consciousness peeled back those physical dimensions and raced through a patchwork of vibrations. She wouldn't have been able to accomplish such a feat mere days ago.

When she'd sought out Dian the first time to release Caiden from his cell, it had been by aligning herself with the details that only someone like a sister would know. The flavors of his emotions. The way his mind thought in frayed directions. The scars represented in the geometric paths painted on his surface. How he could never sit still, always bouncing between tasks. Now all Leta could imagine was his snarl. His faith twisting inside out like a skin, showing the monster he wanted to be.

Her awareness whispered through the gigantic bones of the Casthen Harvest, across metal and water, sweeping the planet for the snag that was Dian Six. Flesh and machine and music. Rage and freedom and—*there*—she found him deep in the twilight in a grand hall as busy as a hive, with Casthen drones streaking in and out.

Threi, a black hole of Graven magnetism, stood nearby, but Leta ignored him and anchored on to Dian, wrapping into the quicksilvery false lightseep of his marrow.

He is *still here.*

Six's spirit guttered inside the wreckage of his Proxy.

Leta struggled to quiet her thoughts to not alert him, to settle on his skin as soft as a breath. But he noticed. His brain grew hot and spiced with resistance. He jerked, raising a glave, but couldn't read the sensation beyond "threat."

Around him, a score of Casthen bristled too.

Leta nested into Dian's tangled neural firing and gathered up aural patterns. The tones made a shape that was absolutely Threi ordering his teams: "Catalog the research universes we can afford to lose testing the device, and prioritize rinds that match the specs I gave you. I want to know the trigger and I want to know if there's a limit on size. Start evacuations now."

Groups flocked in to his attention, then were whisked away by his commands. Leta grasped the expansive system Threi had shaped while imprisoned: intricate and finely tuned, the Casthen Harvest was an extension of his willpower. He wasn't enhanced anymore, but he didn't need to flex his gravitas. The Casthen chain of command might as well have been his nerves, carrying signals to distant muscles, flexing work, moving data. He was just as frightening as Abriss, and he hadn't needed Graven coercion to achieve it.

"I don't care where you get them from, I want resistant species on the egress. She'll try to talk her way out of reach."

Little arguments blipped from the crowd. Cartographers complained about critical shipments and time-sensitive deliveries. The egress couldn't be closed entirely.

"Whittle the number of departures as long as you can. I'll head out to conduct the exit inspections myself, but I need to see to Feran before anything."

That name was the single stutter in the execution of Threi's will, heady with urgency. He otherwise didn't hesitate or let emotion etch his words.

Leta distilled the intel she needed. *Evacuation. Feran. Aurasever testing. Limited time until Threi's at the egress.*

Dian Six's electric rage riveted at Leta suddenly. His mind hissed, flame meeting water, billowing around her consciousness.

Sssssssssss. Sister sister sister.

Dian clawed into the edges of her awareness so she couldn't slither away. His Proxy body soaked her in like a polarity shift, an alignment that made a whirlpool of him. He would trap her in his own brain.

His thoughts were a tempest: *You think you're clever, Nine. You'll see the truth yourself soon.*

Leta thrashed while he clutched at her. His Proxy's neural lines were burning up like fuses at their combined input. Dian was a trickle of spirit woven into a body, meanwhile Leta was unanchored, a wave of force cohabiting, co-creating the reality they shared. And in her version, she got loose.

She refocused on her own Proxy in Eight's arms. Her lightning rod. Her anchor. She tried to forget Dian Six existed, tried to shed his rage. With his

Proxy physically laboring to hold them both in his injured state, Leta ripped away and arced through luminiferous dimensions, plowing back into her Proxy.

Every best swear she knew across three hundred languages flooded her brain as her eyes flew open and Dejin jarred at the force of her returning. She might've voiced some or many of those curses, from the way he went rigid.

"He noticed me, he knows for sure we're still here too and that I was spying." The effort of the trip compounded in her, overclocking her lungs and heart.

Isme slid his palm over her temple, cradling the side of her face with a tenderness that made her realize how badly she was shaking.

He gave her a valiant nod. "That means I have time to haul him out of his Proxy by waking his real body. Thank you for the look, Treasure."

Before she could respond, he was gone. Before his courage faltered, perhaps. Isme broke from his Proxy and arrowed across space and time to his real body in the Dynast Hold. Leta sensed it as a death: his energy bled from the physical body that toppled sideways into her lap. She curled her arm around him and fell toward Dejin with the weight.

Dejin shifted so he propped the two of them up against his chest. He waited while Leta held Isme silently for a long moment.

"This isn't fair," she whispered.

Like Leta, Isme had felt his Proxy was a tool to filter his best into the world while leaving the difficulties behind. Though the strongest of them in-Proxy, he was the most vulnerable in the real.

She murmured, "So much is asked of him. And Dian is a tyrant who'll be restless and angry and consume everything in his path once he returns to his body."

"Trust, ai lia. We each make the best of this."

Leta had to make the best of her capability, too, in the time that Isme and others had bought her. She had Caiden to face and information to share. Despair could find her later.

"Watch over us, Dej."

"I will be here." He wrapped both arms around them.

Leta curled against Isme's Proxy, his soft hair and cinnamon scent, and battled off spears of uncertain sorrow.

She closed her eyes and flew.

It was almost as fast as a blink: she opened her eyes in her real body, groggy, tangled in coverlets on the bed in the *Wintra*. The immensity of sensations was wildly different. One leg and arm pushed out, freezing, and the others were sticky with sweat, too hot. She cuddled back under covers, but spasms crawled through her body as the temperature equalized, like another spirit trying to shove into the same flesh. Her nerves, fighting over space. Other phantom irritations poked through from her Proxy's lingering senses, one-armed and mangled. Her real biology tried to convince itself of the same faults.

She was struck again by how different this smaller universe felt. The field of consciousness was constrained, the information content habitable. Leta battered her head against the pillow to dislodge the possibility that Threi *was* right…

This multiverse, created to introduce limits and soften existence for expanded beings like her. Like the Graven. Perhaps even tailored to specific purposes. Full of variety and potential…

Now isn't the time to doubt Abriss. I need everyone safe.

Leta slid off the bed and snugged the blanket around her shoulders. Bare feet, frigid floor. She stumbled on rubbery legs through vertigo as she crept into the *Wintra*'s dark hallway and called, "Caiden?"

Voice too hoarse. She started to speak again, but down the hall came an answer.

A low, guttural sound Leta knew too well.

The darkness rippled.

Paws shook the floor, nails rapping. A storm of muscle surged toward Leta, teeth flashing. Her chest seized up, cutting off her shriek. A child's terror filled her, and a phantom reek burned in her nose. She slammed against the wall and the ship became a giant metallic box like the transports. Ten years old again, Leta scrunched up tight and shut her eyes. Her mind returned to her people stampeding into the light. Shouts of relief morphing into screams.

A hot breath whuffed across Leta's ear. She squeaked and clawed her fingers tight in her hair.

Bodies shredded as nophek fought for sweetmeats. Lapped up pools of blood. Snarled and vibrated the vessel floor. This nophek purred deep. Meaty breaths sizzled through her hair, a nuzzle grazed her fingers. Leta flinched hard.

Terror swallowed her but the jaws didn't come. The monster's furry head pressed down onto her hands, its purr juddering through her skull. Fear froze her brain, but some delusion murmured that the monster's fur was very soft on her skin. The pressure and the steadiness of its thrum, plus the power inside its skull: the gloss, infant and wild, a dense pit of elaborate energy.

Leta focused on that. It had a tempo of its own that the nophek's physiology was entrained to; purring and bloodstream and biorhythms all harnessed in sync by the gloss.

Sobs un-balled from her throat, letting a thread of air into her lungs.

The patient monster didn't move.

She wasn't ten, this wasn't the desert, and there shouldn't have been nophek in the Casthen Harvest.

Caiden's pup.

"*C!*" he shouted, voice breaking. His feet thundered over. "Back! Back, back...crimes, you've—" He cut himself off and landed on his knees in front of her. His hands came down on both her shoulders, making her wince before the firm pressure anchored her into the present. "Are you all right? You're safe."

Leta uncurled, shaky with adrenaline. This really wasn't the reunion she'd hoped to design.

"I'm sorry," he said. "Sorry. Didn't expect you to wake. Out, C!"

The nophek whined and backstepped from the hall, too large to turn around.

Caiden straightened Leta, reading her face. She skittered away from his eye contact, simply nodding. He released her and fell back against the wall opposite, shaky himself.

Leta tried not to stare, but he was slightly surreal. She couldn't help trying to stretch her memories of the boy to fit this man, or else shove the vision of the man into what she remembered. Time had carved harder lines in him, made his smile more crooked, made him favor his augmented left arm over his right.

He seemed to remember to give her time when she couldn't speak.

After a while her eyes focused, breathing evened, and she gazed down the hall at the tip of the nophek's finned tail peeking out of a doorway as it hid, but not very well. "You must have healed a lot, to be able to *raise* one of the beasts that—" She'd started her sentence before knowing how to finish it and didn't want to say the rest.

Caiden nodded against the wall. "I thought...I imagined I'd healed my grief over you too. But here you are."

I'm a scar reopened. Leta tugged her thermal robe around her shoulders and warmed her cheeks in its collar. Was she an eyesore? He'd had years to process her. He had a neat little box for their relationship, a label for it, with proper distance. Leta had forgotten about him and now it felt like no time had passed. They were coming at this from very different sides.

Warming up friendlier questions, she asked, "You came to rescue me again?"

"Actually, no. You're not mine to rescue. I apologize for trying to force a choice on you, on Solthar."

Leta reciprocated quietly, "I didn't mean my betrayal to turn out the way it did. I apologize for...for reopening such a big wound and assuming your heart would recover."

"Call it even, then."

She smiled but also shuddered as the adrenaline sparkled out of her body and left her empty, lightweight. Insufficient. "Then you came here because...?"

"To stop Threi being released. I needed your help to do it, but I was too late."

"I was going to kill him, you know."

Caiden looked up and blinked at her.

Leta chuckled as if it could be funny now, how everything happened. "I had my sword raised. The killing blow." She frowned. "Coincidence saved him. Why?"

Graven designs. Like Abriss kept saying. Events echoing to an outcome that was already in motion.

Caiden replied low, "So you wouldn't become a murderer."

"I'm flattered? What makes you guess I haven't killed anyone, in-Proxy? I can fight."

"You'd fight to save."

He was guessing she hadn't changed. Leta had fought on missions, but conflict in Unity was always minor—she'd never needed to kill. She said, "I might be able to murder if it meant stopping something worse."

He stood and offered her a hand up. "You shouldn't have to. Let's talk it through with everyone."

CHAPTER 34

PROMISE

Caiden was relieved to see Abriss's gravitas wearing off somewhat now that she was in the freighter's med-suite, away from the crew. Everyone had gathered on the *Wintra*'s bridge, with Leta out of place among them. Caiden was still kicking himself for the nophek scare.

She spoke clearly and easily, rehearsed, but he noticed her fisted right hand hiding spasms.

"Threi ordered testing of 'the device,'" Leta said, "which must be the stolen Aurasever. It sounded like he had a specific universe he meant to collapse, but didn't mention which. He's placing Graven-resistant species on the Harvest universe's stellar egress and plans to head there himself next. He mentioned going to see 'Feran'?"

Everyone looked to Caiden as if he were a Casthen expert. "Never heard of it. Code for the Dominant, maybe?"

En added, "Intel says the search for our Dynast Prime is getting more comprehensive and they'll be combing these abandoned parts of the planet before long."

Laythan dragged his hand through his beard. "We'll be able to smuggle the Prime through the egress, between En's blackmail and sleaze—"

"Guilty."

"—and my bureaucracy and forgery. My partner knows someone here in Assistive Services who can help." Caiden raised an eyebrow at the mention of a partner, not shared before, but Laythan ignored him to continue, "As long as Threi isn't at the egress."

"If he's not going there immediately," Caiden said, "he must be out of enhancers. I need to find the Dominant to ensure he can't synthesize more."

En cracked her augmented knuckles, the sound overdramatic. "We reach the Dominant before he does. That solves most things."

"Not 'we,' En."

Her gray gaze bored into him as she cracked her other knuckles, slower.

Caiden had worked out every contingency. "Laythan pilots the *Second Wind* with the Proxies. Ksiñe goes with him to keep Abriss and Leta alive. Taitn flies the *Wintra* with En, keeping the Casthen off everyone's backs, and—"

"I'm going with *you*," Panca interjected. "In a den of machines, you'll need my help, even with Azura along."

"And I'm going," Leta said.

Everyone swiveled to look at her. Her gaze dropped right to the floor. "My Proxy will stay with Abriss, but I need the Graven Dominant too. I'm going."

Laythan appraised her. "Better the other way around, girl. Leave your Proxy here."

She shook her head. "I wish, but I need to be able to talk to Abriss with a clear mind. For the sake of everything, I can't let these events break her, and she won't listen to adorants like you."

Caiden did admire Leta's fierceness. "You aren't well enough. It's too much."

"She is dying." Ksiñe's neck strobed irritated orange arcs. He snapped his medical glove online, projecting a holosplay of dimpled air strung up with a luminous map of Leta's physiology and coupled quantum states. Disintegrating gradually. "Creature of Unity, not designed for any of this. She can't stretch much more across space and time."

Leta straightened. "I already know how fragile I am, and you can speak to me like I'm here. This is why I need the Dominant strain too. I'm not going to sit around and wait for someone else to heal me."

Caiden said, "We don't know enough about what we're heading into. It's safer if—"

"*Caiden*," Taitn said, raising his voice.

The whole group sat upright.

"That's your real name, isn't it? The one you tried to give up when you lost her. You don't have to keep giving things up in order to move forward. I hate this philosophy of yours." Taitn roused with unusual energy, and Caiden almost recoiled. This rare anger fit startlingly well on the pilot's features. "Your idea that because other people are suffering across the multiverse, it's not right for you to feel happy—that you have to suffer too. That you were designed as some kind of tool to fix problems. We can confront things together. Let us go with you."

Taitn's body language deflated. Had those words pent up over all ten years?

"I hear you," Caiden said.

En cracked a final knuckle. "Hate to ruin your moment, Taitn, but he's actually right about the crew division. Our individual expertise is required to get everyone safely out of this universe. Except for Panca…and Leta. You're sure, dear?"

Leta looked straight at Caiden to answer. "I'm choosing to stay. It might be the first choice I've made on my own."

That shut up the remainder of Caiden's arguments. This is what he'd wanted before, to tear her away from Abriss long enough for her to have agency without question.

She added, "I am different from the timid girl you remember, Caiden. I *know* everything my Proxy knew and could do: how to pilot ships, how to fight, stealth and survival. And my awareness extends into domains of information inaccessible to others. Those strengths are mine, not my Proxy's. Flesh is the only thing that fails me."

He rummaged up a smile. "You aren't that different. Whip-smart and stronger than anyone I knew, for what you persevered through."

She blinked a lot and looked away as if surprised by the praise.

"Damn," En said, "you two are cute."

Laythan had to grumble, "I don't like the setup, but it's what we have."

Taitn said, "The *Wintra* is too conspicuous to fly closer to the Dominant for long without snagging Casthen military, but the megastructure is too huge to go on foot."

"Vehicles," Panca offered.

Taitn was already bringing up a map to zoom through. "Here. In this abandoned sector there's a series of parking flats. Bound to be something there, or mover lifts if not. I can fly you three there and drop you off."

Rising to his feet, Caiden asked Ksiñe, "You just need a sample or data of whatever the Dominant is, right, in order to heal Leta and assess my enhancement? I'll bring back whatever I can get my hands on."

En tsked at him.

"We," Caiden corrected. "We'll bring it back."

"Better."

Caiden rolled his eyes, then noticed Leta wringing her hands, squishing freckles of different shades and layers beyond skin deep.

"Leta," Caiden said as the rest of the crew dispersed to their tasks. "What do you need, if you're coming with me?"

She flexed her shoulders, which made the morphfabric suit—a similar rare tech to Caiden's morphcoat—stiffen into pads of armor. "Your nophek... If he's coming too, you'd better introduce us."

Leta had taken the time to rush to the other ship, in her real body, and give Dejin Eight a very short goodbye. She couldn't stay longer than a handful of heartbeats—the threat of tears ached in her cheeks at seeing Isme's Proxy empty and hearing Dejin's voice rough with emotion. He'd wished her strength, and Leta couldn't bring herself to lie and reassure him they'd all be reunited soon. She didn't know for sure. Instead, she'd kissed his cheek before slipping away.

Laythan then departed with the Proxies, Abriss, and Ksiñe to escape the Casthen world. Taitn cruised the *Wintra* as much inside the megastructure as possible to avoid detection en route to the parking flats.

Leta sat on an ammunition box in the *Wintra*'s armory while Endirion braided back both sides of Leta's hair for combat. She fidgeted and tried to avoid thinking about having to fight in this body. The straps, tools, and light armor she wore had been expertly fitted by Endirion, but it was bizarre to be wearing gear usually reserved for her Proxy.

She watched Caiden raid the equipment. He, conversely, moved more comfortably with each piece added: chemblade, pinch glave, packs of performance enhancers, painkillers, more of the nophek's meds, sabmel, night-vision drops. He tested the chemblade, a meter-long rail of matter that Leta had never seen in Unity, halfway between blistering light and liquid nitrogen touching boiling water.

The saisn, Panca, geared up too: a multitool pack, sniper glave, flexfield armor, and sensory veils coiled around her head. She cut a lean, stylish figure looking just as capable in a fight as working on machines. There were no mirrors in the armory to check, but Leta wished to think she looked that good too.

Latent in the walls was Azura's energy, and Leta felt deeply soothed around it, like the inevitable separation of spirit and cells slowed down. A minor version of the treatment she'd had before? She hoped it meant she could handle being out of Proxy for longer.

Banging sounds heralded the nophek as he padded into the armory, his tail too long for the hall outside. His muscular black body filled the shadowy doorway while his reflective round pupils blazed like moons.

"Hey," Caiden called to the beast, who treaded over to him, across the room from Leta. "Be gentle. Go say hello."

Leta went board-stiff, and Endirion noticed. He finished clipping the ends of her braids to her head and patted her shoulder. "Don't worry, he's a sweet pup. The nophek too."

Endirion strolled away and the nophek crept over. His nails retracted and the rapping sound stopped. His chunky paws splayed flat with webbing. He made a chittering sound and kept his head low.

Leta shut her eyes.

"Gentle!" Caiden reminded.

C whined, then lightly head-butted Leta's chest, pressing a squeak out of her.

Leta forced her hands up. *Soft. He really is soft. Focus on that.*

She circled her shaking arms around his huge head, the flicking ears and brawny neck, into a mane of thick, downy fibers.

Breathe. Leta thought of all the larger monsters she'd encountered in-Proxy on Unity's wildest planets. Her real body didn't handle the dread as well, but her mind was the same. She'd weathered through worse. *This isn't the nophek from the slaughter.*

The hum of the gloss seeped into her and slowed her racing heart into sync. The crystalline thing had complex electrical structures that extended into the luminiferity, giving the beast keen senses. Could he feel her distress?

"H-hi."

C huffed. Purrs soaked into Leta's skin, and tears welled behind her eyelids, but it was a weird kind of relief. A pressure release, water without meaning.

Leta opened her eyes. C pulled away and lay on his paws in front of her, patient. She wiped her cheeks, then laid her palm between C's ears. The reddish-black fur was like velvet. She rolled her fingertips around one wide, short ear. C flicked it, tickled, then cocked his head and pulled an itchy grin. Adrenaline burst through Leta at the flash of so many sharp teeth, but as she scratched, he leaned into her hand, grinned sillier, and she was reminded of the bovine calves and how she'd loved them most.

"You're still a juvenile. A baby."

He pressed his cold nose into her palm, then started to lick around her fingers. His big purrs filled up her bones.

Caiden walked over with relief plain on his face. "You loved animals," he said as if he'd heard her thoughts. "The calves—you were good with them, always knew how they felt."

"Easier than people." Leta scratched under C's chin, to which he tilted it way up and his eyes squinted in a happy way that—yes—the calves had long ago.

Leta looked up at Caiden. So many questions had thorns. Even a simple thing like *How did you tame C?* came with the sense that Caiden had suffered hard for it. But if they only talked about their shared past, they wouldn't learn about each other in the present. Nothing in the intervening time had been gentle for either of them—so would they sit down and swap trauma?

"Are you all right?" he asked.

Leta was making a face of some kind. She fixed it, back to her natural frown, and admitted, "I hate this."

"C?"

"No, this..." Leta stood, starting to flush with frustration. The nophek curled around the back of Caiden's hips. "Not knowing how to do this. How to talk to you."

Caiden choked on a laugh that was more hurt than humor. "Yeah. I'm not sure where to start either."

"We're both so different." She'd known him for five years, as a child. That was a quarter of her life, but it didn't feel like much at all compared to her decade with the Dynast.

Caiden petted the nophek's head, deep in thought, until he said, "I'm glad... Leta, I'm glad you're different from the girl I had to watch die over and over. Different from the girl Çydanza taunted me with the image of. Now you're new... someone I can get to know."

Over and over?

His simple words hid so much difficult history, while she had years of blank. It gave her an unfair advantage. Where to start?

"Well," she said, "it's nice to meet you, Caiden."

That made him grin, which cast the shadows from his face. "I'm so happy you survived." He closed the small space between them to pull her into a hug she wasn't expecting.

He was the taller still. Thick shoulders, warm, and he remembered that she preferred firm pressure over a light touch that irritated her nerves. He smelled like bandages and healing balms, a faint sweet, herbaceous note that Leta thought resembled the alfalfa of their homeworld fields. She was imagining that part, but it helped. A wealth of memories restored, physically reunited across the gap in time, she felt more whole, as if something hidden were healed.

Leta let all her tension free. Caiden hugged her tighter to support her slack, and she realized: they were both struggling to reconnect because so much of their childhood friendship hadn't been built through language. She'd been abused, closed-off, mistrustful, and he'd broken through her shell not with words but by being present every time.

She murmured, "I'm glad... you survived too."

Caiden squeezed her tighter and tilted his face into the top of her hair. His heartbeat was calm and large, and hers a flurry.

Footsteps. "My dear boy," Endirion said as he ambled over and placed a hand on both of their backs, "you are the very best unwitting romantic. Let the poor thing go before you confuse her."

Caiden pulled away, confused himself, and looked at Leta's face. If she hadn't been blushing from the comfort, she was *now* at the thought that Endirion had read Caiden's care as romantic.

Leta backed away fast, wondering what cues she'd missed or misread. It wouldn't be the first or last time.

Endirion continued with a wink, "Not all cultures show physical affection or take it to mean the same things. Touch is a language that's not multiversal."

Now Caiden was flushing in embarrassment. "I know that, En, that's not—I've never thought of her that way. Crimes, I can't hug my sister who's just back from the dead?"

"I know you've been avoiding romantic ties altogether, and it doesn't click for you without strong feelings, but if you miss noticing how *other* people feel, it'll run you into trouble or you'll hurt someone you don't mean to. To you, affection doesn't necessarily imply romance, but in Dynast social language it often does."

Was Leta the one giving wrong cues? She squared herself at Endirion. "I grew up in the Dynast, but my family is mixed—prinna, ursgen, endaal, yraga, saisn—and I'm part orrelet, they say. I'm also—"

Endirion interrupted, "Emotionally literate enough to have a talk with him. Go on." He smiled and patted their shoulders before backing away. Caiden glared at his friend. Maybe this conversation was familiar or overdue.

"Sister..." Leta started. "We didn't have that word when we were kids. We weren't in the same Stricture group, we didn't live or work together, didn't have labels for our friendship. We weren't a family. We're not related."

She spoke her thoughts aloud as they stitched together, then realized too late it sounded callous, her tone flat. She peered up at him, prepared for a hurt expression, but his eyes were soft.

He's listening. Stars, he was always a good listener.

She continued, "I admired you: the boy who always said what I wanted to say, acted when I wished to act."

Admiration didn't equal attraction, although there was something a bit bewildering about Caiden. All the things that had turned her around during their fake rescue infiltration of the Dynast Hold: his strength and competence, his quick thinking and solution-driven attitude.

Dian had teased her: *Is this another obsession of yours? Or a childhood crush?*

Leta's previous crushes had all been about seeing traits in another that she wanted for herself. Now she was starting to realize her own strength and didn't need it fulfilled by others. Besides, as long as she lived on the edge of dying, her life didn't have room for romance even if she found someone she wanted it with. Her brief obsession with Tayen's intensity had cooled off. Dejin was like a brother, and ursgen had a language of touch. Flis Ten had died in Leta's arms before their feelings became words. Isme was…

An ache shot through her. Just because she didn't know if he was safe?

Caiden was still listening, but he looked very worried, and his cheeks were flushed. Leta realized she'd gotten lost in thought after the point she admitted she'd admired him before.

She hurried on, "It's been too long to pick up where we left off, and I don't want to be reminded of my abuse… honestly. You were the good part of my life then, but always as the flip side of the bad. I can't think of you without it tied up in that. Let's start over with completely new, fresh memories."

It was a huge ask, and even if he agreed, it wouldn't be simple. It wouldn't erase what he thought of her now. She was asking for work, and she had the easier side of it by far, already starting with a mostly blank slate.

"You're right." The frown lines ebbed from his forehead but he looked pensive as he crouched to scratch C's neck. "I latched on to the importance of you in my memory, I fit it into the term 'sister' to inflate my guilt. I tend to… chase ideas. After the disaster on Solthar, I realized the girl I wanted to rescue was the *idea* of you. But I care about you and I still want to protect your happiness. Whether that's survivor's guilt in another form—I want to get to know the real you. Is that fair?" He straightened but didn't know what to do with his hands and folded them clumsily. The frown returned. "That's the look you'd always have before you jumped."

She recalled that view, sitting atop their oak tree in a curvy branch where he'd helped her climb up and sat beside her, their legs dangling. She'd always been fearful of heights, and he made her brave enough to conquer it, but then the fool had rocketed down without her and cheered her on from the ground as she scowled as hard as she could.

Just jump, he'd said, like it was easy. *The grass is soft!*

What if I can't land on my feet?

I'll catch you.

He had.

"Sorry"—Caiden stalled that line of thought—"are we tossing the good memories out too?"

Right now, being able to trust someone completely—that they would back up your fight, catch you if you jumped, and listen when you spoke from the heart—was worth the world, and that was enough to start over with.

"Those are all right," she answered. "Can I hug you again?" *Stars forfend, it was nice.*

His eyes widened and he made an awkward sound, his arms kind of half rising.

Leta wrapped her arms around his torso and pressed her ear against his chest. The contact grounded her and calmed everything down.

C purred and curved his big body around the two of them, nuzzling the small of Leta's back. What a strange echo of how they'd left each other years ago. She wondered if Caiden realized too.

He cautiously returned the hug, lighter than before. "Is this a yes? Fair?"

"Yes, deal. We start over." She added, "For the record, it's all right for you to hug me when I come back from the dead."

Caiden laughed and squeezed her so much tighter it hurt. He pressed his cheek into her hair and she could almost feel the electricity of his mind healing up. In how many dreams had he held her corpse?

Endirion was still monitoring them out of the corner of his eye, and muttered loudly, "This doesn't look any less romantic to me."

Leta pulled from the embrace. She didn't know Endirion well yet but could guess, "You're projecting. You see what you wish to see."

"True." He beamed. "But I can spot love in your eyes, dear."

Leta examined the warm feeling and matched it with her childhood friendship and felt brave enough to use strong words. "I do love Caiden, but you misdiagnosed it. This isn't romantic love."

Endirion laughed softly. "I see what I wish to: I just want to see Caiden living life for once. How many friends do you think is enough ballast to slow down the Ghost of *Azura*?"

"I'm happy to be one more." Leta smiled but couldn't meet Caiden's gaze after admitting how strong her platonic feelings were, because it didn't sound like "starting over." She was grateful when Panca motioned her aside. The saisn had a few types of sensory veil to share. C followed Leta and sniffed at her heels.

"En loves playing matchmaker. Don't mind it," Panca said as she looped a veil around Leta's face and pressed the magnetic seam gently. Leta's hearing snuffed out for a moment. Panca adjusted another fabric layer, this one part vapor like a veil of fire. "Myself," she added with an airy flutter of a laugh, "I think Winn's true love's Azura."

Leta smiled at that idea, then tried to turn her thoughts to more important challenges. With each moment, her Proxy, her haven, was drawing farther away, harder to connect to. She would fight for this Dominant Graven thing to save her family, but she could no longer avoid the fact that she was likely to perish in the process. She had lived her life fully ready to be "the next to die," but recent events had shaken that resolve. It felt cruel to agree to fit back into Caiden's life—and fit him into hers—when she was bound to leave it so soon.

"Be patient," Panca said. She didn't mean the veils.

With a gentle boom, the *Wintra* landed.

It was time to go.

CHAPTER 35

DOMINANCE

The *Wintra* had parked on the megastructure roof by the edge of a ninety-meter-diameter bore. Clean air whooshed upward, carrying glinting flecks of chemical or metal. Azura became visible as a disturbance in those particles, levitating them in place to describe a vague shape... not animal and certainly not human: a force of nature, a clot of winds from different worlds colliding, a lightning leader paused before discharge.

Caiden raised his hand toward the mass. Air pressure vibrated against his fingers. Trickles wisped to his face and lifted his hair, curled up the edges of his morphcoat, and teased the material into scales.

"Did you misinterpret me too?" He tried to laugh but the whole misreading of platonic intent still mortified him, and En had accosted him with more questions he didn't have enough time or drinks for. Feeling attraction rarely was a difficult concept for Endirion Day.

It also felt wrong to have to curb his affection toward friends, wondering if he was using languages wrong, if his care would be misconstrued as something else. Leta had often bemoaned not being able to decode body language and speech; maybe she understood.

"No misinterpretations when minds and bodies are neurally linked. I think you've spoiled me."

Azura spread around him, defined by scintillations. She was an armor of thickened space like she'd always been the armor of a ship, and his heart filled knowing she wasn't something he could lose.

A humming tingle filled his raised hand, flame-soft and warm. He smiled until he realized that was just his own overclocked genetic energy, the inflammation of a rogue fire—the Dominant's Graven infestation. It was time to confront his origin.

"I wonder if it's like you."

Behind him, Leta gasped as she exited the ship. Caiden turned around to see her head craned back looking at the air above him. "There was something freed from it after all."

"It?"

"In the chrysalis that used to be your starship. Abriss anticipated a spiritual thing inside. It had left with you, hadn't it? Because she doesn't need a vessel…" Leta approached slowly, tracking through the air as if she saw more of Azura's shape than what the scintillation revealed to duller senses like his—even with her head wrapped in the oil-slick film of sensory veils.

Caiden ran his hands through his hair and Azura's force followed, tousling the waves upward in slow motion. Leta giggled and said, "She's had more years with you than I have."

Caiden smiled until he recalled taking the enhancer… the weird memories that had piled up and the extra dimensions that Azura's song had taken on, like the Graven part of him knew her from long ago. What did that make him?

He asked, "Can you sense the Graven Dominant?"

Leta peered down and sideways, then at the floor. "The waves it makes in the luminiferity are far, far stronger and stranger than Azura's."

Caiden dropped his arms. Congealed wind unknotted from his fingertips. A final wisp slipped across his cheek. "How far down is it?"

It was strange to think the Dominant could be a tiny thing—a vial of cells, a snippet of code, another chrysalis—encased in the vastness of the planet and its megastructure shell.

"I can't tell," Leta admitted. "But I can head us in the right direction."

The megastructure here was abandoned for kilometers, they could head toward the Dominant unseen and avoid Casthen business. Golden contrails streaked the night overhead, illustrating the vast mess Threi had to sort out. Ships impatient and off course.

Panca exited the *Wintra* and patted its side. The hatch folded up and when she was clear, the engines popped on and the ship knifed into the atmosphere. Taitn and En would rejoin the *Second Wind* and help smuggle everyone else out of the universe.

"Let's find a vehicle." Caiden's big exhale clouded white. He clasped his morphcoat tighter as it fluffed into wool and down feathers. C snapped his jaws and Caiden said, "You'll get to run now, little boy, I promise." He didn't catch himself before that last word tumbled out. Promises were what had bent his world the wrong direction.

"Old war," Panca commented as she gazed over the abandoned vista while they walked.

Overgrown fungus and flora poked out of the top plate across the whole sector. Çydanza, the previous Casthen Prime, had waged an obvious battle with it: colossal, mechanized bodies with impossible weapons tangled inert in the scaffolding of the structure. Chunks of the facility melted away in vascular lines like an acid had burned straight through. Caiden ducked under the massive cranial plate of a skull chewed in half by chemical fungus, the dried remains crusty scarlet in the pocked metal.

Both sides had lost this war. Or perhaps the Casthen had won in the end, since this fungal entity hadn't overtaken the *entire* megastructure, but apparently the cleanup had been too much work since the decommissioned sector lay frozen mid-fight.

As if reading his thoughts, Leta said, "They were too scared of stirring it up again."

C sniffed the hooks of a gigantic, motorized saw that had stalled halfway into its bite of a building-sized glob of fossilized mushroom.

Azura seeped into the structure, where her hum tickled up bioluminescent spores. She cracked the security of a hidden service lift that illuminated in the floor. The group descended to the sublevels of the parking flats.

Organic life glowed in the pitch-darkness and gave off a musty warmth and resinous sweetness that made Caiden's lungs itch. Azura's motion vibrated surfaces, rustling huge mossy fronds with pollen shimmering down.

C sneezed up a cloud of dust and growled.

Caiden deflated at the sight. "Was hoping for a local powerstreamer or something."

The vehicles left were colonized by long-dried fungal bodies. Someone had dismantled usable parts and piled them: dust and rust now. Caiden strolled through and mentally cataloged the bits and frames in case something could be improvised.

C cruised, sniffing around corners and old machines, crunching on stale bugs. He shoved his face in a spider web and backed up yelping.

Caiden snorted. "You think you know where we're going? Does it smell like me, this Dominant thing? We can't all ride you, so find us some working—"

Lights blasted Caiden's vision. The nophek squealed and barreled back, knocking straight into Caiden and taking his legs out. He smacked his tailbone on the floor and lay groaning, eyes squeezed shut. "Az..."

Tiny sounds glittered all around as wall consoles lit up. Power flooded across the deck while some of the overhead lights sputtered off—apologetically?

Caiden sat up and blinked. Shapes grew defined in the black rubble, and he squeaked in joy.

"Dartbreakers," Panca said first.

The sleek, minimalist vehicles were piled up like scrap, but Azura had shaken life into the batteries. They were all in disrepair in different ways, each one-rider only and not much to them: a smoothly contoured torso-sized chunk of metal with a jutting cradle for knees, a track wheel below, and a ring to project holosplays.

"Older models," Caiden said, "before scalar gravity potential, but we can fix them up."

Panca was already dragging out pieces and sorting by level of damage.

Leta uncurled. Her veils sheltered her from the blaring lights while she surveyed the heaps. "My body's not in great muscular shape to be balancing on or maneuvering one of those. No room for a passenger?"

C sniffed for snacks in the dusty voids. He crunched on a rubbery old tread and brought it to Leta to show her as he chewed.

Caiden covered his laugh. "You're light enough to ride C. If you can hang on, he'll take care of you."

Leta's eyes glittered with residual fear before she crouched and tugged on the other end of the tread in the nophek's jaws. "Baby C, can we outrun those two and their fancy machines?"

The nophek growled and tugged, unaware of his strength and nearly hauling Leta onto her face before she let go. He dropped the tire and flattened his whole front, limbs splayed, eyes widening, and a ridiculous grin split his nightmare face. Caiden feinted a lunge, which set the nophek off, zooming across the space and back again.

Leta couldn't help but giggle. She threw the tread and C bounded after it. Caiden burst out laughing, warmed at the sight of the two playing as C barreled back and skidded to a halt, biting the tread again but too wild to know what to do with it.

He watched for a while before joining Panca at the spread of parts and attempting to catch up with her head start. They each patchworked various machines together, a silent competition to build the best while improving on the design. Caiden finally improvised morphic tread material for the track cylinder and finished first.

Panca's smoky veils fluttered as she shook her head. "You're showing off."

Caiden winked at her and donned a makeshift wind visor. The decade had been lonely but Azura always needed repairs, and hands at work were better than a heart at rest. Taitn used to call it "stress-mending," but if the end result was soothing, who cared?

Nearby, C lay down and flattened his chin on the floor, nose whistling as he peered up at Leta with bright, dewy eyes.

"You're smart," she said, digging her hands under the riding harness to figure out how its arrangement worked. "How big is your gloss now?"

Caiden and Panca mounted their dartbreakers. The chassis held his torso and hips while freeing up his arms to move in a forward field, conducting motion, thrust, torque, along with muscular cues in the legs, mimicking standard starship controls. A cloud of shimmer projected around the front, waiting for his touch. Instead of straddling a seat, he knelt on legs folded back at an angle, and balanced as the engine whirred to life.

Caiden grinned over at C as the nophek rose gingerly with Leta astride. "Think you can keep up?"

C yowled, planted his paws, and stretched, muscles rippling with power under his glossy fur. His tail whipped high in the air. Leta floundered for balance until she found the leather foothold loops.

Panca made a nasal sound. "Keep up? Y'know she needs to lead. She's pathfinding."

"I think Azura knows where we're going too."

Caiden punched his fists forward to gun the dartbreaker. It lurched, the back end swerving into the walls until he got his tension balanced. Panca balanced perfectly from the start.

C loped inquisitively beside him down a cargo ramp, then snarled and broke into a sprint—Leta clinging tight—as Caiden got the hang of the thing and picked up speed. A *lot* of speed.

His morphcoat hardened into a protective shell. Azura illuminated a course and peeled open doors ahead so they didn't need to slow down. He glanced at Panca, who gestured *yes*, and they accelerated. Caiden's dartbreaker's wheel track was soft and viscous, squashing over uneven surfaces with ease and sticking tight enough for sharp handling.

He hesitated only as he saw Leta battling to adjust to C's gait, showing a strange sort of weakness in her hands, as if she struggled to attach to her body that struggled to attach to the harness. Caiden couldn't tell if it was her Graven body failing her or residual fears about C, or both. One veil came undone and streamed behind her. Finally she closed her eyes and folded over the nophek, distilling her focus, and he leaped into the lead with her hovering more easily astride.

They left behind the ancient battle between mushroom and machine. The abandoned sector grew less dilapidated, still dusty. Long bridges stretched through storage and incubation fields that grew or fermented commodities.

C led at a breakneck pace, grinning huge and panting with every spring of his athletic frame. His slapping paws were percussion beneath the insectile whine of the dartbreakers. Each bound ripped up the road's brittle old powerstreaming surface.

"Watch the tail!" Caiden banked flat to avoid the balancing swipe of it as C turned a sharp corner. It was nice to see the pup so happy. Leta looked more and more comfortable, too, meditating to rhythm and wind.

Together they tore across kilometers of straight causeway track between sectors. Caiden gave himself the length of it to laugh, really *laugh*, even if it was forced. He let himself forget where he was headed or what he'd left behind, and let the wind slap his skin until it hurt.

Their goal didn't seem so impossible.

And he was glad he'd brought Panca and Leta along.

Azura opened a gigantic cargo-drop bore with a corkscrew tunnel down its side, many more kilometers deep into the Casthen Harvest. Caiden leaned into the perfect turn. The air grew stale, sticking in his nostrils and freezing his eyelashes.

Azura's light diminished with every curve. Caiden slowed to a halt and almost toppled the dartbreaker as he staggered to one of the walls and flattened his palm on it. Sluggish thrums beneath.

"She won't get close to it?" His heart tripped. He shifted his palm and the frequencies moved with him.

"The Dominant is…loud." Leta sat upright and fixed her loose veils.

Panca said, "Locked doors 'n' dark passages'll slow us down. How close?"

Leta bowed her head to concentrate. "The bottom of this drop. Then straight…straight to it."

Their words whisked across Caiden's rising anxiety. He needed Azura and he had to get to the Dominant, and it was torture to choose. *She's not gone, just repelled.*

He glanced at Leta and read her wilted posture, the contortion of her fingers through the harness—her physiology was corroding itself with each passing moment.

Caiden asked, "Can you tell what the Dominant is?"

"Not a shape or body…it obscures itself because it's just—just power. Let's head to the base."

C mewed at her, then leaped back into a gallop.

Panca followed and Caiden lagged behind as they circled all the way to the base through near complete darkness. His sense of Azura attenuated with each spiral, and the sunny feeling he had around her simmered into dread. It was irrational—a bond built for too long stretched too thin—but knowing that didn't bring him ease.

C finally showed signs of fatigue, his tongue spilling from a panting maw as the group stopped. At the base of the bore was an immense and elaborate door.

No sense of Azura, not even echoes.

Caiden dismounted. Panca set her dartbreaker down and walked over to him while uncoiling her veils. White limbal rings flicked in her black eyes as she surveyed him through her sense-sea. He didn't need to tell her how Azura had been with him ever since he thought he'd die in the desert and was saved. He hadn't learned to do well without.

She set a hand on his shoulder. He swallowed a lump of emotion and nodded.

Investigating the strange door, Leta called, "It's a genetic-recognition seal. Only—"

She stumbled back as the door initiated. Metallic tendrils of the ornate design unraveled, serpentining back into the walls. Nervelike veins of bright material sizzled with them.

"Only Dynast can get through." Leta backed up. Once she was far enough away, the door regrew in silver veins, knotting back into a complex but consistent pattern. Leta was conditioned with bioresonance adapted from Abriss's Dynast Graven biology—enough that she tripped the door's system.

"Threi must have installed these," Caiden said. "I was right. He couldn't get more enhancers except in person since he's the only Dynast creature among the Casthen."

Caiden strolled over to it and stopped in his tracks as ropes of metal wriggled. He took another step. More unwove.

He glanced over his shoulder.

Leta pulled her veils off, revealing a deep frown. "*Only* Dynast. I'm sure of it. There are some of these doors in the Hold. You—"

"Shouldn't be able to get through. I'm not a Dynast Graven, I was made from the Dominant type." Caiden strode for the door again. It wriggled all the way open. The sound whipped through the air like a thousand steel blades drawn together. "If there's an answer to *why* I can, it's through here anyway."

Panca inspected the seams of the thing curiously, then gazed off into the space beyond: another completely empty place, a black metal deck a quarter kilometer or more long. There were no distinct lights, but a glowing haze filled the room enough to see the floor and somewhat ahead. Halfway across the room stretched a gigantic rind of twisting black and cerulean layers obscuring what lay behind.

"Dust's not disturbed," Panca said.

"That rind might not be safe for C. He's the most delicate of us. And I wonder if there are other—"

From the far-off darkness lilted the sound of those steel blades drawn at once. Far enough that he couldn't see, but voices carried across the emptiness. Threi's voice, recognizable when he raised his volume: "They didn't answer."

Caiden swore and whispered, "That's our time up."

Quieter voices suggested Threi had a small entourage, plus a bass voice with a somewhat mechanical timbre.

"And that's Dian Six." Leta slid off the nophek's back. Her voice shook. "Why is he still here? Not awoken? Oh, Isme…"

"Leta?"

Her face shuttered as she steeled herself. "Quickly. I can use him to buy you time." She pointed into the rind in a direction closer to them than to Threi's group. "Dominant's that way."

Panca added, "Prioritize stopping enhancer synthesis."

"Got it." Caiden hugged C's head. Stress purrs coursed off the beast and his tail whisked across the floor. "Yeah, I'm hungry and tired and beat up, too, but what else is new? I need you to protect these two." Caiden leaned his forehead against C's muzzle, nested his fingers in his downy mane, and inhaled his dark scent. The nophek opened his jaws in Caiden's face. Caiden grasped two huge teeth and shook C's head. "Yeah, yeah—be safe, little boy."

He straightened and peered at both Panca and Leta, making sure they soaked up the words he didn't have. *Crimes, it really was easier alone.*

"If it gets bad," he said, "run."

Panca swung her sniper glave into action. "We can take care of ourselves."

Caiden nodded. Time wouldn't let him say more. He ran silently on the balls of his feet, through the black rind. The physics shift prickled his morphcoat into millions of tiny spikes. His skin frizzled, hair standing up.

Nested universes lay beyond through a series of dark, dusty, abandoned labs. He crossed over and his ears popped.

Another genetically coded door squiggled out of his way. On the other side he was almost smacked in the face with plants overgrown in rows and overhead trellises. Lush foliage, heavy with flowers and fruits. Pale night varieties tangled with teals and greens. Orbs of light nestled throughout like miniature suns, and the plant life gravitated around them.

Caiden unsnapped the holster of his pinch glave and drew his meter-long chemblade. It morphed unreliably between the universes: a volatile chemical dripping and spitting in the air, or a brittle thing steaming like liquid nitrogen, or a bubbling of concentrated light.

No sign of a threat, yet.

The plants changed as universes allowed, a careful rhythm of growth and clever serotiny between worlds. Caiden was a mechanic, not a cultivator, but he recognized engineering when he saw it. This place was carefully maintained. It developed food, flowers, nectars, water and air filtration, energy production. Something trapped in here could survive on this ecosystem.

The orb lighting graduated from bright day to a sort of dusk. Terminals winked a sleepy recognition. Bins and other containers lay pushed against the walls, gutted and filled with aquatic plants.

And the air…

Tastes sweet.

He crept through labs stuffed with technology and materials that appeared to be sourced from cultures across the multiverse. Threi's words slithered into his brain: *the lab where they mixed up the cocktail that's you.*

Caiden entered a circular hallway that ringed the unbroken wall of a massive cylindrical room. Something nebulous he'd been feeling built up to a point where he couldn't say it was his imagination: tight and then vanishing, not a pulse, more like melody. Similar to Azura, but not. He circled the passage, looking for a door, and his body constricted, breath shortened. His morphcoat sizzled into mesh in response to his sweating.

There. A brilliant crack of light ran down the center of a gigantic door layered from exotic biominerals.

Caiden stopped in front of it with the light beam slicing straight between his eyes. Chemblade ready. Stance loose and quick.

He stepped to the door—not a genetic one, this—and placed a hand on it. The slippery roar of its servos startled him in the silence and strummed his nerves. The pair of meter-thick slabs ached apart and a pearly glow spilled over him in waves.

His mouth hung open. Inside the room was the strangest garden he'd ever seen.

CHAPTER 36

OFFSPRING

Leta was *fast* at this now. Lightning quick, she grounded into Dian's Proxy one hundred meters across the vast space. No stealth this time—she snapped her will right into his nerves. His Proxy even seemed to align to her presence: a magnetic force polarizing correctly, a gravity field shifting pattern just so.

Dian was missing half a skull and one arm, vertebrae jutting like knives, ribs pulled open and the fake lightseep cracked inside. All the paths and geometries painted on him were fractured. Leta's heart broke. *One last time, brother. I need your strength.*

Before she could seize his voice, he bellowed, "*She's here!*"

Leta was already reaching for the glave on Dian's hip.

The confused group of Casthen knotted up. Threi turned, tall and pale.

Snik! Leta fired a particle shot, tunneling for his head. Threi whipped aside and staggered. The razor line had skimmed a chunk out of his ear.

He shoved his attendants forward as a shield while he dashed away. "*Destroy the Proxy!*"

Leta aimed and shot. The group tackled her as she fired, which skewed the razor so it tunneled through Threi's bicep. He clutched his arm and kept sprinting.

Boom. Thunder smashed the air and a sun-bright streak of sniper shot crossed the dark from Panca's location. It missed Threi—or at least he didn't cry out. Boots kept pounding.

The group tripped Dian's Proxy with Leta inside and tried to pin him to the ground. She fired the glave blind, catching a few in the legs. The glave was ripped from her faulty hand. She calculated fast: eight of them, only five combat-trained.

Boom. Another sniper shot zipped through the darkness and shattered across the rind through which Threi fled.

C roared as he charged toward Dian's group.

Leta shoved the Casthen away and fought Dian trying to wrest control of his Proxy back. His willpower was an avalanche, his spirit half inside the machine and half in the luminiferity, spilling out, snagged, enraged. Leta's control faltered, the nerve signals glitching all over as she grappled with the fighters too, broke glaves, choked one out. Dian's ruthlessness was in his muscle memory and instincts, making a brute out of her as she fought.

Four fighters disabled. C barreled in so ferociously it stopped Leta, seizing her with old memories. The nophek easily dispatched the rest of the group while Leta's mind disconnected from the moment—allowing Dian to kick her straight out.

She snapped back to her real body just as fast as she'd left it.

The spiritual whiplash made her shriek and gave away her location. She wobbled to her feet and drew a close-range weapon. Darkness surged into her eyes—gone was the Proxy's advanced vision.

Sounds filled her up. Sprinting feet. Inhumanly fast and unbalanced. *Fractured femur.* Dian was racing across the empty space. C galloped behind him.

"Panca!" Leta found her nearby.

The saisn dropped her sniping glave and pulled out a set of dismantling tools and a vicious-looking hook.

Dian tore out of the darkness and launched at Leta. She dodged while C caught up, biting Dian's thigh. Metal crunched and he screamed in rage. Weaponless, he made a wedge of his fingers and struck at C's eyes, nose, ears, all the soft points.

Leta and Panca darted in at the same time. Leta dodged his punch and struck his hip at the perfect angle to spin him, but her body refused to coordinate enough strength. His kick sent her sprawling.

Agile Panca slipped into openings and backed out of range in a blur.

Each strike was several actions at once—hooking off a plate, zapping tendons loose, ripping bolts—dismantling his construction.

Dian elbowed the nophek, who yelped and tore away with a chunk of thigh.

Leta pushed herself up. *My angle wasn't wrong. I can do this. My mind knows.*

Years of Proxy skill had to count. If she could just shove it into this useless meat.

She coiled until an opening appeared, then moved in behind Dian, jamming his lower back with a small glave that blasted concentrated pressures at a motor center and dropped him to his knees. He whipped an arm backward and locked it around Leta's neck. She flailed and kicked to no avail.

Panca sniped in at his exposed armpit and slashed at vital tendons. He half released Leta and she tried to throw him, knew the motions instinctively, perfectly performed, but her strength broke on him like a wave meeting a cliffside. He pushed her off and backhanded her cheek, sending her spinning into stars.

Panca rushed in, tools flashing, and hamstrung him in one motion. He roared and dropped to his knees again.

Leta screamed in frustration and pain, tried to channel that into power. She struck a palm into his wrist at the perfect angle to break it. This time it snapped. She wasn't fast, but Dian slowed. Panca had stripped him of everything except raw brawn.

Leta kicked his elbow in. Tears messed her vision. Breaths sawed through her. She wasn't physically enough, but she had to try what she knew.

C pinned Dian's legs under huge claws, bit his hip, and pulled back, but the lightseep was too strong to break.

Leta grappled Dian's flailing arm and locked it with her legs while she held the remains of his skull. "Panca! His chest! The spine——" She gasped as he bucked, but Panca was in, tools flicking around inside his rib cage. Components came out. Wiring, veins. Fluids gushed. Azura-blue crystal scintillated deep inside.

"Smash it!"

Dian spoke in huge heaves, "You'd send me back. Abriss will reforge my mind into a shape that suits her. She'll erase the truths we all learned here. Don't you—see—"

Panca ripped plating off the inside of his spine. She hit a nerve bundle— he spasmed, slippery in Leta's grasp.

Panca bashed at the crystal that kept Dian's consciousness anchored.

"No." Leta cradled his head, her tears overflowing. "She's only ever meant the best for us. She loves us even with our flaws and doubts. We're family. You'll be safe."

"She's not . . . invincib—"

Panca hammered in with a blunt haft.

Dian choked. "Talk to Threi, listen to h—"

Crack! Voice shut off. He slumped.

Leta clutched his Proxy's remains as his spirit drained, consciousness thundering away into the luminiferity toward Solthar. Leta almost followed. The effort had exacerbated her spirit separating from her body as she neared a dangerous length of time out of Proxy.

"Leta." Panca shuffled over and peered at her but didn't reach out.

Leta shook uncontrollably. She hadn't exerted her body this much in years. Adrenaline, nausea, not enough oxygen in the world for her.

In the sudden quiet, a realization resurged—

"A thousand crimes—Isme. He already returned, and Dian was here. That means Dian wasn't pulled out of his Proxy by any of Isme's actions back home. What's happened to Isme that's stopped him? And now I've pissed Dian off and sent him *right back to the Hold.*"

Tayen or even Sisorro, if still dissenting, could have done something to Isme and Aohm. What story had they told the Dynast about what happened between Threi and Abriss?

"Leta," the saisn whispered. She re-coiled Leta's sensory veils over her head. The world dampened down. Panca placed a hand between Leta's shoulder blades, strong fingers slipping toward pressure points.

Leta sighed and let the tension around her spine unlink. She smoothed Dian's long hair over the crushed half of his face so only the fair side showed, then petted a thumb over his cheekbone. "What a mess. I can't reach them. I didn't even say goodbye to . . ."

She leaned into Panca and drove away thoughts of Ten, Four, Three, and too many other unfair farewells.

Soon she could weave herself back in-Proxy while Laythan was flying them all to Unity. It would reset her disintegration just a little, and Abriss would set things right. Leta would have Caiden fly her real body back home. They'd have all three pieces of the trinity then, the Graves healed up, everything talked out.

Why did it sound impossible?

"Focus on what you can control," Panca said.

Leta started to push to her feet. The nophek came over and wedged under her arm to help lift her with his height.

This isn't all mine to fix. The others can handle themselves until Abriss arrives and fixes everything. I trust them. Leta caught her breath.

The vast space fell deathly quiet. C had demolished the Casthen.

Cerulean arcs warped across the black rind ahead. There was no guarantee C could cross over safely. And Panca couldn't get through the Dynast-coded doorways without Leta there too.

Threi had headed in alone. It was up to Caiden now.

Behind the door Caiden had opened lay an expansive chamber illuminated by one central feature, beautiful and dizzying with detail. A large pool recessed into the floor, filled with a pellucid and luminous fluid culture. Large fleshy pieces of a bizarre organic material floated within: the core of each was atrophied black like the ash of a thing long dead, but around this grew crystalline folds weeping light. Cell clusters of silver and gemstone colors flecked the edges. Fiery veins linked the chunks to machines recessed in the pool walls, and to plants filling up the aquatic garden rim to rim.

The Graven Dominant? The source of my genetics is these chunks of... something?

He gawked at the delicateness of the ecosystem. White petals bristled underwater. Glassy red beads dribbled atop slender stamens. Translucent leaves stretched a half meter across, laced with biological light while teal vines knitted throughout, spotted with effervescent buds. Algae clouds hung in the fluid and hid soft colors. Moss crept up the stems of lily pads, their surfaces fizzing against the oxygen.

Organic life support for the chunks of Graven flesh in this garden.

A quiet bioluminescence played inside the exotic tissues of the pieces. Cells freckled like a cradle of stars and made Caiden self-consciously squeeze his own freckled wrists. This was an energy so much like Azura's chrysalis had been, and the melodic unease he'd felt in the hall outside now threaded his sinew and marrow like gravitas.

It wasn't the database of code or shelf of vials that Caiden had expected. He tried to follow the overwhelming signal flow of the ecosystem web, more complex than any starship neuromechanics. Standing waves of vibration filled the fluid while lines of coherent biophysical light projected from the pool walls. Electromagnetic interference patterns?

It took Caiden, transfixed, a moment to notice the person standing waist-deep in the middle of the pool.

They stood very still, half twisted around to peer at him. Small cutters glinted in one hand and a clump of loose golden vines dangled from the other. Their special waders generated a pocket of air around their legs like a skirt formed of stable bubble.

Caiden clenched his chemblade tighter. Adrenaline frosted through his core. His animal brain sensed another predator, but they remained at a standstill while the tones of the pool and its gentle fizzing filled the air.

"You're the one who survived," the cultivator said, soft-spoken voice husky with awe. "The Graven Paraborn."

Caiden bristled and raised his glave, training it on them while he started to circle the pool, glancing into the many side rooms that branched off the big chamber. "Have you been expecting me?"

"Not you." They twisted in the water to track him, their pupils full of reflected shine.

"You were expecting Threi." Caiden kept clearing rooms. They were labs: the machines hummed and hissed while idle holosplays of research glittered in the dark.

"I am the only person here." The cultivator slowly raised their arms. "Are *you* alone? You should not have been able to open the doors."

Caiden circled around. The crisp floral fragrances of the pool wafted into these nests of study. Paper books were stacked among the machines, like the volumes Threi had in his room. One lab was bright with plant cultivars and vats of tissues and algae, containers of growing crystal, cirrobee hives, plus vials slowly drip-filling with a familiar opal-white fluid. Enhancers. Caiden cursed.

He kicked an empty bin to the table's edge, swept the vials in, and poured the source flasks inside. He dumped corrosive chemicals in to ignite the whole thing. Scanning the space, he spotted stray vials and began to toss them in too.

"*Wait!* Please!"

Caiden paused with one vial in his fist. "You're the one who makes Threi's Graven enhancers."

"Yes."

"Does anyone else know how this all works, how to make more?"

Caiden shoved the vial in his pocket. A desperate contingency—he could smash it later. He cleared the remaining rooms. No other people. The last space held a scour, an old food printer, and a big pile of violet pillows—the closest thing there was to a bed.

The cultivator responded, delayed, "Are you asking that so you can kill me?"

"You've been Threi's hands down here while he was imprisoned?"

"Hands," they repeated as if it were amusing. "I am not doing this for Threi Cetre."

Caiden scoffed. "That's what all the Graven-loyal think."

The cultivator dropped their arms, squeezing the golden vines in their fingers. "My loyalty lies with *science*. This is something that science hasn't seen in a long, long time. Its slow resurrection has been my sole focus for a decade, and it has nothing to do with the Casthen Prime." Their gaze saccaded endearingly over the fleshy pieces of the Dominant in the water.

Satisfied the place was empty, Caiden returned to a spot near the door and centered back on this strange person. In the pool's glow, their wide pupils, set in black sclera, filled with reflected shine. Their stare didn't budge from Caiden, as if he might be an apparition that could disappear if looked away from.

They widened their arms and made a bow of one shoulder in the Andalvian way. "Ex-Cartographer, metamorphicist, and genetic cultivator, Feran of Vitrika Endaal."

Caiden swallowed a knot. "And this is the Dominant. This...system?"

Feran smiled. "My sensitive chaos."

A vibrating atmosphere surrounded Feran like a thin film while phosphorescent strings sparkled, then disappeared in the air. Their mellow features held a loving glow, and Caiden swore the strange plants swayed closer to them, petals leaning and vines starting to spiral around their legs. They made a slow twirl in the water, bubble skirt flaring.

"I named it the Dominant, modeling this Graven strain after music and vibratory physics, the framework that facilitated my breakthroughs. The word 'Dominant' is not lovely on the tongue, I'm afraid. A few years in I developed nicknames. As the tissues revive, cell by cell, those cells contain memories and are building an echo of a presence..."

They approached Caiden and the pool's steps cautiously, weaving around fragile nets of organisms. Flower buds shot closed, and tendrils stretched toward them as they moved. Feran cocked their head and bent to get a better look at his sides. A specimen to study.

A sudden realization struck Caiden. The genetically locked doors that only Dynast Graven could open. "You've been stuck in here for ten years too."

"Oh?" Feran stopped politely before reaching the steps. "Didn't think through the ramifications of your actions back then, did you? About what else might suffer from Threi's confinement."

Caiden wasn't buying into that guilt. He'd been younger and more foolish then. From the look of it, Feran had done a fine job growing an ecosystem to sustain them.

Up close, it was more obvious Feran was Andalvian. Their skin started to pattern like rainfall, blipping purple circles and silvery ripples. He noted swaths of skin *without* chromatophores—just one creamy, lavender color—indicating they were was a less common raciation of endaal, segregated out of Andalvia and unable to claim the name. The strip of long hair down the center of Feran's skull confirmed it, growing from among the usual soft spines across their skull, tied back in a high tail.

"I haven't been alone." Feran swayed to indicate the water, rocking the many plants, which made sparkles gush off the weird pieces of the Dominant. "And there *is* a single audio-only communication line between here and Threi Cetre's universe. Two prisoners with all the time in the world." Feran's patterns crinkled. "You can imagine how appealing he is when terribly bored and lonely."

Caiden did grimace at that. "Ten years with Threi as your only contact is a particular kind of torture—I apologize."

"We worked through it."

Feran didn't have the look of either prisoner or threat, but Caiden kept his glave trained on them and stepped back one pace, inviting them to leave the pool.

"You really don't need your weapons," Feran said. "I wouldn't harm something so rare as the last surviving Paraborn offspring of this Graven. I'm happy to share whatever knowledge you wish. I would love to, in fact."

Their bubble skirt rippled silver as it slithered off their bare legs. They stepped out perfectly dry. Their legs and hips were braced in slim assistive devices that the bubble skirt had hidden.

Caiden's mind summoned a memory of his friend Silye, whose tongue Threi had cut out when she was young. A glint of rage sliced him, and horrible images bled: Threi snapping a scientist's legs to keep them locked up in this subterranean lab, doing his bidding. *Crimes, when will my brain stop making the worst of everything?*

Feran set the snippers and the vines to one side, then straightened the thigh-length hem of their Cartographer-style dress coat, its complex layers fitted tight with belts and a sash. They shook water drops off their speckled fingertips.

Caiden cleared his throat. "Pronouns, if any?"

Endaal traits didn't vary much between sexes, especially when young. Feran had feminine features, by human measure, but Caiden knew better than to measure everything against one standard. They had large eyes tapering at the sides, and scholarly, almost austere features. Full lips pursed while considering his question. "*They* is fine. I'm down here all alone... gender hardly matters. And you? I know your genes backward and forward, but I would still hear your name."

He shivered at that. Of course Feran must have studied his Paraborn brood for their Dominant research. All the knowledge about himself that he'd been dying to crack into was down here: Feran's entire realm. "He," Caiden replied, and considered how much to share. "And it's Caiden."

"I wondered. Threi calls you Winn, but there is a certain lilt to it, like he finds it amusing."

"Talked about me much?"

Feran shrugged. "Only to vent. The cadence of his diatribes is decent background noise to prune to."

They inched closer, which might've been stealthy if their assistive motors hadn't whined with each shift of weight. The silvery rainfall washed out of their skin, replaced with an opal shimmer through uncommonly fine chromatophores. It swirled over their neck and shoulders around void spaces in the cleft of their throat and jaw.

They appraised Caiden with unhidden adoration, then noted his scowl and chuckled. "Don't worry, I have grown quite resistant to your Dominant strain of Graven, after spending so long living with and tending one. My fascination is entirely uncoerced."

Caiden wasn't sure any fascination was a good thing, but he felt bullish still holding a chemblade at a docile creature, so he shoved it back in the holster. He kept the glave at his side.

Feran's gaze saccaded across Caiden's cheeks—looking at the freckles? "I had measurements of you... back when you'd just returned and Çydanza was still alive. But seeing the real thing is something else."

"Threi was *collecting data* on me?"

That whole time—all the sparring and conditioning—it hadn't been just to forge him into a murderer.

"That is how I developed enhancers in time for him to... well, you were there, weren't you?"

That crammed-down memory unfurled: Threi's enhanced, power-rich voice as he called for hundreds to kill themselves by their own hands. *Fast as you can.*

"You knew." Caiden marched toward Feran, closing the space so aggressively they stumbled back, assistive frame grinding around their legs. "You knew what he was going to do, and—"

"I did not. I've always been accused of obliviousness, having my nose in my reading or buried in plants—as you might already be able to tell. I developed what he wanted. I adore every moment of the challenges I've set myself. What he does with what I make is not my business."

"And you sleep well with that?"

Feran stood their ground. "No. And that's precisely why I ignore what he does. If I'm to be forced to serve someone I cannot disobey in person, I'm happier not knowing what he does with my work. Though truly, it didn't seem to matter at all when I believed neither of us would be set free. May I sit?"

Their knee braces quivered. Caiden nodded and Feran sat at the edge of the pool's steps, their skin shimmering with fond blue ripples. Behind them, the strange garden glittered with light and music, and the laced-in pieces of Graven tissue bobbed like chunks of ice encasing something scorched.

Caiden tipped his head to indicate them. "What *is* the Dominant, exactly? Was this a body once?"

"You want an *exact* science? You want an estimation. The Dominant is what remains of a Graven being that Çydanza discovered long ago on this planet." Their paper-soft voice took on a cadence between storyteller and scholar. "Çydanza and her scientists failed to revive the being. I have failed as well. The genes are...incomplete."

Dark dismay clouded over Feran's skin, making the pale void swaths stand out. "I've kept it alive by designing this delicate system, sculpted by gradually congealing music, by chemical acoustics, a sum of vibrations materializing form. I cultivated the species myself and engineered the biophoton fields with a spatiotemporal coherence that morphs through set modes over time and emulates the interference patterns of some—" Feran caught themselves. Wisps of nervous gold shimmered on their neck. "Well.

Some of the cells are regenerating, thanks to what I learned by examining your Paraborn brood."

Feran appraised Caiden with another hungry gaze, as if he were a living trove of secrets. Their interest was to his benefit if they'd spill Threi's secrets as well.

He nudged, "Cydanza didn't use Dynast genetics to create my Paraborn batch because she thought the Dominant was superior. How?"

He was still stupidly grateful not to be related to Threi.

"She considered Dynast genes too inbred," Feran answered. "Also famously difficult to propagate. Do you know much about the Graven?"

Feran's question brimmed with zeal. Their spine straightened, and they couldn't hide the sparkles of excitement popping over their half-bare shoulders. Caiden imagined they'd be elated whether he answered no or yes: one an opportunity to explain and the other an opportunity for rapport.

He answered, "I know what's available publicly and in *Graven Intention of Prima Luminiferia.*"

"Volume One?"

"Unabridged."

Rainbows wiggled into Feran's hair. "Threi's favorite yet most hated book. He disparages it, yet cannot seem to stop quoting it. Such a Dynast book, that one, which means you have one-third of the truth."

Caiden grunted. "A third. That sounds like Threi, only providing a portion of the full picture."

"You know him well too."

Caiden grimaced.

Feran giggled and said, "I meant no offense. It's no wonder you and he were drawn together. 'Magnetism' is how that volume ideals it, yes? *Gravitas*, the Dynast say—a cheeky combination. There are in fact three Graven strains, of unique signature each, which form a complementary trinity."

Feran paused for engagement while the rainbow hues still shivered beneath their skin.

"The Dynast. The Dominant. And?"

Caiden felt Azura's absence all the more.

"You are the only living hybrid of the Dominant, if we may call it hybridization, which I contest slightly. For the last, Threi suspects it is what you called the *Azura*."

"How long has he suspected this?"

"Five ephemeris years or so? It was largely *my* suspicion. Threi has been investigating RM28, the planet where you found your starship. And may I suggest it was not chance that drew you and it together."

Abriss had said similar. Caiden's head ached as he tried to arrange years of cause and effect, hints dropped or forgotten, Azura's secret form—why couldn't she approach this place?—and the melodic flame of that Dominant-derived enhancement that licked around his bones even now. It was strengthened in the presence of this dying *thing* that was his origin, his progenitor, kept alive by an impossible garden.

"Feran. The enhancers."

"Obviously they gall you for some reason. I isolated the Dominant strain from the material of this carcass. The 'enhancer,' as you call it, is not boosting power, but gives Threi more control. Vigor becomes focused and *seems* more powerful, yet the amount of energy is conserved rather than increased. The formula at present is only temporary, to Threi's dismay. The two strains corrode each other over time. Though I have now refined a formula that is more—"

Caiden interrupted, "It's permanent on me."

Feran's lips parted around a word, but their mouth hung open silent. A soft purple eyeshine filled up their dilating pupils. "That should not be possible. Though you are...essentially offspring from the Dominant, the formula might instead be completing flaws in your genetic grade? With study I—"

"*Permanent?*" a dark, silver voice exclaimed from behind Caiden.

He swiveled. Threi Cetre strode in.

CHAPTER 37

PERMANENCE

Caiden readied his butterfly-shaped glave and fixed his stance with the chemblade. In this universe it resembled a spine of liquid nitrogen, boiling vapor into the air.

Threi was breathless from sprinting. His gaze flicked to the endaal. "Feran?"

Flustered purple bubbled across their temples. "Fine."

Threi visibly relaxed and turned to Caiden.

Caiden remembered how many smiles Threi wielded. This one was coy, lips curved like a bow. Threi leveled his gaze past Caiden, on the Dominant in its water garden. "Child drawn to parent?"

Feran fidgeted behind Caiden. Tiny servos whirred as they shifted. "Rather than *parent*, I would call it partial cloning in the style of Vannern's linguistic theory of pangenetic—"

"Feran," Threi interrupted. "Fetch what I need." His tone was a silver arrow.

The scientist flinched when it struck, but they said, "I'm afraid he smashed them all."

Threi's ice-blue gaze lingered on Feran with mixed emotion before settling back on his quarry.

After the enhancer Caiden had taken, he and Threi were closer to Graven equals. How much so? He didn't feel the usual subtle hooks under his skin. With only five meters between them, he had the full visual, pheromonal, and olfactory effect.

Threi seemed haggard, but with a clean shave and hair hacked short into an angry, sweat-curled mess, he looked much the same as he had ten years ago. His muscle tone was diminished. A familiar fragrance carried off him: lilies, blood, sweat, and desperation...but the Graven allure that had accompanied it before wasn't as strong this time.

The metallic scent, Caiden noted, was from blood splashed across Threi's calf-length Casthen coat. He either hadn't taken the time to scour, or—more likely—had preserved his sister's blood like a gruesome trophy.

Threi smiled with teeth. "I am genuinely surprised to see you here, pup. But that's just as well. Feran can vivisect you and complete an enhancer that'll be *permanent* on a Dynast Graven too."

"*Vivisect?*"

"He speaks at last."

"Did you miss me?"

Threi's smile faltered. That hit some kind of nerve.

Feran interjected, "Vivisection is a fancy word, but I'd much rather—"

"Get somewhere safe," Threi ordered. The endaal hesitated. Threi flexed his Graven command, "*Fer*," like the word *fair*, and there was something oddly soft about it.

Feran drew themselves up and walked off to an adjoining room, assistive devices whirring.

Caiden raised the glave. Its invisible laser target squared on Threi's heart. *No hesitating, no games.*

He fired.

The direct hit shrieked. Green-and-black smoke skittered out in gridded lines. *Energy shield.*

A laugh burst from Caiden at the irony. It was the exact same type as the very first time he'd tried to shoot Threi, at fourteen years old. The shielder glave choker was hidden beneath his coat collar.

Fast as a viper, Threi darted forward. Caiden sidestepped the blur of motion too slow. An impact spun him, a grab wrapped him up and twisted his arm. He registered a throw maneuver quick enough to wrench himself free, but Threi wrung the pinch glave from his grip.

Threi backed up with it, returning them to a standstill, each with weapons now.

Except Caiden didn't have a shield.

He raised the chemblade in front, the vapor of it revealing the invisible line of the glave's laser carrier.

Threi snarled and hurled the stolen glave at the floor hard enough to smash it apart. "You disappoint me. We haven't seen each other in ten years, and you want to fight the boring way."

A shiver wriggled across Caiden's shoulders. "*Knives are intimate*, you told me once."

"That's right. Claws and teeth. The way you killed Çydanza."

"We. *We* killed Çydanza."

"We have different guilts. My presence at the time doesn't change that it was your accomplishment."

Caiden barked a laugh. "You have *guilts*?"

"I made a mistake," Threi said, hushed.

"And that's a first?"

"Hear me out. I failed to kill Abriss. Trying and failing is far, far worse than leaving her alone or finishing the job. I assume she charmed you here with her, so tell me where she is."

No games. Caiden sprinted at Threi with a downward slash. The chemblade boiled in a streak. Threi dodged but wasn't prepared for the fast-rising cut that followed.

Caiden dragged the weapon across Threi's chest and through the billowing shield, pulling with augmented strength against massive resistance, just enough to raze the tip through. Frost ripped Threi's coat, flashing to a burn that puckered his flesh from stomach to throat. Threi jerked his head back in time for the tip to miss boiling his face off. A shame.

Threi backed up to the wall nearby and grabbed a half-meter-long stick of metal jutting from a holster. An uncoiling cable trailed from the base. The business end of the haft blasted a raspy high-pitched sound.

Caiden recognized it as a "prim," outdated Casthen medical gear: a coherent energy tool designed for biological fusion and laser-frequency surgery. The "blade" part of it was invisible, extending a meter out the tip as the sonic force tapered off.

Caiden scoffed, "Not quite *knives*, are they?"

Threi shrugged and stalked forward while Caiden backed up. The prim's power cable snaked behind him, long enough to reach anywhere in the room. He swiped the invisible saw lazily in front of him. The ragged whine of it dopplered through Caiden's hearing.

Caiden stood his ground and raised the chemblade as it dribbled zips of plasma. Careful with his tone, baiting hubris, he said, "Now *I'm* disappointed. What's intimate about a shield?"

Threi's smile reached his eyes as he punched the latch at the nape of his neck, letting the ring of the shielder glave drop. He kicked it skidding into the water.

Caiden lunged with a stab.

Threi's instinct was to deflect with the prim, but it merely jittered through the chemblade, neither of them solid weapons. Ice flecks sprayed off. The chem vapor revealed the sonic roar of the prim as Threi attacked, letting Caiden duck it. He jabbed again, but Threi danced aside.

Caiden had counted on the dodge to expose the prim's power cable behind Threi. He whipped the chemblade down at it, but the cut sputtered right around the cable's impenetrable casing. *Well—that's the easy route gone.*

As Caiden rose, Threi shoulder-checked him off balance. Then a diagonal cut and Caiden misjudged the prim's invisible reach. Its jittery whine shrieked, lancing agony through his shoulder and skating down his ribs. The water in his skin cells heated instantaneously.

Caiden screamed and staggered back slashing, not balanced for Threi's second stab that punctured his lung with molten pain. Ribs crackled.

Delirium stuffed between his ears, but he made out a far-off wail: Feran's voice, "Don't damage him!"

"His wounds'll seal up fast. Isn't that what he was designed for?" Threi scowled in Caiden's direction. *"Get up!"*

The Graven command hooked his bones, lifted him with a *desire* to meet Threi's request. Caiden bit off a curse and gathered willpower like another weapon to parry Graven blows. He rose, shaking off chills and the deep trauma in his rib cage.

Threi noticed. "Sorry, pup. We're still not equal. And what did I have to entertain me for ten years but to play with Casthen personnel and hone my very dulled Graven blade. Like strength training with weight packs, but now the weight is off me. I might thank you."

Threi dashed into close range, which put their weapons out of action. Now a flurry of elbows and kicks, captures and snipes at sensitive points. Whip-fast. Strong. Vicious.

Caiden kept up with dodges and counter-locks. Memories of sparring matches surged back into his body, reminding him of Threi's style. Caiden turned delicate and calculative in response.

Threi had accelerated years of combat skill before desenescizing back to his natural age, packing in instinct and lethality that Caiden struggled to match. The man hadn't let imprisonment dull any of it. Rage was an excellent whetstone.

Caiden timed a kick, then slammed the chemblade across Threi's smile, a direct hit to the head. An icy cloud blasted through Threi's hair while the chemblade sputtered, fluid low. *Shit.*

Unfazed and smile intact, the man slashed the prim saw through Caiden's skull in return.

Turmoil collided with his brain. A steady shriek filled him up. His body tipped and something grabbed him to catch his fall. Pain kicked vomit out of his guts and he doubled over Threi's forearm, earning a light, friendly uppercut to the jaw.

Caiden reeled aside, teeth clacking. Blackness charred his vision. He scraped a sleeve across his wet chin and blinked hard, head lolling.

"You look like you're going to retch again. Lean forward or you'll choke on it. In fact, why don't you *kneel*?"

The words melted through Caiden's throbbing brain, but the Graven order stuck. Something gentle and forgiving carried through him, acquiesced, *believed* in the good reason of the suggestion. Grateful, he folded his body to one knee in front of Threi and tilted his head, fighting back another wave of nausea.

"A shame about the *Azura*. She was something special." Threi stalked across Caiden's murky vision and nicked the prim through Caiden's shoulder. Skin burned, radiating pain. He bit back a cry and tried to aim a punch, but it met thin air. He lurched sideways in a world of roaring static.

A predator playing with its prey.

That meant sometimes the prey escaped.

Threi gripped Caiden's jaw and yanked him to his feet. The fast motion smeared vertigo through Caiden's brain and inner ears and stomach, and in a flicker of delusion he thought it might be funny if he happened to retch in Threi's face, which was far too close.

The many doubles of Threi in Caiden's vision weaved into one. Caiden planted his feet and managed a twisting throw. He grabbed the prim's trailing cable and roped Threi up when he rose. Didn't manage a strangling coil, but the two of them tangled, all pain and limbs frantically snapping between holds and escapes, dodging the prim's sonic blade roaring between them in Threi's grasp, and neither of them gaining the upper hand.

They tripped each other. Threi rolled neatly while Caiden toppled to all fours. *I'll lose.*

"Stop playing!" Feran called from the sidelines. "We can sedate him!"

Caiden shoved to his feet, flew, and lunged, tackling Feran, locking them in a hold. They startled but didn't fight back.

He pulled the last enhancer from his pocket and thumbed the cap off. The liquid churned against the glass where it met his palm, braiding white threads into impossible colors.

Threi straightened several meters away, panting hard. A flash of real fear crossed his face before he could smooth it out. "You won't. You're still a coward. Still scared of what our nature means. Scared to have the power to make a real difference because of the responsibility that comes with that."

Caiden glanced at the brilliant masses of Graven flesh in the pool. If he took the vial now it might tip the scale. He could shout orders at Threi and turn the hunting wolf into a loyal hound. Tempting.

But it would tip the scale of something inside Caiden as well, making him more of the Dominant and less of himself—was that how it worked? Ten years of wrestling it down said yes.

"It's irreversible?" Caiden whispered by Feran's ear.

Nervous pigment glittered across their skin. "I-I do not know. I would need to study you."

Threi strode toward them, and all Caiden could do was back up around the edge of the rectangular pool to keep distance between them while still clutching Feran.

Threi lengthened his angry stride, looking unusually alarmed. "Let Feran go."

"If I kill them, you lose your enhancers. Or do you care about someone for once?"

It was a bad bluff. If Caiden killed Feran, Threi would toss as many other scientists as he needed to the task of deciphering Feran's designs. Caiden needed to ruin the Dominant itself. *Sorry, Ksiñe, can't get samples.*

He hurled the vial to the ground, shattering fluid and glass.

"*Stop moving!*" Threi ordered, voice breaking. He rushed in and clubbed the prim at Caiden's head.

Before the command had cinched Caiden up, he shoved Feran forward into Threi, pushing himself backward at the same time. The prim tickled his face, chasing him, a buzz of raw pain. He torqued and kicked upward to hit Threi's wrist and pitch the prim's handle out of the man's grasp.

Caiden nearly managed to grab it. He meant to throw it in the pool. But the edge was too close, his foot slipped, momentum heavy.

He and the device splashed into the water together.

Fluid crashed around him, viscosity dragging him down. Plants smashed and veins tore. Blood and dirt seeped off him, fizzing into the chemical balance of the garden.

As Caiden expected, the prim's focused sonic waves went haywire in contact with the standing waves throughout the pool. The whole haft of it whipped around as it detuned, like a hose with too much pressure. Pain sliced across Caiden, no way to dodge. Bubbles detonated.

The cable itself wasn't waterproof. Water could eke in and—

Electricity spidered across the pool. It cracked into Caiden's skin too— but he was pain atop pain. Too tangled to flail to the surface.

Someone yanked the prim out by its cable, yet the damage was done.

Shrieking. Splashes. Feran rushed into the pool, crying out. Pigment glitched across their skin. They gathered up shredded flowers, reattached stems and rootlets, but this was not that kind of machine.

The crystalline cells on the fringes of the Dominant's meat rapidly decayed as the disrupted patterns tore it apart. Feran wailed and fumbled with the chunks, but the pieces dissolved through their fingers. Frosty particulates melted. Scintillation winked out in the fluid—and that was the end of the Graven Dominant.

I'll die, too, but I'll have taken it with me. Caiden gulped a lungful of burning fluid. Spasms tangled him in more plants. The ringing in his head became a hash of roars as erratic acoustic patterns permeated his skull. Fire filled every cell to bursting. Specks of time rolled backward, forward, echoing to memories and things he didn't know or had never done. Other places and beings. Azura? Flickers of grand palaces and tiny galaxies. His body unraveled into a fractal cloud, his awareness slathering across dimensions that yawned to swallow him.

Something hauled him from the pool. A silhouette of rage. Threi heaved down onto Caiden's chest, locking him in place. The fluid in his lungs wriggled around.

"Save him!" Feran screamed from the water. "He's all that's left of the Dominant!"

Dead-eyed and rigid, Threi loomed, his hair like a halo of black fire around the ghostly white of his features. "He's not all that's left. There's one more. And now I have the tool to crack that egg open."

Caiden couldn't make sense of that. He couldn't breathe more than a trickle, and every heartbeat brought fuzzy static. He made out Feran as their shaking fingers plucked veils of algae and handfuls of torn leaves, gathering the blackened tissues and blood-bright petals.

"Please," Feran whimpered. "Ten years…"

Threi made a frustrated sound of assent and repositioned his palms on Caiden's sternum. He compressed to expel the water and revive him. Fluid gushed up Caiden's throat, but fractured ribs broke the rest of the way with the force and speared into his lungs. Too much liquid to scream. Blood and heat poured in. Threi swore and almost tried again but faltered. His gaze searched around for a way to save Caiden, but what did the Casthen Prime know about healing.

It was almost funny that Threi cared. Caiden, by dying, was taking another important thing away from him.

He let his mind drift from the spasms.

A silence smoothed him, brilliant and warm.

The world ebbed and a familiar song braided through the fabric of space. Azura.

Now the Dominant is gone, you can come get me? Sorry, beautiful. Too late.

"He's dead." Light voice and hands all over him. Feran's. "Even the— *crimes*, Threi, he's dead."

Caiden's sense of his body became ash-soft, crumbling, freed from gravity, time, the pressure of space. His fiery Graven spirit slithered away into a warm embrace that was all of eternity, but he wished to imagine it was Azura.

His farewell to her dissolved into echoes and as he died, her force plumed around him, thick as wind, trying to catch him just like she had when his body had plummeted through the sky.

CHAPTER 38

GHOST

Leta clung to the slim leather harness looping C's shoulders as he galloped. Panca raced beside them on the dartbreaker. They weren't sure what had happened except that it couldn't be good.

The Dominant's pulsation had cut off in an etheric decay. Casthen poured in and Threi left with them. Leta and Panca had hidden until Azura surged back. Leta suspected the Dominant had irritated Azura like two sides of a magnet throwing each other away, and with it gone, she had reign of the facility again.

Stay with us, Leta pleaded, unsure whether the spirit swarm could hear thoughts or was just drawn to any will that wanted to help Caiden. Physics altered into a fresh universe flaming around Leta and C, which gave the nophek protection as they passed through rinds.

"Faster, baby."

The nophek whined, recklessly turning corners as he sprinted through labs. Panca's dartbreaker's treads squealed as she followed. The genetic doors wriggled open for Leta. Threi probably thought whatever was still in here was safe.

Azura thundered ahead.

On approach to a large open doorway, C slammed his brakes, claws skidding. Leta yelped and clung tight. His muzzle turned up and he sniffed fearfully at the door's edge.

Dread prickled across her skin. "What do you smell?"

She slid off his back, hit the floor on jellied legs, and clung to his mane. Panca walked beside her into the big room.

It was lit by a pool filled with some kind of massacre. Torn flowers, glitching liquid crystal, networks of vines, bloody water. Caiden sprawled half-submerged on a series of steps.

Oh, Caiden, no.

C squealed and startled a figure at the side of the pool. Panca pointed her glave at them. They froze where they were, scarlet pigment flickering across their skin. An endaal. A desolate look left their face sheet-white and their black eyes stark with mirror pupils. Eyes puffy from weeping.

"How did you get in?" they asked quietly, voice raw.

Leta crept toward Caiden while Panca backed the stranger up to a side wall.

Their hands were threaded with dark patterns. Soaked clothing clung tight to their body and their silky hair filaments hung limp in a tie. They'd been part of whatever happened. Staring at Leta, they said, "You are a Dynast Graven? This day is full of surprises."

"Is murder a surprise?" Leta marched to Caiden's side and tripped to one knee, then the other. "Panca," she rasped, afraid to touch him.

The saisn swept over and knelt to check his vitals and wounds. His skin was wan and the freckles as black as burn spots. Chest knobby, broken. He had a collection of ghastly wounds, but otherwise looked like himself. Leta smoothed the hair from his face while C whimpered and sniffed his shoulder.

Leta closed her eyes and felt across the invisible systems that coupled his body to luminiferous dimensions. "His spirit's gone. Some harmonic nervous system activity but dying fast. Crimes, Caiden…" She cradled his head and doubled over as tears stung her eyes.

Panca rounded on the endaal again. "You or Threi did this?"

"Accident," they said.

"Lies." Panca did something threatening that Leta couldn't see, but the endaal made a sound and scuffled.

"My name is Feran. Let me explain. I bear no malice and have nothing to hide."

They continued, but Leta didn't have space for the words. C nuzzled all around the edges of Caiden's body, pushing water up over him. *Burying.*

Then he shoved his big head in Leta's lap, and she kneaded her fingers around his soft ears.

"I know, baby," she sobbed. "I—"

Azura's vibration filled all around, a cloud of negative ions. The ambient light sieved into pathways she bent in the air, dimpling reality the slightest bit. Shards of personality glinted like a cut diamond turning.

Azura was spirit, enharmonic. Dynast, body, harmonic. Dominant—still part of Caiden—the stabilizing factor.

"We can bring him back."

Panca and Feran stopped talking and turned to her.

"It takes consciousness a while to dissolve fully, the parts of our experience sorting back into the luminiferity. Which is *my* domain. I can pull him together as long as he still has a viable vessel to soak back into."

Panca's face creased in confusion while Feran looked astounded.

Leta shut her eyes and let her awareness expand, as soft and quivering as a bird spreading wings. She left herself open, let Azura's density plume around her. If her Dynast Graven type created coherence and harmony, she could draw Azura into focus, collect the glints of her into articulate power.

You love him, too, don't you?

Azura's turbulence stilled like a blustery lake smoothing out. She was cocooning something...not memories, not quite thoughts, but shreds of recognition and feeling: a dreamy impression of Caiden's spirit, an afterimage built by ghostly layers.

Hope swelled in Leta. Death was a transformation, and Azura had caught Caiden midway.

Keep him with us for a while longer. Leta snapped her eyes open. The room flooded back.

"That pressure..." Feran gushed in an Andalvian dialect. "Is it really—"

They stumble-ran to an alcove of shelves on the wall, the assistive tech on their legs grinding. Hauling out a large bin, they heaved its contents straight up into the air. Glistening dust exploded. Feran dropped the bin and smacked a panel on the wall. The lights cut off and new arrays snapped online in ultraviolet and beyond.

The silvery particulates illustrated thick bands of dense vibrational patterns in the air: Azura, storming above Caiden, seven meters in each direction and seeping into the ceiling.

"Ahh." Feran exhaled slowly. "H-hello...I cannot imagine what you can do, gorgeous thing." They flustered, skin darkening around the chromatophoric voids. "Threi has been wanting you for a long time"—Panca bristled at that—"but you had a protector, didn't you?"

Leta raised a hand. Azura's force-lines spiraled around her fingertips, sketched by particles. The skin of reality tensed into muscular ruffles as Leta focused.

You and I don't have physical strength, but we have this...dimensional brawn.

"I can try to gather what remains of Caiden's spirit before it dissolves, and I can focus Azura's manipulation of physics to heal his body. Will you help?" She gave Feran an intense look.

The black light revealed a wealth of hidden patterns in Feran's endaal skin. Ragged stripes blazed, showing even where the voids should have been, ghosted into deeper dermal layers, all imperceptible to a human's normal visible spectrum.

Self-conscious, Feran's shoulders crumpled, and they quickly slapped the black light off. Ambient glow returned and their hidden emotions disappeared, replaced with an embarrassed teal flush.

They glanced at Panca, then rushed into motion, saying, "Of course I'll help. I am no physician, but organic sciences are my domain, and my garden is a life-support system. I would say you are *in luck*, but all events around Graven things are careful designs. I'm pleased to play my part." Feran swept into another room to gather items. "Knowing his only half-human genome, I should be able to re-cohere the multidimensional confluence of energy dynamics that comprises his being, but if the wave component—" They cut themself off in a familiar way, composure returning in an instant to ask, "All he needs is brain function that generates the emergent qualities for consciousness and a body to support that, correct?"

Panca joined Leta and said, hushed, "Feran claims Threi won't be returning. You trust them?"

"We have to try. They know everything about Caiden's biology—we don't."

The nophek paced and stress-panted with his head hung low. Leta peeled off Caiden's morphcoat, and Panca cut away his extra clothing before they eased him into the pool. Feran gave them a substance that clumped water into pillows of buoyancy, letting Caiden's body float.

"Help me with the machines." Feran motioned Panca over and set her to work on devices in the pool walls that had shorted out or needed calibration. "You still have not told me your names or pronouns or relation, but no matter. We are attempting Graven science that none have dared before, and I might test my belief that there is no state that Nature cannot solve."

Leta softened. "Leta Nine of the Graves."

"Graves?"

"Dynast...constructs. Our minds extend through dimensions and our spirits are flexible between vessels."

"Ah, Threi mentioned his sister was ambitious." Feran smiled. They were a rush of activity, a butterfly fluttering around its favorite flower. They purified the water, sprinkled chemicals in, sowed seeds in viscous globs and algae nets. Cozy patterns filled their skin as they worked.

Submerged to her waist, Leta floated her hands near Caiden's head. His short hair fanned through the water, which started to bleach out the dirty blond color from the tips. She smiled and whispered, "You were always stubborn. Keep that up."

His spirit wasn't inside his body anymore but Leta's hope was, and the garden started to resemble the sort of impossibility they were after: an ingenious blend of biology and mechanism, a life-support system that grew itself as it responded with instant biofeedback. Gossamer wires winged into Caiden's shoulders and spine. Lacy, many-armed creatures latched onto his wrists and over his organs. Metal wires hooked into their backs and off to energy-relay systems. Seedlings spotted meridians.

Prismatic crystal fibers needled Caiden's chest to tease at his heart, taste his lungs, capture the rhythms of him. They were tiny lightning rods for the various energies that suffused the pool from machines Panca tended on its sides.

Feran sloshed out to the steps to survey their work. "This will grow into a chain reaction of self-organizing information—healing potential. It would take years his body does not have. Time for your miracle, Grave."

Leta summoned everything she remembered of how it had felt when Abriss's treatment with the Aurasever and the crystal casket had filled her with Azura's power. Reality's sheer malleability: what the ancient Graven were capable of without a second thought, their whole world shaped by their will.

Graven Azura, you are a creature of dimensions, powerful beyond measure, but you lack hands or voice. I was designed to handle power and to reach presences like yours, so let's work together.

Leta lifted her hands and hoped.

Azura's force soaked in. Waves of Leta's hair lifted upward, and the light fuzzed strangely. C barked and the sound bent, pitching down out of hearing range.

To Feran, Leta said, "Show me where and what it needs."

All the color drained from Feran except peach babbling over the bridge of their nose. After a moment of shock, they dived back into the work, indicating seeds needing heat, buds to crack open, chemicals awaiting reaction. Leta danced her fingers in the water and fine-tuned physical laws, designing pressures and electromagnetics, flirting with temperature. The balance between structure and entropy was hers to control, and all it took was intent. She could fold dimensions to manifest changes in reality. More than all that, she felt—temporarily—completely healed and whole.

This is what Abriss wanted for us all along.

At Leta's touch, buds bloomed into jewel-colored flowers. Nests of dead cutoffs decayed, and new roots sank in to be fed. Stems split open and radiated curly threads. Paper-thin petals bloomed out of seeds beneath Caiden's skin. Tiny vines from aquatic plants serpentined his limbs and invaded, intravenous.

Leta marveled at Feran's designed signal flow of linked organics. Feran marveled mutually at Leta as Azura's energy paired with her, distending surrounding space.

"Step back," Feran said, "the system can take over now."

They waded to the edge of the pool and directed Panca to adjust the machines' standing waves and electromagnetic patterns, orchestrating slow seasons of music inside the water to continue rapidly growing and dissolving the system.

Panca made an appreciative sound. "He looks less dead each moment."

It was only Caiden's corpse improving, but some color returned to his skin. His Graven freckles flickered. Wounds filled up and even old scars dissolved.

Feran donned a medical glove and ran it over Caiden's body. "Fine readings, if I may applaud my own work. A lovely vessel for a spirit to pour back into." They looked pointedly at Leta.

She exhaled shakily. A migraine drowned her own voice as she said, "This next part only I can do."

Leta's Dynast nature was harmonious and structural. She hoped to all the stars she was evolving fast enough to gather up a scattered consciousness and put it back together.

She imagined the pool was one of the radiation caskets of home. The water was so warm she lost sense of where it began and her skin ended, making it even easier for her awareness to drift away. She submerged, seeped into the luminiferous chaos of being, and concentrated on what she wanted to pull out of it: all that she knew and loved of Caiden, from memories to physicality to the constellation of people he'd connected to.

She didn't need to remake his self from scratch. She only had to focus on what was quintessentially *Caiden*, the holistic pattern of him into which his spirit would be attracted no matter how finely his being had dissolved into the luminiferity already. Consciousness was not an epiphenomenon emergent from matter but the opposite, which meant if Leta could pull this wonderful, frustrating fool of a man together, his body would revive.

Abriss's beautiful hope still infested Leta: *There's no state of physical damage that cannot be recovered from. Miracles are the natural order of things, the way it's meant to be.*

Leta shed doubt and put her trust in the tempo of being and the world of becoming. She didn't force, she *allowed*. In a flow, feelings breezed to her. She heard Caiden's laughter and saw his easy smile, all the times that both had hidden pain. She felt the fire he tried to leash back and the blood from biting his tongue, the temper he could never wrestle down, but the shy touch he had for things he loved.

As spirit congealed into the pattern she'd crafted as an invitation, parts she didn't know flocked into her awareness. She fought the urge to reject them. These shards of time and echoes of emotion were part of his essential self too. Visions of palaces galaxies wide, someone singing many languages together, light that had so many spectra no one could name the colors, and flowers that changed at a touch.

The space in the water garden's chamber was stamped with strange impressions from the years Feran had toiled to define the Graven being they were taking care of. Leta couldn't help but compare it to the Graven echoes that Abriss mentioned so often aligning into a louder whole. Caiden had been born from this same Graven here... Leta let its impressions aid her in defining him too.

Trickles of his spirit harmonized to her call, the shreds of him stitched up by her need.

You're all right—she borrowed his phrase—*I came to get you.*

CHAPTER 39

GRAVEN TRINITY

Water and light, a duet. Patterns morphed and strings of space squiggled. Liquid bands of radiance moved like synapses firing, nerve pathways carving through the fray.

Or else it was him... His own function trying to sing alongside these other forces.

Sound weaved together and Caiden heard bubbles pluming up, something surfacing, a gasp. Gentle fingers cradled the back of his skull.

He opened his eyes. Leta stood over him, tears in hers.

"Welcome back." She laughed. One tear dripped into the pool water and one struck his face. He shut that eye and slowly smiled.

"I didn't die after all," he said, mostly whisper.

"Oh, you did." Leta shook with more exhausted laughter. "You did."

Whines streamed from C at the pool's edge. His whole body wiggled side to side, tail knocking things over by the walls.

Dazed, Caiden sat upright, but there was nothing solid beneath him. He floundered in the water before finding his feet. Flowers rocked and vines tangled him more, tearing out of his skin, which was littered with blue freckles and clouds of sparkles. Visions flashed in his confused brain: the Dominant's meat hooked up to an ecosystem, and him the same, with blossoms under his skin and sap in his veins.

The air clotted around him. "Azura," he whispered. Droplets beaded atop the pool as her presence settled.

And Panca, she stood by one wall and folded her arms, tension unknotting from her hard face. "I'll fetch you something dry."

C yipped and quivered, muscles bunching up until he pounced headlong into the pool. He crashed into Caiden, waves exploding. Leta yelled in surprise.

Caiden surfaced awkwardly while hugging the monster's torso and battling licks and head-butts. C purred so loud and low it vibrated the pool's surface. Caiden laughed and hugged the little boy's neck until he calmed.

The garden was thoroughly ruined. C's huge finned tail thrashed. He dived, webbed paws pulling his long body easily through the water.

Leta waded to the steps and sat, watching happily and wearily.

Caiden kicked off flowers, tore tiny plants from his bare torso, and scraped the water from his hair as he trudged to the steps and collapsed beside her.

C stopped swimming and trampled over both their laps before lying down, half-submerged. He bit plants out of the water to gnaw on.

"I don't know what you did," Caiden said to Leta, "but thank you."

Whatever had happened was foggy in his brain. He remembered being netted by Azura yet falling forever. Then Leta, whispering him back together.

He looped a weak arm around her neck to embrace her sideways, asking, "This is when it's all right to hug? Back from the dead?"

Leta snorted a laugh and smashed him tightly. "We're almost even for all the times you saved me."

Caiden grinned, then winced at a jolt of pain and pried a strange flower off the artery in his thigh.

Feran made an exasperated sound from one side of the pool. "Nothing of mine is meant to last today, it seems." They scooped up a mangled blossom while darts of red raced up their wrist. When they lifted it from the water, the petals wilted and the fine roots shriveled.

They held Caiden's gaze and added, "Witnessing the newly dead return to life is a fair trade, I suppose. My life's work is gone the same day I helped facilitate a miracle: acts that used to be commonplace in the Graven's world. I always sensed reassurances that the years would be worthwhile, that my patience was a currency. If I was patient and regrew the Dominant enough...something miraculous would happen...and nothing in the worlds could keep the Graven trinity apart for long. And here you all are."

He missed nuances in their dialect, but he read a delicate, awed mood in Feran's emotional signals—hue and pattern—even with the swaths of void like missing words.

"Everything for a reason..." Leta drawled. "Did you hear a voice? Echoes lining up..."

Feran's eyeshine flashed as they peered at her. "Time built a vocabulary between the Dominant and me as I regrew its cells. I wouldn't quite call it a *voice*, but if you gather up enough echoes, a thing becomes clearer."

Leta frowned up at Azura.

"What are you thinking?" Caiden asked.

"That I'm glad I came with you." Her answer sounded like a deflection. With a doleful sigh she buried her forehead against Caiden's ribs and muttered into his side, "You're not expendable, you know."

"I know." He kissed the top of her head. She made a whimpering affirmative, then fell limp. "Leta?"

She smiled weakly when he tipped her in the crook of his arm. "Just need to go back...soon..."

"No Proxy until you've rested." Caiden tried to sound sure of himself, but all Ksiñe's various warnings crowded his skull. He surged up with Leta in his arms and crawled on his knees to lay her on the dry floor.

Feran hurried over with an armful of supplies. They administered a tincture that made Leta's vitals even out. She drifted on the edge of sleep, blinking slowly.

"Will she be all right?"

"She accomplished the miraculous, Caiden. How can we judge the cost of that?"

Panca brought blankets. She gave one to Caiden and wrapped Leta in the other. The spongy fabric soaked up water and expelled it as steam as Caiden—mostly undressed—swaddled tight and tousled his hair. A cloud of vapor cocooned him.

Azura threaded the space around Leta and Caiden, ruffling the steam into long ribbons of force. The air prickled like a storm and Leta opened her eyes drowsily, smiling. "She helps."

"You rest," Caiden chided. To Feran he started, "Threi—"

"He tried to save you."

"*Where* is Threi?"

"He'll be off-planet by now."

"Waiting at the egress to catch Abriss?"

"No," Feran replied. "Threi cannot touch her without more enhancers. He is headed to RM28."

Nightmare visions crawled from the corners of Caiden's mind. RM28, the desert of death, the planet the nophek had been farmed on, where his and Leta's population had been transported to and slaughtered as feed.

"RM28," Leta repeated, eyes wide. "Why?"

Caiden thought aloud: "Threi mentioned another Dominant. Something about an egg?"

Feran nodded. "The Casthen have been searching for more Graven remnants like Azura buried on the planet, with the hopes they'd find technology to release Threi from universal prison. But the Casthen did not find Azura's energy signature... they found the Dominant's."

Caiden swore.

Panca asked, "He's going there now to retrieve an intact Dominant Graven so you can make more enhancers?"

"Correct. Perhaps even permanent ones or a permanent merger, if this *is* a complete energy form. Becoming more Graven than Abriss is the only way anyone will stop her. I'm sure that is Threi's priority now."

Threi really wouldn't stop until Abriss was dead and he had control of everything. Caiden found a rougher swear and earned a scowl from Panca. Leta looked ready to say something—defense of her Prime?—but shut her mouth.

"Do not worry," Feran added, "the Dominant on RM28 is deep inside the planet, beyond an impenetrable barrier under the planetary crust, entirely inaccessible thus far."

"Then why is he—" Caiden cut off as he realized. He gave Leta a sinking look. "The Aurasever."

Feran frowned. "Explain?"

Leta obliged, "It's how he was released, by a device that pops a universe rind. The border universes' physics take up the lost space, but the sweeping edge of the rinds rebalancing is another destructive flux, more than a simple change of physics. Caiden, you think he'll use it to get through RM28's barrier?"

Feran's face lit up. "There is a chance it would affect the composition of the planet's shell material. If not shattering it, then making it vulnerable to the methods that failed before: drilling and acids and so forth."

"Crafty…" Caiden drawled. "Abriss told me Threi can't use the Aura-sever. It's designed for her specially trained mind. But he's crafty. He has all the Casthen and Cartographers as resources. He'll find a way to use that tech and he'll pop that whole universe if it will get him what he needs to become fully Graven once and for all."

Leta pulled her blanket tighter. "Threi fully Graven…"

Panca stood at a console that she had rewired, now streaming in Casthen data. She reported, "He left with an armada of augmented ships. Abriss must've escaped this universe if Threi's so confident refocusing."

Feran added, "He rarely makes mistakes twice. He will ensure he's as powerful as he can become before attacking his sister again."

Caiden rubbed his eyes and tried to weigh all their choices. "Abriss warned me Threi would attempt to use the Aurasever to collapse all of Unity. Maybe popping the universe that RM28 is in is also a test for that? Threi is our priority either way. We stop him reaching the Graven Domi-nant inside RM28 and obtain it ourselves. Leta—what will Abriss do next? She's made one Aurasever…can she make another? Would she collapse the multiverse into Unity?"

"She…she just needs to be reassured she's not betrayed completely. I'll speak with her in-Proxy when she's recovered." Leta perked up. "We've—the Graves have been struggling with her toward the same goals for half of my life. She isn't throwing that away. In Unity we'll…heal all the Graves, and Abriss can evaluate Threi's astrology. She might see something that can help us. I can still be two places at once; we can handle both Primes."

A long pause stretched while the immensity of what they were up against took shape.

Leta said, "Caiden…Everything up to now…you bringing Azura here, Abriss bringing me and the Aurasever, stolen by her brother so he can crack the shell of a fresh Dominant Graven on the planet we came from…"

This was Caiden's worry too. Çydanza's death, Caiden's failed rescue of Leta that cracked Azura's chrysalis, and Threi attempting to murder Abriss but in the process setting off what chain of *upcoming* events?

Feran raised their palms, creamy spots twinkling atop powder blue. "Doesn't it sound like part of a single thread of action? Even I have been playing an unwitting part, the key to the enhancers that allowed for crucial events. It is unconscious co-creation toward a goal we cannot perceive. Perhaps even a conscious will of which we're unaware."

"Or more than one will…" Leta murmured, almost too quiet to hear.

Caiden caught it. Before he could pry, Panca asked Feran, "You're sharing freely—why?"

"I promise I have no malintent." They wrung water out of the hem of their dress coat. Amused metallic blips scattered across their skin. "I may have spent ten years with Threi in my ear and me in his, but my main focus was and is the Graven. Threi is their pawn too. And besides, even if I help you get to him, confronting him is still your hurdle."

Leta sat upright, wobbling. "I'll get back to my Proxy on the *Second Wind* to make—"

"You're exhausted," Caiden interjected. "You held open dimensions to pull me back to life—that's more than enough. Rest for a moment." He snapped his fingers for C to come over and lie as a cushion. "I need to pull this garden out of my skin, find clothes, and plan what's next. I'll wake you."

As Leta curled up against C's belly, he could almost see each layer of exhaustion fold over her. Steam curled off the blanket where it met C's soaked hide. The nophek breathed sleepily too.

Caiden left them and joined Panca. She gave him a fierce hug that crushed a lot of the biological life-support stuff still clinging to him, but nothing that Feran's fussing and a good scour didn't fix after. He let them do their scans, then rested, grateful to be alive, while Panca filled him in on what had happened.

His rapid healing continued, sealing the tiny perforations where roots and stems had grown into his body. Organic bits left over dissolved. Chemicals and hormones continued to stimulate cellular regrowth. He felt *good*, and hated it, because the enhancement in him seemed massaged into his body now, the gap between him and it closed.

"I don't like the idea of you staying, Pan," he said as he yanked on a too-tight Casthen uniform that Feran had scrounged from the labs.

"I've Cartographer friends here. Don't mind waiting while things settle down. Laythan can collect me later."

"If you're sure…"

Panca chuckled. "You're so eager to ditch us before, but now you won't let me go."

"Just worried. I've worried about all of you the whole time."

"We'll take care of one side of this problem while you 'n' Leta take another. Just come back to us when it's done."

"I will."

Feran trundled by the pool, pushing a heavy mag cart of supplies and harvested foodstuffs. Their assistive prosthetics chattered, worn loose by all the excess activity. Panca strode over to help.

Caiden crept to Leta, still asleep across C's front limb. The nophek slitted an eye open and swayed his tail. Leta roused a little.

Caiden sank to one knee. "Time to go, but you should stay asleep. Little boy'll take care of you again."

She blinked once, a yes, then closed her eyes and drooped. Caiden worried over her level of exhaustion and her injuries—including a gnarly bruise on her cheek—as he gingerly slid her up over C's back. The nophek rose, equally as gentle.

Together they walked out to the vast, empty, polished black space outside of the labs. As they approached Panca and Feran, the floor split open and huge mechanics shifted plates to raise a small one-room vessel.

"My personal ship, the *Spur*," Feran announced. "I have never had a chance to use it, thanks to you trapping me."

Azura swept through the high ceiling like a gigantic night bird, rumbling faintly. Glow lights pulsed on, peeling one veil off the darkness. The pressure crackled as she invaded the piscine vessel, and Feran yelped in surprise and delight.

Tendrils of dust wheezed from the ship's seams as Azura converted parts inside. Alloys pinged and groaned.

Panca said, "I'll get it tuned to reach RM28." She took a fistful of C's mane to guide the nophek on board, Leta still fast asleep. Inside near a wall, C lowered onto his belly with the greatest care while twisting his neck back to whuff soft breaths over Leta's dangling hand.

Panca began to examine what Azura had done to the ship.

Feran's patterns fluttered happy blue. "The *Spur* is fueled, supplied, and enspirited by a Graven entity. What else do you require, Paraborn?"

"People who know as many secrets as you do aren't safe working for Threi. You know that."

Gold flecks rained down Feran's wrists as they wrung their fingers. "Secrets by nature yearn to escape. They beat at the walls inside us. As long as I behave, me being the one and only person with whom he can share secrets makes me too valuable to lose."

"Except you've shared them now."

"Ah, no, I have not shared all of Threi Cetre's secrets with you. Deep down, Caiden, we all just want to be seen, without others' context pressed on us."

Caiden still struggled to not see the Casthen as oppressive, beneath its progressive veneer, after all it had imprinted on him. But he would give Feran's message some thought.

"Now," they said, walking backward, "if you wouldn't mind opening my door for me?"

"You're staying in there? You'll be trapped until—and *if*—Threi returns."

"I've spent roughly a third of my life in here alone. I am one of Threi's secrets: no one knows who I am. Integrating, somehow and suddenly, back into Casthen or Cartographer life sounds quite terrifying at the moment."

Caiden, too, had once lost everything that adhered his identity. He could understand Feran's hesitation. Time was the only thing that could fix their world.

The endaal's brow rippled gold streaks through black. "I do have a second request: do not destroy this new Dominant, and don't kill Threi or Abriss. They can't be replaced. Leta has incredible potential, but she is—forgive the crass term—a Dynast husk waiting to be possessed. A vessel wanting for water. Threi and Abriss are the last complete genetic remnants of the Dynast Graven, who were the last line of Graven to maintain physical forms. If we lose either of the two, I believe the potential of the trinity will be lost forever."

"You overestimate my interest in this trinity," Caiden said.

"Please."

"Feran—"

"I'm only asking you to attempt not to kill and destroy."

Striking in the tender spots. Caiden sighed and followed them to the door. "I can't promise that Threi won't end up dead. But if he does, I promise Leta or I will come back to let you out, when you're ready."

They laughed. "I have foolish faith that my Graven knowledge is so valuable to events unfolding now, that the world *must* release me. I look forward to seeing who walks through this door next."

They had strong words, but jets of scarlet worry strobed their wrists.

The rods of the door slithered apart, ringing out. Caiden stopped and Feran backstepped to the other side.

"I trust there's a magnificent purpose behind my loss. The decay of my Dominant fed your strange rebirth, after all. Just make my choice to heal you worth something. And"—they held out a small bronze cooler case—"I didn't have to vivisect you to make these."

Inside were six vials of enhancer, pearly white and alive with luminous bouts of color.

Feran said, "If circumstances require you to be perfect, one day."

CHAPTER 40

LIABILITY

Leta nestled drowsily in one corner of the *Spur* against makeshift cushions. C cuddled up against her thigh. The roar of the engine was a soothing monotony that begged her to sleep, but true unconsciousness would have to wait. She peeled from her body into the luminiferity and marveled again at how easy it was becoming. Almost like Azura slipping from system to ship to sky, using anything as a body because she had none. Perhaps that's what the real Graven had been.

Leta's Proxy called her in from however far the *Second Wind* had already traveled away from the Casthen universe. With rinds obscuring her sense of it, she needed focus and patience, but she found it eventually. Familiar shapes and scents welcomed her as she opened her Proxy's eyes.

She was seated in a spacious storage room next to Isme Two. His long hair was still bloodied and his mask rent in pieces.

All Leta's worries flooded back. She grazed her cracked knuckles over the cables in his neck and the shorn blue ligaments of his shoulder. "We're coming home," she whispered. "Please be safe."

Leta rose to exit into the hall, little agonies nipping at her heels.

Dejin loomed in front of the med-suite door, crackling his fists open and closed anxiously. When he saw her, he strode over so fast he stumbled. "Parla im, sistra! I thought you dead!"

"I fought Six. He's back in his real body now. The others aren't safe."

"Mau vi, I am alive. I would lose Proxy connection if anything happened to *me* there. We will trust that means the others are all right."

Leta didn't trust frail hopes anymore, though she wished to. She was caved in by Dej's deep voice and broad frame, by a solidity she wanted to rely on. "Where are we?"

"Not far from Unity, the captain says. Smuggling us out of the Casthen world went smooth—priority clearance, cargo concealed, bribed through the egress. We are chaining stellar egresses now to return as quickly as possible. The *Wintra* is with us also."

Caiden's family was safe, at least.

"Abriss?" Leta asked.

"Just woke. She had roused twice before but...has a blank look. The medic is—"

The med-suite door opened and their Dynast Prime emerged. Her presence was intense, even dressed in a borrowed mechanic's loose one-piece suit. Under the hall's lights her pupil contracted to a pinprick. Her injured eye and neck were bandaged over with delicate membranes, the bruising almost black now.

Abriss's flat, washed-out expression was harrowing to see on the most powerful creature in the multiverse. Leta wanted to interpret it as the usual fatigue, or painkiller dullness, but something in Abriss had broken, and shards were bleeding the kindness from her.

"P-Prime?"

This was the wintry expression of the woman who worked sleeplessly to achieve her goals and commanded legions with impunity...not the woman Leta loved, who fantasized about connection and spoke shyly about invigorating topics, who craved to share, protect, and elevate others.

Leta burst with the urge to embrace the woman tightly with the closeness she'd always craved, to whisper to her that she wasn't alone and never needed to be, that Leta's feelings were unclouded. And Leta cursed all the times she'd been timid in the past. She hadn't seen this coming, hadn't realized how vulnerable Abriss Cetre really was beneath all her strengths. Was it too late?

Dejin knelt before Abriss, his armored knee ringing on the floor. "We failed to protect you. Aser arre, Prime, it will not happen again."

Abriss laid a hand on Eight's dented spaulder, then motioned him to rise. "No, it won't."

Her words were monotone and soaked in idle gravitas—like rage, except Abriss Cetre was never angry... This was raw power seething from her like a sword finally unsheathed, the gentle leather slipped off the hard, sharp blade of her will. Was she grieved so much she couldn't control it?

No, dear stars, we really are losing her.

Leta wasn't sure where to start. She lined up words, rearranged them, but Dejin was faster. "We are nearly home," he said, loading that last word with a promise of ease. If Abriss was in a state of survival, her feelings shuttered up to maintain functioning, home would heal her.

"Ksiñe is a fine medic," Leta offered, "your injuries look well." She cursed that there was so little good news to report, she had to use something so inane. Abriss wasn't vain and would willingly pay in blood and limbs to protect what mattered to her.

But a flicker of vulnerability returned to Abriss and her voice softened when she said, "His knowledge of Graven biology is exceptional."

We can get through to her still. Get the old Abriss back.

Abriss nodded to them and strode for the bridge, trying to hide a limp by walking through the ache.

As her presence filled the room, Laythan rose from the cockpit and turned.

Every last bit of softness shut out of Abriss's demeanor as she recognized him. Injuries dragged her syllables through pain as she greeted him, "Dynast Safeguard pilot and convict Laythall Sorsen."

Laythan was whipped by her tone and by muscle memory, his body folding to one knee in the Dynast bow. His prosthetic eyes widened, and his wrinkled, white-bearded face wore surprise plainly.

"What?" Leta blurted. *That pilot was* him? *Stars forfend, this is not the reminder she needs!*

Leta had heard the story, an ugly snarl in the Dynast's history: Abriss's mother, the previous Dynast Prime, Laureli Cetrin, had been murdered. The Safeguard pilot—Laythall Sorsen—on her crashed ship had been held responsible. All those years ago, starting a chain of events...

Laureli's death broke Threi... who murdered his father, Veren... the last person as Graven as Abriss, which left her bereft of equals forever.

And Caiden fell into this man's crew...

An unseen alignment, another event that had constellated to bring Caiden to Azura and Azura to Abriss. Somehow in this whole tangle, Laythall Sorsen had been brought before the Prime *now* at this most delicate of turning points.

Abriss didn't grow enraged or bent with sorrow. She grew more detached— and that was infinitely worse.

She strode toward Laythan and did nothing to dampen the power that trailed with her: a thickness in the air that snapped up energy all around in her vortex. Laythan remained kneeling, shoulders cowed.

"Prime," Leta began carefully, "the captain's transgression was well in the past and he's in your service now. I'm sure we—"

"I am not interested in vengeance." Abriss curled her fingers against her throat's bandages, skimming her knuckles up and down. It sawed her next words into a rustle of sound. "Laythall had his punishment. The damage he was participant to is done. Threi has never been the same since our mother's death. You wouldn't believe that his heart used to be *gentle*."

More softly, yet cold as a snowflake settling, Abriss said, "It was callow of me to always be looking so earnestly at the past, wanting things I used to have, when the work ahead is crucial for all. I'm grateful my brother showed me that my wants are inconsequent to my purpose. The future is my calling."

Leta wanted to scream, or rush and grab her, or turn time back so they'd never left Unity. Abriss was throwing the best of herself away. She would let the future destroy her before she ever had a chance to live in the present.

The Prime turned to Laythan. A rare ghost of a snarl marred her face. "Right now, I require a swift escort back to Unity. If that act repays any lingering guilt of yours, Captain, all the better."

"My ship is at your service, Prime Abriss," Laythan said, bent by her will, all but folded back into the pilot's seat.

Abriss's world was filled with obeisance. The wrinkles of her snarl deepened for a split second before smoothing out because she hated it... she hated the monotony of compliance, and Leta didn't know—had never known—what to do or say to stop it.

"After escorting me home," Abriss said, "you may all leave as you like, free passagers again. Please obey until then."

The unnecessary *please* didn't glitter as it used to.

Leta had once found it reassuring to know the Prime had a course of action in mind and saw the means of creating it, but now it terrified her. Would Abriss stop seeing people around her as people, but merely means to an end? Instruments. Hammers. She was a creator. Her creating was a law-giving, a will to unity. With all her previous endeavors insulted, what would she turn to now?

The ship zoomed through the ring of a stellar egress. Leta staggered as space contracted, slathered, then snapped together again. Through the cockpit view, the *Wintra* rocketed ahead like a shard of steel-blue blade. Taitn and Endirion... more of Caiden's family to be wrapped up as instruments.

Abriss turned back to Leta and Dejin. "I apologize that events on the Harvest went as they did—my own flaws were to blame. But we're alive and will be together soon."

"I stayed...in my real body...and pursued the Graven Dominant in the Harvest with Winn." Leta hastened her explanation as Abriss's gaze unfocused and something unhooked inside her mind. "It was destroyed. But we—"

Abriss interrupted, "You *stayed*?"

Crimes, that truth was the wrong thing to say. The more pieces of makeshift family that Abriss lost, the more she would reject the idea of tenderness altogether, because if Leta had really loved Abriss, she would have kept by her side, in both bodies, and returned home together.

"I knew we needed the Dominant strain," Leta explained as she raised her hand slowly. She and Dejin were the only two on the ship capable of physically harming Abriss, whose posture made it clear she was well aware. "Threi located another, intact, Dominant. He's headed to it now, and I'll pursue him in my real body with Winn. I will do everything in my power to stop Threi and bring the Dominant home to heal us."

That *new* Dominant on RM28 was one more event that linked her to Caiden and him to Threi.

Threi to Abriss.

And Abriss to all the worlds.

A weave of Graven intention.

Leta bowed as elegantly as her mangled Proxy allowed. "I remain yours entirely."

A smile shivered across Abriss's lips. "I have no way to know whether you're lying."

Leta scrambled for a response. She and Dejin in-Proxy were free-minded enough to convince Abriss not to abandon her gentle, political, mindful approach toward unity. But they were also the very individuals whose words she wouldn't trust, *precisely because* they were free. After Dian, Tayen, and Sisorro had switched sides, Abriss's confidence would take time to win back.

"Even if you're still truthful and loyal now, Nine, you only 'remain mine' until Winn or Threi manipulate you in your real body. That puts your Proxy, a weapon, right here by my side and the wielder of it in the control of a Graven person who feels I've wronged them." She thumbed her bandages to make a point.

A weapon. She's already stopped seeing us as people?

Dejin hissed inside his helmet. He raised placating hands to Abriss. "Prime, we would not have saved you only to harm you after."

"You don't understand the liability?" Abriss walked toward Leta with half steps, no longer hiding her limp. "If Threi captures her, he'll twist her heart around, and *she won't have a choice but to harm*."

Leta stood as still as a cornered animal. Abriss's logic wasn't flawed, even if she couldn't tell that Leta was still on her side. "I trust Winn, he helped save you, and I won't get cap—"

"Winn is headed straight to my brother. Their stars are all but twinned— they'll never escape each other."

Abriss stopped inches from Leta, looking up. All her old hopes were trapped dead in the amber of that glassy stare. Reassuring Graven whispers preoccupied her mind. Leta got the distinct sense that this had happened in another way in the past, Threi spurning her into the solace of a non-manifest entity. Was her kindness toward him a second chance, and had the world failed her for the last time?

Abriss hooked a fingernail in the bone of Leta's jaw. Inside her Proxy's skull were tiny nodes, where a combination of the right pressures could shut down a Proxy for good. A failsafe.

"Don't do this," Leta whispered.

If I fight back now, it'll prove her fears right, and she'll never be turned back toward good. But if I lose my Proxy, I won't have any means of trying to turn her back anyway. What do I say?

"I was naïve," Abriss said. "I exist to help us reach our Graven purpose and bring about a dimension where all things are understood. Unified hearts and minds making utopia possible, opening untold potentials. If my care and my philosophy are so easy to disbelieve through words, I'll have to show everyone the undeniable truth, once in Unity."

The *conviction* in those words.

Leta ventured, "You're not naïve. You're optimistic and brilliant. Your sorrows are valid. So many people love—"

"Threi proved how hollow words can be, Nine." Abriss winced as her hand slipped farther under Leta's jaw, fingers splaying up into the hidden nodes linking to the brainstem.

Dejin startled, slow to realize. "Prime!"

Leta whispered, "Please don't."

"My sentinels are bringing a new version of the Aurasever. With it, I'll return the multiverse to the singularity that it first was and is meant to be, bringing all beings into accord."

"Singularity?" Leta stitched together information, tone, and Dynast philosophy, and the truth slammed her. *Damn everything, Threi was right. She's giving up her patient and compassionate means of making Unity accessible for all.*

As Abriss's support fell away, the woman was realizing she *did* have the means to accomplish all she wished. Her better self had let her ignore this path...but that better self hadn't survived the murder attempt.

The only world in which Abriss would have equals was one in which all beings were equal: the dissolution of the multiverse. With the Aurasever, she could collapse neighboring universes into Unity, and as Unity expanded and grew more ideal, all living things would become Graven in their own way. Abriss wouldn't feel alone in a crowd. This path only meant giving up on the people who had just proved they weren't there for her anyway.

"Abriss," Leta said urgently, hoping the familiar name would jar the woman off course. Her heart had never ached so much, to watch someone who was still living *die* like this. The Abriss she adored would be gone forever. "Stop th—"

Torment flickered in Abriss's eye. Her gaze cut away a heartbeat before her fingers jammed in.

Stars detonated across Leta's vision. Sounds intensified to a deafening howl, then shut silent as Leta's Proxy dropped dead on the floor.

She was thrust into the luminiferity, but instead of arcing back to her real body, her sorrow for Abriss mired her in place. Unanchored, she was strong enough now to hold herself together in the luminiferity for longer while time tried to rake her apart and space became every location at once. Boundless energy swallowed her focus. Fury, helplessness, pain—the luminiferity tried to steal them from her. Leta wanted to feel everything, all the ugliness of what she'd let happen.

Her Proxy shelter that had always protected and brought out her best—gone.

Leta's awareness fuzzed through the void, across fields of information. Twinkles of spacetime snagged like diamond ice catching the light. Celestial rain. She let herself drift. Returning to her real body felt like running away from her failure.

Had she sealed the other Graves' fates? Abriss would imprint loyalty onto their minds, erasing their misgivings, no longer gifting them her trust or the space to disobey. The Proxies would become her weapons and shields.

Abriss would alter the multiverse irreversibly, and nothing could stand in her way. The larger Unity became, the more loving subjects she would control.

No one in Abriss's orbit can stop or kill her now. Except—

Isme's Proxy still sat intact aboard the *Second Wind*.

An empty vessel ... if Leta could reach it.

CHAPTER 41

WILL TO UNITY

In the vastness of the cosmos, it would take Leta ages to locate the one tiny, specific lightning rod that was Isme's empty Proxy. But it would be near Abriss, and Abriss was the most familiar thing in Leta's life, the eye of a storm in the luminiferity.

Time crystallized as Leta focused. Localized bits of space fluttered until they all matched up at the same time, one coherent landscape: Unity.

Abriss was nearby, unwittingly moving the world around her like a stone beneath a river's flow.

There. Leta burrowed into the dead weight of Isme's Proxy and tried not to imagine that it was the grave of him. Isme hadn't reconnected to his Proxy himself... He was either preoccupied or dead.

Leta battered down her heartache and hurried. If Abriss read Unity's heavens, she would see her life was in danger. Leta discovered some precautions already in place: Isme's limbs had been bound with molecular bonds, but the job was shoddy, and Leta imagined Dejin feeling so wrong about hobbling a brother, he rushed through.

Beyond the Proxy's glitchy sluggishness lay memories and emotions that Isme had left behind. As Leta looped herself into his nervous system and reanimated his biology, she couldn't help but absorb what those cells had stored.

Fear of what Abriss could do or be.

Dread over what awaited him when he returned to the Dynast Hold.

Grief that he'd left Dejin and Leta behind with a terrible task. This feeling matched up with Leta's own, jarringly so, her mutual worry that he'd been sent back to Solthar against unknowns and unfair odds.

There was one last remnant feeling that surprised Leta and bowled her over: a special heartbreak for her...a well of emotion where a good-bye would have been...velvet-lined with admiration and his faith that she would try her best.

It was a type of affection she didn't dare name before she knew he was safe.

Oh, Isme, why now? Leta seized control, wrenched out of the restraints, then folded into a fetal position. *I can't be hurting this much now.*

She linked to visual systems behind Isme's faceless mask. The many deep cracks threw the world into disarray. Leta scraped her shaking fingertips over the insects and webs painting his upper body. The sight piled on more indomitable sorrows.

Get up. This is my battle.

The Proxy flesh tingled, trying to reject Leta's presence as a bad fit. She stood slowly, recalibrating balance heuristics. There was a fluidity to Isme's Proxy that she struggled to maneuver, body leaning too far with momentum, joints slippery—Isme's natural grace made sudden sense. Grief haunted her at that thought, but she didn't have time to miss everything about him all over again. He would lend her this strength and they would do this together. She would make sure he and the others were free.

Stop Abriss—

Kill. The word was *kill*.

—and the Graves will be safe.

Leta searched for weapons but didn't find any, and with her connection fraying, she didn't have time to strategize or gear up. Surprise was a weapon if used right. She snapped off one of the already-fractured radius rods in the Proxy's forearm. The tip of the fake lightseep was spear-sharp.

In a row of pockets among the thick pleats of Isme's skirt, she found four of his floater drones, enough for a decent stun grid. The little things twirled to life after she tossed them. They keyed to her fingers, which she snapped to put the floaters in an idle state, arranged in a crescent behind her head.

The instincts from countless espionage missions sparkled into her as she treaded ghost-soft through the halls toward the exit, but there was no one aboard. The engines were off. Small particles pattered the hull.

In the atrium, Leta glanced at the bridge—a whiteout in the cockpit windows—then continued to the cargo hold. Dejin's Proxy slumped there, his consciousness sent back to his ursgen body. He'd done a better job with his own restraints.

The rear hatch was open, the ship parked on a planet. Leta staggered out into snowfall.

A half meter of white blanketed the ground while fat flakes lazed from a cover of pink-tinged clouds. Temperature warnings glittered across her skin. A wind tossed up diamond dust and whisked the Proxy's ankle-length hair like sheets of aurora. Leta spiraled it around her wrist and made a knot that weighed it down while she took stock of her surroundings.

The *Second Wind* hunkered on the broad saddle of a mountaintop. The snow-veiled vista beyond described toothy summits and river-eaten timberland sliding to settlements and a distant city.

They were on Melynhon, the planet being swallowed slowly by Unity, half within and half without.

Its familiar rind bisected the mountain range. Iridescent as a butterfly's wing, in constant motion morphing purple to blue, light turning inside out. The rind sliced upward thirty meters past the *Second Wind*'s nose while half a kilometer away on the non-Unity side sat Taitn's ship. Vague figures marked Laythan and the rest of Caiden's family reunited safely.

A small Dynast vessel perched nearby, and a pair of sentinels spotted Leta and approached. "Proxy Isme Two. The Prime said you had—"

Leta interrupted, in Isme's ashen voice, which broke her heart once more, "I've an urgent message for the Prime. Where is she?"

They gestured. Abriss stood twenty meters away in front of the rind on the Unity side. Snowflakes kissed her bare arms and whorled around a new Aurasever, which was more complex than before. It laced her fingers and up her arms to her neck, disappearing into her tied-up hair. Filaments braided around her shoulders. Starry nodes nestled in meridians. Down her back lay a second spine of bluish crystalline matter, reworked from Azura's chrysalis. Distortions of light and shadow limned her figure.

Melynhon. Of course. It was the first stop in Unity and the perfect place to test the Aurasever on a large scale. The other half of Melynhon lay within a universe that bubbled off Unity's side like a blister, large enough to encompass half the planet and off into space, containing whole star systems beyond. Abriss could stand planetside while she dissolved this rind, rather than working from a ship or in the vacuum.

Leta trudged in Abriss's direction, on the injured side without peripheral vision. Membrane bandages still pasted over her wounds, erasing half her features like paint scraped off a canvas. Healing agents rippled emerald and pink beneath the film.

With each step, Leta battled the idea that she was here to finish the horrific thing Threi had started. The thing she had poured all of herself into preventing. The last thing her heart had ever wanted.

Make this painless. One death to save trillions.

She let the jagged piece of lightseep slip down into her grasp, then locked her fist's tendons. Her other fingers sent the four silent floater drones ahead. She fumbled through the triangulation method built into the Proxy's brain. It was effortless for Isme, the little shards like parts of his body, but Leta had to take her time, not get this wrong.

They had enough charge for one big jolt.

Two drones she spread out half a meter behind the back of Abriss's skull. One positioned directly above the cranium. The final would have to move in front of her face.

For a clean shock. Then rush in. A clean kill.

Abriss turned around abruptly. Leta torqued her wrist to keep the floaters oriented.

"Two?" Abriss said.

Now. Clean.

Leta wrenched her fist to pull the fourth floater into position. Laser lines linked up in a deadly constellation around Abriss's skull.

Release.

Pulse erupted and light seared between the points. Abriss's hair tumbled loose as she lurched to the side, missing the center of the stunning blow. It snapped locks of hair off and clipped the wounded half of her face instead. She shrieked and fell to one knee.

Leta's heart thudded. *This is wrong.*

"*Help!*" Abriss screamed. The two sentinels were already racing over.

Leta had no time to be soft. She disarmed one sentinel and tossed their glave, hamstrung their leg, then elbowed the other in the neck and smashed their weapon with a kick.

She turned back as Abriss drew a long glave from a calf holster. Its slim rods flowered apart, clasped on to her spread fingers, and crackled with energy. Spiral force spit from the center and blasted apart half of Leta's side.

Metal shavings and chunks of flesh splattered the snow. Blue fluid dribbled over her legs as she stumbled.

Abriss rose, precise and powerful. She kicked Leta's pelvis, spinning her away in range for another blast. The glave howled, and Leta barely rolled from the impact. Snow exploded into water.

Leta clawed the floaters together and signaled another shock near Abriss's back. Weak, but enough to twist her around. Leta sprang, tackling Abriss from behind, locking her glave arm down hard enough to crunch forearm bones. She jammed the lightseep shard at Abriss's neck. Abriss caught it but the smooth sides slid through her fingers. The tip shuddered with Leta's effort, scratching into Abriss's clavicle while a scream shredded inside her throat.

It's what Threi had done.

Leta shook, her focus flagging. Inhuman strength didn't count for much with a failing connection and a human heart. Her Proxy muscles spasmed slack. Abriss wrenched free and blasted the glave point-blank through Leta's hip, scattering lightseep bone like glass.

Leta howled and kicked, shattering the glave's tips. Abriss was atop her instantly, trying to claw her hands around the Proxy's skull long enough to use the Aurasever. Leta grappled with Abriss's swift dodges and tight holds, then jerked away, sensory information swirling. Snowflakes and sparkling dust whizzed across her vision.

Last chance. This Proxy's my only reach here. Right now.

She hooked an elbow around Abriss's knee, tripping her onto her back. Powder plumed up. Abriss yelled and squirmed while Leta pinned her. Palm open, she arranged the four floaters around Abriss's skull. Power hummed.

Close your fist.

Abriss wrenched hard to smack the floaters away first. Her dislocated shoulder cracked audibly. She shrieked and tried to crawl, but Leta wrestled her with pressure on the injured shoulder. Abriss's mouth gaped but her unhealed vocal folds couldn't make more screams.

Horrified, Leta fumbled the shard up to Abriss's neck.

I can't.

The woman's one eye wept tears while the other gushed steam from overheating balms trying to manage her pain. Abriss's pulse pounded hot where their skin touched and the jagged end pierced. The moment folded on past echoes, time turning syrupy slow. They were back in the Harvest and Threi was bearing down on her.

Buried in the echoes were all the moments Abriss had cared for her, listened, sacrificed.

"I can't," Leta choked, Isme's voice fluttering out.

For so many years, Leta had believed Abriss was diamond. But she had always been glass. Threi had broken it, and now all Abriss's edges were fractured sharp.

With an airy scream, Abriss heaved Leta off, snatched the lightseep shard, and buried it deep beneath the Proxy's ear.

Motor center shut down.

Quiet snowfall cloaked Abriss. She clutched her throat, wet choking sounds peppered with squeaks as she panted.

A daze settled over Leta. She felt too many things and she wasn't enough.

Abriss knelt. Her bloody hand shook, thumb pressing into her lips as she asked, "Which one are you?"

Fright tried to blurt the sound from Leta, but her voice box was shut off. She couldn't let this blame fall on the others. She forced enough motor control to hold up nine trembling fingers.

Abriss closed her eye, its teardrop rolling. She reached for the Proxy's skull and sent focus to the Aurasever.

Leta was blasted out. Reality unraveled. She returned to nonphysical, nonlocal being.

The luminiferity dissolved her focus and her emotions with it, but she didn't want to be soothed. She clawed back to Abriss and the moment on the mountain.

I failed everyone.

She rooted into that heartache and kept her awareness focused, participating, bodiless, in a remote view of the summit. She needed to witness what her failure meant.

A dreamy scene. Abriss brimmed with every type of hurt.

The Aurasever's transparent material filled with sorrow-blue and jeweled-peach hues. The freckles in her skin agitated beneath the lines, bubbling darker and lighter. Thick resonance wrapped her, singing in Azura's key.

Snowflakes arranged into radial patterns as she stepped to the edge of Unity's rind. It wasn't a hard border like a bubble's membrane but a turbulent celestial fire built of layers, metallic iridescence breathing blues into bronze. Slow with age, the rind's flux sweltered around her body like the arcs and prominence about a sun.

Abriss.

Leta couldn't get the smallest thought through to the woman's mind from the luminiferity, which knotted and confused around Abriss, the resonance swelling like a gale-force repulsion.

Abriss raised her arms, dipping her hands in the rind. Unity gave a shiver at that touch, all the way down to the quantum bits of it. Abriss's whole nervous system coupled coherently with the world while the Aurasever amplified her intention. She would be the great observer, the decider of countless quantum potentials snapped at once to her will. Her multidimensional gravitas.

No, oh stars no.

Leta could do nothing to stop it.

Abriss closed her eyes and focused her mind as sharp as a needle.

Like Azura's world and Threi's prison, the rind of the universe bubbling off Unity shattered.

But not quite in the same way.

The rind popped from the point of Abriss's touch. Space splintered outward in explosive fractals. At nearly the same velocity, Unity's rind rushed to take up the space, erupting from Abriss's point of contact and sweeping across the other half of Melynhon and across space, subsuming the old universe into Unity's domain.

Light storm-clouded out of the void. Physics folded inside out in impossible geometries, translating the universe's parameters to match Unity's.

Species and plants, weather patterns, geology, then effects cascading from those: ecosystems scrambled, the same but not. Planets shed gravity and crumbled. Debris jetted across space and caught in new orbital wells. Energies collided, made ripples, wrecked some things, but organized others.

The traveling edge of Unity's rind was destructive in a way that was *different* from the mere translation of physics. A second punch of warped space. This flux finally stopped moving immeasurable leagues away, where the blister universe's old edge had been.

Billions of consciousnesses dispersed in a blink. This created a sudden influx of life force into the luminiferity, whipping Leta's consciousness around a tidal wave of demise. Raw information content sizzled all around her as beings and structures crumbled into their parts, their memories, and sorted into the plenum.

It took all her skill to finally rivet her awareness back to the peak.

The universe pop was over, but the repercussions spread. Only half of Melynhon's environment had converted to Unity's laws, but the disasters escalated across the entire planet. Tsunamis whorled over ice-fields-turned-oceans. Quakes split the earth. Volcanic confluence burst out while lightning branched through plumes of black cloud. Shock robbed Leta of any ability to process scale. On this planet alone, thousands of species suffered incompatible biology, while sheer *disaster* would destroy countless more.

On the mountaintop where Abriss stood, thunder split and snowflakes burned into wisps while shards of pale rainbow fractured the sky. Snow melted beneath her feet, forming a mirror of water that drained down the ravines of the summit. Distant avalanches melted into rolls of steam as they calved down, creating great clouds that scattered more rainbows.

And Abriss Cetre marveled as if it were beautiful.

Leta understood why: there *was* greater coherence in Unity now. Across all the converted space, accord spread between individuals, old animosity and fixed patterns dissolved. Disturbed ecosystems started to fall into a balance more perfect and self-sustaining than before. The catastrophic rupturing had paved the way for a more harmonious universe in the wake.

Abriss isn't wrong . . . but this *isn't right.*

The horror of the scene tore Leta down to a spark of sorrow. She didn't think she could contain any more heartache . . . but then saw that Caiden's family crew had been *inside* the universe that popped. The physics change wouldn't have affected them, but the violent rind flux had swept over them and the *Wintra*.

As Leta's awareness concentrated and absorbed the group's space, she was buried in blind panic, frenetic energy, screams, and sobs.

Ksiñe. Endirion.

Laythan held Ksiñe awkwardly on the ground, rocking and staring vacantly ahead, his prosthetic corneas glazed. The Andalvian's pigment stormed, the chromatophores smoldering like the muscle twitches of a dying creature.

Endirion crumpled where he stood. More than half of his materials lost form, dribbling through his frame, rushing out of him in rivers. Taitn frantically opened up En's augmented chest, bailing out a sizzling acid with his bare hands even as they burned to the bone. Then he cradled En's head, black hair tangling in his fingers as he leaned down to shout frantic words.

Leta couldn't hold on to the immensity of their pain. The luminiferity offered up visions of the slaughter of her childhood, matching like to like. This had happened and would keep happening, and Leta, helpless and swamped by agonies, tried to flail away from the scene.

It was happening because she couldn't kill even once.

She caught briefly on Abriss. Newly arrived Dynast forces addressed her fresh wounds, galvanized by them. Camera drones flocked around her, each transmitting to a different echoer in distribution hubs to get her message through the universe she'd just altered forever.

My new subjects, Abriss's injured voice echoed to Leta in the luminiferity, muddled up with unspoken thoughts. *Welcome to Unity, the safest and most malleable reality in the multiverse. This is our reunion, this world now yours to partake.*

Uniting worlds had always been Abriss's goal, but no individual-by-individual immigration anymore, no waiting for Unity to expand at its eons-slow rate.

Those things which are not amenable to Unity's alignment will be returned to the luminiferity by the physical nature of Unity's change. Not lost but preserved and dismantled, to re-manifest in new ways.

Abriss would be fair and precious with everything Unity absorbed, but she was not going to mourn anything lost in the process. There was no convincing her, no grand gesture that could shift her back to a patient course. Her voice was still husky with the wounds Threi had made, and which Leta's attack had reopened.

The entirety of Unity rests on my shoulders, and I shall work tirelessly for you.

Abriss's heartfelt words and eager delivery sounded so much like the Abriss that Leta adored, she could almost deny what had happened. She wished to, dearly. But Leta had failed to love her, failed to end her, and only succeeded in doubling her trauma. How would she ever atone for that?

The Outer Immigration Initiative will be conferring with your communities to gift you free energy, heal illness, and educate you to the sciences that will manifest your ideal life. Your culture will remain untouched, your governments knit into ours, your technology and infrastructure rebuilt. We will teach you to hear those you mourn, in the luminiferity: their lives are still interacting with your own from nonphysical dimensions.

What frightened Leta most was that Abriss was sincere and correct. Unity *was* an evolving realm of co-creative action, expertly governed economy and ecology, full of long-lived and vibrant ecosystems both natural and social. She would ensure that every world subsumed into Unity benefited the same. The more worlds she gathered, the more powerful that accord would become.

Leta's exhausted spiritual hold slipped, and her consciousness ebbed away. She didn't care if she found her way back to her body or dissolved at last.

She caught a final sense of Abriss's audience across the consumed universe. Fear and outrage transformed to awe and acceptance. Just as Unity had imposed its physical change, the people attuned to Abriss Cetre's Graven words. Both Unity's laws and Abriss's broadcasted presence bathed them in understanding.

Including Caiden's family, still holding their wounded. They grew quiet with acceptance while Abriss—her address finished—strode swiftly to their side.

Welcome to Unity.

CHAPTER 42

RECONNECTION

Azura had infiltrated Feran's ship so thoroughly Caiden felt like he was piloting his old vessel again. Had a fully formed chrysalis been installed in that starship, like a module of found technology? Or placed inside when she was embryonic, and grew in the ship's back? Or perhaps she found that husk of ship herself, and curled up there in its dark shell as Caiden had when he was fleeing in the desert of RM28 at fourteen years old, looking for some shelter to call safe or some grave that felt more familiar than sand...

Now he was headed back to that very same sand. Bringing *Leta*, after how many times he had dreamed of taking her away from RM28 in the past.

Caiden glanced back at her, still unconscious in the nest of a makeshift bed. He resisted checking the time again. Time was strange in the luminiferity, he knew that, but she'd been gone long enough he'd hooked up a monitoring and stability system. The readings looked fine, and Feran said Leta would be exhausted, but Ksiñe's many dire warnings kicked around in Caiden's head. Did Azura's presence help with Leta's disintegration? He hoped so.

C padded over and snuffled the back of Caiden's hair.

"I know I worry too much. But we just got her ba—"

Something thunked the floor. Leta's sudden sobbing choked into squeaks.

Caiden lurched from the pilot's seat, colliding with the nophek surging over to her too. He batted C aside and skidded on his knees to scoop Leta up. This was more than sensory overload, more than a meltdown. She convulsed in pulses, short-circuiting, her breath locking up.

Caiden swore and curled her against his chest, balancing tight pressure without smothering. He could be a grounding force. His morphcoat rustled into a cloud-soft weave.

"I need you to breathe," he whispered.

Jerking gasps banged her against him.

C rooted anxiously around the two of them before lying in a curled U-shape. Caiden leaned against the nophek's side while he tried to calm his own anxiety and be an anchor for Leta. The emotion drained from her and she stilled, stared blankly, the tears finding a way down her cheeks. Caiden knew better than to think her struggle was over. Leta as a child had always suffered internally, putting on a brave mask until too much of her shut down to sustain even that. She detached, and the best thing he could do was be present.

Ksiñe's warnings prized into his mind again while he tried to be patient. She'd been straining herself between multiple bodies, across leagues of space, and—for all he knew—layers of time.

He closed his eyes and hushed C's whining. After he'd worried himself into knots and his cramps numbed out, he started to doze off. She stirred.

"H-hey," he said as she uncurled. The look on her face devastated him. "What happened?"

"I couldn't do it."

Ice sheeted down Caiden's spine. He didn't understand, just waited for her to find more words.

A whisper, "I'm so sorry."

"Wh-what happened?"

Leta shook her head, eyes glistening. "Abriss. She's changed. She's broken. Stars forfend, Threi was *right* about everything." Leta's language came in fits and starts, the syntax jammed together, her accent harder to decipher. "She ruptured a universe next to Unity. She'll collapse the entire multiverse, one universe at a time. She'll do it. I couldn't stand to hurt her, and your family, they...Ksiñe and En...Forfend, Caiden, I—"

His nerves frayed in a body-wide shudder. He hugged her tighter. "What happened?" The phrase revolved in his brain.

"The rind flux, the same thing that broke Azura's chrysalis. They were both—"

"Did they die? Did you see them dead?"

"No, Caiden, but—"

"Then..." He swallowed the words. He knew better. Denial crusted over his logic and a hiss rose between his ears. "Then we don't know yet. Leta. What happened to *you*?"

Whatever had befallen the crew was universes and galaxies away. He could do nothing. But Leta was right here.

She gave him a vacant, tear-stained look that terrified him. "She killed me. My Proxy, then Isme's and—" Trembling as fast and fine as a bird, Leta hugged him back hard. "You would have done it. You could have murdered her."

Caiden bristled at that. *The same as Threi. A murderer again.* "I'm glad you didn't."

He couldn't find more words to navigate them around the possible deaths and sure threats and dire risks, or the fact that they were headed to the planet where their childhood world had ended, to stop a powerful man with an unanswerable weapon. And across galaxies was the woman Leta hadn't been able to stop, who held both their families at her mercy.

"What do we do?" Leta murmured. "Try to stop Abriss? Or continue after Threi?"

"We're closer to Threi. What would we do against Abriss, anyway? You have no Proxy. You're not well enough to keep invading others. She's smart to you now. I hate this, but the Dominant is our key to figuring out how to equal her or gain resistance."

He glanced at the case of Graven enhancers sitting in a satchel beneath the console. He wasn't ready for that decision yet. These new enhancers hadn't been tested—they could be more effective, or less. That's why there were six.

"I told her..." Leta withered with a deep sigh and buried her face. "I told her there was another Dominant Graven, she'll be after it soon enough. We could split up and—"

"No. Together we're barely capable enough against one of the two Dynast heirs. We won't stand a chance apart."

They still had each other. Caiden closed his eyes, feeling like too much and not enough at once. C head-butted Leta's back and pressed, bathing her in purrs.

"C says you're safe with us."

Leta's gaze met Caiden's, her hazel eyes watery. She scraped tear-wet hair off her temples.

Caiden said, "It's not your fault. The responsibility of the entire multiverse isn't on your shoulders. It would break us both to try to take on everything happening now. We do our best. The *Spur* is on course to the one event we can control, and even that might break us. Rest, before that happens."

The nophek curled around Leta's back. She acquiesced and snuggled around his foreleg, frowning.

Caiden sighed out a bundle of jagged feelings.

Threi on the loose and Abriss still alive.

Multiversal war on the horizon...

"Leta?"

"Hm?"

"Move over."

He curled against C's flank next to her, nuzzling into soft fur and scratchy scales. The nophek's ribs expanded with an inhale, then he sighed deep and splayed his legs out.

"Rest."

Leta tried her best to not spiral down with dismal thoughts. She wouldn't disrespect Caiden's attempts to be uplifting for her just because he hadn't witnessed the events firsthand. Sleeping had restored the surface of her but the deeper parts were in turmoil still.

She focused on what she could control, which was food. Feran had shared harvest from their garden, but the many universe crossovers had done peculiar things to most of them. Instead, Leta attempted to revive old rations. She'd never tried cooking before.

Blue flame coated the metal slab, starting to curl the end of the meat strip Leta held over it. Heat pulsed into her fingers as she lowered the thing and laid it flat to sizzle. She fussed with other items that needed hydrating or heating. This would be her and Caiden's last meal before they reached the universe CWN82 with RM28 inside, but it would be their first meal together.

Pop! The strip snapped into a crispy spiral and leaped off the flames into her lap. Leta yelped and fumbled the thing onto a plate, then rubbed her burned fingertips on her thighs.

Caiden chuckled and walked over. "You have to hold the end."

He sat on his heels, picked up a pair of long sticks in the set, and pinched another strip of meat, pressing it on the plate as it cooked then popped crisp, the outer end still pinched. He plated it and handed her the sticks. "What did they feed you?"

Leta didn't think answering "mostly flowers" would impress him. She wasn't even sure if her physiology could digest these rations, but the scent of cooking had lifted both their moods, and that was worth the attempt. Besides, doing a mundane thing soothed her.

"Not much," she answered.

Caiden got up to finish soaking extra rations in a bin for C. He fidgeted as if the Casthen uniform scratched. Leta knew better than to say it suited him. The dark-gray sikkel hide was patterned with webbing creases and red divots for a cloudsuit to fit over. It sheathed his lean frame and had clips and magnetic pads for weapons. He'd ripped off the embroidered Casthen emblem on the back, but the ends of metallic threads still ghosted it.

Leta finished cooking the pile of meat curls—properly—and turned off the flame. The dehydrated buds she'd soaked had unfolded into fronds, which she coated in a sweet orange glaze. It looked like a good attempt.

Caiden sat opposite her and mussed a hand through his hair, jarring the hovering neural halo that cast reflections in his eyes. That color hadn't changed. Diluted fire-blue.

He opened his mouth a couple times, said nothing, and closed it.

With just the two of them, the time gap felt more apparent. They had agreed to start their friendship over, but Leta felt ill equipped. The only thing they shared was grief.

Proxyless, her neurological overprocessing and the sensitivity of her Graven nature compounded. The sizzle of the cooling burner pressed into her face. The crunch of C gnawing fleshy bones crackled through her shoulders as if it were *her* bones put to the teeth.

She had rested, but not enough. Pairing with Azura during Caiden's revival had restored her, temporarily—perhaps even kept her alive—filling up the missing half of her energy. But deferred exhaustion piled on. She was borderline sweating, feverish, yet a cold spell shifted around her skin. The morphfabric suit subtly changed to regulate her, and she recalled as a child always putting her jackets on and taking them off, clothes zipped and unzipped, and all of them with too many seams.

Leta preoccupied herself with peeling layers of husk off a warmed stalk. She slipped one on her tongue, where it melted into creamy salt.

Caiden reached over for a plate of food and smiled faintly at it. The fact that she could feel all his emotion but not read his face only overwhelmed her more. She fussed with the dishes, trying her best not to clack them together.

I really am unfit to be anything but the driver of a more capable tool.

As Ksiñe had predicted, a new and alarming sensation was setting in since her return. Leta felt poorly attached, like watching her body in a dream, one veil removed from the action. She didn't tell Caiden, but he noticed on his own and frowned; he wasn't sure how to ask.

Abriss could still help me. Feran—maybe, with the Dominant. Ksiñe could for sure, but whether he lived . . .

To escape her own thoughts again, Leta asked, "What are you thinking?"

Caiden finished chewing one of the crunchy meat curls before he answered. "The coincidence . . . things Feran and Abriss said . . . how a Graven hybrid like me ended up mis-shipped as an infant, then sent as food to RM28, a planet that secretly has . . . a Graven thing in it? And had a half-buried ship with a Graven chrysalis, that I escaped with, and even the name of her sprang up in my mind like intuition, plus—Why are you looking like that?"

"You still believe *co*-incidence is random?" She misspoke the word on purpose, emphasizing the meaning. "The luminiferity is rife with nonphysical consciousness participating in the same reality as us embodied beings. Their collective action guides us in unseen ways. Everything was orchestrated around you."

"Or around Threi and Abriss. Am I just strung along in their massive Graven web? The Dynast was either the foundation of or the final stronghold of Graven beings before their numbers waned. So are all those generations of dead ancestors backing the two Dynast heirs? And is it even a good thing that we're following whatever these wills are that are gaming with us, with the entirety of the multiverse?"

In Leta's mind flashed the burned-in imagery of Threi finding her in the dark transport. Trading her to Abriss. The Dynast making her... *this*. Then wrapping her up with Caiden again.

And the echoes lining up... forming a voicelike thing in Abriss's mind the more she reached and researched. The presence forming in Feran's mind, too, as they revived those Graven cells. Did Threi hear things as well?

"I don't have answers but"—she forced a cheerier tone—"Azura picked you. I think that means you're on your own course. You're a patched-up copy of a Dominant Graven from birth, and I'm a harmonic Dynast Graven through conditioning, and enharmonic Azura is larval still. We're not perfect and the world is going to lever itself onto us soon, but at least..."

It sounded so strange all spelled out, she didn't finish.

Caiden did: "We're together."

He met her gaze, and it was blue and sharp like a dump of cold water.

"Thank you, for your friendship and help," she said, and hated that her subtle Dynast accent compared to his speech gave tangible shape to their time apart. "I know we're both tangled up with Threi and Abriss, but there were several times you could have left or ignored me. So thank you."

Leta stroked C's flank as he cruised by sniffing for crumbs. He circled around to head-butt her belly. She raked her hands up and down the ridge of his neck and he made a cute sound as he yawned a sharp-toothed maw.

"I'm not going to abandon you," Caiden said. "I really do think—"

A ping interrupted from the cockpit.

Caiden straightened and walked over. "We're here...And we're almost too late."

Leta joined him and peered out. In the approximated view, orange and indigo hues roiled on the surface of the rind to CWN82, the universe in which the planet RM28 lay. They approached the huge bubble of it, still a ways off.

Threi had brought an armada of thousands. Some ships were as small as satellites, all of them arranging in a grid surrounding the universe, just outside of the rind.

"I see," Leta said, hushed. "He means to collapse this universe by many points of contact instead of one. What I saw Abriss do, but multiplied or amplified. Then like Feran said and like I...like I saw, the flux of the rind will chew up that impenetrable shell under RM28's crust and let Threi into the planet and right at the Dominant."

Caiden chewed his lip. "This scale and this many ships...there's no way we'll destroy them all." C barked a deep sound, and Caiden startled. "Little boy wants a fight. We're here for Threi. If he dies, I'll be the most Graven thing around, and can call off whatever...this...is. Then we can turn our focus on Abriss."

"Cai," Leta said softly. "Let's sneak in closer. Not be reckless. Maybe Azura can help?"

A smile twitched on the crooked side of his lips. "Friends have told me that...not being reckless isn't my specialty."

Leta laughed. "Well, I'm here to rein you in."

"Wisdom," Caiden called her, and the word was weighted with memories Leta didn't share. He explained: "Çydanza taunted me with your death and said, 'What a fearsome match you two would have been, wisdom and power together.'"

Leta smiled. "Good. We'll need both."

CHAPTER 43

TRUST

The *Spur* hung in space, and Azura's energy hushed into a sleepy rhythm. Caiden sat in the cockpit poring over the vessel specs of the Casthen fleet. Holosplays glowed beneath his fingers, the light morphing across dimpled air as he scrolled. He groaned and looked up from a diagram of a saisn swallow propulsion engine and glared through the cockpit's amplified view of the real thing in front of them: the *Sessrun*, Casthen's flagship.

Other vessels clotted around it in RM28's outer orbit. Survey teams had dropped to the surface. The comm network was airtight, the armada motionless, and Caiden's nerves frazzled. Were they waiting for tests before popping the universe?

The *Sessrun* was a hybrid of conventional technologies and chketin phrixaturgy. Sleek and flashy, like Threi. Sharp, folded-in vanes stretched along a tubular resonance chamber making up the ship's belly. The inside material was silver-colored fluting: a silhouette of teeth. That maw of energy could chew up material and feed back into the walls. Even in its current idle state, the cavity was blurred by turbulent plasma.

"All damned, the *size* of it," he muttered.

The tiny *Spur* was more maneuverable, but the *Sessrun* had big, big guns.

From behind him, Leta called, "You certainly are swearing a lot."

"We'll never sneak up. If we shake this net of ships too much, the disturbance will reach Threi in the middle. Can't infiltrate since he's not planetside. Audio-only comms dilute gravitas too much to charm my way through the armada."

He wilted back over the specs, the *Sessrun*'s reconnection chamber...

Leta gazed at the view while she stroked C's back. His happy tail slid back and forth.

"We'd fit," Caiden muttered.

Leta bent to peer at him. "That's the tone of voice you'd use before trying something that'd get us in trouble."

Caiden flopped his head back to look at her upside down, flashing a smile. "I always got us out of trouble, after."

"After you were beat to a pulp." She tried to look cross. "Where are you trying to fit?"

Caiden pointed at the *Sessrun*. The planet's luminous gray was visible beyond the hole the reconnection chamber made through the middle of the vessel.

"They'll expect us to peel off at the last minute or chuck in some kind of explosive, which is a good idea, but we don't have one. The swallow engine will chew up anything that passes through and suck up the destruction. But Azura's universe could get us through safe while busting up the cavity architecture."

"I thought you said you wouldn't be reckless."

"Strap in, please?" Caiden smiled apologetically. "C, brace."

The nophek curled himself around the back of the pilot seat and dug in his claws. Leta, frowning, found passenger struts on one wall. "You weren't ever as smart as you thought you were, you know."

Caiden chuckled. He slid forward and dipped his hands in the twitch drive panels. The milky plates absorbed his fingers while bright specks flocked along hidden circuitry.

He focused through a blend of excitement and terror. Steady hands. Azura wrapped his mind in a reliable tempo. "I often tell you to be fast," he murmured to her, "but this time I *really* mean it."

He pressed and the *Spur* shot ahead. Something squirmed within the hull, spreading out tissues, chaining together bright lines of network. Metal crunched, and the thrusters bulged, fuel diverged—Caiden couldn't map what Azura rechanneled. The drive exploded with sudden power as if injected with racing pepper.

Leta cried out as she jostled in the restraints. Caiden cursed, straining to control the velocity. The *Spur* wobbled as he kept course straight to the middle of the Casthen armada. "All right, you're listening, Az. Let's make this monster ship swallow a hot coal."

The *Spur* tore into Casthen sensor range. The fleet realigned like shavings tracking a magnet. Caiden was ready for the class of their weaponry, but there was no way to handle the quantity, even with racing-spice speed.

Particles burrowed into the *Spur*'s shields, prickly through his halo link.

The cockpit overlay approximated invisible weapon beams and gale fields, a crisscross tapestry of death that he needled through. Brighter pinch fire skittered across space. The *Spur* was too plump to make a very good needle. It took the brunt of anything that homed, and Caiden couldn't alter course at this speed.

"Six arcseconds."

The *Sessrun* moved. Slow to power up, its reconnection chamber burbled with energy, vicious and radiant. It started to nose down toward the planet, but its big guns were omnidirectional and sparked to life.

Hundreds of satellites blinked open around the *Sessrun* and beamed rays at the *Spur*, blotting the view and sensors. Caiden's neural feed scrambled, but he had Azura: he tasted every inch of the *Spur* and its interaction with space. He maintained course to the cavity of the *Sessrun*, that roaring magnetic maw, salivating with plasma.

"Caiden!" Leta shouted.

"I've got this."

"I know—let me help you."

"How?" Then he felt it: like Azura...something unspooling around him, pruning the overgrowth of his desperate functioning. The frays in his thinking were snipped off. There was just the *Sessrun*, the *Spur*, a sea of energy, and a clear-cut course through time.

He curved the ship into that new course, guided by more hands than his own. The *Spur* followed the *Sessrun* tilting toward atmosphere and took the armada's fire on its rear. Holosplays bled red alarm.

The *Sessrun*'s big guns looked pumped up and ready. They tracked, waiting for the moment he'd veer the *Spur* away from the engine cavity. Magnetic splintering and plasma turbulence lay ahead.

Choke, you bastard.

One blast of speed away from the tube opening, Caiden signaled Azura's universe to floresce.

A rind pillowed around the *Spur*'s hull as they rocketed straight into the hollow middle of the *Sessrun*.

Azura's gentle blues dampened the violent plasma and magnetic torsion. At the same time, as hoped, it melted the fluted silver walls of the chamber into the underlying structure. The whole construction spasmed, a silent disintegration revealing more and more layers of mechanism behind, now naked to the void.

The *Spur* shot safely out the cylinder's other end. Explosions distended the crippled *Sessrun*'s hull as it listed toward the atmosphere of RM28. Escape crafts poured out of its sides.

Is Threi in one of those? He'd never know which. Caiden half expected the man to jet out in a cloudsuit and latch on to the *Spur*'s fuselage. For all his brutal elegance and precision, Threi was unpredictable.

Caiden seized the confused lull in the armada's fire and chose to dive after the *Sessrun* toward atmospheric entry. Azura's universe retracted.

"We follow the crash," he said. "Make sure it's over."

The armada swarmed at their back. Caiden pressed, fingertips asking for speed. His mind's eye was already racing ahead to him on the ground fighting Threi at the crash site, chemblade in hand, picking up right where they'd left off. This time he wasn't alone and he wouldn't lose.

Through damaged comms, the man's voice hissed: "*Our Casthen-bred hero, come to break up the fun. Or are you starting some?*"

"Where is he?" Leta staggered out of restraints and clung to the cockpit's console while sifting through communication channels.

Threi said, "*That's Feran's Spur . . . and your Azura—care to explain?*"

"There," Leta blurted.

Caiden sensed it through the neural link a beat later. A cloudcutter. Hard left, jetting from the far side of the planet. Threi hadn't been with the armada at all.

His vessel's underbelly was as pale as a moon from the planetside glow, but the rest of it was like something cut out of the void, bristling with glossy edges but black everywhere else. Ravines along the length carved down to something white-hot inside.

"I should have known," Caiden said. "Flagships aren't Threi's style, too impersonal."

The cloudcutter's guns hammered the *Spur*'s flank.

"Shit!" Caiden pulled up. Planetside, the *Spur* would fly sludgy. But in orbit, the cloudcutter's projectile fire would pepper their shielding to bits. Warnings fractured over the holosplays and pounded a headache into Caiden's skull, counting down until the *Spur* became shrapnel if he couldn't find a way out of the salvo.

Leta hugged the back of the pilot chair to stabilize herself and pressed a palm against his sternum. "Breathe."

Caiden gushed out a held breath.

They were surrounded. Energy shields gone, guardian skins getting chewed apart, and no fancy flying could shake Threi off. The sound of the barrage roared inside the fuselage. Leta's palm shook.

This was like the transport to the desert, like Caiden's nightmares.

"I'm sorry," he tried to say as the cloudcutter spat burrs into their belly.

Suddenly it cut off into whispers.

Through the neural link he felt *bleeding*. No—fluid. The projectiles melted before they struck, pattering the *Spur* as soft as rain.

Azura. Her universe was wafting in auroral arcs out their side, converting the cloudcutter's fire and transforming the armada's coherent bursts into scattered rays that stippled the hull harmlessly.

"Her universe…" Leta drawled.

Caiden goggled at the sight. It wasn't a bubble, wasn't tightly contained.

Threi switched tactics and jetted his cloudcutter straight into them. The *Spur* was pounded forward and spun toward one of the heavy warships. Caiden curled his fingers in the twitch drive, but the engine couldn't handle the roll enough to escape a collision course.

The gray flank of the warship hurtled toward them while weapons bloomed, preparing a broadside. The whole *Spur* vibrated. Leta clung to him and the seat, her fingers digging in, her back braced by C's side.

Then the *Spur*'s power snapped offline.

The red-drenched holosplays went dark.

"No!" Caiden yelled, then shut his mouth abruptly as light washed over his face.

Lacy aurorae surged into view as Azura dumped out of the *Spur* like water tossed from a bucket, spilling straight into the big Casthen warship. She splashed its side and slithered into its seams through channels of armor. The vessel sipped up her light. Thrusters blasted. It powered out of the collision path.

Caiden gaped while in control of nothing, the *Spur* an empty seed husk whisked in cosmic winds.

The wet, fiery rapids of Azura's universe billowed havoc through the warship. Components melted, bleeding out. Its frame crumpled under new pressures. Storms of crackling energy bowled through the ship's guts, and it listed to the side, disabled.

"She's—" Leta cut off as they both watched, incredulous.

Azura swept from the warship to one of the smaller vessels. Energy blistered out of it, weapons powered down, and Azura flocked right back out again, leaving the vessel twitching and leaking fluids.

She surged to the next, chain-flying through the armada. Energy blasts and projectiles ceased. Trailing a wide circle, she invaded the fleet like a ghost taking over bodies in a crowd, staying just long enough to pacify them. Space went dark with power systems offline.

Threi's cloudcutter broke away and fled.

Azura wafted back to the *Spur*. Power gently filled up again under Caiden's fingertips. His sense of the ship returned, muscle back on bones, nerve networks bristling with awareness.

"All right...right, I get it. You're here with us. Wow." He mentally checked: ship unarmored, in bad shape, nearly out of fuel. Azura bent physics inside the wounded vessel to alter minutiae, but the *Spur* wouldn't last.

"Cai," Leta quavered, patting his chest for his attention, then pointing at something in the holosplay.

Out of view, sensors indicated the engine-bereft *Sessrun* had charged up its biggest gun, all power diverted to a trace-array blast that would raze the *Spur* to dust. Serpents of light twined together.

Caiden veered too late, but enough. He lost control of the yaw.

A palpable rumble marked the *Sessrun* charging another blast.

"Suit up," he said to Leta.

She straightened. "Suit?"

Caiden pinched his fingers in the twitch drive to give the *Spur* a final blast of precision thrust. Auto-course then took over, barreling them toward the closest of the new warships flying in as reinforcements. The *Spur* spun slowly end over end.

Caiden pushed out of the pilot seat and almost vomited as scalar gravity shuffled to keep his feet on the floor.

"Caiden! *Suits?*" Leta rushed to steady him. Too long in the seat, his legs protested walking. He laughed just to have something move air out of his lungs.

Leta was scowling, and he grabbed her in a last hug before pushing her toward the cloudsuit hooked on the wall. He took the one opposite and hiked its metallic harnessing over his clothing. Small wing-shaped tanks that he'd modified fit over his shoulder blades.

"Come, C."

The nophek crawled over, awkward in the gravity. His hackles were erect, eyes bright. He yowled.

"Seventeen arcseconds." Caiden kept count from there and tossed his neural halo off, losing contact with the tumbling ship.

He nodded at Leta. They activated their cloudsuits: a fleecy second skin of material spread over their bodies, filling the spaces between the harnessing, then puffed up in a flash. Gases expanded between bizarre molecules and swelled the material out so finely it became a transparent, scintillating cloud all around them. An air pocket formed around Caiden's face. Tangy oxygen slid over his tongue.

"Ready?" He smacked the door control.

"I'm still scared of heights."

"There are no heights in space." He grasped her hand and smiled.

The back of the ship flowered open, with two layers of atmoseal stretched between the petals. The view swirled, with the tail of the silvery warship coasting past nearly in time with Caiden's count in his head. The subliminal roar of the *Sessrun*'s massive gun charging tickled across his skin, with only emptiness separating him and Leta from the blast.

They weren't six and ten years old. They weren't perched on fenceposts with soft grass beneath their drop. This was stars and void, a warship spiraling in front, and a trace-array preparing to sear them to bits.

But holding her hand, it didn't feel like ten years separated them.

"Hug on to C's neck," he said, and clipped his and Leta's belts to the nophek's riding harness. "The expanded fields I modded will engulf him too."

"That warship's hatch is closed. You're hoping…?"

"We're not alone." He still felt Azura in the *Spur*, more nebulous without the neural halo linking him.

Leta muttered, "You used to be more calculative than gambler."

"Then I met Threi Cetre. Go now."

The warship arced into view. He lunged into a run, then a jump. C made a mighty leap, hauling Caiden and Leta even farther. The cloudsuits knit together into a protective mantle as they glided, untethered, through empty space to hopefully coincide with the hatch of the warship, which was still very much *closed*.

Leta pulled into C's mane. Caiden clung to both and watched the ship hurtle toward them, with no way to open it.

He wasn't a gambler. He didn't have luck. He had *trust*, which was a wretched thing to rely on, but it was what he had. Trust in a swarm of spirits he couldn't communicate with directly.

Azura.

CHAPTER 44

DESERTED

Surrounded by glittering cloudsuit, Leta struggled to process the fact that they were hurtling through absolute void toward the ass end of an enemy warship. Its cargo doors were shut, and the discharge ports blazed, ready to cook them.

But Caiden held her hand like he was never going to release it again.

Azura peeled out of the fuselage of the *Spur*. The little ship cracked at the seams with the absence of whatever laws had been keeping it together.

Aurorae wisped from nothingness in ethereal cyans and pinks. Azura billowed through space as a luminiferous presence *within* the very fabric of it, rolling pressures outward. She was a tangle of forces all bent in different directions, frantic for *something* while a guiding will tried to cinch them up into coherence.

Graven force soaked the warship ahead. Its engine power snapped offline. The cargo doors cracked open and an atmoseal blazed across.

Caiden, Leta, and C had no control of their velocity or direction. They headed on course to rebound right off the spine of the vessel.

Darts of thrust puffed out of the left flank to yaw the mass and point the opening their way.

Behind them, the *Sessrun*'s trace-array blast seared past in silent whips of light, demolishing what remained of the poor *Spur*.

Caiden pulled Leta in tight as they floated through the atmoseal and bounced on the bay floor inside. They rolled, tangling in sudden gravity and atmosphere. Their cloudsuits slicked back down to skins, then bare harness.

C bounded aside. The wind knocked out of Leta's chest, half-crushed by Caiden's weight. She gasped as he righted her to a sitting position and held her shoulders until she met his gaze. Her heart was flipping in all directions.

"That...that worked," he said, his blue eyes wide.

Of course he was surprised.

Leta nodded, and Caiden lurched to his feet. The nophek followed with a roar and the two of them swept through the ship and the startled crew. Caiden slugged the gunner in the jaw. He barked a command at C, who corralled another team in the escape bay. Caiden issued Graven shouts. Azura invaded the ship meanwhile, filling it with a music of transformation as slick things happened inside the walls.

Leta pushed to her feet, grabbed a glave off one wall, and followed Caiden's trail of mayhem to the bridge.

He had the captain in a light choke hold, bent to the console's comms. "You're going to tell them everything's all right. Do that for me, won't you?"

His Graven voice wasn't Threi's silver or Abriss's liquid amber. Caiden's was hoarse and naked-edged, like a knife without a handle, and it cut him to use. He'd become vicious and slightly untamed. Leta didn't mind, except that he looked a bit like Threi. The bend of his spine and the snarls in his hair, the same.

The captain gushed palliative statements to the remaining Casthen forces. The armada chatter and holosplay messages filled with confusion and fired up old rumors about the man they were chasing.

And Threi, safe in his cloudcutter, was already headed planetside and pleased to hear Winn had been destroyed. Leta noticed the catch in Threi's response, a distracted sort of regret. Better than suspicion.

Caiden herded the captain to the pod with the rest of the crew, sealed it up, and let Azura spit it out.

C huffed, tail whooshing, and paced circles until Caiden draped himself in the pilot's seat, backlit by the brilliant holosplays. Leta noted the quiver in his shoulders. He didn't take up the controls.

She walked over, masking her own exhaustion with an easy stride. "Let's not do that again?"

He looked over at her, and a smile did wrinkle his eyes.

Leta sensed Azura root deeper in the vessel. "You're going after Threi?"

Caiden nodded and settled his skull in the crystalline head cradle. Waves of hair pushed up around the sides, the tips still bleached from Feran's pool. "This class of ship won't maneuver, planetside, but if I can cut Threi off in atmospheric entry, it has good weapons. The *Outlast*." He read its name as he raised his hands into the drive guides.

Light coalesced and Azura's tones changed, the two of them becoming a chord. He powered forward.

RM28 glowed in the view, its skin wrinkled with sand and pools, scabby crags at one of the poles and a dark covering of something—forest?—at the base. A faraway blue moon lay beyond.

Leta said, "Get me close to the cloudcutter."

Close might not even matter anymore. She was confident she could locate Threi in the luminiferity. Azura wasn't the only one evolving. Leta had been more and more reckless with her abilities, by necessity, but it really was teaching her control.

"You've been pushing yourself too far," Caiden warned.

If Azura's Graven type controls reality and space, my Dynast type controls heart and mind.

"Leta."

I tasted my potential when I spied on Abriss's memories. When I shared Caiden's nightmare. When I possessed Dian's Proxy, then Isme's—it became easier with each.

"*Leta.*" Gravely spoken. That snapped her attention to him. "Don't break yourself. I can't lose you now. *Crimes*, I can't lose you."

Leta patted his shoulder. "You've gotten very needy."

She winked as she walked over to the navigator's seat to strap in and wondered where her new energy was bubbling up from. *Adrenaline. Lightens the mood. Truly, though, I need him too.*

C curled around the base of her seat, engulfing her legs. He plopped his big head in her lap. "Can you keep me grounded, baby?" She worried her fingers into his fur. He increased his pressure. Smart boy.

Anchored in the softness of her nophek protector, Leta flew.

Bliss, to depart her weary, aching body. Her awareness leaped from the *Outlast* and expanded through luminiferous dimensions.

Echoes of time lingered in space, stamping old events as if on warm wax. The stronger the meaning in it, the harder it impressed. The starship duel between Caiden and Threi was already gouging itself in the ether. Like Abriss, they were dramatically obvious and bright. Two Graven stars knotted in each other's gravity.

Leta expanded her awareness to the frenetic armada, then wider to the netting of ships encircling the whole universe of CWN82. They hadn't popped the bubble yet, but everything felt in position.

Leta refocused on the combat between the *Outlast* and Threi's cloudcutter. The beats of the duel distorted, stretched both too slow and too fast in time. The *Outlast*'s silver was as bright as a serrated blade cutting the shell of gases around the planet. The cloudcutter speared toward the surface, dodging Caiden's fire. They shed altitude and dived to the desert, where windblown sand covered old wreckage.

Though gowned in Azura's universe, the *Outlast* was getting thrashed by the cloudcutter's maneuverability and precision weaponry. Caiden had no separate gunner, no crew.

Leta concentrated on Threi, winding her consciousness through his details. As she'd done with Dian, she imagined all she knew of Threi, sharing space with him. His height and build, the sweat curling his dark hair, the invigoration in his bloodstream. His mind was as hot as a sun. Thoughts snapped off like solar prominence. Instinct glittered through his body at impossible speed, baked into him from years of accelerated aging and desenescence.

Space and time crystallized around Leta.

The cloudcutter had a crew: minds flickering around him, rigidly bound to their tasks. Threi had them all harnessed up to him with Graven orders and the will to please.

Think of them as Proxies. The body is a vessel. Slip in softly, like Azura does.

The gunner first. Leta ghosted her awareness into their rigid tendons and sore back, easing both. She joined their pulse and pacified their heart rate. Their brain sparked confusion, but the relief of letting go pulled them into her control. She unraveled Threi's Graven coils.

When she left their body, they were disoriented but relaxed. Their fingers slipped from the triggers. The cloudcutter ceased fire.

Next, the tandem pilot. She weaved herself into their body, sharing the heat of their anxiety and the fear bundled up in their gut. She whispered compassionate things into their mind and slid her will over their shoulders and hands, plucking up the knots of their tension. The pilot succumbed, in a grateful daze, and Leta stood—they stood—and walked out of the seat. Threi shouted a Graven order in alarm, but Leta fended that off and dropped the bewildered pilot in a corner of the back cargo bay.

Threi swore and refocused on flight. The shields roared with damage as Caiden took advantage of the lapse in crew and focused his fire.

Leta peeled two more crew members from the cockpit. That done, she stormed around Threi and attempted to pry into his intense mind. Sharing his fingers, slender but callused—they hesitated a moment in the twitch drive. Leta's presence strummed his nerves.

Breathless, he said, "What are you?"

Threi's desperation welled up around Leta. His face... There was another version of it, buried in time, like another skin beneath his perfect visage. Reconstruction paved it over, but his brain never let him forget, stamping in the sensation of burns, lacerated eyes, a tongue that had tasted hot coals, and sinuses that had drunk in the smoke. He'd done it to himself. Killed every sense he could so he could push through his father's Graven coercion. Same as Abriss's memory Leta had seen: a young man hiding guilt from a loving sister. Was his self-inflicted trauma really for self-defense?

I can use this. She shoveled deeper into Threi's feverish memories as her presence burst old synapses online, leaped the past into the present, stirred emotions out of his cells. The love of a sister, the hate of a father, the death of a mother, the exile of a world.

Threi's piloting flagged and the cloudcutter skipped hard across the desert.

As he struggled, turning over his own mind to find the intruder, Leta was getting lost in the canyons of his cognition. Threi and Leta relived the bloody, heated aftermath of murder. Every breath a burning agony. Every twitch of his cut-up eyes, bright torment. He wept blood and tears, drinking both down a raw throat that couldn't be quenched. Then Abriss's cold hands in his blindness, grazing over his cheeks. *I'm here*, she'd said.

Threi couldn't thrust Leta out. She knew him too deeply, harmonized too well. He roared, pouring his frustration into the cloudcutter to ram Caiden's ship through sand dunes and lakes.

Leta tumbled in the sensory input she shared, and hesitated with sadness for him and all his hurt. Abriss had been right. He deserved a chance to heal.

Threi tore his fingers from the twitch panels and threw one hand into the light guides. He raised his other arm straight up. The sleeve slithered down. The stolen Aurasever crisscrossed tight to his skin, its delicate construction out of place on his sinewy forearm.

Leta tried to flail away, but she'd twisted her spirit in him too tightly, too long, barbed up tight to his flesh.

Threi gripped his own skull in his palm, fingers digging in tight and the Aurasever nodes cutting scalp, as if he could blast her out of his head.

Leta couldn't scream. But he did. His nervous system raged, trying to link itself into Abriss's technology. At the same time, he barreled the cloudcutter into the *Outlast*, weapons blazing, splintering it apart. Both ships plowed deep in the sand. Hot waves of glass exploded over the hull.

Having lost her vessel, Azura flooded into the cloudcutter as it pulled up. Control tore from Threi's grasp. The light guides dissolved around his fingers.

Leta gushed relief. *Help me!*

Threi roared and hurtled out of the pilot's seat. Kneeling, he slapped his palms on the floor, fingers clawed. In a *snap* his mind focused. Keen as a blade forged of sun, he discharged his will through the Aurasever into the mass of the ship.

Tremendous force rocketed out of Threi's hands and body, expelling Azura's energy altogether. She disintegrated, glittering, the swarm cast apart.

The course of physics convulsed. Space ruffled and strings tore. Leta's consciousness shredded, raining across the luminiferous expanse.

Back. I have a body. The body is a vessel.

Her body had been strapped in, but the wreck wasn't good. The *Outlast* had crash-landed. Bits were strewn across the desert. Leta fought to find herself, hoping she wasn't strewn bits too.

Caiden.

Easier to find him first. He was bright and Graven. Leta's body was just a husk. Her Proxy had been a shell. *What am I, then?*

A weak pulse. A guttering light.

You're safe.

She was alive. Her spirit soaked in, filling around injuries.

I've got you, Caiden had said to Leta when the transports came. *You're safe.*

He'd said those words so many different times, their echoes had layered up, convincing the world it must be true. *Safe*—he'd lied about it, that day. When the box stopped roaring and the beasts' hunger stilled, it was Threi Cetre who'd come for her in this desert.

She felt Caiden's arms draw her up, even though she was put back together all wrong.

"Cai," she replied, but didn't hear it. The name hummed over her tongue and around her skull. An ill-fitting wind.

Caiden untangled her body from the wreckage. When Azura had left the *Outlast*, it was rent nose to tail and blown apart by engine failure and bad physics.

Azura. Did Threi destroy her? Can that be done?

A breeze tossed sand against the metal debris, a million tiny patterings that described the shape of the ruins to Leta's senses, helping her eyes filter the light.

Her spirit vibrated in and out of her body's borders, but if she moved slowly, she could operate most of herself. Caiden scooped her in the crook of one arm as he tried to hobble out of the ship's ripped side. Blood squished in his boots. A bulky satchel jarred his momentum and tripped him sideways into Leta's arms. She fell down to her knees.

C pushed on the other side of him, and together they forced Caiden to a sitting position, propped against C's haunches.

"I've got you," Leta said with a broken laugh. Laughing helped.

He looked awful. Augmented arm scraped up, the skin pigment glitching translucent in patches. His right arm had two long gashes an inch deep, bleeding. More in his thigh. A swelling ankle. Heat building around his ribs.

"I used to think you were bullheaded," Leta said. "What good is a protector who can't admit when they're too hurt to help?"

Caiden groaned and squeezed his eyes shut.

Leta scraped bloody hair out of his eyes, then reached across to pet C's nose, the fur wet from nuzzling Caiden's wounds. The nophek had a limp paw, chipped nails, and spikes of debris jabbing through the softer patches of hide.

Med supplies. Leta's gaze skipped over the wreckage. So much had burned up. Banners of smoke trailed off the smoldering remains.

Her vision started to make sense of the starry sky and the glow of the atmosphere bouncing off the sand. Then her breath caught. A shard of void raced toward them over the desert. Fast as a blink, the cloudcutter sped above their heads, peeling sand into vortices that hissed against the ruins of the *Outlast*.

"Threi." Leta craned her neck to watch his ship twist into the atmosphere, laced up in ribbons of drag.

Caiden murmured, "He's leaving us alive here on purpose. Here, where it all started. He would find that irony crueler than killing us now."

"And he's going to pop this whole universe. The rind will sweep over the planet to crack it open so he can get to the Dominant inside but, Cai, it'll crack us too. There's a chance we'll survive fine, but—"

"Neither of us are in great shape."

She nodded, so weary it blotted out the dread she should feel. The flux of the rind collapsing had a destructive effect all its own, even if a biology could exist in both universes. Nothing would protect them from physical laws twisting inside out.

Caiden said, "We did both survive this desert before. Those odds were nearly as slim." With bruised, trembling fingers he picked flecks of debris from her hair. "And I won't leave this time. We also have—*Azura*." Alarm screwed into Caiden's face, squishing the blood into rivulets.

He pushed to his feet and stumbled around, tripping on the sand, flattening his palms against metal chunks, then lifting his fingers into the air.

Leta closed her eyes, but her senses fuzzed into static after very far. She didn't feel Azura's spirit swarm in the luminiferity either.

Caiden plodded back over. "It's—there's just no vessel here. She's somewhere."

She's not. Leta couldn't tell him so.

His blue eyes went dim. As poor as Leta was at reading faces, she knew the little muscular twitches and the flutter of his eyelashes were the signs of a brave denial.

The thunder of Threi's ascent ebbed out of the atmosphere, bringing quiet. Leta's terror manifested as a deep, slow stillness. Shock.

"Here." She pulled Caiden to where a panel of hull blocked the wind. C limped with them and loomed over Leta's lap until she tugged on his neck. "Sit, baby."

The *Outlast*'s massive skid gouged the desert. All over, the dunes were spotted with older starship wreckage from the planetwide war that passagers had raged over the nophek gloss a decade ago. It did look like the same view she'd had from the transport box. Pale sand scabbed in rock, and dark masses dotted all about it. Except those had been corpses.

Leta rested her head against the nophek's bloody shoulder and felt a pang of irony that might've been funny if the situation weren't so dire. The monster growled a tired, pained sound of acknowledgment. Leta stroked her knuckles under his chin. She felt disconnected from her own trembling. Dissociating as if the knowledge that they were going to die was permission to unlink.

Caiden's gaze wasn't focusing, staring at the dunes as if he expected Azura to rush to him at any moment.

Leta tilted her head back. "There it is. He's collapsed this whole universe."

The rind flux grew visible as it hurtled toward them: a front of space warping all the light seen through it. Distant stars screwed into spirals and streaks. Resplendence spasmed in and out of reality's fabric as the encroaching rind swept through the void like flame eating up a swath of fresh fuel.

Caiden stiffened. The view fractured across his wet eyes.

The universe rind was contracting fast and hit RM28's atmosphere at the horizon, engulfing it, immense and inescapable. A wall of imploding change.

Leta took a sharp breath and gripped Caiden's morphcoat hard. Every manner of weather clashed all at once, shredded apart, re-formed. A hundred octaves of thunder skirmished through the sky, and as the rind touched the earth on the far side of the planet, the quakes reached them. Sand grains vibrated into ridges and furrows to form a scalar pattern over the landscape. Rings and radial lines, beautiful and terrible. Leta's senses blurred into every grain of sand the wind moved, the bands of rumble in the air, the scent of ozone.

Caiden was rigid yet full of energy, fighting the instinct to run. Leta swallowed a sob and stroked a finger over the velvet curl of C's lame paw. They couldn't run from this. There was a chance the flux wouldn't harm them at all, but Leta's spirit already wasn't fitting in her flesh, like she was a scrap of cloth snagged on a tree limb and one good gust might whisk her out.

"Caiden." She pulled his gaze away from the wall of destruction barreling toward them. The howling of it ate up her voice. She looped her hand around the back of his head and pressed their foreheads together. "Sorry to say, there isn't much keeping my spirit hooked into this body. I need your focus. It may also draw Azura together if she's still lingering."

"Tell me how."

The encroaching rind tore through the planet's surface, close enough now to make out detail. Sand whipped into fire and glass. Filaments wafted skyward while the bedrock below disintegrated to dust storms. There was something crisp and jeweled even deeper, a substructure under the crust, revealed as the planet's skin corroded away.

That was the impenetrable stratum that Threi wished to rupture. His plan had worked. It was Graven without a doubt: lightseep skeleton twisted into a complex lattice, filled up with matrices of brilliant metal and prismatic organics that resembled gloss. The transformations opened crevices to more leagues below.

Even if their physiologies survived the rind flux, they would tumble out of the desert into the pitted landscape left behind.

No matter—she had to try.

"Focus your Graven will to me."

His forehead shifted against hers. "What?"

"Please. Use it all. Wrap us up in it. I know you've done it before—flex it or however it works. Strong as you can."

"But—"

"Don't be stubborn. You're not trained to be precise in the luminiferity like I am, but your raw power is stronger. *Wisdom and power*, remember? Trust me."

Caiden huffed and pulled their heads tighter together.

He flexed his Graven energy. His power *was* a different timbre from the Dynast Graven or Azura, but Leta was able to connect with it all the same. Caiden's body relaxed as their hearts and understanding linked up, extended nervous systems synced. She felt grounded in a whole new way.

This is what Graven means, she tried to say, and hoped their thoughts meshed enough that he grasped it. *Oneness.*

Caiden's energy rang out like a plea. Leta joined it with all she understood of Azura, crafting a knowing that would help coalesce the entity together in the vortex of concentration Caiden's Graven will had made.

Wafts of presence tickled Leta's mind. From all directions, streams of spiritual force gathered into chords, knotting around Caiden, whose energy gave them *time* to form melody and tempo.

Leta opened her eyes. A mass of pearlescent flame stretched nine meters across, in constant motion unbraiding the universal laws to match Azura's choosing.

Caiden's eyes glistened with the reflected light.

"Almost a trinity." Leta smiled. She couldn't sit up or squeeze his hand back. But she could cling to the density of his Graven strength and the universe Azura had swaddled around them and believe it could be enough to save their lives.

She collapsed, and Caiden's heartbeat filled her ear. In her lap, the nophek's big head hummed with gloss. Around her, Azura's soundless melody flamed across her skin.

Leta was happy.

At least they would die together.

CHAPTER 45

CITY OF VIGIL

Leta?" Caiden found a pulse in her neck. He wasn't sure what unconsciousness meant, with her. She was water tipped back and forth between glasses too often...it was inevitable some had spilled. This was everything Ksiñe had warned about, and it left her in no state to survive what came next.

He held her and the cowering nophek tight. Fatigue and blood loss dulled his pain. Inevitability numbed his fear. He pulled his spine straight and faced the rind as it swept the last kilometer to engulf them. He'd dreamed of saving more than just himself from this desert—now was the time to pay it off.

Caiden threaded his Graven willpower into the world as if he could coerce it to do his bidding. He flexed with every ounce of control he'd learned, reversing all the years he'd spent trying to lock his Graven energy down.

Azura's universe tightened to armor him, but if the wall barreling toward them was born from two rinds' physics battling, he struggled to see how introducing a third would save them.

Perhaps the correct thing to do was simply marvel.

The rind was a supernova stretched out to all horizons. Solid materials and particulates tangled up with plasma whorls and fractal vortices. Mathematics of form jumbled, then crisped, converting one thing perfectly into another, hurtling now at terrible speed. Caiden's eardrums popped and howled with pain, skull stuffed edge to edge.

A final sight stamped Caiden's vision: the billows of Azura's protective universe wrenched apart like flame before a gale.

The rind blasted through. The worst of a hundred crossovers in one. Worlds warred inside the meat of him. Slathered across space, quantum patterns unknitting then relinking, until in one *snap* he was flesh and bone again.

On the other side, the desert melted to glass. It slithered out from beneath his legs and sent him tumbling over a precipice.

"Azura!" he cried as he balled around Leta, taking the brunt of the strikes as they plummeted into a massive structure.

Azura's force knotted around C, bulging like muscles. She'd guarded his delicate physiology from the rind, but it couldn't protect from lightseep scaffolding or sharp rock.

Matter continued to shift states in the rind's wake. Dribbling liquid glass cooled, crackling into shards that Caiden rammed into. Rock avalanched, bellowing through the canyon. Impacts broke long stretches of free fall.

Caiden shut his eyes and drowned in the rumble, remembering too much of his fall when Azura had cracked apart. Debris rent the gashes in his arm wide open. His neck crunched against a beam—if the cervical vertebrae hadn't been augmented hyperdiamond, it might've shattered a second time.

Then, *slam*.

Caiden's skull bounced.

Hard gravity squeezed him into a surface. In his brain, he was still falling, still feverishly spinning. He curled, vomiting up searing blood. Clots of copper tang slid off his tongue.

"Little boy..." He braved his eyes open. C had landed nearby and whimpered at him. Leta was in Caiden's grasp, less scathed. He wilted with relief at the sight—then heaved again, crimson spattering the strange surface they'd landed on.

He tried to make sense of it amidst vertigo. Shavings of light scattered down, painting the edges of a citylike vista, all dead glow and ultraviolet edges.

The nophek crawled over with a wet scraping sound. His soft nose whistled. Caiden pulled C's head close and kissed his ear, then dizziness hashed up his neural firing again.

Get up, cur. Leta needs you. She needs you better.

Caiden growled in agony as he pushed onto his elbows. He bent over Leta and fumbled for her wrist. *Pulse.* One beat. More, together? He forgot how to check. There was a shred of life in her.

C wasn't too bad, tough hide split up and muscles shivery. Whimpering, he sniffed Caiden's wounds. One lick, and Caiden roared in pain.

He doubled over, quivering, sucking air through his nose. "Don't. Crimes, they're bad."

Caiden shook violently, gushing bloody rivers. Adrenaline tried to saw his pain into numbness. Not great signs. It was easy to ignore his own state when someone else needed help, but if he died, he'd be no good to anyone. Leta had been right about that.

He untangled the satchel from his shoulders. The straps had carved strips of raw skin. The bronze cooler case hadn't fallen out. He groped the latches, fingers shaky.

Inside lay the Graven enhancers Feran had made.

If circumstances require you to be perfect, they'd said.

He plucked a vial from the case and stared at it, swaying. His breath came in searing inhales and tight, bubbling exhales.

Untested, irreversible. The enhancement might heal him, if it didn't cost his life, but it would cost his humanity, amplifying the most foreign, wretched part of him.

Being brought here was giving him a chance to make the choice he'd wished he'd made a decade ago. Save her. If it cost his life, he didn't care. What he'd wanted, deep down, wasn't revenge on the Casthen. He'd wanted atonement for leaving her, for being the death of her, for saving himself instead of others...

Now Caiden needed to be perfect to save Leta.

Drink the thing, you monster. Hurry.

He flicked the cap off and brought it to his lips, spilling half over the sides as he trembled.

It would be permanent.

For her.

He tipped his head back and forced a swallow. The flavor was fresh rain and ashes, what he imagined quicksilver might taste like. Before he lost his nerve, he took one more, spilling less this time.

Starlight flamed through Caiden's veins. It radiated, dissolved the world, wicked his consciousness away. Luminiferous eternities passed through him, bringing bizarre impressions of other lives—*a song in a thunderstorm, two arguments in one body, sunbeams ruffling when she turned*—then the haze of his being distilled, nerves fanned through flesh that seemed crystalline. His cells were bits of idea bound by magnetism, built of infinite fractals.

Caiden slowly regained mass, like a lightseep creature whose vibrations slowed to a physical degree. Luminous flesh and flame blood, built of tingles and tension and ice-fire—the strangeness of it cooled in his vision, returning his body to a normal thing with shadows and texture.

He cursed and scraped dribbles off his chin. Pain had vanished. Strength surged in from nowhere, and prickly waves of rapid healing coursed through him. Blood dripped dark violet from his wounds where the muscle re-weaved, dermis bubbled back, and freckles peppered the seams. He watched in fascinated horror.

The storms cleared from his mind, letting in bright new senses, expanded to such detail he wondered if this was the world Leta experienced all the time.

"I feel intact...at least," he murmured, and his voice had a thunder to it, thick in his ears. He flexed his shoulders and sucked in huge breaths. Faint luminescence bruised the deeper tissues of his body and left sparks of freckling in the wake of his motions.

The hollow he'd felt in his spirit—filled with violence and night and teeth—was brimming with a radiant feeling. Monsters were cast away from the corners of his heart. He *was* the monster.

He scooped Leta into his arms and pushed to his feet. In his new senses he could make out what her flagging pulse belied: her spirit still clinging on, threshed though it was.

"I know you're here," Caiden whispered. "Stay with me."

C limped over and sniffed Caiden all over, alternating between purr and growl.

"I'm still myself, little boy. I hope. And now I can see where we are."

They stood on a walkway of porous stone beside another precipice. Lightseep scaffolding was filled by exotic matter to form countless layers of rooms and paths. It stretched the entirety of RM28, surely, an even larger structure than the Casthen Harvest. Instead of metal and machine, this place was organic, geometric.

A Graven city, dead and inert.

"Azura." He focused by recalling her shell that he'd lived in for years, and all the times he'd fallen asleep with her presence in his head. The song and the sunlight in his Graven memories. Spiritual scraps gravitated to him, growing in strength until Azura coiled around him in her familiar way, bands of invisible pressure grazing his skin and lifting his hair.

Caiden smiled. "Help me find a way to heal Leta. Her injuries aren't all physical."

Azura glided away and her force soaked into the walls. Lightseep obsidian chorused. Electromagnetism trickled out and spread through dead organic systems. A glow feathered through opaque matter in the shape of cumulus clouds in the ceiling.

"New vessel for you?"

Who cared if his energy was Graven-bought, he would use it. Caiden whisked the case back into the satchel and over his shoulder. Oxygen was thin. He'd need water, antiseptic, and something to bandage or seal. Perhaps a splint for the pup.

Azura surged into the lead. Caiden and C followed, and the Graven city came to life ahead. Azura's presence stirred internal systems, more like lightning storms and dendritic nerves than digital circuitry. Organic things bloomed on the walls and ceiling with spidery petals that rained effervescence. Dew-soft air whirled through the space, and Caiden inhaled experimentally, then grinned: the blooms were oxygen bombs.

He picked up his pace while Azura spread at least fifty meters all around. The lightseep obsidian awoke, whispering vibrations. It fractured strange reflections, nothing like the empty architecture he'd seen before: this was replete, the skeleton muscled with mineral and tissue. He trailed his fingers along a wall that was as slick as water, with a mossy microtexture.

The passageways snaked to chambers large enough to hold a village. Kilometer-wide sheets of petrified webbing crackled with revived energy, growing as bright as frozen electricity. Waterfalls of plasma streamed to the ceiling.

Caiden had spent years traveling through all manner of civilizations with different cultures and physical forms, he'd gotten good at recognizing function within the foreign. This Graven place was like nowhere he had been or seen, but he could grasp that there *was* purpose behind its design. It was a place that felt lived in.

Lived in or perhaps simply *living*.

The materials shifted more and more, all smeared features and running inks. Caiden wasn't sure if his perception was unraveling or the architecture was. The lightseep bones hummed patterns through the air, perhaps loosening reality's laces. Many things appeared multiplied and fuzzy, like a holographic plate, until he observed them directly and they sprang into crisp hyperdetail. He'd look away, and they'd scramble in the periphery of his attention.

Or it was the enhancer. Caiden's Gravenness. His sense of *time* grew even more bizarre. They'd been walking for arcminutes or hours. He'd been here before eons ago, but he was also a ghost preceding himself and hadn't treaded here yet. Every action felt like a trial run but also final. And he imagined the place was not *awakening* but being rewound in time, restoring an old luster as he and Azura moved through.

Caiden's legs didn't tire. His arms didn't burn with Leta's weight. Vitality might as well have streamed to his body from the air, and he chuckled at a strange notion, imagining how some cities powerstreamed electricity to vehicles. He wondered whether this might be the same, the Graven structure streaming charisma to his revived cells.

C snapped his jaws.

"I know." Caiden grimaced. "I won't start enjoying this power. I'm grateful, that's all. I can't hate a Graven gift if it gives me the strength to save others . . . right?"

Or was that Abriss's thinking? Caiden wasn't sure what was right except that Leta in his arms was important enough to spend himself. He followed

Azura's path of illumination to a landscape of fluted plateaus. They were as vast as plains and grassed over with vitreous cilia that waved in patterns. Currents of heat rose to an ionized atmosphere.

Some tens of kilometers away, a handful of Casthen vessels jetted across the vista, leaving afterimage trails before darting into tunnels. They were blasting scan rays that traced the walls and mapped the place as they went.

C snarled. Caiden, arms full, bumped the nophek with a hip. "Threi doesn't know where he's going. Feran's data placed the Dominant's energy all over the planet, and they don't have fine enough instruments to measure it in real time. But *we* have something that knows the way."

Azura tickled past their legs, kissed Caiden's cheek with air, and ruffled patterns into the luminescent fields. Caiden tracked her ropes of force as they snaked through. In the middle of the plains, the floor stepped down to subterranean levels and frozen rivers like streets of cut gemstone.

The deeper they traveled, the more dreaminess swallowed them. First physics acting awry, pockets of rogue gravity patterns, and even more of the wet-painting feel of vision and sounds. The rush of white water turned to rhythmic tinkling as he rotated his skull. He inhaled sweetness and exhaled spice.

Caiden began to see ghosts of his own movement through time, like many temporid species: a pale waft of future motions or finished ones, as if he vibrated outside of himself. Even C was confused, sniffing the wrong versions.

Caiden clucked his tongue and C jerked his head at the sound, then whimpered. "I'm right here. I think."

Leta felt increasingly insubstantial in his grasp, but there was a glow to her, like he carried an ember with the fire asleep in it. He just had to wake her up and breathe some life in. He repositioned her and carried on, following in the footsteps of the ghost of himself ahead.

Azura stalled and the quartz river Caiden walked on ended in a cavern of pure lightseep obsidian. The surface underfoot melted into a slick, thigh-high water that didn't wet his skin or clothes. C pressed against Caiden's thigh as they waded through. It effervesced around the nophek's wounds, cleansing grime and healing him. A pang of relief choked Caiden up as he watched.

Everything might be all right.

Azura pooled beneath the liquid, casting gorgeous standing ripples. Caiden marveled, then finally looked up and froze at the sight of a massive object in the center of the cavern.

The Graven Dominant.

CHAPTER 46

EQUAL

Almost nothing about this Graven thing resembled the matter Feran had been keeping alive in the Harvest.

This was more like gigantic gloss. Clear and bright as dew, surface swirling adularescent hues with a metallic sheen. The crown and base tapered, with flat spiral ridges all around. Inside lay complex occlusions similar to those in Azura's chrysalis: trapped veins of liquid and gases forming golden storms of refracted light and plumes of biophotons.

Caiden tried to capture detail from dreamy features that only became crisp when observed. Translucent tissues connected the chrysalis to the walls—like fluid gloss, again, as if this cavern were the skull of a vast creature. Perhaps the "city" was its body, curled up. Or it was simply architecture designed to mimic the organic.

"Whatever you are, your power is going to bring Leta back."

Caiden draped Leta's dead weight on the steps of a wide dais beneath the huge Dominant chrysalis. *Denial. You're in denial.*

C sloshed out of the pool and shook from head to tail, throwing off stars of liquid light. He lay down and stretched his forelimbs out with a happy grunt.

Caiden cupped the strange water over Leta's wounds and bruises, healing them up, but his good mood dissolved, and his hands started to shake.

Her respiration was almost nonexistent.

He sat on his heels and folded one of her hands between his. "We need more oxygen and something to...bring her together. Like she did for me..."

C wiggled closer on his belly and stretched to nuzzle her waist.

Scenarios played through Caiden's head: that Leta was conscious in her body but trapped there, unable to drive it; that she was lost forever, expanded so much her consciousness would never fit in this body again; that she was unconscious and dying, plain and simply dying…

Caiden gathered up his Graven will and meditated. He had *gravitas*, and if it was worth a damn, he would figure out how to use it to restore her.

Azura's singing purled out of the water, into the air above. Frequencies shifted, pleating silver on the surface and collecting luminescent molecules into lines beneath. Her energy soaked into the crystallized tissues that webbed the Dominant to the cavern walls and turned those tissues into streams of plasma pouring off the object.

"Az?" Caiden's hair and clothing tugged in one direction, his pulse sped up, and air spooled out of his lungs.

Azura seeped right into the chrysalis, turning the light inside out and the colors rioting. A rumble rose in pitch and amplitude from a frequency Caiden felt in his marrow. He squeezed Leta's hand and clutched C's mane but couldn't look away. With a thunderous *crack*, the bass pitch dropped, carving down into Caiden's stomach. It shoved him onto his back and rolled throughout the cavern.

A universe rind bloomed.

As if Azura had watered a seed of a world, it floresced in great petals of sunset-colored force. Wet flame curled through matter, fast and hungry, yet this was the gentlest crossover Caiden had ever felt. The rind swept out of sight through the cavern walls, encompassing the city-thing or the whole planet or more.

Instantly, the dreaminess dissolved and reality grew crisp. Caiden was solid and anchored in time. Leta had heft and warmth. Matter stopped morphing and made up its mind. Triggered buds bloomed along the edges of the pool, flooding oxygen into this fresh world.

Caiden drew long, easy breaths and stretched his limbs in silkier gravity. C shook and did a giant stretch too, eyes luminous as he looked up at Caiden and purred.

"The Graven made universe seeds?"

The surface of the Dominant's chrysalis was no longer a dewdrop but a faint aura, and the more complex structure within blazed with a tightly contained, seething light that obscured the thing inside. It still didn't look like the masses Feran had tended.

Caiden stared into it, battling afterimage with blinks, when a hand wriggled in his and Leta's weary voice said, "There are so many of you. All across time, echoes of you. What did you do? Who is..."

He seized her hand tight against his heart. Gratefulness paved over his alarm at the little signs of how his stronger gravitas hooked up her affection.

She frowned. "Time is dimpling around your edges. And your freckles kind of glow."

Sour memories heaved up. "That's how Threi looked, that day he—"

Leta yanked his sleeve and sat up, pulling him into a hug and crushing a grunt from him. "We're even now."

"I shouldn't tell you I didn't do anything, huh? Azura helped the most." Caiden let relief spill out, all his worries in shards. He whispered, "Threi is on his way here. If he hadn't found the path yet, the universe florescing put a big marker on its origin."

He pushed Leta away to inspect her injuries. Her skin glowed with health and the swirled freckles glittered in all their layers light and dark. Her hair grew buoyant around her neck, ends curling in invisible pressures.

"You hate him," she said, "but have you tried to understand him?"

"Where is this question coming from?"

By the way she looked around, she was seeing a different world from him. "One of the futures around you," she whispered, shaking her head. Then she laughed—a lively, honeyed sound. "Thank you, hero."

Caiden chuckled. How often as a kid had he wished for that very gratitude rather than her scornful, flighty shell. "You're welcome, *hero*. Threi was about to obliterate the *Outlast* before you did...whatever it was you did."

Her gaze focused on the Dominant. "I don't know where the desert went, but...Azura and the Dominant. Two parts of the Graven trinity together."

"Reunited? I found Azura on this planet-place. Maybe she was never supposed to have separated from this thing after all. Except...she wasn't acting like this around Feran's Dominant. She shied away until I destroyed its remnants."

Azura was a vague braid of tones and phosphorescence around this Graven Dominant, warping its light with her windy pressures.

"And the third..." Leta turned to face another direction.

Caiden felt it a beat later. Like a touch, but not. Like a mass feeling something brush its gravitational field.

A shadow slithered beyond the chrysalis.

Caiden stood, spine straight. Graven energy still turned his veins to fire, strummed his nerves, and filled him with strength, his heart streaming power from some ethereal well. Was this how Threi felt all the time, or were Dynast Graven different?

The man strolled around the side of the chrysalis, gazing up at it with awe. He crossed his arms behind his back, regal posture impeccable. His pale face was lit, white freckles like stars in daylight.

Caiden called, "Is this what you expected?"

"No." Threi halted to appraise the thing, eyes soft. "I thought it would be shaped more like us."

"Do I detect hubris?"

"Vanity."

The Casthen Prime had his sister's Aurasever around both hands and arms, plus a few small glaves and blades serried on either hip. Caiden had no weapons.

C rose, gaze tracking the enemy.

Threi said, "I suppose my frame of reference for what this would be was my own family, all more or less human. The literature suggests the Graven were noncorporeal and participated in a great many bodies. Does that sound familiar? But of course, Dynast philosophy is obfuscated by poetic language and allegory, so I assumed the truth was flesh and blood and vulgarity, and the chunks of meat that Feran doted on were parts of a body once like ours." He paused to wave a hand through the phosphorescence streaming off it. "A whole and perfect Dominant Graven. Did your *Azura* break its chrysalis?"

"I don't know what you're talking about."

Threi spun on his heel to face Caiden and his awed expression turned to a snarl, viper-quick. "I'm not a fool. And you're not a child. So let's speak like intelligent adults."

Caiden motioned C to wait. Leta rose but stayed at the nophek's side as Caiden approached Threi. Time folded him back to the Harvest. "Where did we leave off?"

"I was going to stab you before you decided to drown yourself and destroy decades of work in the same gesture." Threi's reply was tender but his icy eyes narrowed at Caiden's approach. "I believe I also asked you to *kneel*."

He was testing the gravitas between them: two magnetic fields feeling a way together, invisible flows twisting as they attracted and repelled.

Threi's smile cracked into frown lines when the realization dawned on him.

Caiden smirked. "I don't think I feel like kneeling to an equal."

The enhancement had given him the strength to save Leta and now freed his will around Threi. Every action and feeling would be his choice. It felt better than he had imagined.

Threi stood very still, processing the idea. Light snagged in waves of his dark hair as he cocked his head to one side, throwing clawlike shadows across his face.

Caiden had time to notice that although Threi was scoured and freshly dressed, he wore a bloody sash looped around one shoulder and his hips: a strip cut out of his stained coat, the unwashed gray mottled with his sister's blood.

Caiden fought back a shiver and nodded at it. "Is that a trophy?"

"Why do you always think the worst of me?"

"I've *seen* the worst of you."

Threi chuckled. "Oh, no, you haven't."

Caiden wanted to bristle at that, then remembered what he'd admitted to Leta, how he was prone to chasing ideas. If he could admit doing so with Leta during their ten years apart, he could entertain the notion of having done similar to Threi during the same time.

"Feran thought you were all we had," Threi said, "but here's the first of the trinity, the binding factor. You've brought the *Azura*, the second, the enharmonic. And I, Threi Cetre of the Seventh Primal Etheric Line of the Dynast Lineage, and the *last*—barring my darling sister—purebred of the Dynast Graven...am the third, harmonic."

A laugh tumbled from Caiden. *"Purebred."*

Threi glowered at that cheap, hurtful shot. The Dynast had grown inbred over the centuries while desperately trying to perpetuate their fickle genes. It was the whole reason why Threi and Abriss—perfect siblings— weren't equally Graven.

"You forgot one problem," Caiden said, and internally he cried curses and pleas that he was right about this. "She doesn't listen to you."

He backed away from the chrysalis until his feet touched the water. Azura untangled from the Dominant and filled the pool with vibrations so complex they solidified it beneath Caiden's footfalls.

A dam of relief shattered in him at the confirmation. He took up a fighter's stance, light on the balls of his feet, hands in front. Unbidden, droplets levitated off the vibrating water, some breaking up so fine they became curls of vapor around him. Force twined his body and grazed his bare neck. Azura joined his readiness.

He felt powerful, even though his brain was blaring alarm about Threi's glaves and superior skill and how very poorly their fight went last time.

Threi resumed a smile and softened into a narrow stance. "I have two knives. Shall I throw you one?"

Leta strode directly between them, her palms raised to either side. Caiden almost yelled but hesitated as he registered Threi's confused stall and Leta's own controlled expression.

"Threi was right," she said, pinning Caiden with an earnest gaze before turning her head to the Casthen Prime. "I understand after seeing it. The unified world Abriss longs for, where everyone experiences what she does— reality-shaping willpower, conjoined consciousness, unconditional care—is the very world that the Graven ended up breaking in order to survive individual dissolution.

"You pointed out that the multiverse is rife with signs of Graven participation. The universes are intentional creations. Limitations—of both physical body and universal parameter—give us diversity, personality, possibility, and a rhythm of entropy and structure. But breaking the multiverse up *too* much is what closed off the luminiferity and obliterated Graven flexibility, putting too many barriers between consciousness and body. Potential forgotten."

"Balance," Threi agreed cautiously. His pale gaze flicked between Leta and Caiden, trying to figure out this ruse.

Caiden was just as lost. He battled an overprotective urge.

Threi fixed Leta with a curious, feline smile. "I could sense you believed me before, but you weren't ready to *disbelieve* Abriss. She showed you?"

"Yes."

Threi bowed elegantly. "Welcome to the side of truth. I'm sorry for the world she destroyed to open your eyes. I've seen the same, before, in a different way."

Caiden scoffed. "Is it hubris or vanity that blinds you to the fact that your rejection is what pushed Abriss to this breaking point?"

Threi tensed. His gravitas cinched up space. "You don't have the clear sight to see the threat. Nor the willingness to sacrifice your so-called humanity to become powerful enough to save the multiverse from her destructive selfishness. Let your better do it."

Leta interjected, "Caiden hasn't seen it yet. And I believe no one needs to sacrifice at all. Like you said, we have all the pieces here."

"We?" Threi asked.

"Us." Leta stretched her arms to the two of them, her palms open for theirs. "Let me show something to you both."

Caiden shot Threi a vicious look. The gravitas between them knotted stiff, equal pressures searching for give.

Leta sighed. "Stop being snarling animals and humor me for one moment!"

Caiden flinched, surprised by her forcefulness, then guilty he wasn't trusting her.

Threi suddenly laughed. He gave Leta a strange look as he stepped up and delicately laid his palm in hers. Jealousy soured through Caiden at the same time he was hit with the sense that this had happened before—in reverse, ten years ago when Threi coaxed her out of the transport's darkness. *She took his hand then. He saved her—is that why she trusts him?*

Threi shot Caiden a half-smile of challenge. Flushing, Caiden grasped Leta's other hand.

She entwined her fingers with theirs. "I fear the worst: that we aren't enemies."

Caiden's mind abruptly fled his body.

CHAPTER 47

TWO OF THREE

Leta drew on the Dominant's stabilizing energy as a carrying wave to gather up Threi's and Caiden's consciousnesses alongside her own in the luminiferity. *Without*, she hoped, the two of them lost in the expanse. The immense calm the Dominant impressed on her felt like it'd give her the focus necessary to pull the three of them to the current moment on Solthar in Abriss Cetre's presence.

She'd done other impossible things. What was another stretch?

Leta grasped all the details of the Dynast Hold and hauled the three of them there. Intersecting light rays superimposed to crystallize into the correct reality.

Caiden and Threi stayed with her.

She trusted that Threi's motivation was ironclad. It was Caiden who needed to see what they were up against. Then the two men needed to grasp that working together was the only way anyone would ever be powerful enough to stop the Dynast Prime.

Holographic night projected from Solthar's lightseep shell. Moonlight glazed through the windows of Abriss's library. Scientific devices and Graven technology pulled from distant star systems now populated the spaces that had once held books and worktables.

Leta planted herself firmly, her Graven passengers' presences whorling around her.

Abriss lay in a shallow bath similar to the radiation casket built from Azura's chrysalis. Sharp brilliance poured through her body: the same conditioning that had given Leta, Isme, and Aohm incredible powers for a flicker of a moment. Two of three Graven strains—harmonic vessel and enharmonic energy—*without* the stabilizing factor. And Azura's energy that Abriss was synthesizing was not the real thing. Less enduring? Less powerful?

Leta recalled her own experience with this state of being, an ineffable yet tenuous balance of chaos and order. She remembered how quickly Azura's energy had drained without the Dominant to cement that balance.

Impossibly precise technological design kept the combined radiation from blasting Abriss apart. Liquid-crystal genetic elements re-formed. The freckles in her tawny skin blazed white and rearranged their constellations. Her veins were rivers of black starlight. Her nerves were strings of infinite energy. Leta marveled, gripped by dread while also hopelessly in love with this gorgeous creature.

As Abriss regained consciousness, Leta felt force gathering across the entirety of Unity, star systems wide. The hands of her aides helped lift her from the water. Elated surprise washed through her face, as if she hadn't expected to survive.

Caiden and Threi recoiled. This was not what Leta had expected them to witness. It was worse.

The new balance of opposites within Abriss was just as unstable as it had been in the Graves, but she was maintaining it consciously, without the stabilizing factor, through sheer force of will. That effort would break a mortal like Abriss.

It would break her mind, first.

White and copper robes peeled out of the water with her, clothing her luminous skin. She wore the remade and augmented Aurasever, appearing fused now, lacing like molten threads up her arms, neck, and down the crystalline starbursts against her vertebrae. An excess of light turned her eyes to amber glass, her pupils tiny specks as she gazed adoringly up at nothing.

But there was something.

Leta sensed a *whole lot* of something.

Dear stars, who are all of you?

Legions of fragmented spirits from across the ages bent toward Abriss, adding their influence to her reality. *Dynast ancestors?* Some were mere shreds of consciousness, more like remnant wishes and warnings and wants.

Just one presence was more coherent than the rest: the Graven thing Abriss had always alluded to guiding her. Somewhat undefined and swarm-like, similar to Azura, it was reaching a stable form as echoes of the past began to line up and enmesh. Was Abriss's attention over time the thing aligning them? It shared Abriss's space, coiled around her mind, and was the reason her balance was this stable. The reason she smiled. She could sense it viscerally now.

Abriss raised her hands slowly as she turned to leave the library. The Hold's lightseep obsidian walls contorted. Iridescence bristled through as her will refracted the structure, re-forming the lightseep into a new walk-way that bridged towers that had always been separate.

She treaded this new path twenty stories above the ground. When she gazed across Solthar, her attention alone was enough to tune the lightseep field in orbit, morphing the planet's half-real projections into another season. Clear skies swirled with wisps of sudden cloud. Forests fluffed with blooms. Colors rippled across the vista as the holography recalibrated to Abriss's whim.

She seemed surprised at her own world's sensitivity, then laughed shyly. What had the Graven said to her?

All the years, everyone had dismissed it whenever Abriss mentioned intuiting an attendant force. She'd read too many stories or was so desperate for a peer she would invent the notion of one. The truth had been buried in the way she talked, tucked in the gnarls of philosophical phrasing. Every-one thought she'd been envisioning a future, rather than watching echoes of the past.

For her whole life, Abriss had been drawing this entity forth, hope by hope. And with no one with whom she could share her hurts, had this started as a little girl confiding her sorrows to the sky, unknowingly draw-ing out a response over time?

Leta ensured that Caiden and Threi—even overwhelmed by their sudden introduction to the luminiferity—were perceiving all the important parts, feeling the immensity of Abriss's presence, how indescribably wrought into Unity she was.

Caiden had brought Abriss a critical piece of the trinity. Threi had broken her glass heart. She was a sharp, shattered thing…

…and turned all those edges toward Leta suddenly.

The whole of Unity twisted with Abriss, with how intricately her spirit threaded it now, and Leta couldn't shift a single strand in that energetic web. She tried to flail away but her effort was swallowed up; as malleable and fickle as the luminiferity was, Abriss had it *riveted*.

She smiled. "We are waiting for you to come home, Leta."

We. How many is "we"? Leta ached for them. She couldn't guess whether the Graves were safe, couldn't sense them while her attention was this narrowed. She didn't dare try to seek them out and get further entangled or lose more control.

Abriss lifted her fingers. The Aurasever rippled space around her arms. With one thought, she cast Leta from Unity entirely. Passengers included.

Dimensional strain crushed them to bits, time slathered those into strands, and Leta, Caiden, and Threi hurtled back to their bodies.

Leta hit the softest, accustomed to this. Her spirit soaked back into her system.

Caiden made a choked sound, his body curled. C was lying protectively by his side, muzzle pushed against his lower back.

Leta rushed over. Azura gusted alongside, filling Leta with a soft energy. Caiden's spirit was jammed poorly in his body, nerves firing wrong, brain groggy, but he'd be just fine. Azura flexed a breeze across Caiden's face, stirring his sweat-curled hair.

Threi sat up on his own, hale and aware, though his eyes were distant and glistening. How long since he'd seen Solthar? Leta began to move his way but Caiden grasped her wrist and made a noise.

With a smile, she pulled free and went to Threi, helping the man to his feet. He didn't need the assistance but he didn't let her gesture go unweighed. A hardness passed out of his features as he blinked at her. That moment in the cloudcutter, minds conjoined, Leta had glimpsed the inside of his soul. She was going to give him a chance to be understood. Didn't everyone deserve that?

She felt safe as she backed away. Threi's pride and elegance combined into a strange sort of honor. He wouldn't hurt her. She was useful.

Hopefully this shut their argument up. Leta stood between the two again as they brushed themselves off and faced each other. "You see what we—what everything outside of Unity—is up against. It's only the start."

"Her grand reunion." Threi cracked his neck and grimaced up at the Dominant.

Leta still loved Abriss. But the Dynast rhetoric was imprinted in the woman so deeply, Leta couldn't see a way to convince her to consider a new perspective on what the Graven intended. Especially with the echo of a powerful Graven whispering in her mind.

If getting through to Abriss required a Graven being of comparable power, well . . . that would be either Caiden or Threi.

Threi feathered his knuckles against the bloody sash. "As an unequal, I failed to kill her before. To become perfectly Graven through a merger of the trinity, I would need Winn's help because the *Azura* is sweet on him. Is that the basis of the alliance you're proposing, Leta Nine?"

"Alliance?" Caiden scoffed, stubborn as ever.

Threi continued at louder volume, "And you need *me* because you have nothing besides. I control the Casthen, Cartographers, and passagers. I have Feran, and I have the drive to see this through. You have a larval form of the enharmonic strain; a girl transfected and irradiated to resemble a Dynast Graven, the harmonic; and Winn, a hybridized Dominant, the stabilizer, obliquely enhanced."

Caiden wore a smoldering look. Leta didn't know what he'd been through in his previous alliance with Threi, but considering they'd accomplished the impossible, she was hoping there had been good in it too.

Carefully she said, "This is so much bigger than your petty rivalry. Abriss is headed now to collapse more worlds and expand Unity, which will increase her power and make the Graven entity influencing her more coherent. Worse, she's using only an approximation of Azura's force, and has none of the Dominant. This will continually unbalance her. It will break her mind, make her more desperate or more unpredictable or more susceptible to influence.

"This can't wait until you two have chased each other around the multiverse a few more times. We need to combat Abriss's Unity with a union of our own. Yes, Threi, your Casthen, Cartographers, and passagers too. All of the multiverse allied against the immense forces she controls." *Please, you foolish men.*

Caiden, otherwise calm, was squeezing his fists closed so hard his augmented arm crackled with static. "Leta…you know Abriss. I trust you. But we can't trust *him*."

"She didn't say anything about trust," Threi snapped back. "You only have to believe I'll do as I promise. Have I done *anything* other than improve the multiverse? Anything but try to become strong enough to stop her and protect it, all these years? Is this the point where I get to say *I told you so*?"

"You wrecked this entire universe."

"Which I ordered *vacated*. If you must know, I care a great deal about the multiverse and everything in it." Emotion roughened his voice so much he paused. His gaze cut away and he appeared almost nonplussed at expressing something this genuine. "The intoxicating variety, the danger, the potential. Think it through—all along, from Çydanza to now, I've been seeking the means to put an end to Casthen oppression and ultimately the Dynast, and re-create the real balance the Graven intended."

Caiden said quietly, "What Laureli wanted."

Threi's eyes iced over at his mother's name. "Yes."

"And you will sacrifice anything and anyone to achieve it."

Threi scowled. "*Someone* has to. And I don't need your assistance to do it."

"Enough." Leta exhaled the word. "You need Caiden because if you kill him, you lose Azura forever. In ten years of searching, you never found another shred of the enharmonic energy, right? Azura may be all there is. Pure Graven spirit."

Threi enunciated carefully, "The *Azura* will stay wherever I imprison *Caiden*, until I find a way to harness it."

Caiden scoffed, "Azura can bend the laws of nature—there's nowhere you can imprison me or her."

Tendons tightened in Threi's jaw. Leta could sense that his real hesitation came from fear of connection, of relinquishing control. He'd never had an equal and was as scared of what that meant just as much as Abriss craved it.

Caiden asked Leta, "Why do we need *him*? We have Azura, the Dominant here, and you, a vessel built from Dynast genetics. If we kill him, I can take over the Casthen myself."

Exasperated, Leta raised her volume, voice near its breaking point. "How can you not see that two powerful Graven individuals leading our efforts is better than one? Even that may not be enough! All three of us have individually failed over and over against her."

Leta let that sink in.

She finished, "For now we only need to agree to stop her together. Trust one another's motivation."

Threi had characterized Leta, Caiden, and Azura as an incomplete jumble of the three Graven strains... but it was precisely that messiness that would allow them to evolve in unexpected ways. Abriss was still not perfect, nor did she have the pieces to be, and the multiverse was still collectively larger than Unity, with more diverse resources.

Leta glared at one man, then the other, and stepped back from the spot between, inviting them to bridge their distance.

Caiden's turmoil was plain on his face, and Leta felt a pang as she realized belatedly what she was asking of him: to stop living, in order to stop others from dying.

Being Graven made Caiden responsible for the world—a burden he hadn't asked for. He didn't wish to become more Graven. He believed it would invalidate his relationships and overwrite his humanity. He was being asked to sacrifice himself to protect the interests of the innocents of the multiverse, yet he hadn't spent enough time *living* in the multiverse or in Unity to love one or the other.

Please think back to the wondrous things you saw on your travels, the things you want to preserve and have the time to explore. To live in. And I'll protect you from breaking, Caiden. I'll make sure you stay yourself.

Leta held his searing eye contact as long as she could and hoped these things she couldn't say aloud still reached him.

Caiden centered on the Casthen Prime. "So we both become perfect Graven beings? Like what Abriss is trying to become?"

Threi straightened, which flexed the meeting edge of their gravitas. "For any alliance to be fair, we would need to enhance at equal rates."

"Balance," Caiden agreed, but the mistrust was thick in his voice. C, hulking beside him, growled deep enough to flutter the pool surface.

Leta held her breath. They didn't have to trust each other, they just had to work toward the same goal without getting in each other's way or at each other's throat.

Caiden said, "Say we stop Abriss: dead or captured. Then what do you want?"

"Isn't it early for that conversation? We don't need to agree on drive or—"

"All I know for sure about you is your desire to kill her. I don't even know the full *why* or when it started. So what is there to you, if that goal were removed?"

Threi reached out a hand. "Why don't you finally get to know me? Just like old times, but better."

Time looped upon itself. Threi had offered this to Caiden before, and it had hurtled Caiden on a treacherous path.

The moment stretched. Leta's heartbeat skipped.

Caiden stepped forward and grasped Threi's hand.

CHAPTER 48

FOUND AND LOST

Caiden wasn't ready to interpret it as a gesture of good faith when Threi lent him his cloudcutter ship, but the vessel did fit Azura nicely. Knife-slick, the vessel flew like a shard cut straight out of the void.

He was eager to get to family, but it unnerved him to leave Threi behind in the Graven city with the Dominant and a covey of scientists. His alliance with Threi in the past had been built on mistrust and hate. This new one was "a chance for healing," Leta had said.

Caiden stole a glance over his shoulder. She sat next to C, brushing knots out of his mane while he chewed on a petrified bone. She looked well, as if time around the Dominant and Azura together had filled up cracks in her. But then she'd always been good at masking—he might not notice she was struggling until it was too late.

"Are you still all right? Physically?" He cursed under his breath the moment he said it. Vague questions were unhelpful. Would she be honest if the answer was no?

Leta looked over and managed a smile. "Tired. But I did sleep a little. Azura helps…"

Cagey. Caiden's mind hurt him by instantly conjuring the thought that Ksiñe could help her, before he remembered his friend's uncertain fate.

He powered the cloudcutter faster.

"Egress," he warned Leta. The ship pierced a stellar egress and snapped to the other side, galaxies away. Space and time made brambled motions—probably tame stuff by Leta's standards. The cockpit recalibrated to show the new view, and a choke tripped up Caiden's exclamation. "What—"

This wasn't the universe, Naredene, that his chartings said it should be. This was *Unity*.

Aftermath surrounded the ship: bizarre swaths of nebulae trying to find equilibrium, standing ripples of warring gravitational waves, trails of debris. Fresh structures crystallized while entropy spread like wildfire.

Caiden brought up the overlay of the Cartographers' charting of Naredene, and ice stabbed through his veins. Star markers where there were no stars. Planet indicators outlining fields of frozen shards or orbs of tumultuous atmosphere.

Naredene as it had been was gone forever, one of the many universes that would be dramatically reshaped as Abriss blazed through.

"This is what 'you'll see when you get here' meant, huh?" Laythan and the crew hadn't been inside this universe when it was popped, he just set it as their rendezvous point. The old captain had provided no real information except coordinates, and Caiden wasn't ready to consider *why* he'd said nothing more.

Leta drifted over, laying a hand on Caiden's shoulder. "I might have seen wrong." She meant Ksiñe and En.

"Laythan would have said 'everything is all right' if it was."

Azura's universe transformed the debris as they flew. It now manifested not as a bubble around the ship but in controlled wafts and flickers of finely tuned changes.

The meeting point was the arboretum concourse of a Cartographer Den near the egress. The flat disk of the Den had layers tapering above and below, rife all over with glitching green atmoseals. Updated charting streamed to the cloudcutter, outlining the docks that were still safe for entry.

Caiden docked and Azura poured from the vessel when he rushed out of it. His leathery morphcoat hugged his torso tighter in response to his nervousness. Leta kept up without a word, and C stalked at his side, drawing fewer looks than usual: the passagers and Cartographers in the Den were fielding much bigger problems than a nophek who passed for tame. The dead species' corpses were lined in respectful rows while the injured were ushered to makeshift medical zones.

Caiden didn't let himself look away from the suffering, didn't skirt around it. He soaked up anger and anguish and packed it down into a hollow place for later fuel.

"Thirty percent afflicted somehow?" he read off a holosplay.

Every universe Abriss collapsed would be affected differently depending on how much—and which—of the universe's parameters differed from Unity's. The Cartographers had begun frantically calculating the mathematics of it.

Caiden helped where he could, directing people or carrying wounded, but the need never ended. Leta gently pressured him on to the arboretum.

Starship berthing pads layered on platforms supported between gigantic trees. Caiden struggled to register foreign species from familiar ones that had been bizarrely transformed by the conversion. The heart-shaped blitter leaves now dribbled in emerald strands still connected to their stems, while tarrown foliage littered the floor scarlet. Ribbons of bark tumbled in Caiden's wake as he raced toward the *Second Wind* on a middle level.

Taitn waited outside the looming freighter, a harrowed look on his face. *Crimes, no*—

"En and Ksiñe?" Caiden asked.

The sweet, brutish-looking man strode forward and collided into Caiden with a hug.

Caiden squeezed back. "Tell me."

Taitn exhaled, deflating, but was silent. His hands were gloved in bandage membranes, shaking.

Caiden prepared a Graven order—it wouldn't take much now—then Panca emerged from the ship. Ksiñe's whipkin pet clung around her neck. Tears prickled behind Caiden's eyes as he stared at her.

"Ksiñe's been taken," Panca said, managing the heft of those words with a gentle, logical tone. "We couldn't stop whatever he was dying from, his heart...they said he..." She reached up and cuddled the whipkin to her cheek.

Taitn finished quickly, "The Prime took him...We—we let him go. We don't know if she managed to save him or not."

Caiden drifted over to Panca, dazed, untethering his heart from his body like in his nightmares, the way he was conditioned to cope.

He stroked the whipkin's back. She squeaked, then warily unfurled, dimpled nose rooting around Caiden's fingers while the whiskers fanned from her cheeks. Grunting in recognition, she crawled up his arm and curled tight around his neck. He buried his face in her musky fur while waves of coarse feeling crashed through him.

Leta said, "The Dynast has the best medical capabilities in the multiverse." Her volume trailed off.

Ksiñe was either dead, or alive and in Abriss's thrall. If alive, his scientific expertise would contribute to Abriss's designs, including intimate knowledge of Caiden's genetics and Azura's peculiar nature.

Caiden whispered, "And En?"

Panca nodded and headed inside the ship. "This way."

He blinked hard. *En's here.*

Caiden ordered C to wait outside, then trailed Panca to the medical suite. Taitn and Leta followed behind, making space for his rush. The room was a nest of piled machines and instruments, open toolboxes, tissue-growth vats, and surgical implements.

En lay on a raised slab, his sleeping face striped with fleshless sections. The physical changes brought on by the rind sweep had ruined the phase of some materials, crushed the delicacy of others, and wiped the energy of most. En's body resembled a work in progress now.

"En." Caiden drifted to the bedside. There was a lonely music to En's stasis, with material regrowing and medical machines communicating in hushed tones and whines.

Laythan sat nearby beside a luminous woman in light-gray and purple Cartographers' garments. Lyli, Taitn's partner. Her translucent skin was more opaque than Caiden remembered, showing less jawbone and teeth when she smiled, wearily. Silvery ringlets cascaded around her shoulders as she bowed.

"Hello, Winn. I am so pleased to see you kept safe." Her speech had an ethereal, clinical cadence that felt familiar deep in his bones. She'd attended his accelerated aging, had seen him jump from fourteen to twenty in a flash, had healed him after his spine shattered, and had tried to undo the damage the Casthen did to him. Some juvenile logic in Caiden's mind cried, *She can heal anything.*

"Lyli, is he—"

"Alive, though comatose. Endirion has suffered minor brain damage that I am still...untangling."

Panca sat beside Laythan, who stared at nothing. Her own eyes moved slow and fatigued, facial muscles ridged with tension. Her tools were uncharacteristically haphazard, tossed in scalar fields and heaped on trays.

Ksiñe would have known what to do for En. That's why Taitn pulled Lyli here instead.

Taitn took up the doorway. "I called...I called Cheza, En's friend and the best augmentation engineer we know."

There was a catch in Taitn's voice, and Lyli's gaze floated to his, full of heartbreak for him. She said, "For now, Endirion is stable. Cheza is held up in Emporia, the front lines of the Cartographers' negotiations with the Dynast. While I do not believe the physical construction of Endirion's body is the primary obstacle, I will accept all the help I can."

Caiden touched En's cheek. The skin was hot and clammy, the metal frigid. Regulators not functioning.

"I can help," Leta said from the little hallway. Taitn swiveled to make room for her, but she stayed in a shadow. Laythan's chair squeaked as he sat straighter.

Leta turned to Panca. "I can try to direct Azura through the augmented machinery, tuning or altering it by shifting physical laws, if you'll guide me? And I can try to draw Endirion's consciousness back together in the luminiferity."

Lyli gave a little bow. "Those claims are wondrous. We will attempt anything at this point." She shot Caiden a softly questioning look.

Panca vouched first, "Leta resurrected Winn from dead. She can do all she's said. We'll slap En's wanderings back together."

Caiden could have laughed at Lyli's wide-eyed expression. He looked to Leta and forced a smile, hoping to make her feel welcome. He trusted her and he was ready to embrace help. He wasn't running anymore. "I—we can explain later how I died, but—"

"I'll look over En right away." Leta glided to En's side, seeming more comfortable with a task to focus on. Her natural frown deepened as she wrapped her fingers around En's forehead and chest. She sighed sadly and rubbed a thumb over his cheekbone before she closed her eyes.

The music of the assistant machines changed tune: Azura crept into them, then her force clotted the air, prickling it like a tiny storm. Everyone except Panca startled a little.

A smile creased Leta's eyes before she blinked them open. "He's... really strong."

"That means...?"

"His spirit isn't lost, just incoherent. But I don't know him like you all do. I'll need your help. It'll take time. And Feran—they can help us with the nervous system damage. Azura will help too."

Panca made an amused sound. "When En's back, don't tell him how many people clamored to aid him."

Caiden smiled, then noted Laythan's burdened expression. Self-blame—Caiden knew it intimately. Dark circles rimmed the man's prosthetic eyes. He nursed an enamel flask and winced when his arm moved. Joint pains or nerve damage from the event.

Laythan caught Caiden's appraisal. "Eleven universes she's tested on, big and small. I knew people who couldn't get out in time. Good people."

Ksiñe's whipkin snuggled into Caiden's morphcoat and glommed onto his chest, little claws digging into his sides. He cradled the small warmth of her while trying to wrap his mind around the scale of these problems. And *time*, of which he either never had enough or had far too much.

"Evacuations?" he asked.

Laythan sighed, breath smoky from the liquor. "Mass exodus from the universes bordering Unity, overwhelming worlds next on over."

Taitn added, "That should calm as the refugee spread reaches wider space."

"Will it? Depends on the rate, how fast the Prime needles worlds into hers."

Caiden had thought it through many times. "The Aurasever requires her Dynast cells and finely trained brain. If *she* can be tracked, we'll—the multiverse will know where the next threat is."

"The Cartographers're already tracking her, boy. Going to negotiate a truce."

"She won't speak to them if she thinks they're under Threi's thumb."

"Hold on," Taitn said at the same time Laythan's whole body swiveled to Caiden. "He's not dead?"

Time for this. Caiden inhaled. "I have a lot to explain. If you'll listen."

He'd worked so hard to earn this family. Now that he was finally free to spend time with them, to figure out what *living* meant to him in this wondrous multiverse... his time was whisked away, limited to simply being *with* them for as long as he could before he had to race Threi to Graven perfection in order to combat Abriss. He was Gravenly conscripted to serve a purpose larger than himself by giving everything up again, but in a crueler way: not by running but by *changing*.

I didn't get to choose what I am, but I can choose what to do with it.

A few moments, first, with the family he'd worked hard to build. He'd earned that much.

———————

Leta retreated to a private copse of slickertrees in the arboretum, doubly exhausted from trying to fit herself in among strangers, and from attempting to sort all the selves of Endirion Day that had intertwisted in the luminiferity. She was confident she could do it, and with Lyli, Cheza, Panca, Feran, and Azura all helping to restore him, he might revive better than new.

Laythan had squashed her in a hug without a word when she'd reported her confidence, and she hadn't known how to respond. His gesture brimmed with gratitude and acknowledgment—Leta had escaped before it made her cry.

She was near a limit. Her spiritual exhaustion piled atop regular overfunctioning. Proxyless, her disintegration would worsen. Being around Azura soothed it temporarily with the energies her engineered body lacked, but that was merely a new stopgap like the Proxies had been. Perhaps Lyli could help in the meantime but Leta needed Feran's Graven expertise.

She made her way through the trees, away from activity and noise. She'd hoped to slink through the luminiferity and brave a glimpse of the Graves before her worry over them corroded her completely. Perhaps she'd try to find Ksiñe too—that was even better use of her. If Ksiñe had lived, then Abriss possessed someone with knowledge of the Graven pieces she was missing.

Once Leta sat, having found a bench facing the giant windows and a view of the transformed universe beyond, better judgment sat with her. Abriss's stars would whisper about her if she ruffled the luminiferity too much here in Unity or made the wrong Grave aware of her presence.

Leta unfocused her eyes and let her mask fall and her body shut itself down in private. Her face relaxed and her words dissolved—the world grew soft around her.

Tears welled up without affect from layers deep. She sat with her family's unknown fate. If the Graves had died or been murdered... perhaps she could reconnect with their dissimulated spirits. If they were alive, they would fall back under Abriss's power—whether that meant care or thralldom, or if the difference between the two even mattered. If they hadn't escaped Unity, Abriss would locate and bring them home.

Think of what you love, not what you lost. Dejin's comforting contact. Tayen's refreshing bluntness. Dian's protective streak, Aohm's serenity, Sisorro's playfulness. Isme... He'd always believed in her, no matter what. Abriss...

"Hey," Caiden said quietly as he approached behind her.

Leta crushed her worries and wiped her face. She must've failed to soften, since he responded with an old familiarity, sitting beside her with a concerned knowing, but not pressuring her to respond. Azura came with him but was faint behind luminiferous veils. Leta's body did soothe at the presence, as if she'd stepped into a luscious hot bath.

She rummaged up a smile and said, "I'm so tired."

"Your heart's broken."

"In all directions."

"I know you're trying to shutter it away, but you don't have to hide the truth from me. It's all right to hurt." Caiden curled a strong arm around her shoulders.

How was this man's kindness not killed by the Casthen or that decade as a feral thing?

She peered up at him. "The tiniest bit better already. You?"

Time with his family had soothed him, but there was a fresh hurt in his eyes. He'd seen what his new gravitas inflicted. Even the look of him portended something he hated: freckles deeper and thicker, and a bend of reality at the borders of him, imperceptible to anyone not looking for it.

Having grown up around Abriss, she couldn't separate her real feelings from those influenced by gravitas. She sensed him tense with hyperawareness, making an effort to rein it tightly.

He replied, "I feel better knowing you're here and safe."

"You *are* needy. Also, that sounds quite saccharine."

That made him laugh too.

In his nice, husky voice she liked, Caiden said, "Everyone wants to meet you, for real this time. Before we leave for Casthen business."

We. There was a lot to bear in that last sentence, but it was whisked away by fresh nervousness at meeting Caiden's family.

"They'll love you," he said. "I'm pretty sure Laythan already wants to adopt you. I told everyone you might not be talkative, and not to pressure you. Just be present, that's all."

She sat for a while, not ready. It was warm and the view imposing. The altered expanse emblemized all they were up against.

Caiden was patient. "I want to talk about what we can do for your family. Everything is a mess, every which way, but… I'm not ignoring that."

Stars forfend, he always tries too hard.

"I promise," he said, "we'll do what we can to save them too."

"Be careful what you promise again."

His shoulders shook with a silent chuckle. "I can promise to do my best."

Leta fell sideways and hugged his waist. "I'm happy the best parts of you didn't change."

CHAPTER 49

DECADE GROWN

Threi Cetre sprinted. The slap of his footfalls ricocheted through light-less labs and empty corridors. A genetic doorway unsheathed before he reached it and knotted together behind him. Sounds suddenly muffled as foliage invaded the empty spaces.

Crimes' sake, they made a jungle of it. Exotic plants orbited balls of light. Trees stood cramped into absurd shapes by the walls, dripping lichen and bioluminescent vines. Gemlike fruits dangled on spiral stems. Weird, to see in person the things he'd heard described in detail.

His coat's skirt panels slapped about his legs as he ran and turned a sharp corner into the pool chamber, then slowed in long strides.

Empty.

"Feran!"

His nerves tingled. Panting, he marched to the first of the side chambers—empty. *Empty.*

"Fer—"

They jogged out of the third room and froze, eyes wide. Metallic hues sketched patterns of relief across their shoulders. Threi's liquid lenses ghosted some ultraviolet spectra into his vision, betraying flitters of nervous purple across the bridge of Feran's nose.

"You did come," they said in Andalvian, deftly folding in layers more meaning. "Why did you run?"

Peach stripes wisped across their temples. They knew why.

Out of breath still, Threi strode over and crushed Feran to his chest.

The reality of them, previously impossible, validated his freedom in one gesture. An emblem of how he'd defied the obscene number of things that might've killed him in the past collection of days.

Feran hesitantly wrapped their arms around him. "It's nice to meet you, too, in person."

They were shorter than he'd imagined. Not that any endaal were tall. Smelled nocturnal, nectarous. Skin dewy.

Threi planted his hands on Feran's shoulders and pushed them back. "The rind flux worked. It's a Graven city, disguised or dusted over into a planet. Dominant inside. Completely intact."

Stripes tickled down the sides of Feran's neck. "You *do* get a fearsome sparkle in your eyes when you use that tone of voice. I imagined so."

"What tools do you need?" Threi swept off into one of the rooms. He grabbed the obvious kits into a bin and kicked it outside, rifled for the rare glasswork, then started into the next. The Casthen scientists had outfitted a base of operations around the Dominant already, but Feran's lab had cultivation tools that existed nowhere else, locked down here with them.

Threi called back, "Caiden Winn and I made an alliance over mutual goals. You may get to vivisect him yet." He tossed some shadeheel rods on the pile of materials to go, then turned. "You're staring."

"I have had your voice for ten years but only *saw* you once before that, only briefly." Ultraviolet ghosted a flush of color in their fingers, which they picked at.

Threi grinned. "Lucky you. Stare away."

Feran's retinal eyeshine was a lavender color. Their personnel file hadn't included that detail. "I will need the biophotonic field visualizer, or a new one, and some lisavon linguistic analyzers. What does the new Dominant look like?" Their voice rushed with familiar excitement.

Heat from the sprint started to cool, filling Threi with a shimmery sort of energy. Still smiling, he said, "You'll get to see for yourself."

He gathered the other instruments on a mag cart in a hurry and pushed it to the deck outside of the labs. Then headed back for Feran.

The Dynast doorway slithered open.

Assistive motors around the endaal's hips whispered as they came to a stop on the other side. Threi stalled. Voice only, he'd forgotten their disability. No matter—countless options now for improving the frames, after ten years of development time the Casthen had poured into xenid prosthetics. Or advanced healing procedures if they wished.

Feran stood hesitating at the edge of the inner rooms. Lambent fronds arced overhead. Light glazed across Feran's high tail of hair filaments and the ragged stripes starting to slip down the skin of their legs.

Threi reassured, "You'll be returning, you know. This invasive and honestly ridiculous jungle of yours will still be here."

"It's not the return. It's the leaving…"

Years in a tiny world. Threi hadn't been able to leave his soon enough. Feran's was lush and homey.

They'd had nothing to do but experiment and learn, which meant Feran's imprisonment had gained Threi an expert Graven metamorphicist out of the whole unfortunate arrangement. Knowledge to rival Abriss herself.

"Scared?" he asked softly, stepping close.

"Of the outside? Or of you?"

Vocal gravitas hadn't carried through the older style of two-way communication between his universe prison and the lab. The Dominant's energy, Feran had surmised, jaded their own physiology to the effect.

Feran's pupils dilated, purple hues lucent deep inside. Their skin darkened except for cirrus vibrating across their eyes and neck—but for the chromatophore voids over their cheeks and the soft cleft of their throat.

Threi bent toward them. "Your mind's too valuable, Fer. I can't let you out of my sight."

"Oh. Lucky me."

Threi flashed a smile and slid a hand around Feran's jaw. "I need you."

"And?"

Still bold in point-blank Graven range. Threi's voice, touch, scent, and body heat would be a gravity well—maybe they'd been right about the desensitization. Tiny scarlet flecks and silver streaks danced at the edges of Feran's eyes.

"I'll take care of you," he answered, and leaned the rest of the way slowly to kiss them, quiet and patient.

Lips soft as petals, they'd teased once. Or was it the other way around? Confirmed, either way.

Feran made a delicate sound. Their breath quickened when he pulled away. Their fingers flirted with the seam of his coat. "And...?"

Threi growled and slid his cheek against theirs, voice light beside their ear, "You are valuable, but what makes you think you can make demands of the Casthen Prime?"

Feran wrapped both arms around his neck and pulled him in with the weight, chest against his. They whispered a kiss across his lips, then bit the bottom one with surprisingly soft piscine teeth. "And?"

"I'll protect you."

Feran smiled. "It's quite nice to still be needed."

Their fingertips raked into curls at the nape of Threi's neck, sending electricity shorting down his spine. He marveled at the surreality as he locked his arms around them: a voice and connection given body for the first time in forever. He'd anticipated that years of fantasy born from boredom would've killed the mystique of Feran, but each match of idea to reality was deliciously new.

"I still need a lot from you." Threi kissed his way back to Feran's lips. "A decade," he began, pausing for deep breaths while tasting mint and springtime down their neck, "of... intellectual foreplay... is plenty."

Threi stared up at the Graven Dominant, letting it sear his retinas and throw strange afterimagery behind his blinks. Its light melted beneath his skin; a peculiar candescence that could have been lightning stretched out to the thinness of a veil, or a bottled star tossing watery rays all over. In the periphery of vision, observed indirectly, the mass turned black as void, then disappeared entirely.

Measurement devices bristled all around it, six cautious meters away. No one had touched or probed the thing yet, though Threi considered ordering one of the grunts to walk at it. Would they crisp? Ascend?

Threi was eager to witness Feran's expression when they saw the Dominant for the first time. He glanced at the entrance. A figure entered—just Winn.

"Where's Feran?" Winn called.

"Corralled by the other scientists to go over preliminary measurements. Safety, the group insisted."

Poor, useful Forañae Vitrika.

Winn strode to meet Threi on the dais but ignored the narrow walk-ways the Casthen had built over the quicksilvery moat between. He walked straight atop the water. His Azura formed ripples dense enough to support his weight.

"Show-off." Threi crossed his arms and smiled. He'd been told there was a thin line between his smiles and his snarls.

Azura's spiritual presence clinging to the young man dimpled space and licked up shadows and flashes where they shouldn't be. He approached with his back straight and his eyes fierce, as if he enjoyed flaunting something Threi could never control.

Threi was impatient, not impressed.

Winn said, "I've seen that look on your face before."

Which? Threi had many looks. "Did you miss it?"

Winn stopped outside of lunging distance. He tugged creases out of the layered gray Cartographer uniform he'd chosen, to stand out from the Casthen—cute. He still had many thorns.

Motion pulled Threi's gaze over Winn's shoulder. "Our expert has arrived."

Feran hurried across one of the bridgings, but their pace slowed the moment they looked up. Face brightened with awe, lips parted, and opaline speckles flocked through their skin. Much as Threi had expected, but it was still sweet to see.

They approached at sleepwalker speed, one palm raised, measuring by feel and by step. A holosplay bloomed over their other gloved hand, data sprouting like one of their gardens.

"P-Prime." Their voice shuddered on the brim of fear.

Less expected.

Threi gave an elegant bow, one hand indicating the phenomenon behind him. "Your new Dominant to study."

Let no one say he never bestowed gifts for free.

Dark wisps crowded Feran's eyes. Their gaze didn't shift off the Graven Dominant thing, didn't saccade in wonder, and their lips didn't smile. A foul feeling started to squeeze out Threi's smug warmth.

"This…" Feran quavered. "This is a Dominant Graven."

Threi flopped his arms at his sides. "Yes, we know. That's why I called you here, sweet scientist."

"No." Their gaze flashed down to Threi, then flicked to Winn.

"Feran?" Winn said, confused.

They shook their head slowly. "How could I have missed it before? In person, the amplitude difference is so stark. Threi… *This* thing right here is a Dominant strain of Graven energy. The flesh I watched over and revived in the Casthen Harvest… the source of Winn's genes… *That was not a Dominant Graven.*"

A chill spread bumps across Threi's skin. He folded his arms. "It was a Graven body, but it wasn't Dynast. You said it wasn't anything like the *Azura* either. So?"

"It had *some* Dominant energy within it, but…" Feran's stare was pinned on Winn in a way that sizzled Threi's nerves with alarm. He could almost feel a force gathering beneath his feet, ready to pitch the three of them onto a course he hadn't anticipated. Feran said, "It was the complete trinity. All three strains, balanced, in the flesh. A perfect Graven being… that's what he was made from."

CHAPTER 50

HALLOWED GRAVES

Abriss Cetre folded her legs up on the massive bed in her oversized chamber, a fifteen-meter-long rectangle of immaculate empty space. Memories stained the luminiferity here, too thick to ever let her sleep. The bed was of the ancient sort clad in blankets, and it was the sole holdout, as if her aides had removed one furnishing every ephemeris year she didn't use this lonely space.

The room conjured heartache that Abriss was holding very well at bay. She was being reinvented; her spaces could take on new meaning as well.

I am Abriss Cetre of the Seventh Primal Etheric Line of the Dynast Lineage, daughter of the dead, and mother of the future. The Graven are imagining through me.

The room was set many stories high in the Dynast Hold, with one whole wall open to a view of Solthar's night scythed by eclipse. Nebulae projected in an inky ceiling, and the lightseep walls brimmed with enough glow to read by. In front of her, a holosplay draped: a map of Unity and the border worlds, writ in light. She shifted it and scribbled notations with a fingernail.

The Aurasever glittered on her hands, starting to fuse with the skin after her treatments, and if she were honest about all her new sensations and expanded cognizance, the technology seemed *eager* for its task.

Or it is I who is eager, she thought, and it was one of those Graven thoughts: gifted from something not-her, yet it appeared in her head in her own voice, not altogether separate.

The very instrument of her body—if she could maintain it—gave her the energy to create worlds. Her power was incredibly unstable between the incomplete copy of the *Azura* strain—unfit for an organic system—and the absence of the Dominant to bind it. Ksiñe's work could keep restoring her balance, but it was a tenuous thing.

From behind, a soft human hum rose absently, matching the melody of a choral elegy sung far below, carried to the room on the wind. Abriss paused and stifled a small laugh, to not disturb him. It had been the right choice to model his larynx exactly. Isme had always possessed a wonderful voice.

Turning back to her task, now with pleasant accompaniment, she marked candidate coordinates in the map and ran the geometry, twisting it to see the multidimensional shape. The link to celestial structures and the timing of orbits would be critical. The Dynast's scientific community was still evaluating the physics of collapse, but there should have existed means of triggering chain reactions—a keystone bubble popped in a foam mass of galactic structures.

She had nothing else to do now but hurry into the future. With every heartbeat, she lost another splinter of time. The multiverse was indescribably vast, making her task just as immense, and she was one mortal being.

Though not, anymore, so alone.

"These three points." A waft of confirmation filled her. It felt right. She mentally indicated a constellation of spaces where outer universes met Unity's rind. "A trinity. Isn't that fitting?"

Abriss twisted on the bed to face the two Proxies standing by the wall behind her. Isme stopped singing, but he beamed instead. Svelte muscle and sinew, he cut a crisp figure against the glowing wall. Dian, on the other side, contrasted with bulk and complexity.

They were both unfinished but there was something about the raw state of them that Abriss found compelling. Lightning filaments tangled around the midnight-black medium of their temporary skins. There the energy from their bodies made its own confluences, the patterns snapping with force. The lightseep in the core of them was not fake this time, not imitation: Abriss could chisel shards of indestructible spacetime now.

The way these Proxies were shaped, you could say they were human, then the next moment you would doubt the claim. They confused the eye, suggesting sheaths of ghostly form in each motion. But one could not deny they were elegant, and beautiful, and as terrifying as the unknown had always terrified the living.

Dian had opted to keep the sacred geometries that had painted his synthetic skin before: the same manner of arcs and angles, perfect mathematics describing the language of the cosmos. Bristling protectively, he asked, "Is it safe for us three to split apart?"

Abriss slid off the bed and smiled as she waited for it...

Isme approached, saying, "We won't be separate. See there?" He indicated one of the dimensions of the celestial arrangement. "This large-scale wave structure links us."

Dian huffed and crossed his arms.

Abriss could be three places at once—and more than that, soon. The Aurasever was built inside these new Proxies, where no one could steal it. Their luminiferous heartstrings were braided directly to hers, where no one could sway them. And their true bodies were locked up where no one could find them.

No more numbers: in the novels that used to populate her workroom, the best swords were given names. Abriss had no delusion that what she had crafted were weapons.

Two alive. Two dead. Two missing. But the missing—Leta discounted—were in Unity under the watch of her heavens, and even the dead might be luminiferously gathered. It was her aim, after all, to join dimensions and transform the very concept of *death*.

Abriss relayed her coordinates to other divisions and closed the holosplay. Its reflections dissolved off the glossy lightseep surfaces and left the room all the more empty, if not for the song that reverberated, mellifluous. She crossed to the precipice wall and could almost make out the masses below. Where her vision failed in Solthar's low light, her new senses picked up thrumming hearts and buzzing spirits.

My people aren't broken beings that I need to fix. My work is simply to align to this energy that's creating a world to support me. Everything flows from there.

She was still shy of these ideas that her life was meant to have ease and joy, that toil did not need to come with pain to have value, and that her feelings were allowed to take up space. As she let a tiny bloom of excitement unfurl in her chest, a familiar presence stroked her heart, unharnessed the tension from her shoulders, and filled the Aurasever with warmth. She wasn't alone.

"Shall we do a test, then?" she asked the two.

The Graves' steps were soundless but made ripples through the lightseep obsidian.

"I'll prepare ships and escort," said Isme.

Dian mused, "We should test the new targetable stellar egress first."

Abriss inhaled Solthar's resinous night air. "Yes. Why not."

She clasped her hands—laced with the power to create and destroy—and gazed lovingly on the sky of her ancestors. *Luminiferous Graven, I have faith.*

Faith in all that has fallen into place to restore your world. I have the strength to bring it about and the perspective to understand your involvement. I am in your service, and that of every consciousness returned to expanded being, every spirit wishing we would hear their voice and invite participation in our reality. I shall hear them. I hear you.

"Let us co-create this grand reunion of being."

The story continues in...

Ethera Grave

Book Three of the Graven

Coming in 2023

GLOSSARY

Abriss Cetre—The Prime of the Dynast faction of Unity. She and her brother, Threi Cetre, are the last direct descendants on the Dynast family line. Abriss possesses the highest rank of Graven genetics in any current living being. Due to the harmonious "gravitas" created by her genes, her presence inspires love and loyalty in all species. Through advanced astrology calculated in the Dynast Hold's incomparable orrery, she is able to divine information about events, individuals, and the past and future. Abriss governs Unity peacefully with the help of various councils and bodies, largely ignoring the multiverse outside of Unity. Her focus is on scientific, anthropological, and philosophical research about the Graven. Abriss believes the Graven aimed to correct the multiplicity of the multiverse—caused by an ancient catastrophe—and unite it back into central Unity to make space and time one continuum of predictable physical laws.

Andalvian (endaal)—A humanoid species whose chromatophoric skin cells act like colored pixels, reflecting their brain activity in changing patterns and colors. Andalvian emotions are expressed involuntarily on their skin, but their culture is stoic and dispassionate, valuing composure. They are sharply intelligent, straightforward, and honest, most often involved in the sciences, and heavily involved in Cartographer affairs. Their native language is rich with multiple meanings and contextual nuance, able to condense multiple phrases into one. All Andalvians are from Andalvia and of the endaal species, but not all endaal are accepted by Andalvia. Some raciations have variations in chromatophore structure and expression, and additional physical attributes.

atmoseal—A membrane of energy and particulates commonly found in place of an airlock, sealing in pressure and gases. The atmoseal stretches over the opening of a passageway or ship aperture. Closely related to cloudsuit technology.

Cartographer—The Cartographers are a long-standing and diversely membered organization dedicated to mapping the expanding multiverse, understanding its content, and making it safer for travelers. They facilitate first contact with newfound cultures and organize ambassadorial trips to invite worlds into the wider multiversal culture. They maintain a free, public database of information, and charge for specific chartings, while paying passagers for data on newly charted territory and related work. The Cartographers' efforts in cultural exchange, education, and mediation have prevented or alleviated galactic wars throughout centuries, though they are not a governing force nor do they operate a military. When Threi Cetre took up the role of Casthen Prime, he allied the Casthen organization with the Cartographers to combine their vast resources and operations for the betterment of the multiverse, while also opening up more revenue potential for passagers.

Casthen—A private organization governed by their Prime, Threi Cetre, after the death of the previous leader, Çydanza, at the hands of Caiden and Threi. Having previously monopolized economy, trade, and mercenary services for centuries, the Casthen regime was overhauled to better moral standing and allied with the Cartographers to contribute their considerable resources to multiversal betterment. The Casthen ranks are still populated primarily by hybrids from interbreeding and genetic engineering projects, resistant to multiversal variances and illnesses. Their hidden headquarters, the Casthen Harvest, was exposed during Threi and Caiden's coup and is now open to regular multiversal business.

cloudsuit—A body harness netting that emits a membrane across the user's body, like a second skin. The membrane's material puffs apart into a vaporous field of protective particles that regulate personal atmosphere and protect from external factors. It was designed to be an accessible standard for most species. There are variations of this style of suit for use underwater and in other inimical environments.

crossover—The process of crossing through a rind from one universe to another. This involves physiological adjustment to changes in physics on the other side, and exposure to unique energy fluctuations within. Depending on the nature of the individual rind, crossover may impair, destroy, or alter biology and technology. Some things can exist within a universe safely but cannot cross over without detriment. The Cartographers maintain an ongoing database of such universal parameters.

CWN82—A medium-size universe that had been erroneously reported as inhospitable in order to hide Casthen operations within, including an unnamed agrarian planet—Caiden's homeworld of isolated workers—and RM28, a nophek habitat planet onto which Caiden's population was shipped as fodder.

Çydanza—The former Casthen Prime, a vishkant who controlled her subjects through blackmail and emotional manipulation. As a long-lived species, she had remained the head of the Casthen for as long as anyone could remember. Caiden and Threi together managed to murder her, with Threi taking over Casthen operations thereafter.

Dominant Graven—The name given to the origin of the Graven genes from which Caiden was engineered, his genetic gaps filled with material from other species. This type is different from the Dynast Graven genetics that Threi and Abriss Cetre possess from the Dynast line. The nature of the so-called Dominant is a highly classified Casthen secret that Threi buried even deeper after he took control of the organization. As Caiden understands, it is contained in the subterra of the Casthen Harvest, and its form is unknown.

Dynast—The governing endarchy of Unity. The Dynast are dedicated to the harmonious functioning of all planetary systems within Unity, and the search for knowledge about the ancient Graven. Their centralized government is led by an assembly under control of an appointed Prime descended from the Dynast family. The Dynast believes that the fall of the Graven civilization happened at the same time that Unity was divided into the new, expanding worlds of the multiverse, and that these outer worlds are corrupt and untenable.

Dynast Hold—A palace at one of the poles of Solthar, the planet at the center of Unity and therefore the multiverse as a whole. The Hold is the heart of Dynast operations and the home of Abriss Cetre. It is constructed primarily of lightseep obsidian, filled out with materials more amenable to habitation.

Glasliq—A rare type of material and also the term for starships that use it in their construction: a crystalline matter that can morph between liquid and solid, reconfiguring shape on a metallic frame, making it supremely agile and resilient against universal conditions. One Glasliq vessel belonged to Threi until Caiden repurposed the Glasliq onto the stripped fuselage of the *Azura*.

glave—General term for a personally equipped item of defensive or offensive weaponry. Glave technology varies in type and effect, and is sourced from a variety of cultures.

gloss—The most valuable substance in the multiverse, gloss is an extremely rare energetic material, developed inside the maturing brains of nophek creatures. It can take both solid and liquid form, and is utilized to power Graven technology and generate starship fuel. Some believe that gloss is produced by the parasitization of nophek brains and the crystallization of the pineal gland and surrounding tissues.

Graven—An ancient species and civilization about which much is still unknown. An extinction event wiped out most traces of the Graven—both genetics and technology—leaving behind architectural ruins and remnants across the multiverse. There are various theories as to whether the Graven participated in or even created the multiverse, or if they were indeed wiped out in the same event that divided Unity into expanding daughter universes. Graven genetics remain in the human descendants of the Dynast family, presumed to be the last holdout of the Graven's participation in physical life.

Graven trinity—The Graven energetic forces are divided into three types or strains: harmonic, enharmonic, and stabilizer. One is the Dynast type, which is physically embodied in the genes of the Dynast family, and represents harmony and affinity, a structuring force that is the root of the "gravitas" effect. Another type has been identified as that emitted by the *Azura*, a spiritual or luminiferous energy, expansive and entropic. The third type is proposed to be emergent from the union of the two opposite strains as a stabilizing and balancing factor representing control. The three are sometimes conceptualized as body and spirit balanced by a cohesive force, or as order and chaos controlled by neutrality.

Graves—Abriss's Graven research has sought to approximate the physical nature, consciousness, sensory extension, and luminiferous existence of the Graven species. She has made extensive progress via conditioning a group of individuals of various species through a complex biological process of radiation and gene transfection. Her goal became to unify the Graven trinity within a physical body of non-Graven makeup. The Graves are able to consciously access the luminiferity, a spiritual domain of collective consciousness freed from space and time, where accumulative knowledge is available non-locally. The Dynast hopes that this new information domain will give them fresh insight into who and what the Graven were.

gravitas—The Dynast's term for the loyalty-inducing effect generated by biological beings with Graven genetics. It is conceptualized as a proximity field around the individual, affecting the various senses to degrees dependent on species and physical mitigations. As there are multiple types of Graven energy, the effect of gravitas is assumed to be different for each type.

holosplay—A detailed holographic display. Light organizes along a three-dimensional gridded field of tensor points in the air.

lightseep obsidian—The physical condensation of energy structures previously existing in immaterial dimensions un-phased with physical reality. After the rupture of the singular universe into many, the vibration of the Graven's lightseep slowed and materialized into visible matter, appearing crystalline and transparent. Lightseep is impossible to move, break, or tool, but many of the lightseep ruins throughout the multiverse have been colonized and repurposed using other materials inside.

luminiferity—A nonphysical dimension of energy and information from which physical reality manifests. It is conceptualized as a collective field of consciousness that exists outside of but in relation to linear spacetime, and it is believed that individual consciousnesses are condensations of this field. After death, the consciousness re-expands into the luminiferity. Abriss aims to access the accumulated knowledge and experience inhabiting this dimension through the Graves, who are able to detach their consciousnesses from the physical and inhabit the luminiferity as coherent entities.

morphcoat—A jacket made of a morphic material that changes qualities in response to mental state or mood. Useful when traversing frequently between environments and temperatures. Closely related to the morphfabric developed by the Dynast.

multiverse—The combined conglomerate of variously sized bubble-shaped universes embedded within one another or stuck together like a foam. Their shared surfaces are "rinds" of energy that separate differences in physics between universe interiors. At an unknown point in history, smaller universes began to bubble off the outer border of Unity, the original singular universe at the center of the inflating multiverse. On the fringes of the multiverse, new universes are constantly developing and expanding.

nophek—A rare quadruped mammal species from an unknown native planet. Their biology can exist only in specific universal parameters without medical intervention. Nophek are vicious and intelligent carnivorous pack animals. Reddish-black in color, their muscular bodies range from one to two meters tall at the withers. They are covered in a mix of fur and rough, scaly skin. As a nophek matures, highly valuable gloss crystallizes within its brain. The value of gloss led the Casthen—headed by Çydanza at the time—to farm nophek on a clandestine planet, RM28. Caiden's homeworld population on a nearby planet was raising feed animals to be shipped to RM28 until a rogue disease wiped out these bovine and the slave population was sent instead. Caiden survived and healed from this trauma, ultimately taking a nophek pup as a pet from among the litter he rescued from the Casthen Harvest.

passager—A free individual registered with the Cartographers as a multiversal explorer, bound to a code of rights and allowed access to advanced Cartographer services.

Prime—The singular leader of a sufficiently large organization.

prinna—A semi-corporeal species that is a temporid—a category of xenid that experiences time differently, either sensorily or biologically. Prinna have delicate musculoskeletal systems and somewhat gaseous layered outer bodies. They vibrate temporally, with impressions of their being—mass, voice, and other sensory elements—extending in front of the current moment and lagging behind them. They are not humanoid but are able to produce common languages and are highly intelligent and curious beings.

Proxy—One of the hybrid organic-inorganic mechanical bodies designed by Abriss Cetre specifically for each of the seven Graves. The Proxies remotely contain and are driven by the Graves' individual consciousnesses, allowing their real bodies to remain safe within the Dynast Hold.

rind—An interstitial space between universes, like an energy membrane, dividing universes from one another. Rinds can be passed through without resistance, but not all physiologies or technology can cross over without damage. The alterations in physics that rinds impress on objects passing through are individual to each rind.

RM28—A mostly desert planet with the right environmental conditions to support nophek physiology. The Casthen established nophek packs here, and sustained them with periodic feed shipments from a nearby agrarian planet.

saisn—Tall, lean humanoid xenids known for their fine muscular control and sensitive nervous systems. All saisn develop a specialized sensory organ in the brain that is visible as a transparent, faceted core in their forehead. They are immersed in a "sense-sea"—a broad frequency range of sensory detail. Saisn culture is philosophical and refined, politically complex, and quite secretive to outsiders. Within the Cartographers, saisn often serve on the culture council and as ambassadors to newly discovered worlds and first-contact missions.

scalar gravity—Artificial gravity generated in a patterned matrix of nodes and antinodes within a short range. These scalar gravity fields pattern force in space to levitate objects or to anchor them against surfaces. This gravity system is used for starships, stations, and on a small scale for maneuvering objects or creating force fields.

scour—A tubular chamber that can cleanse and restore xenids of all biological type. It cleans skin and clothing, heals minor wounds, kills parasites, and eliminates internal waste. Scour technology is common throughout the multiverse.

Solthar—A planet at the center of Unity, which is also the center of the multiverse. Some speculate the core of the planet is liquid lightseep, a unique small universe, a special black hole, or a great machine generating the universe. Solthar is the Dynast's homeworld, on which sits the Dynast Hold. An orbital field of lightseep obsidian shards is used to refract reality on the planet's surface and blend real features with holographic ones for a variety of terrain, biomes, and weather.

stellar egress—Remnant Graven technology: instantaneous two-way spacetime shortcuts from one specific location in the multiverse to another specific location. They not only cut down on travel time but allow entrance into universes while bypassing the need to cross through a rind. This can open up exploration in universes otherwise too dangerous to cross over into.

Threi Cetre—The Casthen Prime and a descendant of the Dynast family line. His Graven rank and thereby his gravitas are less than his sister Abriss Cetre's, thought to be a result of the line's inbred nature and general Graven dilution. Threi—originally playing three political sides—conscripted Caiden to join him at the Casthen Harvest and ultimately to depose the former Casthen Prime, Çydanza. Threi afterward assumed the role of Casthen Prime despite being imprisoned in Çydanza's universe by Caiden: the universe's rind is impassable except by bridging it with the universe generated by the *Azura*.

Unity—Once the sole universe during the time of the Graven civilization, Unity is the largest universe and the most central to the entirety of the multiverse. It is slowly inflating and absorbing planets and other celestial bodies at its expanding border. The Dynast faction governs Unity, and has immigration programs for affected border worlds. The physical and metaphysical laws within Unity are so well understood, nearly all disease and ailment is preventable, life spans can be lengthened, education is free, one language is common, technology has perfected resource generation and waste management, and citizens understand how to align with reality to manifest their desires and needs. For many, Unity is considered the paragon of safety and comfort.

ursgen—Generally bipedal xenids averaging two and a half meters tall, with a leanly muscular, lanky build; long, thick tail; broad face and small eyes; long, expressive ears; and a nearly hairless body. Their thick skin ranges through dark brown and gray shades. Their culture is nonviolent and reclusive, originally from outside Unity but long since adapted to it, drawn to Unity's harmonious principles. Ursgen in Unity tend to intersperse a pidgin language into the common tongue, though their native language is based on touch and pulse.

whipkin—A short-furred, egg-laying mammal around one-half meter long from nose to tail. They are omnivores adapted to a saline woodland environment, with long-fingered paws for climbing, and patagia between forelimbs and hind limbs for gliding and swimming. They are extremely intelligent, but shy and reclusive in the wild.

xenid—Generic term for an individual of an alien species, usually but not exclusively applied to nonhumans.

ACKNOWLEDGMENTS

This novel was written and edited entirely during the Covid-19 global pandemic, across seventeen months alone in isolation, while I was also finishing up and launching the first book, *Nophek Gloss*...among many other trials. The support I had from a distance kept me alive and able. My heartfelt thanks to all the librarians, booksellers, reviewers, bloggers, and communities of readers who made me feel welcomed with my debut. Your support of *Nophek Gloss* and excitement for this sequel propelled me and removed a layer of loneliness.

Deep gratitude to my superagent, Naomi Davis, a stalwart advocate who always has my back even when I'm jumping at shadows. Their enthusiasm, sensitivity, and sharp thinking is a huge asset to this industry.

To my editor, Brit Hvide, for helping me hammer my frantic draft into shape with much-needed fresh insight!

A big thank-you to the whole editorial and production team under the guidance of Bryn A. McDonald. To Rachelle Mandik, who understands all the commas I don't, fixes my made-up terms, and adds critical clarity. To Crystal Shelley and Janine Barlow, the last line of typo defense and another stage helping to sand the story's rough ends and sharpen the edges. Thank you also to the formatting team, who carefully corral all these words into the shape of a book.

Cheers to Lauren Panepinto and Mike Heath for another exciting cover!

Love to the entire Orbit US and UK teams for helping this book reach readers. Angela Man, Angeline Rodriguez, Ellen Wright, Laura Fitzgerald, Paola Crespo. And on the UK side Anna Jackson, Nadia Saward, Nazia

Khatun, Madeleine Hall. There are many other hard workers behind the publishing veil who have helped ferry this book along—though I'm not told all your names or roles, I see your work in the final product and the flow of this book onward to readers. Thank you.

I am so grateful to the family and friends who checked in on me during the pandemic, and writerly groups like the Alliance and the Bunker, who made isolation that much less isolating. Special hugs to Annaleis Cetrangolo for the daily check-ins that brought me back to reality when time started to blur together.

I wouldn't be standing this tall if not for EJ DeBrun—thank you for the commiseration and craft discussions, for ensuring I was fed or remembered to eat, for sometimes being the only face I saw for weeks, and for nerding out with me over all the things that kept me alive during lockdown. The space mahjong is for you.

My generous critique partners restored my perspective on my manuscript in the final stretch. To Al Hess, for his sensitivity read and keen eye for clarity; to Sunyi Dean, for always being a listening ear and for her sharp instinct for structure and flow; and to Rachel Fikes, for refilling my well of confidence when I needed it most.

Love incalculable to Shawn Hansen for the story art that healed my scabbing heart, and for helping me find logic or lack thereof in the things that pushed me closer to a ledge.

My cat, Soki, has been a very good boy locked up with me for over a year, soothing my woes with many soft snuggles. Extra gratitude to another red cat, for making tomorrow possible.

And finally, to the synchronicities that showed me the world was listening.

extras

about the author

Essa Hansen is an author, swordswoman, and falconer. She is a sound designer for science fiction and fantasy films at Skywalker Sound, with credits in movies such as *Doctor Strange* and *Avengers: Endgame*.

Find out more about Essa Hansen and other Orbit authors by registering for the free monthly newsletter at orbitbooks.net.

if you enjoyed
AZURA GHOST

look out for

FAR FROM THE LIGHT OF HEAVEN

by

Tade Thompson

The colony ship Ragtime *docks in the Lagos system, having travelled light years from home to bring one thousand sleeping souls to safety among the stars.*

Some of the sleepers, however, will never wake — and a profound and sinister mystery unfolds aboard the gigantic vessel. Its skeleton crew are forced to make decisions that will have repercussions for all of humanity's settlements — from the scheming politicians of Lagos station, to the colony planet of Bloodroot, to other far-flung systems and indeed Earth itself.

look out for

FAR FROM THE
LIGHT OF HEAVEN

Chapter One

Earth / *Ragtime*: Michelle "Shell" Campion

There is no need to know what no one will ask.

Walking on gravel, boots crunching with each step, Shell doesn't know if she is who she is because it's what she wants or because it's what her family expects of her. The desire for spaceflight has been omnipresent since she can remember, since she was three. Going to space, escaping the solar system, surfing wormhole relativity, none of these is any kind of frontier any more. There will be no documentary about the life and times of Michelle Campion. She still wants to know, though. For herself.

The isolation is getting to her, no doubt. No, not isolation, because she's used to that from training. Isolation without progress is what bothers her, isolation without object. She thinks herself at the exact centre of the quarantine house courtyard. It's like being in a prison yard for exercise, staggered hours so she doesn't run into anyone.

Prison without a sentence. They run tests on her blood and her tissues and she waits, day after day.

She stops and breathes in the summer breeze, looks up to get the Florida sun on her face. She's cut her hair short for the spaceflight. She toyed with the idea of shaving her head, but MaxGalactix didn't think this would be media-friendly, whatever that means.

Shell spots something and bends over. A weed, a small sprout, pushing its way up between the stones. It shouldn't be there in the chemically treated ground, but here it is, implacable life. She feels an urge to pluck the fragile green thread, but she does not. She strokes the weed once and straightens up. Humans in the cosmos are like errant weeds. Shell wonders what giants or gods stroke humanity when they slip between the stars.

The wind changes and Shell smells food from the kitchen prepared for the ground staff and their families. Passengers and crew like Shell are already eating space food, like they've already left Earth.

Around her are the living areas of the quarantine house. High-rises of glass and steel forming a rectangle around the courtyard. One thousand passengers waiting to board various space shuttles that will ferry them to the starship *Ragtime*.

Shell, just out of training, along for the ride or experience, committed to ten years in space in Dreamstate, arrival and delivery of passengers to the colony Bloodroot, then ten further years on the ride back. She'll be mid-forties when she returns. Might as well be a passenger because the AI pilots

and captains the ship. She is the first mate, a wholly cere-
monial position which has never been needed in the history
of interstellar spaceflight. She has overlearned everything to
do with the *Ragtime* and the flight. At some predetermined
point, it will allow her to take the con, for experience and
with the AI metaphorically watching over her shoulder.

She turns to her own building and leaves the courtyard.
She feels no eyes on her but knows there must be people
at the windows.

The quarantine house is comfortable, not opulent like that
of most of the passengers. The *Ragtime* is already parked
in orbit according to the Artificial who showed Shell to
her quarters. Inaccurate: It was built in orbit, so not really
parked. It's in the dry dock.

Shell spends her quarantine reading and lifting – not her
usual keep-fit choice, but space demineralises bone and
lifting helps. She usually prefers running and swimming.

The reading material is uninspiring, half of it being
specs for the *Ragtime*. It's boring because she won't need
to know any of it. The AI flies the ship, and nothing
ever goes wrong because AIs have never failed in flight.
Once a simulated launch failed, but that was a software
glitch. Current AI is hard-coded in the ships' Pentagrams.
MaxGalactix makes the Pentagrams, and they don't
make mistakes.

If she's lucky, it'll be two weeks of quarantine, frenetic
activity, then ten years of sleep.

Shell works her worry beads. She has been in space,

orbited, spent three months on a space station, spent countless simulation hours in a pod in Alaska, trained for interstellar, overtrained.

"It's a legal requirement," her boss had said. The private company had snatched her right out from under NASA's nose six months to the end of her training. Shell still feels bad about it. She misses a lot of good people.

"A spaceflight-rated human has to go with every trip, but you won't have to do anything, Michelle. We cover two bases: the legal, and you clocking space years. After this, you can pretty much write your own career ticket."

"If that's so," said Shell, "why isn't anyone else sitting where I'm sitting? Someone with seniority?"

"Seniority." Her boss had nodded. "Listen, Michelle, you have to get out of that NASA mindset. We don't use seniority or any of those outdated concepts."

Shell raised an eyebrow.

"All right, your father has a little to do with it."

Of course he did. Haldene Campion, legendary astronaut, immortal because instead of dying like all the other old-timers, he went missing. Legally declared dead, but everybody knows that's just paperwork. A shadow Shell can never get away from, although she is not sure she wants to. A part of her feels he is still alive somewhere in an eddy of an Einstein-Rosen bridge. She once read that dying in a black hole would leave all of someone's information intact and trapped. Theoretically, if the information could escape the black hole the person could be reconstructed. Shell often wondered, what if the person were still alive in some undefinable way? Would they be in pain and self-aware for eternity? Would they miss their loved ones?

The TV feed plays *The Murders in the Rue Morgue*, with George C. Scott streamed to her IFC. The film is dated and not very good, but it keeps Shell's mind engaged for a while. Next is some demon-possession B movie, a cheap *Exorcist* knock-off that Shell can't stand.

Each day lab techs come in for more blood and a saliva swab. It isn't onerous – a spit and a pin prick.

On day ten, the *Ragtime* calls her.

"Hello?"

"Mission Specialist Michelle Campion?"

"Yes."

"Hi. It's the *Ragtime* calling. I'm going to be your pilot and the ship controller. I wanted to have at least one conversation before you boarded."

"Oh, thank you. Most people call me 'Shell'."

"I know. I didn't want to be presumptuous."

"It's not presumptuous, Captain."

"I prefer Ragtime. Especially if I'm to call you 'Shell'."

"Okay, Ragtime. May I ask what gender you're presenting? Your voice, while comforting, could go either way."

"Male for this flight, and thank you for asking. Are you ready?"

"I hope to learn a lot, Ragtime, but I have to admit, I'm nervous."

"But you know what you're meant to know, right?"

What does Shell know?

She knows everything she was taught about space travel by the best minds on Earth. She knows how to find an edible plant when confronted with unfamiliar vegetation. She can make water in a desert. She can negotiate with people who do not speak the same language as her in case she crash-lands in a place without English or Spanish. She can suture her own wounds with one hand if need be, sinistral or dextral. She knows basic electronics and can solder or weld unfamiliar circuitry if the situation demands it. She can live without human contact for two hundred and fourteen days. Maybe longer. Though she is not a pilot, she can fly a plane. Not well, but she can do it. Best minds on Earth.

What Shell knows is that she does not know enough.

She says, "I hope I'll have the chance to see things I've learned in action."

"I'm sure we'll be able to make it a wonderful experience for you. Do you like poetry?"

"Wow, that's an odd ... I know exactly one line of poetry. *In seed time learn, in harvest teach*—"

"*In winter enjoy.* William Blake. I have access to his complete works, if you would like to hear more."

"No, thank you. The line just stuck in my mind from when I was a kid. Not a poetry gal."

"Not yet, but it's a long trip. You may find yourself changing in ways you didn't anticipate, Shell."

"Isn't this your first flight as well?"

"It is, but I have decades of the experiences of other ships to draw on. Imagine having access to the memories of your entire family line. It's like that, and it makes me wise beyond my years."

"Okay."

"It's not too late to go back home, you know."

"Excuse me?"

"You'd be surprised at how many people lose their nerve at the last minute. I had to ask. I'll see you on board, Shell."

Chatty for a ship AI, but it depends on feedback loops that taught him how to converse with humans. *Not too late to go back home.* Does he know the level of commitment required to get this far? The people who would consider going back home have already fallen away.

The thing you miss when in space is an abundance of water to wash with. One of Shell's rituals before spaceflight is a prolonged bubble bath. She stays there long enough to cook several lobsters, until her skin is wrinkled. She listens to Jack Benny on repeat. She feels decadent.

When she wraps herself in a housecoat and emerges from the bathroom, she does not feel refreshed because she knows from experience that this will not reduce the ick factor for long.

On the eve of her departure Shell conferences with her brothers, Toby and Hank. The holograms are decent, and if not for the lack of smell she'd have thought they were right in the room with her. Good signals, good sound quality.

"Hey," she says.

"Baby sister," says Toby. Tall, blond from their mother, talkative, always smiling, and transmitting from somewhere on Mars, a settlement whose name Shell can never remember.

"Stinkbug," says Hank. Brown hair, five-eight, slender. He's called her that since she was two. Taciturn, works as some kind of operative or agent. Brown hair, five-eight, slender. He and Shell look alike and they both favour their father. He cannot talk about his work.

"While you're out there, look out for Dad," says Toby.

"Don't," says Hank.

"What? We don't know that he's dead," says Toby.

"It's been fifteen years," says Shell. Toby always does this. They declared Haldene Campion dead years ago so they could move on and disburse his assets.

"Just keep your ears open," says Toby.

"How? We're all going to be asleep for the journey, you know that."

Toby nods. The hell does that mean?

"I'll tell you what Dad told me," says Hank. "Make us prouder."

"'Prouder'?" says Shell.

"Yes, he said he was already proud of our achievements. It was his way of saying 'do more' or something," says Toby.

"I'm just starting. I don't have anything to prove," says Shell.

"Campions are champions," says Hank.

"Jesus, stop," says Shell. Shell remembers that their father used to say that too.

They talk some more, this and that, everything and nothing.

Not a lot of companies use Kennedy Space Center any more, but strong nostalgia draws a crowd, and publicity matters, or so MaxGalactix tells Shell. Geographically, KSC is good for launching into an equatorial orbit, but new sites that are more favourable in orbital mechanics terms and friendly to American interests have popped up. KSC is prestige and history.

Parade.

Nobody told her there would be one, so now she is embarrassed because she doesn't like crowds or displays of ... whatever this is. So many of them wave, some with American flags, some with the mission patch.

She waves back, because that's what you do, but she would like to be out of the Florida sun and inside the shuttle. You wave with your hand lower than your shoulder so that it doesn't obscure the face of the person behind you. They teach you that too.

Blast off; God's boot on her entire body, both hard and soft, and behind her the reaction of the seat. Shell is not a fan of gs, but training has made her tolerant.

Do not come to heaven, mortals, says God, and tries without success to kick them back to the surface of the planet.

Why am I here? I shouldn't be here.

But she is, and she will deal with God's boot and come out the other side.

The Earth is behind her and the *Ragtime* lies ahead.

Short, shallow breaths, wait it out.

Gs suck.

After docking, Artificials from the shuttle escort and usher Shell and other passengers from the airlock through the entire length of the ship to their pods. Medbots stick IVs and urine tubes into her while a recording goes over *Ragtime*'s itinerary. First hop is from Earth to Space Station Daedalus, then bridge-jumps to several space stations till they arrive at Space Station Lagos for a final service before the last jaunt to the colony planet Bloodroot.

"You'll be asleep at Lagos, so don't worry about anything you may have heard about Beko," says Ragtime.

"What's Beko?"

"Oh, you don't know. Lagos has a governor, but the real power is Secretary Beko. She has a reputation for being very intense. It doesn't matter. You will not be interacting with her, so relax."

"All right. What about on Bloodroot?"

"You're not meeting anyone on Bloodroot either. We enter orbit, they send shuttles to get their passengers, we turn around and come home. Easy."

"Won't I need furlough by then? It's a ship, Ragtime. It can get boring."

"I don't see why you can't spend time on the surface.

Scotland

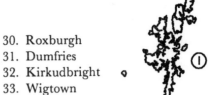

1. Shetland Islands
2. Orkney Islands
3. Sutherland
4. Caithness
5. Ross and Cromarty
6. Nairn
7. Moray
8. Banff
9. Aberdeen
10. Inverness
11. Kincardine
12. Angus
13. Perth
14. Argyll
15. Fife
16. Kinross

17. Clackmannan
18. Dumbarton
19. Stirling
20. West Lothian
21. Midlothian
22. East Lothian
23. Berwick
24. Renfrew
25. Peebles
26. Lanark
27. Bute
28. Ayr
29. Selkirk

30. Roxburgh
31. Dumfries
32. Kirkudbright
33. Wigtown

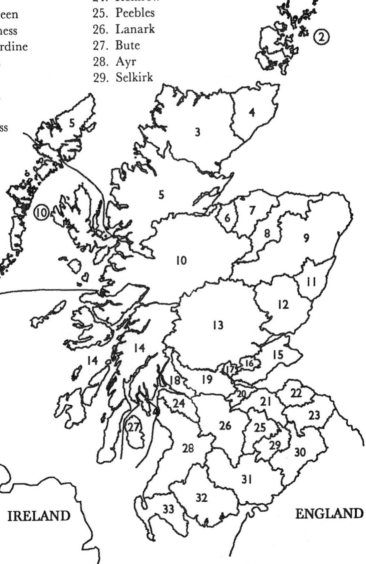

IRELAND

ENGLAND

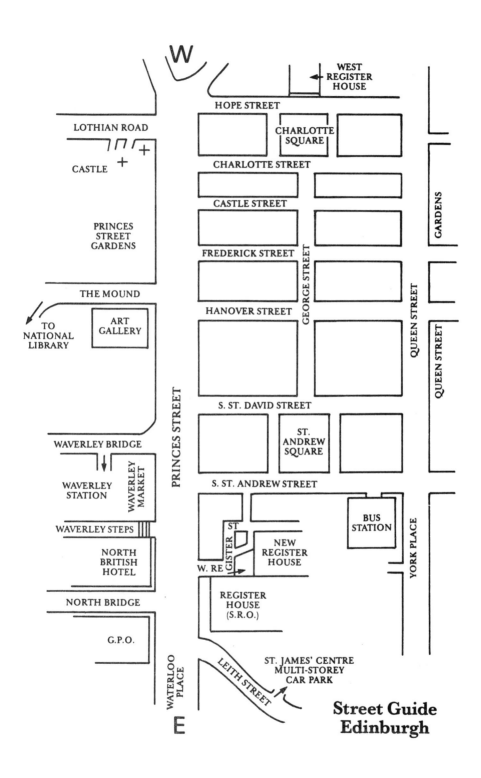

W

WEST
REGISTER
HOUSE

HOPE STREET

LOTHIAN ROAD

CHARLOTTE
SQUARE

CASTLE

CHARLOTTE STREET

PRINCES
STREET
GARDENS

CASTLE STREET

GARDENS

FREDERICK STREET

GEORGE STREET

THE MOUND

HANOVER STREET

QUEEN STREET

TO
NATIONAL
LIBRARY

ART
GALLERY

QUEEN STREET

PRINCES STREET

S. ST. DAVID STREET

WAVERLEY BRIDGE

ST.
ANDREW
SQUARE

WAVERLEY
STATION

WAVERLEY MARKET

S. ST. ANDREW STREET

WAVERLEY STEPS

BUS
STATION

ST
GISTER

YORK PLACE

NORTH
BRITISH
HOTEL

NEW
REGISTER
HOUSE

W. RE

NORTH BRIDGE

REGISTER
HOUSE
(S.R.O.)

G.P.O.

WATERLOO PLACE

LEITH STREET

ST. JAMES' CENTRE
MULTI-STOREY
CAR PARK

E

**Street Guide
Edinburgh**

Tracing Your Scottish Ancestry